FINDERS KEEPERS

FLASH FINNEGAN SERIES
BOOK 1

WALTER SUTTON

"Does the flap of a butterfly's wings in Brazil set off a tornado in Texas?"

Edward Lorenz paper entitled "Predictability: Does the Flap of a Butterfly's Wings in Brazil Set Off a Tornado in Texas?"

Presented at the American Association for the Advancement of Science (AAAS) meeting in 1972.

CHAPTER 1

F lash looked down at the vibrating phone:

> Upstairs, chief's office, debrief, ready now.

Jesus, I need a vacation, he thought. *Just to break free, hit the pause button, anything to have a breather from this nightmare.*

His wife had a boyfriend, or so she'd told him the previous week. Someone special, she said. After seventeen years of marriage, she'd found someone special, at last. She'd told him in the middle of an argument about—God, he couldn't even remember what they'd been arguing about.

Then, too, he'd just suffered through six months, six long months, twenty-four hours a day, of being buried in human slime. A dirty, long dive into the mindfuck world of drug trafficking and big, big money.

Well, that at least was done. Next stop to be indictments all around, and jail time for the bad guys, lots and lots of jail time. So, Flash had celebrated—a twenty-five-year-old scotch celebration, alone.

He took a deep breath and pushed himself out of the chair,

his head feeling as though it were stuffed with steel wool. He really needed that vacation. He'd put in for three weeks, starting right after the debrief. That was it, hangover be damned; do the debrief, go on vacation. Finally, a chance to breathe, get some sleep, maybe even sort out the rest of his screwed-up life.

At the chief's office, he knocked twice on the partially open door. Flash straightened his tie—Italian knit, scarlet, slim, very un-cop-like. He summoned a smile and pushed through into the room.

They were waiting for him, sitting at a small round meeting table off to one side of the monstrously large corner office. The light in his eyes, Flash winced. This morning in Seattle was intensely bright, rare in the land of perpetual gloom and rain. Flash worked harder at the smile, tried to ignore his headache, and sat down.

The chief's hands were folded in front of him. Malcolm Forsyth, Jr. was in formal kit, dark-blue dress uniform with gold braid, ribbons, and medals on display. *Always ready for a news conference*, thought Flash. The chief was a glittering example of Authority, a very political, very public Chief of Police.

Like Flash, Lieutenant John Horan wore a dark Italian suit of the type that detectives in the fraud squad adopted to look like business people—well-to-do, professional-type business people.

"Jesus, Flash, what happened to you? You look like hell," said John.

"Thanks, John! I was celebrating last night. I assume you were too. The goddamn case. What a monster!"

"Yes, indeed, a monster," said John flatly.

Flash looked over at Chief Forsyth, back to John, and said, "And just so you both know, I've put in for some vacation. Gonna go sailing and spend a couple of weeks on a beach where you guys can't find me." He grinned. "So, how do you want to do this? Any news from Zurich? Did we arrest the bastards yet?"

"Mmm, the bastards," said John, opening a red manila folder in front of him on the table. "We'll get to that in a bit. But first, we have to ask you a couple of questions about what went down on your end, Flash. Just some details—a couple of loose ends."

"Okay, fire away," Flash said, eager to finish up the whole escapade.

"I'm wondering if you would go over what steps you took to move the money yesterday."

"Sure, but you already know what I did."

"Just go over it, if you would, please."

Flash stared at the chief. The man could have been a statue, not moving a muscle.

"Flash!" John was gently tapping one finger on the tabletop, a twitch-like tap.

"Yeah—sure, John. Where do you want me to start?"

John looked down at his hand, stopped tapping, and said, "Start with how you put ten-million dollars in the Zurich account, *your* Zurich account, I mean."

Flash let out a breath. "Right, so, I signed into the account, then sent the triggering text you provided to the address you also gave me, and ten minutes later, the Zurich account showed a balance of ten-million dollars. I signed out of the Zurich account, then exactly ten minutes later signed back in, and as we had hoped, the money was gone, sucked into their accounts. They received the money, the trap was sprung. Bingo, indictments secured. And at some point, the money went over to Interpol and the FBI, I presume."

John looked up from the red folder and said, "So, Flash, if I'm hearing this correctly, you're saying that the money did appear. You sent the texts per the plan, and as far as you know, the money was transferred to the bastards. Is that correct?" He was tapping the tabletop again.

"Yeah, that's exactly what happened." Flash was nonplussed. Shouldn't they be joyously backslapping one another by now?

"Well, Flash, how would you explain why the money didn't reach the bastards' bank accounts?"

"What?" He felt as if he had been struck on his already throbbing head.

"I said—well, you heard what I said. Answer the question."

A shockwave traveled from Flash's belly straight up through his chest, his neck, his jaw, his eyes, and straight down through his genitals, through his anus, to the soles of his feet. The red-hot vibration engulfed nearly every segment of his body. "Are you telling me that the money wasn't transferred?"

"I'm telling you that the crooks didn't get the money. Explain to us how that could have happened."

His two colleagues were staring intently at Flash, gauging his reaction.

He swallowed hard to prevent himself from throwing up. He shook his head in disbelief and finally said, "Look, I don't know what the hell you're talking about."

Getting no reaction from his superiors, Flash took a deep breath and began speaking again, but this time more deliberately, slowing his cadence and raising his voice. "Hey, I accessed the Zurich account. I confirmed that ten million was in the fucking account. I cut and pasted the text with the hidden tracking codes, the ones you gave me to use, and then I pushed the fucking send button, and the text messages were sent. I logged out of the account." Deep exhale and inhale.

"Ten minutes later, I logged back in, and the money was gone. Zero balance, just like we planned. That's what I did, all according to plan—your plan." Flushed, he watched the two, trying not to react to all the crazy signals his body was sending every which way.

The chief leaned forward, brown eyes unblinking, and said, "What did you do with the money, Flash?"

"With all due respect, Chief, I did exactly what you told me to do, using the codes you gave me. If the money is gone, it's over to you, not me."

"Well, Flash, that's one interpretation," said the chief. "What you're conveniently glossing over, however, is that you were the only person in the whole universe who was authorized, electronically authorized, I mean, to access the Zurich account. Any transfer to or from that account could only happen with your authorization—your coded authorization."

The chief's face had turned red, and his voice rose with each phrase. "Every nickel in and every nickel out, under your control. You and you alone, Flash! And this morning we find ourselves without ten-million dollars and fighting a holding action with the bastards, who didn't get the money. They are mad as hell, and so am I!"

Flash was dizzy, his body in full fight-or-flight, his senses amped up and screaming. Then he had the out-of-body, wildly surreal experience of seeing himself caught in a life-and-death ambush by John, his boss and friend of fifteen years, and the Seattle chief of police—these two animals were about to kill him. That's what he felt like: They were about to kill him. Right now.

The chief, still red-faced, said, "Why don't you just tell us what you did with the money, Flash, because we're pretty sure you've sucked it into some hidey-hole on the back of God's head, thinking you could somehow explain it away. Believe me, that game is over now. What. Did. You. Do. With. The. Money?"

"Someone is setting me up." Flash forced out the words. "I know what I did, and I didn't steal your money. I want a lawyer before we go any further!"

John said, "Wait, wait, wait, wait a minute! Just hold on here, a lawyer isn't going to help anyone with this. We have a big problem and, somehow, we have to work it out. So, just to be clear, you're saying, Flash, that you didn't cop the money? Is that what you're telling us?"

"Yes!"

"Well, exactly, so you understand where we stand, Flash, we think you did take the money."

Flash looked at John, at the chief, back to John. No one blinked.

After a long silence, Flash said, "So here we sit, and you're telling me I have a problem. But what I'm thinking is that you have a problem. I told you what I did, which was exactly what you instructed me to do. I don't know what happened to that money, and I certainly am not going to take the fall for any of this. Whatever this is."

John said, "You really, really need to listen now. We've been over every scrap of data, coding, reporting, and surveillance intel relating to that transfer, that so-called transfer, a dozen times. I have plenty of evidence to hold you, to jail you, for sure without bail, for stealing some or all of that money.

"And as a consequence, your career in the police department is ending this morning. The only question is how it ends—that's all we're talking about."

"I want a lawyer now," Flash said.

"Okay," said John. "That will trigger one of the two options that are open to you at this point, Flash. So listen carefully—the rest of your life hangs in the balance. We're going to hold you under suspicion of theft, fraud, extortion, aiding terrorists and terrorist activity, and aiding and abetting organized crime. That means you go from here to a jail cell, and then you can talk to your lawyer, who won't have a chance in hell when it comes to bail or—"

"Jesus, I don't believe this. You can't be serious!"

"Believe me, we are," said John. "This is not going to go your way, buddy, it really isn't. I've got the paperwork right here. I've signed it. I give this to my clerk."

Flash looked hard at John. "Or?"

"Or the other option is this." John held up a letter printed on the official Seattle Police Department stationery. "Your resignation from the police department, effective immediately. You leave by the back door and go live your life as anything other than being a cop."

Flash sat back in his chair. "So, John, why the back door?"

"Well, think about it, Flash. The bulletin reads, 'Police sources report ten million lost in mysterious dealings with international drug gang.' The perpetrator appears to be a high-ranking and trusted police inspector, etc. Questions arise as to why this officer was entrusted with ten-million dollars, and how the hell could you lose ten-million dollars, and, of course, who was in charge of the case, who are the bastards, followed by a special police review panel and on and on and on."

John sighed. "But Flash, old buddy, if it were up to me, I would hang you by your balls from the Space Needle."

"Enough!" the chief barked. "Which one will it be, Flash? Jail, or resign?"

Flash sighed and said, "I need a vacation."

John slid the two-page resignation letter across the table toward Flash. As an afterthought, he took a ballpoint from his inside coat pocket, removed the top, and placed the pen next to the letter. He then pointed at the second page, where Flash was to sign, and sat back.

"Just so you understand, this letter waives your right to bring any action against the city or any individual or the police department," John said. "It also incorporates a nondisclosure agreement. If you talk about this case or this meeting or this agreement with anybody, *any*body—in the universe—we will come and get you, throw you in jail, and we invoke option one. Do you understand?"

Flash, his hand shaking, initialed and signed. Pushing the letter and the pen back across the table in front of the chief, he looked directly at the man—his medals, his eyes, his red face—and whispered, "Like I said, I need a vacation. I really need a vacation."

Flash stood up a little unsteadily, pushed the chair away, turned, and left the office, letting the door slam behind him.

CHAPTER 2

Driving south on the freeway, Flash felt sick to his stomach—bile and reflux were rising. The Rolaids weren't working, and the traffic—well, it was rush hour. Interstate 5 between Seattle and Tacoma had an advanced case of arterial sclerosis. They'd widened the interstate four times that he knew of, but every time they added a lane, more cars and trucks somehow materialized, once again constricting the flow. The drive was, in the main, a sequence of slow, creeping advances punctuated by long stops. Go a little, stop for two minutes. *Jesus.*

How could he not be acclimated to the trip by now? After all, he had made the pilgrimage two or three times a month to see his dad. But, today, the traffic wasn't the real problem. What he had to tell, or not tell, his dad, that was the difficulty.

Lieutenant Colonel Tom—not Thomas, just Tom—Michael, formerly of the Army Criminal Investigation Division, lived alone in the same 1,200-square-foot house he and his wife Amelia had bought two years before Flash was born. The neighborhood had been built as part of a development in the late 1930s, on the then-fringes of downtown Tacoma. Many of the houses had similar lines, similar windows, and were on similar postage-stamp-sized lots, each fronted by uneven ribbons of cracked sidewalk.

Three-quarters of a century's worth of added dormers, porches, decks, hot tubs, and garages transformed into workshops or carports gave an impression of architectural diversity. The Michael house had white clapboard siding, red trim, a black asphalt shingle roof, and sagging, worn steps leading up to a weathered front door, long-ago painted red. Amelia, Flash's mother, had chosen the color.

Tom and Flash were sitting at the kitchen table. Tom was slightly stooped, with a full head of neatly trimmed and combed white hair, parted on the side. A ruddy, thickening nose and red cheeks played off the crimson in his Pendleton shirt. He was wearing khaki slacks, and black, highly shined shoes, as though his bottom half was still in the Army, but the top half had retired.

The two had taken, by habit more than agreement, assigned seating. Tom was facing a window that looked out on a plum tree which had dropped most of its fruit on a spare patch of ground one might call a lawn. Amelia, Flash's mom, had bought and planted the plum tree while Tom was away on assignment, and ever since, every year, came an explosion of plums. The crows loved it. Too bad they didn't clean up after themselves.

Flash sat opposite Tom at the other end of the square oak table. Amelia, too, had a seat in the tableau. Her chair was to Tom's left, pulled back from the table a foot or so as if any minute she might walk into the kitchen. She had died of breast cancer six years before.

Amelia, a high school English teacher, named her son Finnegan, from *Finnegans Wake*, and Augustus, for the emperor who transformed Rome from a republic to an empire.

"Dad, I'm going to be traveling for a while. I may be out of touch," Flash said, immediately wondering if his father had heard him—Tom was hard of hearing. "I just wanted to let you know. I don't want you to worry."

Tom shifted in his chair. The two were both drinking coffee

from olive-drab US-Army-branded mugs with the white Army star insignia. *Dad is shrinking,* thought Flash. Today he seemed smaller even than two weeks before. Of course, that was crazy, but that's what he thought. *Dad is getting old.*

"A vacation," Tom said. "Well—of course. Good idea, son. Give you a chance to catch your breath. I guess with all that's going—gone on—gosh, you and Samantha, Flash—You know, I'm so sorry about all that."

"Thanks, Dad. Me too." With what else was going on now, the issue of Samantha was retreating into the far background.

"Where are you going on this vacation, if you don't mind my asking?"

"You know, Dad, I'm not sure yet. This whole thing has just happened so fast—But now that you mention it, maybe a walking trip. Ireland, or England, something like that. Get away, turn off the electronics, and chill."

Tom smiled. "You're certain to have plenty of chill walking in Ireland or England, that's for damn sure. Don't you want to go someplace warm?"

"I'll let you know, Dad."

Tom drank some of his coffee, then put the mug down on the table. "But why would I worry, son?"

"Well, I may be away longer—longer than just for a vacation. You know, some work stuff, an operational thing. Something I can't discuss."

"Well, what are we talking about here? Weeks? Months? What about Pippa?" Tom looked away and said, "Sorry, son, I know you can't say anything."

Flash smiled at his dad. Tom's blue eyes, crow's feet, and a permanent half-smile gave him an air of perpetual optimism. Flash's heart hurt.

"You know the job, Dad. And really, Pip will be fine. Sam is a good mother."

"Of course she is. I really wish everything had worked out. I'm just sorry. But Pippa, I'll still be able to see Pippa, right?"

"Yes, sir, absolutely. It's all part of the deal, the divorce agreement, I mean. Visits to granddad are stipulated in black and white, and Samantha's all for it, too. She thinks you're a wonderful granddad. And you know Pippa, she just, well, she really loves her granddad."

Flash smiled at his father and rose, collected the mugs, and took them to the sink.

"Don't bother with those, son. I'll do the dishes after you leave."

Flash grinned and said, "Okay. KP duty for you, and I've got to hit the road, Dad."

"I know you do—oh, gosh!" Tom's face flushed. "Wait a minute! Did I tell you about the FBI guys? No, I couldn't have. Let me see now."

"What? FBI guys?"

"Okay, well, two of them. You know the type. Slick, white shirts, blue or red ties, short hair, shined shoes, you know—FBI guys."

"Yeah, I do. When was this?"

"Just last Wednesday. They showed up out of the blue at lunchtime."

"Yeah, thoughtless jerks. What'd they want?"

"Oh, well, they framed it as simply a friendly chat, a few questions. They said they were updating, or upgrading, they may have called it, upgrading your security clearance. A sort of maintenance activity, one of the guys said. You know?"

Flash nodded.

"They had lots of questions, ah, mostly about lifestyle. They knew about the divorce, of course. They asked if you had come into an inheritance or had any sort of financial windfall. They also asked if you had any new friends or people you socialized with. Well, I told them no new money, I didn't think you had a new group of friends, and that the divorce was sad for everybody—full stop."

"Did they show you their IDs?"

"Oh, heavens, yes, and I double-checked. FBI, Washington State office, on Third Avenue in Seattle. I called their office, got confirmation."

"Do you remember who they were? What their names were?"

"Ah—damn, no, sorry. As soon as I checked their bona fides, I was satisfied. They knew I was an Army cop, too, so we got down to it."

Flash nodded, trying to grasp the whole situation. "Well, that's that then. Thanks for letting me know, Dad. Sorry, but I've got to hit the road."

Tom got out of his chair and went toward Flash. They hugged. Looked at each other at arm's length, hugged again.

As Flash closed the front door, the pain started in his gut, then moved upward as he walked down the four worn, wooden steps leading away from the house. He took a deep breath, then another, and another, as he went to his car.

What a bullshitter I am, he thought. *Sorry, Dad.* And then the question of the FBI. Just a friendly visit, security refresh? No way.

What was going on at the Seattle Police Department? More worrying was what his ex-buddies at the SPD might be telling other agencies—Interpol, the FBI? Shit!

"D-Day." That was the first thing Flash's said to himself the next morning. D-Day for divorce day. Finally. All the separating, shredding, sorting, the disillusioning and painful process of ending their marriage would finally emphatically be over. Thank God!

Flash and Samantha arrived separately at the divorce mediator's home office, both early. Samantha was wearing jeans, a purple University of Washington sweatshirt, and white high-top Keds. She was standing on the sidewalk, smoking a cigarette, talking on her cellphone. Her black hair was pulled back into a ponytail, and gold hoop earrings danced as she spoke. She gesticulated with her free hand while she walked back and forth on the pavement. Flash could hear her from half a block away, where he had parked, five minutes early.

Italians—God, what a tribe! Although she had been born in Seattle at the Swedish Medical Center, her parents were immigrants. Samantha's olive complexion, almond eyes, black hair, and the ever-moving hands and body were all sublimely orchestrated by Northern Italy. She made her father and mother effusively proud—like parents, like daughter, Italian through and through.

"Okay, but look, you need to be ready for the opening Friday morning at nine, not Friday noon. Friday morning, do you hear me?" She held the phone in front of her and pushed the screen with a long forefinger, grimacing. "Jesus," she said at the phone.

She looked up and saw Flash. "So, let's start a little early with Ursula, shall we? I really need to get back to the office," she told him.

Samantha Orsini, who hadn't changed her name when she and Flash married, owned a marketing research firm. She was an entrepreneur, consultant, a business phenomenon. In the market research and future prediction world, Samantha Orsini was of the class known as "Seattle Famous." She was a popular, well-known force of nature, the mother of their child, and soon to be his, Flash's, ex-wife. Their sixteen-year-old daughter, Phillipa Orsini (they had agreed to give their daughter Samantha's last name too), would live with her mother as part of the joint custody agreement.

Flash's chest ached. He noticed Samantha was wearing her engagement ring on the middle finger of her right hand, the giving-you-the-finger finger. *Nice emerald, though,* he thought.

Ursula Shepherd, lawyer, licensed mediator, and friend of Samantha, was always well prepared. Flash was convinced Ursula was obsessive about everything, including being prepared. A good trait for a lawyer and mediator, indeed, but way too persnickety and punctilious for his taste.

Flash and Samantha seated themselves on one side of the blond, all-wood, smoothly finished Swedish-style dining room table. Ursula had the documents laid out, one pile in front of Samantha and one pile in front of Flash, yellow tabs jutting forth, the piles arrayed equal distance apart, stair-stepped from the bottom to the top of each stack—a black Bic Stick conveniently on the right-hand side of each place setting.

Ursula was six feet tall. Henna-colored hair cut in a bob, she wore no visible makeup, spoke in a soft but clear voice with the ease of a therapist. After greeting them both, she opened the meeting with her slow-paced, carefully enunciated official explanation of the process. "Okay, you two, today, if you choose to go through with this, your divorce and property settlement and financial agreements will be final and binding."

Samantha nodded and said, "I'm ready."

Flash nodded. He wasn't ready, but who cared?

"Now, before you sign, I like to ask clients to take a couple of minutes in silence, just right at this point, to consider—or reconsider. Do you really want to go through with this?" She raised both hands in front of her in a stopping gesture. "Don't say anything, just sit for a couple of minutes, and be sure."

"Ursula, dear, we're sure," said Samantha, her gold earrings jumping as she nodded. "Could we just get on with it? I really need to get back to work."

"Me, too, Ursula," lied Flash. "Let's do it now." Before he threw up.

They signed the child support agreement; Phillipa Orsini would live with her mother as part of their joint custody agreement. They then signed the transfer of proceeds from the sale of their house, and the big one—an agreement about personal property, divided. Samantha got to keep her business, Flash got to keep his 401K and retirement fund. Page after page, each initialed, each agreement signed, until everything that had once been the Michael-Orsini marriage was allocated to one or the other, with nothing left in what had been the middle.

Samantha pushed back her chair, looked at Flash, said, "Well, I'm sure we'll see each other from time to time, but goodbye for now," and walked out of the dining room, closing the front door behind her with a bang.

Flash smiled and shook his head.

"Flash, how are you doing?" asked Ursula.

"I'm fine. Thanks for helping us through this, by the way. Don't know if we could have survived the shitshow without you."

"How's Pippa?"

"You know, she seems okay. I mean, we've been living apart for three months now, and once the house was sold, she was able to settle into the new place with Sam and— Well, so that helped. I'm seeing her tomorrow."

"Good luck to you, Flash. I wish you both, all three of you, the very best of luck, really."

Just like that. Luck. The word rattled around in Flash's mind, a pebble in an empty beer can that someone was shaking simply to annoy him. He smiled, stood up, and left.

Yeah, he had to agree with his own evaluation—*just like that.* He started his car, pulled out of the parking space, heading for, of all places, the REI Co-op.

Seattle was the original home of the national chain of stores known as the Recreation Equipment, Inc. Co-op. Complete with a many-storied climbing wall, it was a vast, outdoorsy, Northwest icon, a wood-and-glass mecca for shoppers who wanted anything to do with the outdoors.

Flash moved from section to section, assembling what he was calling his erasure pack. Buy the gear to get lost, really, to be erased. That's how he thought of it. Erased—

Forty-five minutes later, Flash joined the checkout queue. He'd selected a black, waterproof duffle bag; a practical but straightforward hiking wardrobe; and equipment and extras for wherever he was going: a headlamp, a rechargeable battery pack, a GPS device that wasn't dependent on a cellphone signal, a water bottle, some strong nylon cord, a toiletry kit, a rain jacket and pants, and a knit watch cap—everything in black.

The appearance of the FBI guys at his dad's place had convinced him that he might be under surveillance, so Flash also had picked out several guidebooks and foldout maps for hiking in Yosemite National Park, Grand Canyon National Park—the south side of the canyon—and Grand Tetons National Park, just to confuse the watchers, because he wasn't going to any of those places.

The checkout line was moving slowly, and he looked ahead at the cashier, who was finishing up with a young man—tall, blond, late twenties, athletic, crew cut. The young man was wearing a red t-shirt with North Face in black, oversize letters down the front. The clerk returned the young man's credit card.

As he inserted his credit card in his wallet, the young man looked back down the line of customers, made eye contact with Flash, smiled and, with his thumb and finger, made a shooting motion. The kid nodded his head as if in greeting, then turned and walked toward the exit.

Flash rocked back on his heels. *What the hell?* Flash wanted to jump the line and run after the jerk. He took one quick step forward, then stopped himself. *No way*, he thought.

That's just what they'd want him to do. Break the law, do something to bring attention to himself, make a public nuisance, then all bets would be off. No. He breathed slowly to calm himself. The line began moving again, and eventually he'd paid for all of his shopping and settled it in the black duffel, which he slung over his shoulder as he headed for the underground parking garage.

Flash was still anxious, though, wary, unsettled, and moving carefully. He scanned left and right as he walked into the poorly lit concrete underground. He was, after all, a trained law enforcement officer. He had worked undercover, too, among evil people. He knew how to be watchful for the slightest anomaly in the space around him.

The North Face fellow seemed to have disappeared. But that was small comfort. Flash needed to get a move on. Something was up, and he didn't want to be caught in the middle of the impending shitstorm.

CHAPTER 3

I t was a dark moment. Not only was it the middle of the night, but he was finally feeling the pain of losing his career, his whole adult identity. This was supposed to be a time when he was promoted into the elite level of police work, to undertake real crime fighting on a large scale, working against money laundering, organized crime—parasitical offenses against decent society. All of that was gone, his brilliant future destroyed.

Four years before, in what he thought was a good career move, Flash had volunteered to go undercover, to invade and spy in the land of the international bastards. He'd spent a year and a half preparing for his first assignment, which turned out to be this money laundering operation whose queen bee was apparently located somewhere in Switzerland.

Flash completed a rigorous curriculum of courses dealing with how to be a crook, focusing on money laundering. These courses included the complexities of international finance, the economics of dirty money, and, more practically, acting classes, as well as several courses in the psychology of perception and deception.

He'd had two years of training and had been six months

undercover, during which time he'd also learned a lot about feinting, ducking, hiding out, and disappearing.

In short, Flash was well trained to make his next move: At 2:30 in the morning, dressed in black, he left his month-to-month apartment on Queen Ann Hill, and drove his beat-up green and tan Subaru Outback down the hill, lights out, watching to see if he was being followed. After winding through a maze-like, low-traffic, residential neighborhood, he pulled over and parked, then sat and waited for ten minutes to see if anybody came by. Nothing.

He drove for three more blocks, then turned the headlights on and, wheels squealing, raced out to the freeway. He had smeared greasy mud on his license plates to confuse data-gathering cameras on the main roads, and had scanned his car for tracking devices. He was on his way, low and fast. First stop: Aberdeen, Washington.

"Yeah, yeah, I know you—I can do that. How much are you moving?"

"When?" asked Flash.

"Today, if you're locked and loaded. How much are we moving?" William Jones—his real name, at least so far as Flash knew—leaned across the battered old desk and gave Flash an intense look, picked up a crumpled napkin, and blew his nose.

Flash said, "Six-hundred-fifty-thousand."

William—no one ever called him Bill—lived in Aberdeen, a defunct mill and logging town on the Olympic Peninsula, less than a hundred miles west of Seattle, but in another world altogether. Drenched by rain, covered in moss, surrounded by thousands and thousands of brooding trees, encased by fog and mist when it wasn't actually raining, Aberdeen was a boom town that had lost its boom. Downtown Aberdeen consisted mostly of abandoned buildings, with sections of the town center falling in on itself, beams exposed, roofs rotted. The place was depressed, and depressing.

Flash assumed William lived there because it was a great place to be lost. William was a denizen of the underworld, so a deep hole in a forested, rain-soaked wilderness was a perfect place to practice dark arts unobserved.

"You know this will cost you sixty-five?"

Flash sighed. "Yeah. And you know it's highway robbery! Sorry—okay, okay, what do you need?"

"Did you read the email, son?"

"Yes."

"Then you know what I need. Do you have the information or not?"

"Yeah!"

A person on the street might see William and think he was one step away from being homeless—he was short, bald, over-weight, always dressed in stained and ill-fitting clothes; he smoked, and he mumbled—but he was far from homeless, let alone destitute.

William was a money mover and hider for the wealthy, crooked, or paranoid of the world. Everyone knew that Switzer-land, Panama, and the Cayman Islands were places to hide money. William's big trick was that he would settle money in other places—places that could never be found and, more impor-tantly, would never be exposed in some WikiLeaks or Panama Papers dump. His reputation was ironclad, probably because if he had been the slightest bit unreliable, he would be dead by now.

When William moved your money, his 10 percent would go in one direction, and your money would go in another direction: off the radar, spread over a dozen or more accounts, lost to him and anybody looking for you or your money. He also claimed that any knowledge about a client was simultaneously deleted, lost for all time.

"Here are the codes," said Flash, handing a piece of paper across the cluttered desk to William.

William looked at the paper, flicked the ash from his half-smoked cigarette, and said, "Okay, fine. I'll punch it through in exactly ten hours. You should leave Aberdeen and go somewhere else, so when the money moves, you aren't in Aberdeen, or anyplace close, understand?"

"Yeah, sure. Are you being watched?"

"I certainly hope not, son, but let's not risk it, shall we?"

Flash rose and held out his hand. William looked up, a little surprised, and waved off the handshake, saying, "Nah, we're good, son. Get out of here."

Leaving Aberdeen, Flash drove old Highway 101 toward Forks, one-hundred miles north. He had put his car, a 2005 Subaru Outback, on Craigslist for sale there and would deliver it in person.

The sale of the car might trigger something once it was re-registered, but Forks, Washington? Nope, the location wouldn't help whoever might be after him. He'd be long gone by the time the change of ownership came through the system, anyway.

After he dropped off the car, finding his way to his next stop, Port Angeles, Washington, was a simple matter of hitching a ride on a backhaul logging truck. He spent one night in a motel near the waterfront, paid cash, and left Port Angeles at 8:15 a.m. on the Black Ball ferry to Victoria, British Columbia, Canada.

The passport Flash used that morning was a souvenir from the underworld. It was part of a kit consisting of a valid passport, a working debit card, a working bank account with a thousand dollars in it, a credit card (Visa or Mastercard, never American Express), and a current Washington State driver's license.

The underworld existed in parallel to the legit world, only its institutions and commercial operations were insulated, well-hidden and, therefore, essentially invisible to the legit world. A bona fide underworld citizen could buy almost anything. Just as a legit shopping center had specialty stores, the underworld had specialty stores and specialty services too. In the underworld, identification was big business.

Flash had secretly bought the ID package as a way to escape, a fire exit from the underworld and the bastards, just in case the worst happened and he needed to leave in a hurry; the legit world might not be able to protect him in an underworld emergency. He never would have guessed that the fake ID would be his ticket out of the legit world instead.

And so, Flash Finnegan Michael disembarked from the Black Ball ferry in the beautiful inner harbor of Victoria, BC, Canada with a new name, Thorsten Francis Tucker.

Mr. Tucker's passport picture showed Flash. Once he cleared customs, Flash felt like a new man.

At Canadian customs, he used his new passport, which showed him with a black mustache, black buzz-cut hair, black-rimmed glasses, and blue eyes, and stated he weighed one-seventy-five pounds, along with other particulars that couldn't be dyed, changed, or modified. He told the immigration officer he would be visiting for three days, then leaving as a crew member on board a sailboat in the Victoria to Maui International Yacht Race.

"One of the big ones?" asked the customs officer.

"One of the big ones," agreed Flash, hoisting his black duffel on one shoulder. He thanked the officer and headed toward the exit, more erased with every step.

Ten days later, the Maxi 72 ocean racer *Perfidious* sailed into Lahaina Harbor on Maui. After a farewell celebratory glass of champagne with the other crew members, Flash boarded a flight to Lihue, Kauai, took a cab from the airport through Lihue town going south to Maluhia Road, where the cab turned left and sped through the locally famous Tunnel of Trees, also known as the gateway to the South Shore. Five minutes later, he arrived in Old Koloa Town.

Flash paid the cab driver in cash, thanked him, then shouldered his duffel bag along the covered boardwalk in the old section of the old town. Soon he was seated at a table in Koloa Roasters, a local coffee hangout and roasted nut emporium, sipping a cappuccino and flipping through *Kauai Magazine*.

"Hey, you must be Thorsten—yeah, funny name, you know? Where'd you get that name from?"

He looked up to see a woman standing close by. She was sixtyish, looked like a Hawaiian native, thin, perhaps five feet tall. "My mother. Are you Mia?"

"What you think?"

"Got it. Hello, Mia."

She spoke in a sharp, high-pitched, attention-getting voice, and talked very fast, so fast that her words ran together. She was wearing a muumuu with giant blue flowers on a white background, a pink coral necklace, and a simple gold wedding band.

"So, I got your application and the deposit. You know you shouldn't send cash like that. So now, you have to convince me I should rent you the rooms. Okay, who are you, why do you want to live above an old grocery store and restaurant in this one-horse town two miles from the beach? Huh? You tell me, okay?"

"Well, I'm retired. Between relationships. I like the tropics and I want to be left alone."

"Oh, I see you're maybe a bank robber, lying low, huh? No way I want a bank robber in my rental. No, I give you your deposit back. No bank robber!"

"Wait, wait, wait! Slow down."

Mia nodded.

Flash said, "Okay, let's try this again. I filled out your damn application. I'm guessing you checked it out, and that it didn't come back with me being a bank robber. I just want to get away from the workaday world. I can afford it—on a budget, mind you —and I know how to find the beach when I want to go there. I don't want to pay resort prices to have some rest, get warm, maybe surf, drink a little beer, and have a tropical experience. That's me."

"How long you stay, how long?"

"Well, say at least six months? Who knows? Maybe longer?"

"Ha ha—boy, you must be in a lot of trouble, you want to lay low six months."

"Well, yes, that's one interpretation. But maybe I simply want to take my time, maybe to find a place to buy or lease around here. How about that?"

"So, maybe you're wanted for murder or something, huh?"

"I'll pay six months in advance. Are you going to rent me the place or not?"

Mia's stony face broke into a smile. Not a pretty smile: more of a half-grimace.

"Give me the money first, and I'll bring you over there."

Flash took out his wallet, counted six months' rent in fresh bills, and offered it to Mia. She extended one bony brown hand, took the cash, stuffed it in the canvas book bag she was carrying, and they shook.

Surrounded by farmland, mostly sugar cane fields, Old Koloa Town had as its center feature the covered boardwalk that connected several old commercial buildings, including a market, a pizza joint, an ice cream store, and a surf shop. The Front Street collection of buildings looked like one building. Between the supermarket and the pizza place was an enclosed hallway, at the dark end of which were stairs to a second-floor landing and two doors facing one another on the landing. Each door had a plastic sign, green with white lettering, screwed to the door face; one read "Apartment A" and the other "Apartment B." Mia unlocked Apartment B, and they went in.

Apartment B consisted of three rooms: a living room/kitchen combination, and off to the back of the kitchen, a small bedroom and an attached bathroom. Windows invited a breeze on the side of the living room facing the street; in the back, a small, pebbled window opened in the bathroom.

The living room had two faded-yellow director's chairs, a coffee table, a small flat-screen TV against one wall that stood on an old end table with brass-tipped legs. Watercolor prints hung askew on both walls, picturing a sugar mill, two hula dancers, and a surfer launching down a glowing aqua-blue wave.

The kitchen area had a white porcelain sink, what looked like salvaged cabinets on both sides, top and bottom, and a mottled linoleum countertop. In the center of everything was a four-foot-square, battered and scarred, once-painted-red table, with two plastic chairs—one red and one yellow—on opposite sides of the table.

A half-size refrigerator sat against the wall opposite the sink, next to a green plastic garbage can lined with a black plastic bag. Flash could hear the refrigerator hum as he looked around at his new home.

"Who's in apartment A?" asked Flash.

"No one. Apartment A not for rent."

"Why is that?"

"None of your business."

Flash shrugged and moved through to the bedroom. Most of the floor was annexed by a twin-size bed frame, bare metal with wooden slats. Next to the frame was a small table painted forest green, with a single-bulb cork lamp adorned with a red-cloth lampshade. Like the rest of the apartment, the floor was old, worn wood planking, and the walls were walnut-colored chipboard paneling. The space was tiny, hardly a room. *Bed nook is more like it*, thought Flash.

"You'll have to buy your own mattress. The tropics, you know? Bugs. So, get your own," said Mia.

Flash grunted in reply and looked into the bathroom. It had a stained porcelain sink and toilet, no toilet paper, a metal medicine cabinet with a mirror that was hung off center, and the pièce de resistance was a stand-up shower enclosure with a rusted-

25

steel floor pan. The shower walls were Formica, made to look like stone pebbles. No shower curtain, but several red plastic curtain rings were hanging on the rusted chrome curtain rod.

"You should get your own shower curtain, too, Thorsten," said Mia.

"Okay." Flash nodded his head. "And you can call me Flash, a nickname, better than Thorsten."

As they walked toward the front door, Flash inhaled, and for the first time noticed the place smelled like Pine-Sol.

Home sweet home, he thought.

Erased, home, Pine-Sol in paradise.

CHAPTER 4

Lava rock, death black, had absorbed the heat of the day, as if trying to return to its natural state as a red-hot, fiery, molten dragon, free to flow and roam, destroy or encase, ultimately to subsume anything and everything it touched. Flash's flip-flops stuck to the pocked surface, soft rubber against the flint-hard, sharp rock, which was covered by an inch of water at high tide. With no breeze, the air was hotter than hell, though two beers for breakfast might have had something to do with his discomfort.

Flash was sweating like a pig as he flip-flopped his way across the black plateau, making quiet splashing sounds with each step. He imagined that if he stopped moving, he would rot on the spot, so on he went, sticking and stumbling until he reached the beach. And then he was confronted by the damn sand, dragging him down and multiplying the effort needed for each step.

He was breathing hard, but he had to make it to shelter, out of the sun. Another hundred yards or so and he could rest at the picnic table ahead and double down on the beer. *Jesus, what a place. Aloha, my ass!*

The picnic table was one of several scattered on the shore

beneath bent, top-heavy palm trees along a section of beach called Brennecke's, named after a long-dead dentist who'd lived in a shack at the edge of what was once the best-kept body-surfing secret in the islands.

Finally in the shade, Flash popped another Foster's, deciding it was as good a place as any to nap. He'd wait for the trade winds to start up before heading back. As on almost every other morning for the last three months, Flash felt a curious mix of numbness and relief. He'd done it. He was truly lost, erased even, no doubt about it.

As he was dozing off, he felt a gnawing anxiety in spite of the beer buzz. He was beginning to wonder what exactly was being erased.

Two years prior, in Seattle, his doctor had noticed a spot on his cheek that turned out to be a basal cell carcinoma. He remembered the scraping, a crunching sound, and pressure as the surgeon removed one layer off his cheek, then more flesh, then later still more flesh. He'd thought she was going to tunnel so deep she would break through into his mouth.

This escape, the expectation of erasing himself, was beginning to feel less like erasure and more like surgery, and he didn't know if he trusted the surgeon.

"Hey, buddy, want to come join us?"

The voice, at first, didn't register. "Hey, buddy, buddy! How about some coffee? Come join us."

Flash jumped, startled but still drunk. "What?" was all he managed to say.

"Come join us."

Flash looked at the man, fifty, maybe sixty years old, loose-fitting jeans, Hawaiian shirt, flip-flops on tanned feet, bright piercing blue eyes, a strong jaw with two-day stubble. Holding a white Styrofoam cup, he was offering it to Flash.

"Why, who are you? What do you want?"

"Just a passing friend, buddy, just a friend. We have coffee over here every morning, and we've seen you here before. I just thought you might like to join us. Here, here's some coffee."

Flash wiped the drool from around his mouth, shook his head, and squinted to look beyond the stranger at a group of men and women, mostly men, over at another picnic table, talking, standing, and sitting, all sipping from white Styrofoam cups, some smoking. A large brown air pot thermos sat in the center of the table.

"Why—join you?"

"Well, because we've seen you out here a lot, like I said, and I thought you could use some company today. Here, take the coffee."

"What kind of company? I don't get it."

"You don't have to get anything, buddy. We're just offering coffee and some companionship."

"Oh, shit." Flash slurred the words. "Jesus, you're a bunch of AA types."

"Yup, we are, buddy, drunks one and all. Want to join us? It's just coffee, buddy. Coffee and companionship, that's it."

"Look, I don't need your company, okay? So, see ya around!"

The AA guy just continued smiling. His eyes squinted slightly, but he otherwise stood stone-still. After an uncomfortable moment, he finally said, "Well, have a good day, buddy, and if you ever want to join us, just come on over. Here, here's my card, in case you want to talk to someone."

Flash recoiled.

"Hey, it's okay. It's just a card. Here. We'll be gathering tomorrow and the next day, and, the good Lord willing, the day after that. Pretty sure we'll see you again."

Jesus, thought Flash, *I'm going to have to change my morning route.* And then he wondered why he hadn't noticed the AA meeting before. He took the card. It read "Fred. Call AA, ANYTIME," and gave a local phone number.

Shrugging his shoulders, Flash pushed himself to his feet, grabbed the plastic bag with three full ones and three empties, dropped the card into the bag to keep the cans company, and flip-flopped away, looking for a new place to nap far enough up the beach to escape the Styrofoam cup brigade.

In Princeville, dark clouds opened up for what would be a day-long deluge. Sachiko Allen, a painfully fit, twenty-nine-year-old woman with black hair, was running from the tennis court, where she had abandoned her lesson. She ran up along a flag-stone path lined with low outdoor light fixtures, brass turned green, up to the house. She passed through an open sliding glass door into a covered lanai, cursing.

"Shit, I'm soaked! I've got to get out of these wet things. Get out of my way!"

She ran past her housekeeper, who was in the doorway that led to the back of the house. The woman, a diminutive Filipina named Mary Joy, jumped sideways with practiced ease as her mistress pushed past.

Sachiko glanced back to see the tennis instructor, Mateo, still out on the court picking up tennis balls and tossing them into a nearby basket.

Princeville was forty miles from Poipu Beach, driving north along the eastern coast of Kauai. Not a town, but an unincorporated area, Princeville was a big-play real estate development, one-thousand acres atop a plateau that sat above Hanalei Bay. The complex featured a pristine collection of golf courses, upscale homes, expensive resort hotels, a private airport able to accommodate executive jets, a community center, a handful of specialty stores, upscale restaurants, and a gas station.

Once a plantation, later a cattle ranch, Princeville had been constructed of several large parcels of land that had been pulled together in the early 1960s to make what developers were sure would be a one-of-a-kind, world-class enclave for the well-to-do.

After changing, Sachiko walked backed into the lanai, stopped, and stared in perplexity at Mateo, who was sitting there with a green beach towel around his shoulders. His white shirt and matching shorts were soaked, his hair still wet and pulled back into a two-inch ponytail.

"What the hell are you waiting for?" she demanded. A glass of mango juice in her hand, she now had on black shorts, a black turtleneck silk top, and black Nike runners. These were set off by black fingernail polish and black lipstick.

"Well, I thought we'd go for lunch," he answered.

"Well, no, we won't. What makes you think I want to go to lunch with you? You're my tennis instructor, for God's sake. Honestly, Mateo, get real!"

"Well, Sachiko, Ms. Allen, ma'am—what about last night?"

"Don't you say another word about last night, or any night for that matter if you ever want to see me or any of my money again. Do you understand, tennis instructor? Now get out of here."

Her cellphone chirped. As she raised the phone halfway to her face, she looked hard at Mateo. "I said get out of here. Go. I've got to talk to Daddy. Go!"

Rolling out of his chair, Mateo whispered, "Yes, ma'am. Daddy. Jeez, what a bitch," and headed for the patio door.

"Daddy! Where are you?"

"I'm in Honolulu, but the bigger question might be, where are you?"

"Very funny, Daddy. You know where I am. Princeville, fucking Princeville."

"Jesus, Sachiko, I hate it when you say that word. Clean up your act, will you? And, in case you haven't noticed, you live in paradise. You ought to count your blessings, for once."

"Daddy, I want to be with you. I don't want to be on Kauai. I want to be Benjamin. I could really help you. I'd be good. I promise, please."

"Sachiko, Benjamin makes the business work. You don't. I'm not sure anyone could replace him. Besides, I want you to be happy there on Kauai. It's time you built a useful life of your own, on your own."

"Daddy, I'm your daughter—he's your employee. There's a big difference. I can keep your secrets." Tears rimmed Sachiko's eyes.

"Stop right there. Benjamin isn't going anywhere, and neither are you. End of conversation. Now, about your birthday. I think we'll fly over so we can celebrate in style together. How would that be?"

"Oh, yes, Daddy. Can I throw a party?"

"No party, just us—the family—dinner, I think. You and me with Benjamin and Minette. We'll fly over and be there by six. Dinner will be my treat."

"Oh, thank you, Daddy. I can't wait, and we can talk more about it. Well, you know, Princeville can't be forever."

"I'll have Minette arrange it. See you next week, sweetheart."

He hung up.

Of course it's your treat, Daddy. Everything in my fucking life is your treat, for God's sake! Sachiko looked at the phone and shook her head. Then came the flood of tears and her exasperated, strangled scream.

CHAPTER 5

J esus, *another day in paradise,* Flash said to himself—slurred to himself, actually. The blinding sun shocked his eyelids, then they ripped open. "Ouch!" Moaning, he tried to sit up, only to fall back onto a nest of a dirty linens down at the foot of his bed, half of it on the floor. His head was swimming, his eyes burned, and his stomach felt as though he'd been punched hard recently. He was dizzy and afraid he might throw up.

Eyes closed, Flash reached for the institutional-size bottle of Advil on the table next to his bed. He opened the bottle and felt one, two, three, then four of the little coated pills, pushed them between his lips and swallowed.

He dozed off for a few minutes, maybe days—*No,* he thought, *not days, certainly not days.* He was relieved that the pain had dulled a little.

The nausea hadn't eased, however. *I need to feel better right now,* was all he could think. *Maybe by this afternoon?*

He had no idea what day it was. Not just the day—he wasn't even sure what month it was. All he knew was the sun was out.

Part of being erased seemed to be a kind of hangover deja vu. One long Groundhog Day, featuring nausea, headaches, disorientation, and, well, beer. Flash closed his eyes and dozed again.

He dreamed of lying on a beach towel at what might have been Poipu Beach, eyes closed. He could both see himself and feel himself on the towel. Flash on the towel, in the sun, was magically, completely, in an otherworldly sense, without pain, anxiety, tension, or fear. In this dream, the absence of everything upsetting and physically taxing was better than any high or any drink he had ever experienced.

Then from above, Flash noticed his skin was turning pink, and he felt the tingle of sunburn. He wanted to wake the sleeping Flash, but he couldn't. Sleeping Flash was oblivious to everything, including the tiny pinpricks as he began to burn. Then Flash heard his daughter Pippa's voice calling him. "Wake up, Daddy. Please wake up!"

Flash sat bolt upright in bed, sweating, heart racing, gulping air.

Chief Malcolm Forsyth dismissed his department heads after yet another month-in-review meeting. John Horan was one of the first to reach the door.

"John, a minute please," the chief said.

John, who was always in a hurry, mostly because he believed movement made him look good, stopped and turned around.

"Close the door, John."

John came back into the office. He sat in one of the chairs in front of the chief's desk, straightened the crease on a trouser leg, looked up at the chief, and said, "Yes, sir, what is it?"

The chief leaned back in his chair, which squeaked. He said nothing for a long moment.

"John, I need an update on our ex-inspector Michael. And anything you've learned about the missing money."

Long pauses, John knew, were one of the chief's favorite interrogation devices. He was wary of the chief, not just because of the chief's power and position, but because he knew the chief would hang him out to dry in a heartbeat if he had questions about police impropriety. *Screw him*, John thought. *Wait him out.*

"John?"

"Yes, sir." This was the tricky part. How could he tell the chief the same story he'd told him a month previously, only somehow make the answer sound new, or at least newer?

"Yes, sir, so you know we saw Flash at REI, purchasing what looked like camping gear."

"Yes, you told me that."

"Well, I've also heard from a friend at the FBI that they, too, are interested in our boy. They reviewed his security clearance history, which gave them a good excuse to interview his father, his ex-wife, and several friends. It turns out no one imagined he would do a runner. They seemed to suspect that his leaving the department wasn't voluntary, and one friend reported that Flash uncharacteristically clammed up and refused to discuss any of the details with them. That's a good thing, don't you think?"

"Hmm. Do we have any idea where he has gone? Yet?"

"No, sir. None. But, well, you know, as long as he's out of the picture, we have no missing money issue. It's completely locked down."

"What about the bad guys?" asked the chief, seeming to be deep in thought.

"Well, sir, they've gone completely dark. Disappeared, just like the money. I really wonder if they didn't somehow outflank us."

"What do you mean, outflank us?"

"Why else would they have gone quiet? Couple it with Flash disappearing, and the circumstances just make me wonder if they didn't get at least some of their money, after all."

"You mean they made a deal with Flash or got rid of him?" The chief sounded interested.

"Could be, sir. I wouldn't be surprised. Say the bastards found him—they'd kill him in a heartbeat. Or maybe he's done a runner with the money, and they're busy looking for him. Part of me wants to dig to the bottom of this, but part of me thinks we should leave the whole mess alone. He's gone. The money's gone. Why stir the pot? We have nothing to gain other than more exposure."

The chief steepled his fingers, his face twisted into a scowl, and he said, "I don't like it. I don't want exposure, either, but if we could find out where he is, we might be able to manage the situation if and when. No, we need to keep looking, stay in touch with the FBI too. Interpol? Anything from them?"

"No, nothing. But you know Interpol. They make the FBI look nimble, and we all know how far from nimble the FBI is." John paused, thinking, *Let the old man worry. If any of this leaks, he's between a rock and a hard place.* "As for our people, we've put ears and eyes on phone and data traffic, but nothing so far. We're also trying to find out how it was our boy got out of town so cleanly, if he did leave town, that is."

The chief smirked, shook his head and said, "Well, let's not forget he worked undercover, and he's smart. I'll give him that much. Sometimes I wonder if sending people undercover is just training them to become crooks." He paused in thought. "No, I don't mean that. Those people are heroes. But I sure as hell wonder about our friend Flash."

John sat quietly while the chief prattled on. All of this was nothing but self-indulgent crap. He might be the chief of police, but clearly, he was scared. His worst nightmare was that this situation might morph into an indelible, end-of-life blemish on his spotless record.

Well, good, the more the old man worried about his pristine record, the less he'd fret about where the money went. To John, that was a big win.

John said, "Yeah, I wonder about him, too. One good thing, though, Watson and Internal Affairs seem to have forgotten about him. We don't need those snakes sniffing around the nest."

The chief sat up at that and said, "No, John, we don't. We really, really don't. I'm counting on you to see that nothing happens to renew their interest in our little fuckup. Do you think you can manage that, Lieutenant?

"Yes, sir!"

"Good. Then I think we're done here."

"Yes, sir." John rose and headed for the door. *Nice try, you prick! Just like you to put me between you and Internal Affairs, you self-righteous jerk. Well, we'll see how that plays out, because I'm not going down for this, and I'm certainly not taking a bullet for you. If I can just hang in here for a year or so, then, well, nine-million dollars and the rest of my life, baby!*

CHAPTER 6

S till breathing hard, Flash pushed himself up on one
elbow. Perhaps he could use a hangover break. After all,
he had been hung over for—well, months, a long,
almost endless, string of hangovers.

Flash had gone all in on erasing what he was calling his "old
self." As best he could figure, that seemed to be working. But
apparently, a massive physical and psychological price was associated with the process. *Goddamn it,* he said to himself, *no beer for
breakfast. Well, at least not for today. Lunch maybe, or dinner maybe,
but not for breakfast.*

That decided, he swallowed four Advil, brushed his teeth,
and pulled on his tropical paradise uniform: khaki hiking shorts,
a faded t-shirt that said, "Kiss Me I'm on Vacation," flip-flops
permanently bent from wear, and a Seattle Mariners baseball cap
—faded blue on top, dark blue around the sweatband.

He checked himself in the bathroom mirror.

He needed a haircut. His black hair was long, so he pushed it
off his forehead to the right, and swept it back over his ears. His
gray-blue eyes were slightly bloodshot, of course, but that was
the only real sign of his dissipation—he hadn't gone to flab, at
least not so far.

He noticed he was slouching, though, so he stood up straight. *There*, he thought, *still one inch short of six feet.* A good height for running, and high school football. He'd been a quarterback then and had been physically active ever since. He didn't think of himself as handsome, but women often did—the face in the mirror seemed kind. However he looked, anyway, people appeared to like him; he always had friends. Past tense—*had* friends.

Out on the street, Flash walked along the covered boardwalk that fronted Koloa Town's center, a string of old and older buildings, all wood, dark brown, and weathered. As he did every morning, beer or no beer, he headed west, past the Garden Island Grill, which occupied the main floor of his building, past Sueoka Market—a real honest-to-god small town grocery store—and, as he reached the parking lot adjacent to Sueoka's, he stopped. He would usually crack open a beer in the lot, then turn left to walk along a footpath that would take him to Poipu Road, and eventually the beach, where he would further indulge in his beer-for-breakfast routine.

But since he hadn't gone into Sueoka's, he hadn't bought any Foster's, the breakfast of retired champions, and he wasn't opening one in the parking lot. So he set off, not turning left toward the beach, but straight ahead, across the bridge over Waikimo Stream, flip-flopping along another boardwalk to Koloa Roasters.

Koloa Roasters was one of those inside/outside places so common in the tropics. Protected by two huge banyan trees, the café was open at the front where a number of big tables invited guests, and a bakery and a coffee counter served treats and meals across the back interior wall. Flash ordered a double mocha and two mango scones, picked up his order at the far end of the bar, and took his breakfast out under the two trees' impossibly long and majestic arms.

Despite the usual crowd, Flash found an open table with one chair. He took one of the scones out of the pastry bag and put half of it in his mouth. Then he slurped at his hot mocha. Sugar, butter, mango, cocoa, whipped cream, caffeine/coffee—repeat. The experience was absolute heaven, almost as good as Foster's.

He leaned back in the wooden chair, folded his hands in his lap, closed his eyes, inhaled deeply, and sighed. *Aloha.*

"Hey, beach bum, you slumming? Hey, you, beach bum, are you slumming? Vacation over?"

Flash opened his eyes and looked around. He couldn't see if someone was talking to him, or what. So, he closed his eyes again.

"Hey, beach bum, you should come over here."

Flash opened his eyes and looked around again, more slowly this time. He spotted a hand waving on the far side of the patio and then recognized Mia, who was wearing a red-and-white muumuu and motioning at him. He was impressed that her voice could carry through the din. He picked up his cup and the crumpled, empty pastry bag and walked over to greet her. She held out her hand to shake, then gestured to an empty chair.

"Have a seat, beach bum, I want to introduce you to my friends. You've been here long enough. You need to meet some real people."

"Hello, friends," said Flash, surveying the two women seated across from Mia. He hesitated for a moment, then sat down.

Mia gestured to a young woman with short blonde hair wearing a khaki-and-green police uniform. "This is Officer Kellie Peterson. She's the daughter of an old friend of mine."

Officer Kellie was a strong-looking woman. "Stout" would actually describe her best, and like so many officers Flash had known, her tailored uniform was tight fitting. She was shorter than Flash by a head and dark complected, which against her blonde hair made for a kind of well-groomed beach-bum look. Her eyes were black and her smile seemed natural. She extended her hand to shake Flash's. Mia smiled.

"And this is another dear young friend, Emma Pookalani. Her mother and I went to high school, did Girl Scouts, and had babies together, but she's gone now. Her mother, I mean, by way of the cancer. We were just discussing Emma's son, a boy. You were a boy once, so maybe you could help us, beach bum."

Emma seemed young and old at the same time. She was perhaps in her early thirties, with black hair, shoulder length. She was dressed in designer jeans and a Hawaiian silk blouse, purple with a painted bird of paradise pointing toward her left shoulder. Her eyes were black, and she was slight, with olive skin, thin arms and neck, and high cheekbones. She extended her hand politely in greeting, but she wasn't smiling.

Flash said, "How do you do, Emma?"

Emma held his hand and his eyes for a moment, then released his hand and looked over at Mia.

Mia said, "Oh, we've had better times, but you know about boys, so sit." She looked at Mia and continued, "Flash here, I call him *beach bum* because he is a beach bum. He's renting the apartment above the grill."

The two younger women nodded, both looking at Flash. Kellie asked, "Where are you from?"

Before Flash could say anything, Mia jumped in. "Kellie, dear, Flash, my beach bum renter, he's a good renter. He's living the life of a beach bum, you know. Haole boys, men, they all dream of doing it! The mystery is a big part of it, dear, a guy thing. Don't interrogate him about his dream. He'll leave town if you badger him, and I'll lose my renter."

"Sorry, Auntie," the officer said. Then, looking at Flash, she added, "Pardon me, Flash. How are you enjoying our island, then?"

"It's great, just like Auntie says, a beach-bum dream come true."

Mia and Kellie laughed, and Emma smiled weakly.

Mia's face darkened, and she said, "Today we're sad though. Paul, Emma's nineteen-year-old boy, has gone missing! Did you ever run away when you were a boy, Flash?"

"Ah, only once, overnight. Came home the next day with my tail between my legs," Flash said, trying to be encouraging.

"Yes, well, we wish Paul would do the same. Kellie is working on the missing person's angle. He's been gone a week, so we're sad and kinda worried."

A week. That didn't sound good. "I hope you find him soon," said Flash.

"Me too." Kellie sighed. "It's strange, though. He goes to work at a fast-food place one morning—Burger King in Lihue—does his shift, leaves, and vanishes. Poof."

"This is a pretty small place," Flash said. "No one has seen him, none of the kids? How about his hangout places, surfing beach, cellphone?"

"No," said Kellie. "Nothing—phone, media, credit and debit cards, all silent, too."

Emma spoke for the first time. "We've put his picture out there, social media, all that stuff. Nothing." She looked over at Flash. "Where would you go if you were going wandering away, I wonder?"

Flash spoke without thinking. "You would know better than anyone, especially if you're close to him. Parents and siblings are always the primary sources, followed by peer groups, teachers, coworkers, then his social media, cellphone, and well—" He looked around at the three women. "I have a friend who's a cop. He told me about a runaway case once. But Kellie here has probably done all that stuff. Sorry. I don't mean to butt in."

Kellie smiled warmly. "Don't worry about butting in. You'd have to get in line behind Auntie Mia. She's relentless at interrogating me about our police work, like over and over!" She rolled her eyes and looked at Mia, then at Flash. "You sure you're not a cop, Flash?"

"Kellie!" Mia barked. "Leave him alone. He's my renter, not your business!"

Flash didn't answer her, just smiled and said to Emma, "I hope you find your son soon. This must be hard for you."

Emma swiped at a rogue tear with a crumpled Koloa Roasters napkin, shook her head, sniffed, then whispered, "Yes, it's very hard. I feel so lost without him, and I'm scared for him."

Flash stood up and gave the women a little wave. "Nice to meet you guys. See you later, Mia. I need to get back to my beach-bumming. Places to go, things to see."

He thought he could feel Kellie's eyes following him as he left the table and walked out into the warm morning sun. He shrugged it off and made his way back toward the bridge and the grocery store parking lot. This time, he turned right and flip-flopped down the road toward the beach.

CHAPTER 7

*H*appy birthday to me, happy birthday to me, happy birthday, dear Sachiko, she sang in a an uncharacteristically soft voice. *Thirty years old. No, that can't be right. Happy birthday to me. Shit, it is right. Oh, well, Daddy is coming, and he's got to let me back. No, not just let me back—he's got to get rid of that bozo, Benjamin. That's it, he needs me to help him run his business, now! Please, Daddy, please, please, please, Daddy! I can do it! God, he must know I can do it. I'm thirty, goddamnit, Daddy! Yes, I am. Thirty and ready, Daddy, aren't I?*

Sachiko stood in front of a full-length mirror in a cavernous walk-in closet/dressing room with open, backlit shelving and stacked hanger bays, all framed in polished Koa wood, wearing shiny white silk panties and a black lace bra. She raised her arms above her head and cocked her hips to the right and then to the left like a hula dancer. *Great figure, babe. A little tummy, maybe, but you're the bomb!*

This room was her sanctuary, or maybe more like her vault— a windowless room deep in the center of the house, where all of her secrets were safely stored. The look, the image, the vibe, and the secret sauce were all stockpiled in here. She examined her two rows of hanging shirts—one for black, one for white—then studied a lower bank of five rows of shoes, all black or white, or black *and* white. In an adjacent bay were dresses, black and white.

She turned to the open-faced drawers holding folded shorts, sweats, rolled socks, and bathing suits, all black or white. And on to another bank of drawers, where her underwear, scarves, and leggings were stored. Behind the middle shelf was the secret compartment that held her drug stash and a gun.

The young woman moved to the other side of the room and sat down at a built-in makeup table. She examined her carefully shaped black eyebrows, small mouth, thin lips, and high cheek-bones. She made faces at herself. Scrunching her lips, then baring her white teeth, she surveyed her neck and her shoulders, then tossed her head back and said to herself, "It's showtime, baby."

Touma Allen was in love with the airplane. Each time he entered the cabin and fell into the azure-blue leather seat, the one with his name stitched in yellow script across the headrest, he was revisited by a wave of excitement mixed with relief. He nodded in satisfaction at his guests across the aisle.

He could have subscribed to any of the several executive jet services at the Daniel K. Inouye International Airport. But Touma, a superstar property developer in a land overrun with property developers, had always wanted his own jet, namely a Hawker XP—what a vehicle! What an extravagance! His own personal winged chariot, his, and his alone.

Settling in for the short flight from Honolulu to Kauai, Touma breathed in and smiled, savoring smells of new leather, the floral bouquet on the table next to his seat, coffee brewing in the galley, and a hint of the perfume the flight attendant was wearing.

The cabin intercom came to life, startling him. "Good after-noon, Mr. Allen, Mr. Benjamin, and Ms. Minette, welcome aboard," said the pilot. "We're planning a twenty-four-minute flight from wheels up to touchdown at the Princeville Airfield.

It's raining in Princeville, so we may experience some turbulence during our approach and landing. But not to worry—the Citation 560XL is equipped with the most advanced avionics equipment that is commercially available. So, rain or shine, we can see and safely navigate through anything Mother Nature can throw at us."

Touma nodded in appreciation. He loved hearing the spiel, even though he knew it was being read from a plasticized card by one of several rent-a-pilots on staff at the executive terminal. But the pilot had read it about Touma's jet, not anyone else's jet, which Touma liked most. He felt like a proud parent as his child was presented as valedictorian at graduation.

That thought ruined his reverie; he realized he'd never had, nor was he likely to ever have, the experience of his child being a valedictorian or anything like it. Yes, he was a parent, of an only child, a daughter. Was that a double curse, only child and girl child? It sure as hell felt like it. Sachiko had never come within a country mile of being a student, let alone valedictorian. Sachiko's legacy, as far as he could tell, was as a troublemaker. Wherever she went, she seemed to be hell-bent on creating discord.

At the Mapplethorpe College Preparatory School for Girls in New Haven, Connecticut, Sachiko Allen was renowned as the most difficult—her headmaster used the word *challenging*—girl in a class of seventy-five rich, spoiled, difficult, and challenging girls. Mapplethorpe was made for rich, difficult girls, for God's sake. She was routinely at or near the bottom of her class in academics while rocketing her way to the top as the queen shit disturber. She managed to graduate—Touma had poured enough money into Mapplethorpe that they couldn't deny her—but in spite of the girl's four years of elite education, what he got back was a much more clever, more deceitful version of the brat he had sent away.

"Please fasten your seatbelts low and secure for takeoff."

Sachiko lived on Kauai because he had banished her from Honolulu right after her twenty-ninth birthday party.

That party had been absolutely the last straw! She and her band of privileged millennial hooligans had damaged several rooms in his house and made such a disturbance that the police came and threatened arrests three times that night and early into the morning. The music had been so loud that neighbors a mile down the beach repeatedly phoned in complaints, and the neighbors closer in had been treated to swimming in the nude, with everything punctuated by shrieks, shouts, screams, and curses.

The following week, Touma had been tasked with arm twisting and outrageous payouts to members of the press to suppress the news. Even so, the party was mentioned as an entry in the police-blotter column in the *Honolulu Star Advertiser*. Thankfully, no names were used, only an address with the charge of disturbing the peace. Talk about an understatement!

Being Sachiko Allen's father had become a liability, considering how much of his business depended on a certain aura about his wealth and prominence. So, Mr. Touma Allen, founder and chairman of the Allen Group, gathered his daughter and her belongings and moved her lock, stock, and black-and-white wardrobe to Princeville, on another island altogether.

One particularly mouthy girlfriend wondered why Sachiko would let her father control her life; however, most of her friends didn't question the matter, because they were in the same boat as Sachiko. Taking Daddy's money meant living by Daddy's rules. And in that social stratum, the rule above all other rules was behave, or get cut off.

The Allen Group jet landed in the rain and was met by a limousine. Touma, accompanied by his COO, Benjamin Akamu, and his CFO, Minette Hale, were driven to Sachiko's home.

"Daddy!" Sachiko shrieked as Touma walked in the front door. He smiled. His celebrated sunshine smile—that's what the *Honolulu Star*'s society columnist called it—was always at the ready, white teeth showing alongside slight dimples on each cheek set in a light-brown complexion. His carefully cut and combed black hair was parted on the left with a boyish spike at the front, above black eyes.

Touma was a short, trim man, perhaps five foot two, elevated by bespoke Ferragamo loafers made to lift him some; and today wearing a tailored white dress shirt, floral tie, and a perfectly fitting dark-green dress suit with light-pink pinstriping.

"Daddy!" Sachiko shrieked again as she buried her face in his neck and kicked one foot back. They twirled around in a choreographed embrace. She was in white, all white, from her tight-fitting cocktail dress, white Jimmy Choo glitter stiletto high heels, and white mesh stockings, to a white beret.

"Daddy! I'm so happy you came."

"Of course I came. This is an important birthday for my important daughter. Happy birthday, dear heart, Sachiko."

He kissed her on the cheek.

She looked over his shoulder. "Benjamin, Minette, hi! Thank you both for bringing Daddy all this way."

Benjamin said, "Oh, Ms. Sachiko, he brought us, not the other way around. Happy birthday."

"Yes, dear, happy thirtieth birthday," said Minette.

Benjamin was short like Touma, only he was as wide as he was tall. His arms never settled at his sides, as he simply was too large. His sand-colored gabardine suit was wider than it was long. He was a finely dressed stump, a two-thirds-scale sumo wrestler. He had olive skin, a shaved head, and the gasping breath of a very fat man.

Benjamin extended a hand to Sachiko; she took it, gave it a shake, and nodded.

Minette stepped forward beside Benjamin. She was taller than all of them—a blonde Amazon bitch was how Sachiko thought of her—and olive complected, like the rest of the Allen tribe. She wore a black silk pantsuit with a Nehru collar and a big smile. She opened both arms and hugged Sachiko. "Oh, my, to think you're so grown up, Sachiko, just so grown up!"

"Yes, Minette, I am, aren't I? Thank you for noticing. The big question is whether Daddy will notice."

Minette leaned over and whispered in Sachiko's ear. "Try not to be a bitch, tonight, okay? Your father is making a big effort—actually reaching out to you, for once. Try not to ruin it, okay?"

"No, of course not, Minette. It's my birthday, after all, isn't it?"

"That's it, dear. It's your birthday, your thirtieth birthday."

Why the hell are they here on my birthday? Benjamin was Touma's majordomo, for God's sake, his fixer. Yes, he was called a COO, but *gang boss* was more like it. And Minette was the damn penny pincher, a purse-zipped, tight-assed bitch. Sachiko took her daddy's arm and pulled everyone into the living room.

Drinks at home were followed by a short drive to Bar Acuda, overlooking Hanalei Bay, where Minette had reserved a private room for the party. Sachiko was nervous, so she drank. Her black-and-white shtick was accompanied by her insistence on drinking only Champagne whenever she drank alcohol, which was often. Like teetotalers who bring fizzy water or ginger ale with them to cocktail parties, Sachiko often showed up with one or more bottles of Dom Perignon, or Louis Roederer Cristal, just in case the host didn't know her preferences.

She was working on her second bottle when the cake made its way into the room, three candles adorning a baked-Alaska-like confection placed in front of her for the blowing-out ceremony, accompanied by words from Touma, naturally. The flickering candles cast a soft light over the cake. Sachiko stared, fixated, at the brown lettering on the white meringue: "Sachiko At Thirty.."

"To my lovely daughter, on her thirtieth birthday. Go ahead, blow them out, and then I'll give you your present!"

Sachiko blew, the candles went dark, and her audience, including their server, clapped and then sang "Happy Birthday." After more clapping, Touma rose, slightly tipsy, placed his hand in his coat pocket, slowly revealing a silver paper envelope with

SACHIKO in large red calligraphy on its front. He tapped the envelope against the fingernails of his right hand as he spoke.

"Sachiko, my daughter, today you're thirty years old, a grown woman. You're eight years older than your mother was when you were born. I can hardly believe how fast time has passed. I'm presenting you with this birthday present in the belief that you will at some point soon make your mark in the world. And, being your father, I decided that the best thing I could contribute to assist you on this journey was something foundational, a reliably solid base as it were, a centered place from which you might venture forth to a life of accomplishment and significance. At least I hope that's where the next phase will lead you. So, in spite of everything, I am doubling down on you with this."

He handed her the envelope. She beamed up at him, thinking it was either a great big check or more likely an invitation to become one of the Allen Group's senior executives. Over and over, she'd told him that was what she wanted. Now she would earn lots of money and get on with what she could only imagine as her soon-to-be-spectacular business and social career: Sachiko Allen, vice-chairman, chairperson-in-waiting of the mighty Allen Group of Honolulu, Hawaii. She would be her father's right-hand woman, and of course, his successor.

Tears spilled down her cheeks as she read the first two lines of the two-page document. "Deed of Trust" and "Free and Clear" were there, and a red circular stamp had been affixed on the second page: "Seal of the State of Hawaii." And another blue stamp said "Notary," with Minette's signature and a date in the center of the marking. These were the only words she could make out before her sight was blurred entirely.

"What is this?" Her hands trembled as she held the Deed of Trust out toward Touma. "What is this, Daddy?"

"It's the deed to your house. I've paid off the mortgage and put the house in your name, a two-and-a-half-million house, Sachiko, free and clear. Happy birthday, dear."

"But, Daddy, I don't want to live here. I want to come back to Honolulu. I want to work with you, Daddy. I want to be your—"

"Sachiko!" he barked. His smile was gone. "Sachiko, you may not return to Oahu. You live here now!"

"But—"

"No! There is no *but*! You're thirty years old, and you live here. The time has come for you to grow up and make your own way. Don't worry—as long as you live here, I'll support you with the allowance and all, but if you try to return to Oahu, I will cut you off entirely, and I'll take back my gift. Do you understand me? You either live here, or I'll stop the money —permanently."

"But why?"

"You know why!"

"No, I don't. I just want a chance."

"A chance? You've had nothing but chances, and look at you! White, black, drunk, thirty fucking years old, and you need a chance? Your life is a mess. You're a walking, talking menace to everything I've worked my whole life to build. No, goddamn it! You really need to grow up, Sachiko—on Kauai, not on Oahu, and certainly not anywhere near my business!"

"Don't—"

"Don't what? Don't give you a two-and-a-half-million-dollar house? Don't keep you in the lap of luxury on this beautiful island? Don't support your ridiculous habits, shopping, spending, partying, and God knows what? Don't?"

His face was flushed pink, for once not smiling. She thought, *Fuck it, I hate him!*

The whole scene was a blur; overcome by tears, snot, and adrenaline, she just let go and screamed, slamming both fists on the table. Minette jumped up from her seat and tried to embrace her. Sachiko pushed the other woman away.

"Fuck you, Daddy!" She stood and walked unsteadily toward the door, and Minette followed. They left and went across the main dining room, weaving through the tables, and into the reception area, where Sachiko suddenly stopped, fists clenched at her sides.

"Sachiko, oh, Sachiko, you are such a puzzle, girl."

Minette hugged Sachiko, rocking her back and forth through the crying, gasps, snuffling, and tears.

Sachiko finally went quiet, and in a halting, hoarse voice she asked, "Why is he doing this to me, Minette—why?"

"Because he doesn't know what else to do with you, girl. He's as confused as you are."

CHAPTER 8

The glacial gusts whipping across Lake Zurich bumped Zigfrids Erebus off his stride. His ears were already tingling, despite the upturned collar of his pea coat. He might have appeared drunk, if not for other people walking along the promenade also weaving and sliding, making slow and jerky progress. Erebus hated the cold. Winters in Klaipeda, Lithuania, his childhood home, had been, for him, long, brutal, and soul deadening. He pulled his collar closer with one hand and checked his watch on the other. Ten minutes early. He was always ten minutes early—best to scope out the stage before making an entrance.

Erebus approached the rectangular, glass-enclosed building, pulled open the heavy glass door, and passed under a stainless-steel sign: Konditorei Zürichsee. Inside, the air was warm, redolent with smells of meat grilling, pastry baking, coffee brewing, and a whiff of alcohol. Erebus chose a table in the far corner looking out over the lake—seating for two where he could sit with his back against a wall. A waiter appeared as if by magic, pad in hand, pen at the ready.

"Bonjour, monsieur."

"Bonjour. Cafe latte, bitte—um— s'il vous plaît."

"Cafe latte, bon." The waiter moved off.

Now to wait.

Fifteen minutes later, Erebus rechecked his watch. He had finished his coffee and was working on the accompanying glass of water and thought, *God—inbred Brits, always late. They just love to keep you waiting.* Forty-three minutes later, he was ready to stand up and leave. Maybe he could catch an earlier flight back to Nice.

"You must be Erebus. What are you drinking?"

"Coffee. But I was just about to leave. I don't like being kept waiting." Erebus was pleased to express his anger in a tight statement.

"Really! Well, I don't give a shit about what you like or don't like—how about that, eh? Never mind, I'm here now. Assuming you can spare the time, that is."

Erebus sat back in his chair, considering whether to just blow the whole thing off. He despised this man, Malcolm Haysmith, special counsel to what was known in the dark world as the Laundromat; his actual client was Heinrich Dietrich, chairman of the Banc Schaffhausen GmbH, Zurich, who'd asked Erebus to meet with the Englishman.

The Laundromat's public name was LM Global Ltd. It acted as a private investment fund. In fact, it was an aggregator of dirty money, managed by three international underworld syndicates to launder money and return it to the conventional marketplace to buy things and make more money.

Dirty money laundered and invested becomes clean money. Clean money invested begets more clean money; enormous sums of money issue forth as immense political power, which leads to more of everything. This tautology was a kind of aspirational mission statement for the underworld.

This Haysmith was a nasty piece of work, a weasel. His boss was Michel Planc, the founder of LM Global. Planc and two other directors of LM were crooks, who, having climbed out of the sewers of society, were obsessed with staying above the fray, far from the dirty world they had helped to grow.

One thing these three criminals could agree on was that utilizing Haysmith to rummage around in the primordial ooze was infinitely preferable to any of them doing it themselves. Now here Haysmith was, calling himself an administrative specialist and auditor, charged with protecting the investment interests of LM Global..

Haysmith's assignment was to investigate a deal that had gone off the rails. LM Global Ltd. planned to move five-hundred-million-dollars into an investment fund run by Erebus's client, Heinrich Dietrich, at Banc Schaffhausen GmbH. The legitimate Swiss bank would cleanse the money by loaning it out to finance legitimate mainstream investments, such as hotels, real estate developments, and infrastructure projects.

Erebus's relationship with Dietrich had begun eight years previously, when Dietrich had hired him to deal with a journalist from Bern. Dietrich's boss, the then-chairman, had developed a taste for young girls, and the journalist apparently had proof that the old man was squandering bank funds on a bevy of young concubines.

Within a week, the journalist was dead, shot in an apparent burglary at his farmhouse outside Bern. Dietrich then led a palace coup, quietly ousting the old chairman. Immediately thereafter, Heinrich Dietrich had been unanimously voted into the old man's seat.

Over the years, Dietrich and his bank had occasionally called on Erebus for similarly forceful action to smooth the way for the bank's progress in the turbulent and often violent world of finance. Erebus's current assignment was to cooperate with Haysmith in an investigation into some missing money and to take the pulse of LM Global, and to see if he, Erebus, could defang Haysmith before Haysmith derailed LM Global's promised five-hundred-million investment.

Erebus said, "You know, I could just as easily have reported my findings by phone in fifteen minutes."

"Why don't you cut the crap? Tell me what you've found out so far."

"Ten-million dollars went missing. You know that. It was deposited in a special account you asked us to set up in Banc Schaffhausen. Then, apparently, your agents, whoever they were, issued instructions for an electronic transfer, after which the money just disappeared. As we understand it, the money was supposed to end up in France, but it seems to have gone astray. What I know, though, is that your so-called agent, the people providing the ten-million you wanted to be moved through our bank, were not on your side. They were your enemies, Herr Haysmith. What do you have to say about that?"

Malcolm Haysmith was a chubby, half-bald, rosy-cheeked English ex-pat. He removed a clean yellow handkerchief from the pocket of his tweed sports coat and dabbed sweat from his brow. He looked puzzled.

"Our enemies? What the hell do you mean?"

"I mean they were not people seeking to launder some money. They were people wanting to entrap money launderers like you. Everything points to it being a sting. Apparently, you thought you were dealing with a rogue cop. Unfortunately, you were only half right." Erebus smiled.

"But in this case, someone was setting you up, someone who wished you harm. I can't prove it yet, but I'm guessing the ten million was a trap, a lure. Fortunately for your bosses, fate intervened—at least that's what I think—and for some reason, the trap failed to spring, because the money didn't go where you wanted it to go. It disappeared into thin air." Erebus stopped smiling.

"If on the other hand, the money had been delivered where it was supposed to go, your enemy, the authorities, would have followed it right up your ass, with investigations and indictments all around. You and your bosses would be fending off the forces of law and order, and Banc Schaffhausen could have been in the dock too." Erebus chuckled and took a sip of water. "What were you thinking?" he barked.

Haysmith's eyes bulged with undisguised anger. "That's enough, I'll do the speculating, thank you. What else do you know? I need names!"

"Well, for starters, at the center of this were three police types in Seattle, Washington and probably a bunch of bystanders, including FBI, Interpol, US Department of the Treasury, and Federal Drug Administration—that crowd," Erebus said quietly. "A Seattle cop named Finnegan Michael was the undercover agent, and his boss was Lieutenant John Horan. They both were working under Malcolm Forsyth, the chief of police. Those are the likely perpetrators."

"And?"

"And the money was deposited by the Seattle types into our bank, then moved. We haven't figured it out yet, but either the Seattle people moved it, issued the transfer instructions, or your LM people did. In any case, your mysterious payee, whoever it was you were trying to send the ten-million semi-clean dollars to, didn't receive the money."

Erebus leaned forward and said, "And here you sit, accusing us of screwing up a transfer that was entirely under your control. As I see it, you let the fox into the hen house, and the fox ate your money. Tough shit. You invited the cops in, and you're responsible for the loss of the money. Not us."

"Very funny. You know better than anyone that our people never make mistakes," countered Haysmith. "This cock-up needs to be someone else's fault. That's where you come in. You need to make it someone else's mistake, and soon. Oh, and you need to find that goddamn money! It needs to appear some-where in a hurry!"

Erebus's eyebrows shot straight up, signaling disbelief. "So, you're asking me to find your money? It's your problem, Haysmith, not mine. The sting may not have worked, but that doesn't mean that anyone wandering around this minefield will make their way across it alive. The only people more vindictive and self-righteous than crooks with money are police officers, especially crooked police officers, and it is a distinct possibility that's where the problem lies. A crooked police officer would throw a spanner in the works, don't you think?"

"I'm not the gravedigger in this churchyard of yours, Erebus. You are, or so your boss tells us. Your boss, your client, fucked this up," Haysmith insisted. He grabbed Erebus's water glass and actually dared to drink down a gulp. "We're sure of it. So you need to get out there and discover what happened, and as soon as you do, report back to me. Oh, and send your bill to Chairman Dietrich, not to us. He tells me I'm authorized to accept whatever terms you ask for. If you don't mind my asking, though, how much will this cost, just out of curiosity?"

Zigfrids Erebus smiled and said, "It will cost what it costs. But we're getting way ahead of ourselves here. First of all, your bosses were idiots. Your masters appear to have crawled in bed with undercover cops and agreed to launder ten-million dollars. We both know that ten-million dollars is a fortune to some people, but to you guys at LM Global? Why start a shitstorm over a pittance? Something stinks, and I want to know what it is before I agree to anything."

"Of course it's not big money," the Englishman said. "It was, in fact, a fuck-up. We don't like fuck-ups. As a result, the Laundromat, as you call it, has closed its purse strings to the Banc Schaffhausen. LM Global was prepared to make a five-hundred-million contribution to Banc Schaffhausen's investment fund, Herr Dietrich's golden project." Haysmith glared.

"This special project, the ten-million-dollar transaction, was a precondition to our investment. In other words, LM Global asked Dietrich to orchestrate a simple transaction, as a test, if you will, as a courtesy, to demonstrate your competency and goodwill. As we see it, you fucked it up, not us. The so-called sting or whatever it was, needs to be explained and put to bed, and our ten-million dollars needs to be restored and delivered as promised. In short, as we see it, you screwed it up, and you're going to have to make it right. Unilaterally."

"You people are nuts." Erebus smiled cheerfully. He pushed his water glass over to the other man since obviously he wasn't going to drink from it again.

"Yes, Herr Erebus, we are. We also have half-a-billion dollars Dietrich would like to invest. It's over to you."

"And so here you are, the Laundromat's goon," clarified Erebus.

"Call me whatever you would like. If Dietrich wants our money, he pays you to do what I tell you to do. Is that simple enough for you?"

Erebus now signaled to the waiter and said to Haysmith, "Yes. Very plain. So, here is what I know: Two of the three cops are both pretty much sitting ducks in Seattle. Therefore, if you'd like me to go duck hunting, just say the word. I can have it done within two weeks."

Haysmith wiped the sweat from his forehead. He was taking short breaths now, panting as he listened, his cheeks glowing.

The waiter appeared. "Oui?"

Zigfrids Erebus said, "Un double brandy." He nodded at Haysmith. "Et Perrier avec citron."

Haysmith eyed the waiter nervously and waited until the man was well away from their table before saying, "God no, whatever you do, no killing! Not yet. Jesus! Your instructions are to investigate this mess, find out what happened, get the information about these cops, documented information about *live* perpetrators. Once we have answers and the missing money is replaced, then and only then will we decide how to deal with the cops. Do you understand?"

Erebus nodded. "All right, but be sure to tell our masters that this is the least efficient option. A more direct and forceful method would acquire the same information faster, for pennies on the dollar."

"We aren't looking for a pennies-on-the-dollar solution! We're instructing you to do it our way, which means you stay inside the lines that we draw. Quiet, thorough, in the background, and above all, leave no trace. Do you understand—no trace?"

Erebus paused, nodded, and began speaking in a calm voice, just above a whisper. "Very well, Haysmith, here are my terms. I need a retainer for this delicate investigation and a significant bonus if I deliver your evidence. Specifically, I want five-hundred-thousand Euros in advance as a nonrefundable retainer, and the same upon delivery of the evidence. And if further action is indicated, that will be extra, a fee to be negotiated after I provide the evidence."

Haysmith shook his head. "God, man, someone up there must be protecting you. If it were up to me—Never mind, I am authorized to accept your terms, no matter how outrageous."

"One additional caveat, Haysmith."

"Really?"

"Yes, really! It's about you. I understand I am to work with you, not Chairman Dietrich."

"Yes. But you work *for* me, not *with* me."

Erebus bared his teeth. "Only I don't trust you, nor do I intend to allow you to represent me to Chairman Dietrich, who is my friend, or Banc Schaffhausen or their board. If the terms of my engagement are violated, or if I feel I am being cheated in any way, or if I feel you are obstructing my work or misrepresenting my commission to Dietrich or his board, I will exact retribution—personally—on you. Be very, very careful about how you characterize me to your masters at the Laundromat. If you aren't careful, Haysmith, this could well be your last assignment on earth, contacts or no contacts. Do you understand me?"

The brandy had arrived, and hand shaking, Haysmith reached for the glass, and tossed the drink back in one swallow. He said, "Don't you threaten me, you bastard!"

Erebus smiled but said nothing.

"Fine," said Haysmith. "Fine. Planc expects you to start work right away!"

"I'll start as soon as the retainer appears in this bank account." He slid a three-by-five index card across the table. The bank name and account information were neatly printed in black ink. "When will that be, exactly?" he added.

"Tomorrow," Haysmith rasped and picked up the card. Then he took a napkin from the table, wiped his whole face with it, and threw it down next to the empty brandy glass. He stood and held out his hand.

Erebus hesitated, then took the proffered hand and shook it just once. Haysmith turned and moved unsteadily toward the exit.

Erebus leaned back in his chair, pushed away the untouched Perrier, and signaled to the waiter for a check. He took out his iPhone and sent a text to Dietrich: Met with H. You may indeed have a problem. Who the hell hired him?

Erebus paid the bill in cash, took the receipt, crumpled it into his pocket, and then felt his phone vibrate.

The LM hired him. Planc is his boss. Do what H tells you to do. Just remember to tell me what he told you to do first!

Erebus answered: He authorized investigation. No menace, is that correct?

He put on his coat, buttoned it, pulled up the collar, and pushed his way out the door, back into the swirling wind. The time of day was noon, the temperature was below freezing, the sky was black with storm clouds, and he couldn't wait to return to Nice.

Forty-five minutes later, Erebus checked his phone as he paid off the cab and entered the airport. Correct, no menace of any kind. All activity behind the scenes, no visible evidence of investigation whatsoever. Planc very short fuse. Eggshells, complicated, urgent need for info.

CHAPTER 9

Hot, sweat drenched, and breathing hard, Flash was in the home stretch of what he called the almost-daily grind. Up at six, out the door by 6:20, down the road toward Poipu, past the funeral parlor and the white clapboard church, past several strip malls, through the sprawling Sheraton resort complex, then out onto the beaches—Poipu and Brennecke's—across the black lava rocks, along another beach to Jump Cliff, touching the tree next to the parking lot, and returning. A round of 5.2 miles, three days a week.

Per usual, he was winded, and he felt great, invigorated even. He didn't see himself as a new Flash; for one thing, this was only his second week doing the grind. He'd settled on *Flash, who was not so much recovering exactly, but Flash getting his legs back, becoming stronger—a good thing*. Who knew, maybe a new life would follow? His cellphone buzzed.

"Hi, Mia. What's up?"

"Where are you now?"

"Just back from a run, in front of Shave Ice."

"You should get some coffee. We should meet for coffee. How about now?"

"I need to shower—"

"No, you don't. We need coffee. How about right now?"

"Mia, you stopped drinking coffee."

"Of course I did. Now I drink green tea. But you need coffee now."

Flash sighed. He needed coffee now? What the hell?

"Why exactly do I need coffee now, Mia?"

"I tell you when I see you in ten minutes. At Roasters. Good coffee and pastry. You need a scone too." She disconnected.

Mia had already commandeered a table when Flash arrived, and she'd laid out a double espresso with a papaya scone for him and a small white pot of what he presumed was green tea for her. The settings were complete with napkins and spoons. He sighed.

"What, no scone for you?" he asked.

"No, of course not. Scones make you fat. My sister Lili, she's fat. Being fat is no good."

"How is your sister? I haven't seen her around," he responded.

"That doesn't matter right now. She's fine, but I don't want to talk about her. I want to talk about you, and a friend of mine."

Flash drank half his espresso, broke off a piece of the scone, and ate it, all the while holding eye contact with Mia. She had deep black eyes and the stare of a witch. Not an evil stare, just piercing. He chewed the scone, and waited.

"Her name is Emma. You met her once. She's very pretty. You'd like her."

When he said nothing, she resumed her talk. "She's single and pretty, and you could help her."

He ate another piece of scone, still waiting.

"Flash, you need to be less self-absorbed. Me, me, me, that's all you think about. Time to help someone else for a change. You've been a beach bum long enough!"

Flash smiled, chewed more scone, and swore to himself that he'd wait her out. A particular ask was in there somewhere, for sure.

Mia plunged ahead. "Her son, Paul, he's eighteen, went missing. Very sad, very mysterious. Gone for four weeks now. You should help her. The police are useless—you should help."

He wasn't surprised, and he wasn't sure if he should be annoyed, but—whatever. She'd bought the breakfast, so he'd listen. "I'm sorry? I should help? Why, exactly?"

"You think you fool everybody, big beach bum appearing out of nowhere, drink and feel sorry for yourself all the time. But you don't fool me. I know you were a cop, so you should help her. She's not just sad, you know—she's very pretty too." Mia poured some tea in her Styrofoam cup.

Flash felt blindsided, sucker punched by a witch. This was not good. He bent down, moved his face closer to hers, and said in a hoarse whisper, "Mia, what the hell's going on? Where in God's name did you hear about me? Who told you that?"

"It doesn't matter who told me anything," she said. "You should help her find her son. That's what matters."

"I might help her," he blurted out without thinking, "but only if you tell me why you think I was a cop. If you do tell me, and I believe you, I might help. If you don't, I won't."

"See that proves it. Only a cop would make such a one-way deal." She let the tea sit, not even raising the cup to sip.

"Sorry, Mia, you'll have to do better than that."

"Well, you met Kellie. She's a cop, and she says you act like you might be a cop, might have been a cop—something like that. Kellie is really good at sussing people. That's why she's a good cop."

"That's it? Kellie, the cop, thinks I may have been a cop?" His heart settled back into his chest somewhat.

"Good enough for me," Mia declared. "Besides, come to think of it, when you aren't acting like the local drunk, you act like you could have been a cop. My uncle was a cop, too, and he turned into a kinda drunk. My friend needs help, and she's very pretty also. If you're a cop or not a cop, or were a cop, you could help, I think. I've been watching. So will you help her?"

"What about Kellie, a real cop? Why aren't you strong-arming her?

"You're very self-centered, you know that? Kellie is doing everything she can, only she has lots of other duties, and too many cases. She can't spend so much time on a kid runaway. But Emma is freaked out, and she needs help. Here's her number, you call her and help."

Flash remembered Emma and tried to think how he could help without "having been a cop." Mia was immovable, but he was satisfied she was just acting on a hunch.

"So for the record, I'm not a cop, but I do know something about people from a past life, and I'd be willing to help your friend on one condition."

"See, cops do that, they dig the hole deeper and deeper right in front of your eyes before they tell you to jump in. I knew it!"

"Mia, stop! The one condition is you do not tell anyone else that you think I was a cop. I wasn't, and I'm not. You'll ruin my retirement, my beach-bum dream. Who the hell wants to go surfing or drinking with a cop? I might be able to help her, but not if people think I am or was a cop. Deal or no deal?"

Mia screwed up her face and looked hard at Flash. He met her eyes. He wasn't going to be stared off his perch.

"Deal or no deal?" Flash insisted. "By the way, if it is no deal, I'll rent someplace else. The time may have come for me to move on, what with everybody on Kauai thinking I was or am a cop. Deal or no deal? Your call."

"Deal. You may not be a cop, but you act like one. Okay, okay. I'll just keep telling people that you're enigma man on vacation, early retirement, haole beach-bum wannabe. How's that?"

"Better." He smiled.

Flash took the slip of paper from her. He was wondering how to approach Emma about her son, when another permutation of being erased came to mind. What about the bad guys? As far as he knew, they'd lost a bunch of money, and when bad guys lose money, they— They what? They hurt people. That was what. *Where are the bastards?* he wondered.

Heinrich Dietrich, chairman of the board and chief investment officer of Banc Schaffhausen, Zurich, had insisted they meet at his private club. In his own deliberate way, he had decided that the time had arrived to assert some authority, to bring a semblance of order and predictability to what was a festering problem for him and for his bank, in that order.

He had been patient, very patient, with the others. Questions about what appeared to be missing funds were circulating, quietly, among members of his executive board. At first, the missing money was thought to be just a clerical error, but ten-million dollars was, well, ten-million dollars, and his board— and one notable potential bank investor in particular, LM Global Ltd.—was making quite a lot of noise.

Behind this noise was a threat by LM Global to withdraw from participation as a cornerstone investor in the Bank Schaffhausen Investment Fund. If they made good on this threat, the investment fund would be short by five-hundred-million dollars and be forced to renege on promises made to finance projects on three continents. The chairman refused to renege on any such promises and he wasn't going to eat the ten-million dollars, either. Nor was he willing to kowtow to LM Global's hired weasel, Malcolm Haysmith.

The two men were in a small side room at the club, seated in green leather easy chairs, facing each other. Their waiter delivered a silver tray of coffee in a carafe alongside thin bone-white china cups, sterling silver spoons, plus matching creamer and sugar bowl. He placed it on a serving table next to Chairman Dietrich, bowed and left, closing the door behind him.

One large window was the central focus of the room. Dark-green velvet curtains were pulled back and tied in place on either side, letting in the light and a view out across Lake Zurich.

This day, the sky was steel gray, and frozen lines of snow on the glass distorted the view.

"Mr. Haysmith, I wanted to meet with you privately to hear what you've learned so far. Additionally, I'd like to offer assistance to the extent I can help you with your investigation into this anomaly. Coffee?"

"No, thank you," said Haysmith.

Haysmith was, to Dietrich's eye, a British cliché, dressed in an ill-fitting brown tweed suit, brown shoes, and a Jesus College Oxford tie. At least the shirt was pressed, and the socks were black. Haysmith was chubby, and his lips were held tightly shut under round cheeks in a kind of grimace. The chairman didn't like sloppy men, and as he surveyed Haysmith, he could smell cigarette smoke, sweat, and perhaps alcohol.

Haysmith said, "Herr Dietrich, let's call a spade a spade, shall we? This issue, our issue with you, is not an anomaly—it is a very real problem, your problem. How about you start by making good on the missing ten-million dollars today, and while you're at it, how about trying to explain what happened. Because my client, your board member and prospective investor, is royally pissed. Herr Planc feels that you breached the terms of your deal, and he's on the warpath. I am merely his warrior. Albeit one of many."

Momentarily breathless, Dietrich tensed. He swallowed and asked, "What do you mean, one of many?"

Haysmith crossed his legs casually, seeming pleased with the effect he'd had on Dietrich. "I mean, Herr Planc is determined to be vindicated. Our agent was promised a payment through your bank, a payment that somehow failed to appear. We are surprised and alarmed by this sequence of events. And so, at this moment, my client has decided to withdraw from your board and take his money with him. As you will recall, his promise to invest was predicated on your delivery of a simple, relatively insignificant payment to an agent, which you agreed to make, then didn't."

A fury of a sort he hadn't felt in years seized the whole of Dietrich's body, head to toes. "No! You were not part of our deal, and you're intentionally mischaracterizing the events. I'm going to have to talk to Herr Planc directly, not through you." He put his coffee cup back on the saucer with a hand that had begun to shake. Haysmith was grinning at him like a fat gargoyle, shaking his head slowly. Dietrich tried to hold eye contact with Haysmith, but couldn't, and looked instead at the snow-streaked window.

Haysmith said, "Herr Dietrich, just so you know, Herr Planc has given me absolute authority to investigate this mess. The one you've made. It would be best for you to cut the crap and cooperate with me. Your only hope of reaching Herr Planc is to convince me that you have satisfactory answers to all of our questions and a believable path forward, one that would fully heal this self-inflicted injury to your relationship with LM Global. Until then, Herr Planc has instructed me to tell you to go to hell. He won't talk to you, nor will he release any of the funds."

Dietrich found himself in the unthinkable position of having to appeal to this Haysmith nobody. "Look, we've made commitments on behalf of the bank, based on Planc's promises. We're duty-bound to make good on our commitments to the marketplace!"

Haysmith looked unfazed. "Don't let LM Global stand in the way of you doing that, Herr Dietrich," said the Brit. "Only, as things stand now, you won't be using our money. That is, unless you can figure out a way to quickly plug this breach, completely fix it. Otherwise, count us out."

Dietrich took a deep breath. "Look, be reasonable. I really don't know what happened, or how it happened—the error in the payment, I mean. I'm sure it was just a glitch or perhaps a clumsy oversight, a clerical mistake, whatever. But I won't be held hostage by you. If LM Global is unwilling to go forward with its investment, I'll look elsewhere. We have an excellent reputation as a merchant bank. We don't need your money."

Haysmith screwed up his face in what might have been a smile. He uncrossed his legs. "Really? Well, then, please, go right ahead. Only for your sake, remember who you're dealing with here. I wonder if you can imagine how disruptive Herr Planc could be as a disillusioned ex-board member. Can you see him resigning quietly, for example? Not likely, Dietrich! He doesn't do anything quietly—he explodes first, then moves forcefully and vindictively. You know him. You know what I'm talking about. Are you ready for that? Is Banc Schaffhausen ready for that? Do what you must, certainly, but—"

Something in the chairman's neck felt as though it had snapped, and he blurted out, "Look, I'll have all the answers you need within a week, then we'll meet again. Until then, say and do nothing!"

"A week?" Haysmith's small brown eyes seemed to pin Dietrich to his chair as the bank head waited. "One week? Fine. But be sure you bring answers, not excuses, and restore the missing money. This is not a bluff. We'll smear your reputation across the whole of Europe and beyond, like fresh shit on a newly painted wall, if you come up short. Oh, and just so you know, we're aware of the side deal, your personal side deal for, what was it— five percent of that Hawaii project? I wonder what difficulties you might experience if the regulators from the Swiss Financial Market Supervisory Authority found out about that little off-the-book arrangement. I wonder what your comrades at the bank might think about it too. Don't fuck with us, Dietrich. One week!"

"Yes, yes, fine, one week. One week."

CHAPTER 10

"Look, man, this isn't no party. It's serious fucking business. You gotta get that straight to begin with. You got that?"

Keanu, at the wheel of the pickup they were in, was driving Paul Pookalani nuts with his I'm-older-than-you-and-you-have-to-listen-to-me attitude. Paul said, "Okay, okay. I get it, dude. Stop raggin' on me, will ya?"

"Fine, but I got to school ya," said Keanu.

Paul couldn't even look at him. Keanu just wouldn't stop. This wasn't the way their relationship had been in high school. Keanu hadn't acted this way when they'd met again, either, and Paul had agreed to move in and pay some rent. But now, all of a sudden, Keanu was the big boss teacher, and blah, blah, blah.

Keanu said, "You got a lot to learn. We can make good money in this, real good money, but you fuck up, and it's over, man. I mean really over. Not like the movies when they stop shooting the scene, and all the dead people stand up and walk off the stage. I mean we could get real dead, like no-getting-up dead, ya know?"

"Yeah, I get it," Paul answered. "You told me that before. I already said yes. So can't we just do this?"

"Okay, bro, but just remember—"

"Shut the fuck up and drive, will ya?"

"Okay, Paul, but just remember, this is your first time out. You're a rookie until I tell you otherwise. Got that? Just keep your mouth shut and follow my lead."

Paul hated this rusted-out piece-of-shit 1971 Datsun pickup. But he needed a ride here and there, and more than that, he needed money. No way would he ever be able to live in his own place with his own stuff by working at the fucking Burger King! His mother had told him over and over that the job was a first step to independence. But after six months, he'd realized that fast food was a very long, boring first step—really just a half-step, if that.

Every paycheck disappeared in a week, and if he wasn't living at home, eating his mom's food, he would be no better than those drunks that hung out with each other on the skids. He'd had to do something, and his buddy Keanu Akoni said he had the answer. They were the same age, but Keanu lived in a house and drove this piece-of-shit pickup truck. Keanu Akoni always had money. That was a real first step!

"So, dude, when we get there, we park next to the docks. We get out together, walk over to the port security office. An officer will come outside, and I'll introduce you to him. You don't say nothin' until I tell you to, got it?"

Paul was fed up with being a kid. So Keanu treating him like a kid pissed him off—only he was begging here, looking for a break, so yeah, he would shut up and just take it until well, until he could fend for himself. Keanu let him crash at his crappy little dump of a house on the edge of Kapaa. Piece-of-shit truck and piece-of-shit house.

Keanu had inherited the house from his grandma, who had hated her daughter so much she left her shit house to her only grandson. Keanu didn't like his mom, either, so he'd been happy to leave home and move into the shit house.

Keanu pulled into the parking lot and stopped. Paul

unbuckled his seatbelt and looked over at Keanu, who had opened his door and was standing in the sun next to the truck. Paul opened his door, stepped out, and stood, waiting to follow Keanu's lead.

Paul was wiry thin, Hawaiian brown-skinned, with black hair that hung over his ears and across his forehead. He was wearing a colorful short-sleeve shirt, jeans, no belt, and flip flops. He was slightly bowlegged, mostly because of all the surfing. Years of springing up on a moving board made his movements smooth, while his walking seemed a little like dancing. With a smooth gait, he joined Keanu, and they walked across the pavement to a security office near the entrance to the Nawiliwili Harbor docks.

Keanu was wearing the same island getup as Paul, except he was sporting Air Jordan 32s, the "Italy" tributes, the only Air Jordan 32 "Italy" tributes on the whole island—Nike had only made 323 pairs.

"Mr. P., this is Paul. I vouch for him and would like to have him as part of our gang."

Mr. P. was in the doorway of the security office. Wearing a blue starched and ironed uniform with an embroidered badge on his shirt pocket, he exuded *rent-a-cop*. He was bareheaded, with stringy gray hair, a side-slanting nose, white skin, and a cut for a mouth. Closing the door behind him, he stepped toward the two boys.

He motioned with his head for the boys to follow him, and all three moved toward the chain-link fence and a cigarette-butt receptacle beneath a sign that read "Designated Smoking Area." Mr. P. took out a pack of cigarettes, removed one, and put it between his thin lips. A Zippo lighter appeared in his other hand, and he lit up. He closed the Zippo with a clunk, inhaled, then turned and stared at Paul, squinting in the glare.

"This the runaway kid?" Smoke came out of both his nose and his mouth as he spoke.

"Yes, Mr. P., but he's living with me now, so not a runaway anymore."

"What about the cops? They know where he is?"

"No, sir, only because his father is a real badass, so best to keep below the radar. You know what I mean?"

Mr. P. forcefully exhaled a mouthful of smoke. "So why should I trust him?"

"Because I'll stand for him, sir."

Mr. P. was quiet again, still looking at Paul. He then pointed at Paul's chest, looked over at Keanu, and said, "So it's your ass if he fucks up. Is that what I'm hearing?"

"Yes, sir."

"He had the indoctrination yet?"

"No, sir."

The cigarette glowed as Mr. P. inhaled, then he crushed it on the side of the butt receptacle and dropped it in the bin. He reached into his pants pocket and took out a small package. He palmed it, holding his hand behind his back.

"Good. So here's a starter pack, and you bring him back if he passes the test. You have till Monday. After that, you fucked up —and I'll expect retribution. From you first, then we take care of him. Got it?"

"Got it, sir."

"Get out of here." Mr. P. handed the candy-bar-sized package to Keanu, turned, and walked back toward the security shack. Paul jumped slightly when the door slammed shut.

The boys went over to the pickup and slid in. "What does indoctrination mean?" Paul asked.

Keanu reached toward the key in the ignition but didn't turn it just yet. "It means you gotta learn some shit about being a runner, a seller. It's pretty easy, but you really gotta be careful you don't get caught by the cops, and even more careful that you come give me the money, all of the money, every time. You give me the money you collected, and then I give you some back.

That's how it works, each and every time, all of the money to me, and something back to you."

"Sounds simple enough," said Paul.

"It is simple, bro, but remember, always be careful, and always—all the money! Whatever you do, don't ever fuck with the money— No kidding, dude."

"Or else what, asshole?"

Keanu screwed up his face. "Or else a couple of guys show up when you don't expect them and take you someplace and beat the shit out of you, maybe kill you. That's what else."

"You're kiddin', right, just trying to scare me?"

"No, I ain't kidding." Keanu shook his head. "The price for fucking up in Mr. P.'s gang is broken bones for sure. Maybe never walking again, and maybe being planted in the middle of a cane field where no one will ever find your body."

"Jesus." Suddenly Paul felt an ache in his gut.

Keanu nodded. "Yeah, *Jesus* is right—only Jesus won't be here to help, so don't fuck up. That's the most important part of the indoctrination. I'll teach you the rest of the job tomorrow night. We got a rave over at Waimea. It'll be easier to show you than to try to explain it all. You know, like training wheels, selling to those crazy rave dudes. They love our stuff, and the cops usually don't give a shit about rave crazies. Great place to learn, and you'll finally make some easy money too. Hot shit, right?"

"Yeah, right." Paul made a brave attempt to smile. Keanu reached across the seat and punched him in the shoulder.

Paul was shaken. This new gig was way more than a first step—it was a bunch of steps into the dark. He'd known Keanu forever, but never thought his buddy could be so edgy, blunt, menacing? He shook his head. The shit pickup truck sped along the highway out of Lihue toward his new shit home in the sticks, Outer Kapaa.

. . .

"But why? I don't understand," Touma Allen barked into his iPhone. He clenched his jaw to keep from shouting.

Touma was talking to, of all people, his ex-wife's husband, Bartholomew Singleton II, the chairman of the Hawaii Board of Trade and special advisor to the Honolulu city council.

He didn't like to talk to Bart at the office, so he'd left at 10:30, canceled the afternoon's appointments, and had driven home to return this call.

He was sitting next to the swimming pool at his house in Kahala on Oahu. His suit coat and tie were draped on a chair next to him, the ocean was calm, and a light, warm breeze caressed Touma's skin.

"Touma, listen, this was always a condition in the deal."

"Bart, I've been busting a gut for three years to make the Village in the Sky happen. All of the horses are lined up at the starting gate, for God's sake!"

"Yeah, all but one horse, Touma. The money-in-the-bank horse! Look, I want the goddamn thing to go through, too, but the terms of the project permit are—well, hell, you know what they are. A fifty-million-dollar bond, and deposit of one-hundred-and-fifty million in escrow, before, I repeat, before, you can break ground. When that happens, the permit is perfected, and the project is off and running. Your project, our project, big fella, Village in the Sky."

When Touma's wife had filed for divorce six years prior, money hadn't been the real issue between them. The issue had been Maryanne's freedom, as she put it—freedom to make a once-in-a-lifetime move way up the Honolulu society pecking order. So the fact that Maryanne had been having a fling with Bart, super-rich Bart, entitled and untouchable Bart, socially prominent and politically influential Bart, hadn't been a surprise. She would go from being Wealthy Commoner Maryanne Allen to Entitled Princess Maryanne Singleton by exchanging Touma Allen's money and status for Bartholomew Singleton II's money and status, simple as that.

Touma had managed to keep this fabulous beachfront property in the great battle that had ensued after Maryanne moved out, no small feat.

She was now living in a much bigger castle with twice the property on the same beach, a mile up the road. He was happy to be rid of her, and he had tenaciously held on to his business ties with Bart.

"I told you, Bart. We were granted preliminary funding approval, then something happened with those idiots at Banc Schaffhausen. I've been calling like crazy, and every now and then, they answer the phone and cut me off with 'Yes, yes, not to worry. Goodbye.' That's it, and no signed commitment. You're the one who put me on to these guys, you know what they're like."

"I do know what they're like," said Bart. "But look, this is your deal, Touma, not mine. You need to focus, get them off the fence. Do you have any idea what's gone sideways?"

Touma got up and walked toward the outdoor bar, trying to relax. "I don't know what's gone wrong," he said. "I have another call into Dietrich now, and I'll let you know when he gets back to me. If he gets back to me."

Bart grunted. "Touma, does he know the project permit expires in ninety days if it's not perfected?"

Touma put ice in a tumbler and poured himself a drink—just a little brandy to calm him down. "Yeah, he knows all of that, only he's, you know, an uptight prick, chairman of an uptight Swiss bank, plays his cards close to his uptight chest. But yes, I told him. I couriered him a copy of the permit with the expiration date highlighted and with a damn post-it attached, for Christ's sake. He knows that if we aren't funded before the permit expires, Village in the Sky goes up in smoke." Along with tens-of-millions Touma had already put in.

"So, what does he have to say to that?" Bart sounded as if he might be having a drink himself.

"Say—say? Nothing, other than prattle on in his condescending accented English. *'Oh, you tropical islanders. You shouldn't worry so much, just slow down. We're working diligently at our end—and remember, we're the investors here, and you're the builder.'* What a prick! He treats me like I'm some stupid native carpenter, living in a jungle hut."

Bart made a sound that Touma couldn't interpret. "You might try reminding him that we have plenty of other developers here, with lots of their own money champing at the bit, waiting to pounce if their deal falls through."

Touma sighed. "Yes, Bart. I'll remind him. Again. Hell, look, Bart, can't you do something, maybe to get us some breathing room here? Could you take a run at an extension with the city council? Wouldn't they grant one? It sure would take the pressure off."

Bart chuckled. "No way. Not a chance in hell that they would extend. A couple of our council buddies just hate your guts, Touma. As simple as that. They've been working overtime complaining about granting the permit to you in the first place, whispering stuff like *proceeds of crime, illegal practices*, spreading rumors about drug money—blah blah blah."

Touma shook his head. He did what he could to not be hated, but some of the council members wouldn't take bribes, as hard to understand as that was. Even subtle bribes, like a golf club membership worth a couple-hundred-thousand.

"Touma, ninety days! Well, eighty-nine days now. That's all the time you've got, old buddy. You know I'm behind you on this, but you're the only person who can make it happen. I'll keep my fingers crossed."

"Yeah, sure. Fingers crossed." Touma disconnected, then collapsed back in the strangely uncomfortable patio chair. For the first time, he noticed that the maid hadn't put the cushions out today. Everything and everyone must be conspiring against him.

CHAPTER 11

First, Keanu did a couple of handoffs, just to show Paul how easy the transactions were: a little baggie with two pills, palmed in one hand, the money received in the other hand, and then—and only then—the baggie hand extended, palm down, and the goods placed in the buyer's hand.

Each deal was done with as little eye contact as possible. Get the money, pass the goods, then slide on through the crowd. After a couple of these exchanges, Paul and Keanu moved away through the dark, music blasting and hot bodies swaying around them, over to the side of the throng. It was Paul's first time at a rave—a Friday Night Rave, way at the far end of Polihale Beach, a bit of a walk away from the parking lot where the cops would have to leave their cars if they felt the urge to show up.

Standing shoulder to shoulder, Paul and Keanu looked at the tableau of beach fires burning, pools of light flickering, animated silhouettes moving, all under a heavy blanket of music, the booming bass relentless. Every now and then, the DJ on the stage would shout something over the sound system, and the mob would cheer.

Paul never liked crowds all that much. He was more of an

introvert, not given to a lot of shouting. This scene made him nervous with all these crazy people, but the money—well, that would be good, great even, as long as he didn't lose it or wasn't robbed by one of these crazies.

"See, no problem." Keanu had to shout in order to be heard. He leaned closer to Paul's ear. "Just make sure that they're giving you the right amount. Some of these jerks try to scam you. They wrap a five-dollar bill around three singles to make you think it's twenty dollars." He paused for a breath and leaned in again. "If they fuck with you, keep the stuff, walk away, don't give them anything."

"What about their money?" Paul shouted back.

"Drop the money they slipped you. Keep the packet. Move away. You don't want an argument, no fuckin' fights."

Paul had another question he wished he'd asked before. "How do they know what I have and how much to pay?"

"The price for E is stable. Ten bucks a pill. If they don't know, tell 'em."

"So all I'm selling is E?" The song changed, but the noise remained way too loud.

Keanu pulled Paul further away from the jumping, jerking, rotating bodies. "For now just E," he said in a softer tone. Paul wiped Keanu's hot breath from his ear with his hand. "We'll see how you do, and maybe expand what you sell. Maybe some speed. But right now, get out there with the E and sell it. Mr. P. needs the money. I need off the hook."

"What hook?"

"The hook that came with this packet Mr. P. gave us." Far enough away from the crowd, the two were speaking in almost normal tones. "You need to sell it, and I need to give him the money. Then he gives us more, and you become part of my crew, and Mr. P. has a new runner."

With a nod and a push from Keanu, Paul moved back into the crowd and was soon being approached by prospective clients. A couple of times he had to explain the price, and once a young girl tried to grab the E without paying.

When he jerked the baggie back, she shrieked, "Come on! Look, I'll give you a blow job. How's that?"

"God, no way!" He quickly walked off to another part of the beach, disappearing in a group of fire-lit dancers. He was sure he could feel Mr. P.'s hook.

"Are you the E guy?"

"Huh?"

"I said, are you the E guy? And if you're a fucking cop, I'll deny I asked, so—are you the E guy?"

Bare feet partially buried in the still-warm sand, white t-shirt, white sweatpants, and a white fedora tilted atop a head of straight, long black hair, she shifted from foot to foot to the booming bass, black eyes shining with the light of a nearby beach fire.

"Yes, or no?" She looked neither old nor young, but to his eighteen-year-old sensibilities, she was definitely pretty—very, very pretty.

He nodded and said, "Ah, yeah, that's me."

She smiled and said, "Three packs."

"Sixty."

"Naw, I'll give you forty. You're gouging me!"

"Six pills, sixty bucks—or nothin'."

"Shit," she said. She reached into a white fanny pack, pulled out some bills, folded them over, and extended her hand. He hadn't noticed before, but her fingernails were painted black, matching her lipstick, which he also hadn't noticed. He was down to his last three packets. He reached out his hand, palm down, and she brought her hand up beneath his, smaller than his, to make the exchange. Her hand felt warm, and he thought he felt her tickle his palm with her fingers as he released the stuff.

"What's your name?" she asked.

"Why do you want to know?" he said, checking to make sure

she'd given him the right amount—three twenties, and crisp.

"What's your name?"

"Paul, Paul Pookalani." He winced. He shouldn't have told her his last name. He had to be more careful.

"Got a phone number?"

"Yeah," he admitted. Keanu would probably kill him for being so loose-lipped. But maybe she would buy more from them—from him.

"Well, give it to me, in case I need something."

He told her the number, and she typed it into her phone then she put it into her fanny pack, zipped it shut, and flashed a grin.

"See you around, Paul Pookalani, my new E guy!"

Adjusting the brim of her hat, she pivoted on one bare foot and walked toward a beach fire, disappearing into the mob. His heart was pounding. He was handling this. He was doing great.

Erebus flew into Seattle, rented a car, and drove through the rain —Seattle, after all—then checked into the W Hotel downtown. There, he holed up with a digital file, a collection of personal data, some legally obtained, most illegally obtained, regarding three of the main actors in the missing ten-million fiasco. The file had been prepared by a computer hacker, a dark-world contractor calling himself Bingwen, who supposedly lived in Shanghai, although these days geography was, well, relative.

In this way, Bingwen and Erebus were alike: secretive, suspicious, being nowhere and everywhere at the same time.

After completing each assignment, Bingwen would gift Erebus with a coded text, a kind of key. Bingwen communicated using a dark-web messaging application that allowed him to call you; but you couldn't call him, at least not directly. Erebus could use the key to let Bingwen know he wanted to be contacted, if and only if he wanted to employ Bingwen again for hacking, or "special research," as he called it.

Bingwen, or whatever his real name was, was dark-world

famous, and in demand. As a result, he was very expensive, a master practitioner of covert digital alchemy.

Bingwen was fast, too. When Erebus had most recently sent Bingwen his trigger text, he received an encrypted internet audio call fifteen minutes later. Erebus had explained the assignment, was given a price, completed a money transfer, and two days later had received two-hundred pages of material, the result of a deep-dive invasion into the lives of Flash Finnegan Michael, Malcolm Forsyth Jr., and John Horan, including the names of all family members, associates, and friends.

Sitting in an oversized purple-velvet chair, Erebus read through the material and made handwritten notes in a Moleskin journal. Next, he consolidated the information into a surveillance plan, all elements diagrammed hierarchically. The final version was hand drawn using a Mont Blanc Meisterstück Platinum-Coated 149 Fountain Pen, his instrument of choice. Jet-black ink glided smoothly from the gold nib, forming carefully printed, painfully small letters, boxes drawn around each node, and lines connecting the nodes of the diagram, eventually leading to one center node, a double-lined rectangle labeled TARGETS.

Erebus needed to see the actors in person, see them *in situ*, where they lived, worked, and circulated around the city. This invasion was to be a careful, discreet, relatively soft process. He was under orders not to be seen or to make contact.

Learning where to reach out and find any one of the twenty-five or so people associated with the three cops would constitute success. That thought made him smile. He wondered what would happen if the cops knew what he knew. No matter. It also occurred to him that he'd never taken out a police chief before. Several cops, of course, but no chief of police. It would be a first, a notch on his belt, as practiced by the gunslingers in the old American West.

The next afternoon, Erebus sat tapping his fingers on the

steering wheel of a rented white Chevrolet parked on the tree-lined street leading past the Woodhouse Academy campus, three miles north and east of downtown Seattle. Pippa Orsini's Facebook pages had been a big help, as had been her email and instant messaging activity. That's how he knew she would be leaving school today after volleyball practice. He also knew she would be driving a black BMW and its license plate number.

This was day one of what he presumed would be a three- or four-day crawl through the rain in and around Seattle. He would shadow Pippa Orsini just long enough to build a picture of her habits, hangouts, and her day-to-day life.

Pippa was Flash Finnegan Michael's daughter. Flash had fallen off the map six months earlier. If Erebus needed to find her father for some reason, he wanted to make sure he could get hold of the daughter. Leverage. This game was all about leverage —and force.

Woodhouse was an exclusive private high school for rich kids in Seattle, buried in a wealthy residential neighborhood that meandered along the western shore of Lake Washington. The black BMW pulled out of the parking lot, heading south on Lake Washington Boulevard. Erebus followed.

During the following week, Erebus put eyes on all of the key players, except for Flash Finnegan, of course, and Celest Forsyth, Police Chief Malcolm Forsyth's current wife, who was in Bali at a weeklong batik workshop. But he knew where she lived, where all three of her children lived, where her housekeeper lived, and where her psychiatrist's office was.

Finally, most of the nodes on the hand-drawn diagrams were checked off. The next day, he left the W Hotel, its edgy modern vibe, and headed out to the Olympic Peninsula, where no W Hotel could survive. Forks, Washington was the last confirmed Flash Michael sighting before he had disappeared.

Erebus drove down Interstate 5 and turned right to Highway 8, out onto the Olympic Peninsula. He mentally reviewed his research. Sifting through his observations was an excellent way to deal with the boredom of driving through a dark rainforest punctuated by odd, depressing, moss-covered towns that were littered along the remote highway.

The biggest surprise had been that John Horan lived a strangely modest, mostly nondescript life. He certainly didn't live like someone who'd hijacked millions of dollars, as Erebus had been led to believe he had. It was widely held among the concerned parties that Horan, Finnegan, and perhaps Forsyth were behind the stolen ten-million. But Horan lived a boring, ordered, low-key life as a divorced, forty-something bachelor.

Horan's home was in a high-rise apartment within walking distance of police headquarters. He did drive a new Audi—had apparently paid cash for it—but dressed, off-duty, like a Seattle tree hugger. He belonged to a hiking club and a book club, and always drank at the same downtown watering hole near his apartment. Horan didn't have a Facebook page, had no LinkedIn presence, no Amazon Prime account, no dating service, nor had Bingwen found any personal internet presence other than a Gmail account. Horan even did his banking in person.

Erebus shook his head. Nature abhors a vacuum. Horan must have more to him, but where was it? What was it? And what was he hiding? Other than then millions of dollars.

Horan was an enigma. Erebus recognized the MO, having spent years developing cover for his criminal profession. Erebus's approach was to live in plain sight, a regular person who traveled a lot, someone who rented his flat, bought his groceries with several credit cards, and even paid taxes. This fictitious person currently lived in Nice and had for the past four years. He loved Nice, a warm town with great food, lots of Russians, and plenty of tourists and seasonal residents—a perfect place to hide in plain sight.

The final unchecked item on Erebus's surveillance plan read "Finnegan in Forks, Subaru." He knew Finnegan's 1994 Subaru Outback had been sold via Craigslist to a Forks resident, a retired postal worker. Erebus had the new owner's name and address and visited him. The transaction had been in cash. Finnegan had given the man a handwritten receipt, signed off on the car registration, handed over the keys, and then literally turned and walked away, refusing a ride, walking toward town carrying a black duffel bag on his back.

The ex-postman knew nothing about Finnegan, didn't want to know anything about Finnegan, and seemed a little pissed off that this foreign-sounding stranger was interrupting a fishing program on television at three in the afternoon.

For Erebus, the obvious question was: Why Forks? Other than being remote. But was there another reason? More to the point, where the hell did Finnegan go after selling the car? Forks was in the middle of nowhere. Continuing north on Highway 101, the next stop was a place called Port Angeles, an old mill town with a dying fishing fleet. Going from Forks to Port Angeles was leaving nowhere, going nowhere.

Highway 101 was one big circle around a vast, sparsely populated rainforest. Had Finnegan gone to ground somewhere up here, say, near the Hoh River, or Kalaloch, or La Push? Who knew? What Erebus did know was that the one person in Forks who'd met Flash didn't have a clue. So, for now, this godforsaken place was the end of the Flash Michael trail.

He drove toward Port Angeles. Might as well finish the circuit of dying towns of the Pacific Northwest. He ate lunch at a place called the Oyster Hut, down near the waterfront. Returning to his car, he noticed a street sign directing traffic to the Black Ball Ferry Line terminal on the harbor front. He'd read about the ferry on the back of the restaurant menu, daily service from Port Angeles to Victoria, British Columbia.

Canada? Maybe. Anonymously crossing an international border is an excellent way to become invisible. But Canada was a very large place, and besides, Erebus didn't actually need to find Finnegan on this trip. He just needed to have available options for smoking him out. Pippa was the most obvious option. A good one. As for Horan and Forsyth, well, they weren't going anywhere, were they?

Erebus tapped Seattle Tacoma Airport into Google Maps on his phone, then pushed the start button. Job well done, money in the bank, probably more work to do, more money in the bank. Soon, he would be back under the Mediterranean sun.

CHAPTER 12

"Thanks for coming." Emma wrung her hands. "Look, I know Mia can be sort of overbearing, but I've been at the end of my rope ever since Paul went missing. I'm sure she was only trying to help, but, well, here you both are. I'm embarrassed, but thank you."

Flash nodded, happy that Mia herself hadn't tagged along.

The drive from Koloa to Emma's place in Waimea had taken twenty minutes. Kellie, perhaps a little nervous about Flash's inclusion in Mia's Save Paul mission, had treated Flash to a lengthy account of the Emma Pookalani story.

Emma worked as the vice president of accounting and finance for a Kauai chain of t-shirt shops. Her father had been a superior court judge, and her mother had owned a travel agency.

Even though Emma was only thirty-nine, her parents had both passed away, leaving her with a lovely house in an upper-middle-class development and a nest egg. She had been married briefly, something like eleven months, to Paul's father, a stevedore in Port Allen. The man liked to drink and often engaged in fights when he did. One night, he hit Emma and threatened to hurt baby Paul. A quick and nasty divorce followed.

The three of them were sitting on Emma's back patio, which faced a low, blossoming hedge in front of Waimea and the ocean beyond. The sun was warm, and the sea breeze hadn't started up yet; the temperature underneath the canvas umbrella was perfect.

Emma carried out a wooden tray with a sweating pitcher of iced red hibiscus tea, three jam-jar glasses, a dish of ginger snaps, and white paper napkins. She placed the tray in the center of the round, glass-topped table and said, "First of all, I have news—Paul's okay, he called me this morning!" Emma smiled as she spoke, looking first at Flash, then at Kellie.

Flash smiled back at her, then glanced over to see what Kellie's reaction was.

Kellie said, "Oh, my gosh. Good. Where is he? Where did he go?"

Emma continued to smile happily as she poured out the tea and passed around the napkins. "Oh well, the whole thing is pretty embarrassing. Teenage boys. What can I say? So I don't know exactly where he went, but apparently, he's with a friend in Kapaa. Keanau Akoni, a boy he went to school with. Do you know him, Kellie?"

Kellie shook her head. "No, I don't."

Emma slid the cookie dish toward her guests and said, "Well, Paul is really uptight about his life right now, so he wouldn't tell me where he's been. But he said he was staying with Keanau, who apparently has a house, so that's good. When I asked him how he could live without a job, he said he could take care of himself, and that was none of my business. So I didn't press the issue. Anyway, the conversation was short. I was just so relieved to hear he was okay."

Kellie was smiling, but Flash noticed the smile didn't quite reach her eyes.

Kellie repeated the friend's name slowly. "Keanau Akoni, you say?"

Emma nodded. "Yes. They were in school together, kindergarten through high school. I don't think Keanau went on to college, though, because I don't recall Paul talking about him over the past year. I don't exactly know how someone his age could own a house, either, but Paul says he does."

Kellie took a sip of her iced tea, put the glass down on the table, took a ginger snap and bit half of it, then chewed, looking down at the pitcher in the center of the table.

Then she looked up and said abruptly, "You know, this isn't police business anymore, so I'll cancel the missing person alert. I could find out where he's living, though, if that would make you feel better. Not officially, mind you, but if it would help."

Emma sighed with relief. "Oh, of course, thank you, yes. I should have thought of it myself. We always think we'll behave calmly and rationally under pressure, but then when something happens. God, I just fell apart." Emma shook her head. "Anyway, thanks, Kellie, I'd appreciate your doing that for me. I'd feel good knowing exactly where he is." Emma smiled, tearing up. Then the dam broke, and she ducked her head and began to sob.

When he was sure Emma was done crying, he said in a quiet voice, "Finding out that Paul's okay is a big relief. So, it sounds as if he has a place to stay and is with a friend. I propose we see what happens once Kellie has the address, and maybe you two can find out about this Keanau guy."

Flash and Kellie drove back to Koloa, taking a shortcut away from the main highway. Off duty, she was wearing khaki hiking shorts, a colorful flower shirt, a white shell necklace, and flip flops.

"So, Flash, why do you think Mia insisted I bring you along today? Just wondering. Glad to have company, so don't take that question the wrong way."

"Because I was a boy once?" he tried.

Kellie chuckled. "Interesting thought—maybe that. Only she made a really big point with me that we needed you to be part of this Save Paul thing. For some reason. I'm not convinced testosterone was the only attraction. Any other guesses?"

Flash shrugged. "Nope. Well, maybe she finds me a good listener and values that quality?"

"Yeah, that might be it, certainly adds to your allure. Only she intimated that there might be more to your appeal than that. She mentioned to me a hunch that you might have developed your fine listening skills, as you call them, while maybe being, say, a law enforcement officer of some kind? Could it be that we're fellow cops, Flash?"

Flash looked over at her. She was navigating the twisting road around an abandoned sugar mill and a roadside pineapple stand shaped like a pineapple. This time the smile did reach her eyes.

"Kellie, if people get the idea that I was, or am, a cop, my whole social life around here goes up in smoke. Not that I'm saying I am, or was, a cop. Just if I become known as having been one. You know what I mean? The gossip would ruin my whole adventure. You don't want to be responsible for that, do you?"

"Me?" She looked over at him, then back at the road. "Me? I'm not ruining anything here. I'm just curious. You did seem to know a lot about runaways the other day. Mia is the one who has a big mouth. We all love her, but God, what a mouth!"

The conversation suddenly felt exhausting. "See, Kellie, that's just what I mean. Mia gets a crazy idea, and you think you've discovered an important clue to a puzzle. All of a sudden, I'm a cop. That borders on slander. Worse, it flies in the face of the much-venerated aloha spirit."

Kellie chuckled. "All right, all right already. I feel as if I'm being buried in bullshit here. Not a cop. Thornton F-for-Flash Tucker is not a cop. How's that?"

Flash smiled. "There you go. Doesn't that make you feel better?"

"Not really, but since you aren't a cop, just an ordinary beach bum who Mia the manipulator assigned to the Save Paul committee, what do you really think Paul's up to? Speaking as an ex-boy, I mean?"

"A lot depends on who he is, meaning what kind of kid he is, who this Keanau fellow is, and how desperate Paul is to do his own thing, since the Burger King option seems to have been shit-canned," he answered at once.

"Agreed. Whatever he's up to depends on his innate character."

"What kind of kid is he, do you know? Drugs, booze, rock and roll, surfer, Bible thumper? What's he about?"

Kellie turned serious. "I've heard he's a good kid, not into the drug scene or part of that group. He's a surfer, not a Bible thumper. His father is a dock worker, drinks often and fights a lot. Paul avoids his dad. Seems to love his mom. Sounds like he's an introvert. But I'd say he's acting like a kid who somehow felt trapped and just took off. Oh, you know what? I forgot, he's an artist, a really good one, carries a sketchbook with him, great at drawing faces, scenes. He paints some." Now she smiled again.

Flash nodded. "So he needs some money, probably a job—we hope a legal job—and now he can live with his friend, maybe fifty-fifty he can stay out of dumb-young-man trouble." Flash mused this over for a minute. "You said you didn't know anything about that friend, Keanau?"

Kellie slowed behind a truck. "Yeah, but I'm gonna find out about him," Kellie said. "Missing person case or no missing person case."

"Good," he told her. "That information will help us. Sorry—help you, and Emma. Figure out what to do next."

Now smiling again, Kellie said, "And you wondered why I thought you were a cop, Mr. what was it? Mr. Thurston F for Flash Tucker, from—"

"Over the ocean, far, far away." He sighed. Jesus, the list of bad people who might be after him right now.

"Yeah, that rings true, the faraway part anyway," Kellie said.

"Well, wherever I come from, I'd like to help you guys if I can, for no other reason than to keep you and Mia from spreading lies about me and ruining my island escape."

"Escape? Is that what you call it?" Kellie's smile was now a permanent feature on her rather handsome face.

Pippa was sitting at the dining room table in front of an open laptop, when the house phone chimed. She looked over and saw the caller was Granddad, so she ran to pick it up.

"Hey!"

"Hey yourself, young lady. How was school today?" Tom's scratchy voice always seemed to have a smile in it.

"School was good, Granddad. I'm a better student than Dad was, so you don't have to worry about me. Mom says all she has to worry about is that I'll get a fat head, not bad grades."

"Well, my beautiful girl, if you do get a fat head, I'll still love you. Is your mom in?"

"Not yet. Granddad—Granddad, have you heard anything from Dad? I really, really miss him." She couldn't understand why he hadn't contacted her from wherever he was.

"Oh, honey, no, but I'm sure he's fine. He'll be back soon. I'm sure of it. You know his work."

She felt a hollow sensation in her chest. "Yeah, I know, but usually he can call. Well, sometimes. He's never been gone this long before, either."

"So, your mom hasn't heard anything, has she?"

Pippa sighed. "I don't think so. I'm pretty sure she would have said if she did. But I'll ask. Do you want her to call you when she gets in?

"Oh sure, but no rush. Just tell her I called to say hi and asked about your dad, and to give you a smooch on the phone, of course."

As she disconnected, Pippa could feel herself in an instant falling from Wonder Woman to little girl. Her heart hurt. She started to tear up. She whispered, "Dad." That was all she could say.

She pushed herself to her feet, wiped tears from her eyes and her cheeks using both hands. She took a deep breath, blew it out, walked into the kitchen, opened the giant stainless-steel refrigerator door, and pulled out a cold Jumbo Juice bottle—Raspberry Rumble. She twisted open the cap and took a drink. Sugar, cold, tangy. She wiped her lips with the back of her wrist and ambled back to her laptop.

At her computer, she flew through the folder containing her special pics, selected from the thousands of photographs in iPhoto. She found one from long ago, a happy picture of her and her dad taken when she was six years old, at Brennecke's Beach in Hawaii. He was kneeling in the sand while she was standing with her little arms around his neck. Both of them were looking into the camera, laughing. She pinned it onto her Facebook page and typed a caption in red: "I really want to be with my dad again." She clicked "update" and closed the laptop.

CHAPTER 13

Lufthansa 1126 shuddered in the dark as it began its descent into Zurich. The sudden drop strained Touma's seatbelt for a breath-altering moment. One jolt in a nauseating parade of jolts. Honolulu to Los Angeles, Los Angeles to Frankfurt, Frankfurt to Zurich. Twenty-five hours and counting. He was exhausted. He was hung over too. Jet lag, for starters, plus lots of wine and brandy on the killer leg from Los Angeles to Frankfurt, and a seven-hour layover in Frankfurt in the first-class club room, where he consumed more wine—not good wine——just more of it, along with a brandy or two.

Several times during the endless passage, he had been visited by the image of his very own private jet sitting in its rented hanger. But his beloved jet couldn't make so long a trip. Oh, it could fly to Los Angeles, just, but not to Europe and back. *Yes, yes*, he kept thinking, *first-world problems*. Once upon a time he'd been poor, blah blah blah. But his head was aching, his gut hurt, his back was sore, and he felt as if he had the flu. And he never wanted to be poor again.

His thoughts spiraled on to that weasel, Dietrich. What was up with him? Eight days in a row, he'd ignored Touma's phone calls, then, finally, when tracked down on his cellphone, Dietrich had agreed, with some arm twisting, to a meeting, but only in person: "Here in Zurich, Touma. That's my first and last offer for a meeting. Take it or leave it. Your call."

In the past, Touma had been buffed to a mirror-like shine by Heinrich Dietrich's warm and attentive sales pitch which promised a life-changing sum of money. Touma, playing coy as long as he could, eventually relented, and gave the nod to borrowing five-hundred, million from Banc Schaffhausen.

All games aside, they both knew that he had always intended to take Dietrich's money. The reason was simple: On paper, Touma was severely overextended, a glaring credit risk. He'd been summarily turned down by seven different commercial investors, mostly big American lending institutions. He'd been surprised that an uptight, mainstream Swiss bank was courting him.

As he soon learned, though, Dietrich's money was a special kind of money. It needed a place to go, according to Bart Singleton II, who'd introduced him to Heinrich Dietrich. The deal was part a boatload of dirty money on its way to being cleaned up and circulated in the legitimate world.

At Flughafen Zürich, Touma was met by a car and driver who took him to Baur au Lac, an ultra-high-end hotel Minette had chosen for him, a 175-year-old landmark with its own park on Lake Zurich. He'd had enough to eat and too much to drink, so he crashed onto the Schweitzer Linen six-hundred-thread-count bed sheets under two cashmere blankets and slept fitfully till noon the following day.

Banc Schaffhausen GmbH occupied a four-story, bunker-like building constructed of lots of glass and polished stone, facing Bahnhofstrasse in the heart of Zurich's financial district. The building had no ATMs or tellers as it was not a retail bank—it was a commercial bank. Clients made appointments; they didn't just drop in. Based on financial status and one's relationship with the bank, the client would be escorted to one of the bank's four floors, starting at the first floor for Level One clients, who held the smaller and less important banking relationships, ascending to Level Four, the top tier, gold star, world-class clientele.

Touma was greeted by a woman seated in a slate-colored Philippe Stark office chair behind a polished gray stone reception desk. She watched him as he approached. He detected no visible signs of real work, or business, or busyness on or anywhere near her station. She was dressed in black, which suited her black hair, bob-cut in precise level lines, perfectly shaped to frame her face.

She presented a warm, practiced smile, glanced down at a screen embedded in the desktop, and said, "Good day, Mr. Allen. It is a pleasure to welcome you to Banc Schaffhausen. My assistant, Elke, will escort you to the third-floor dining room, where you will be meeting with the chairman."

Elke stepped out of a hidden space behind the bank of elevators across the entry hall. She, too, was dressed in black, an unadorned silk pantsuit with no jewelry, careful makeup, slightly rouged cheeks, red lips, her blonde hair held back by a gold clip on one side. She was thirty-something, and spoke in a soft voice with a German accent.

"Mr. Allen, this way, please. We will take this elevator." She pointed at one of the elevator doors, and the door opened as if by magic. The walls, ceiling, and floor were brushed stainless steel, and the elevator displayed no buttons. Apparently, it had an intelligence of its own and knew where they were going.

In high heels, Elke was taller than Touma. She clasped her hands in front of her, and bending at the waist slightly, looking down, said, "Welcome to Zurich, Mr. Allen. I trust you had a relaxing journey, although I don't know why you would ever want to leave a place as beautiful as Oahu." She blushed and laughed.

"Neither do I," said Touma, who still had a sour stomach. "Neither do I."

A scotch with just a splash of water was how their meeting

began. Dietrich Heinrich settled adjacent to Touma in a clubby, wraparound, soft, brown leather chair. The two sat at the far end of the room, facing floor-to-ceiling windows looking down at Bahnhofstrasse.

Dietrich was older than Touma and much taller—six foot three or four. He was folded into his chair, comfortably hunched in the way tall, thin people often settle. His painfully simple black suit, radiant white shirt, black knit tie, gold and jade cufflinks, bespoke black wingtips, fiercely creased trousers, carefully combed dark-brown hair—parted on the left—patrician nose, blue eyes, groomed-into-submission eyebrows, and gold signet ring, where a wedding ring might otherwise be, all announced his social position, and of course his control of this meeting, or, as Touma imagined, any meeting he might deign to convene or attend.

Dietrich's voice was surprisingly soft and unhurried. "We'll eat in a few minutes, but I wanted to give us a chance to relax first and for you to tell me, Touma, where you stand on your project."

Touma wanted to explode all over this patrician asshole! To mess him up somehow, to punch him in the nose, or worse. But he knew his temper and knew this really wasn't the time or place. He needed this man to let him pass Go. He needed to pass Go to continue in the game, and he needed it to happen quickly.

And so he recounted, re-recounted because he knew he'd already told Dietrich where they were, and he'd written several memos about the state of the project. He'd done it all before, but he did it again, patiently and businesslike. The recitation ended with the bottom line: They needed the money to be released in the next two weeks, or the permit would expire, and the project would be lost.

"Hmm, yes, of course," said Dietrich when Touma had finished. "Alexander, would you pour us another, please? I think we'll have one more before lunch."

Alexander appeared from the shadows in his waiter's white

tuxedo, and in an eerie silence, dispensed the scotch and the flavor-releasing splash of still water in both their glasses. He bowed, then moving backward, disappeared.

"Timing," said Dietrich. "Timing. This project has a grand scope, Touma, but the timing."

"What do you mean?" Touma shifted.

"Timing. I wonder if it isn't a bit too soon for you and your company? Don't you feel that way?" He lifted his glass and sniffed at it.

Touma told himself to calm down. "No, I don't feel that way, Heinrich. We have everything scheduled out, contractors lined up, resources sourced, and the permit and approvals are in place. I've explained this to you several times. I agree with you, however, that timing is an issue, since we have to move forward now or we may not be able to move forward, hereafter, ever. That's why I'm here." He restrained himself from reciting the flights he had taken and the number of hours he had flown, in fact, to be here at this very moment.

Touma shifted again, uncomfortable in his chair. He put his heavy glass down on the table and folded his hands in front of him. "Look, I've had enough to drink, could we eat something?"

Dietrich seemed to be pulled back from a sort of a dream or reverie. "Of course, Touma, you're on Hawaiian time, aren't you? I apologize for forgetting that."

They moved to a small, oval dining table with chairs at each end—Chippendale, or some Germanic equivalent. The polished wood surface shined, complementing the sterling silver place settings for each of them: three forks, two spoons, and two knives, highlighted by large, off-white dinner napkins with hemstitched borders, bound in bone napkin rings. *God*, Touma thought, *we're headed for a fucking fish course, and I'm getting sandbagged.*

Touma's legs were aching with anxiety, a pain that increased with each passing, patronizing moment. At one point, he thought he might just scream.

The banker returned to the subject. "So we were talking about timing, weren't we? Yes, so I'm quite concerned about timing, and coupled with the project size, which is much bigger, more comprehensive, I'd say, than anything you've done before. I'm right about that, aren't I, Touma? Yes, I think I am. So I must ask, do you really think you can handle so large a project, on budget and on schedule?"

Touma blurted out, "God, yes, of course. We can't miss this opportunity! It's going to be *the* vacation destination for half the world."

"Well, my dear Touma, I'm afraid—"

"Heinrich! Why the hell are we talking about this now? You said you would fund this project. Four months ago, we agreed. We drew up a contract for the funding. You weren't worried about timing then. What the hell has happened to make you doubt us?"

Heinrich Dietrich seemed taken aback by Touma's outburst. He set aside his appetizer. "Calm down," he chided. "I'm just trying to derive a sense of your self-assessment, your feelings about your capabilities, now that we have more of the hard data in front of us—how you feel about Allen Group, its balance sheet, its competence in light of past projects, and its ability to make a quantum leap in attempting this Village in the Sky. We need to know. I need to know."

Touma glared at Dietrich for a full ten seconds, exhaled, and asked, "Why now?"

Dietrich cocked his head and responded, seeming incredulous, "Why now?"

Touma felt his composure slipping. Impulsively, he reached for his drink, but then thought the better of it. "Yes, Dietrich, why now, goddamnit? This deal was put to bed. Along with your little bit on the side. Are you doubting that, too? Why are we talking as if you're still vetting us when you *have* vetted us and agreed to fund the project, as long as you got your secret piece of the pie?"

Dietrich pointed at Touma and said in a quiet, ominous tone, "The contract to fund this project has not been signed, and our side deal, as you call it, was a sworn secret between us."

With that, Touma decided to go for broke. As things stood, he had nothing more to lose. He looked down at his plate of roasted monkfish with chanterelles, swallowed the impulse to throw up, and said, "If you're thinking of withdrawing from our deal, I'll tell the world about the kickback you demanded. I may live on an island in what you consider the middle of nowhere, but I'm pretty sure I can make your world blow up. I don't want to do that, but if you force me, I will."

Dietrich smiled, an I-don't-believe-you-just-said-that smile, shook his head, and said, "Touma, you're delusional." After a long pause, he continued. "You could talk to every major bank board in the world, trying to convince them that I would take a bribe. They wouldn't believe a word you said, and then they would shoot you, like a mad dog."

Dietrich's cheeks flushed a deep red. "You, my little Hawaiian friend, are way out of your league. We have no deal, and if you value your life—and I mean this, Touma, your life—you will go home and make arrangements to stand down from this ridiculous project of yours and hope that we never meet again. Because if we do meet again, ever, you'll be a dead man. We have never had a deal."

Touma couldn't believe what he was hearing. Dietrich appeared to have gone completely mental. This whole dance, the time and money he had spent to get this deal. Dietrich's courting him, the offers—Touma's mega-project was suddenly as insignificant as a puff of wind, a falling coconut, a flea on an elephant's butt. Shit!

Dietrich stood and said in a matter-of-fact voice, "This concludes our business, Touma. Elke will escort you out."

. . .

Later that afternoon Touma boarded the Lufthansa flight to Frankfurt. As he sat in his seat, he wiped his face with the perfumed hot towel provided to all the first-class passengers, then tapped out a text to Minette: VERY CONFIDENTIAL: For your and Benjamin's eyes only. This is an emergency. Village in the Sky is about to crash and burn. We need to sell the jet. How? I need a list of salable assets (Allen Grp) and ideas about quickly turning them into cash. We must move quickly before the sharks circle. Back in the office late tomorrow. We have a lot of work to do in very little time. No one else to know.

CHAPTER 14

J ohn Horan deplaned Alaska Flight 190 at Cancun International Airport. The lines to and through immigration were moving, but they were long and cleverly folded back and forth, so he couldn't tell when or where he would finally be processed. The illusion of anonymity, one stupidly dressed tourist among hundreds of stupidly dressed tourists, comforted him. He eventually answered a uniformed agent's questions, handed the officer his immigration form, and showed another officer his fake passport.

John was waved through into a reception hall with national police stationed at intervals along the sidewalls, machine guns lowered but ready.

He pushed through the throng, then through the automatic doors to the outside, where he was blasted by hot, moist tropical air, reminding him how lovely being out of the rain and cold in Seattle was.

He waited curbside with a carry-on backpack at his feet, all the luggage he would need for this carefully planned and staged two-week vacation in Mexico.

A blue 1998 Toyota Land Cruiser with a jungle grill and off-road lights pulled up and stopped at the curb. The driver jumped out. "Señor Butterfield? You Señor Butterfield?"

"Yes, I'm Butterfield."

"May I see your passport and driver's license, please, señor?"

After comparing the driver's license in one hand with the passport in the other, the man handed John the keys to the SUV along with the documents. He then nodded his head and walked away. Curbside delivery, of sorts. One of many carefully thought-out parts of John Horan's "Vacation in Mexico" project.

Soon, John was accelerating up an onramp, on his way to Tulum, an hour-and-a-half drive south along Highway 307, the coast road, through Puerto Morelos, Playa del Carmen, and finally to the outskirts of Tulum. John was staying at a boutique seaside resort made up of many separate, three-room casitas strung along winding palm-treed pathways, each unit land-scaped, with its own reflection pool, each some distance from the main building with its restaurant and bar.

In such a place, among the rich and semi-rich, the special people, John could be "at the resort" and not at the resort at the same time, and no one would know, notice, or care. Tonight, he would make his arrival visible, though. He would go to the central building, have a bunch of drinks, eat a good dinner, chat up the bartender and servers, disappear into his luxury casita, and crash. The next day, he would need time and solitude to prepare for phase two.

John's so-called vacation would have been a lot less stressful if he could have organized more in Seattle. But international travel made things complicated. He'd had to come to Mexico ready to be flexible, alert certainly, and able to make plans on the fly. This was the only way he could ensure success.

The central issue was that only one sentient being knew for sure what John had done. Just one. As long as that person roamed the planet, even if her roaming was in a sleepy, out-of-the-way Mexican backwater like Tulum, he was at risk.

A long time had passed since the ten million had disappeared —six months. In Seattle, the dust had settled; the event seemed to have fallen from urgent and alarming to ancient history, distasteful ancient history. No one even wanted to talk about it, no one.

So now was the right time for John to free himself from the woman he had paid a million dollars for assisting in the heist.

John was a high-IQ, high-intensity, high-energy detail fanatic, a fastidious planner, and a profoundly secretive introvert. As a result of rigorous training, he had developed a cutthroat and even violent set of survival skills, yet he gave others the impression of being an open and socially affable creature. People tended to be sucked in by his relaxed confidence. Many who knew him considered John to be a special friend, even a confidant. This glow of camaraderie had somehow pierced the rock-hard defenses of Tilly Good.

Tilly and John had met in a low-life suburb of Las Vegas called Henderson. At the time, Tilly was being held for tax evasion, attempted murder, and supplying industrial quantities of drugs, mainly cocaine, to the Las Vegas community, the one that never sleeps.

While raiding her home on suspicion of tax evasion, Treasury agents literally stumbled across Tilly, carving away on a small-time dope distributor in her rec room. The twenty-two-year-old pusher had been duct taped to a high-backed wooden chair and had suffered seven stab wounds, none inflicted in a way that might kill the poor bastard, but precisely placed to elicit terror and pain. John had been liaising with Treasury on Tilly's case as the resident expert in money laundering and drugs.

As the evidence of her crimes piled up, Tilly, a quick and wily adapter, a cat with twice the lives allocated to regular cats, convinced the various aggrieved agencies that she had more to offer them than the satisfaction of adding her to the already overflowing prison population for twenty or more years. She not only knew how to stab people in ways that would maim and scare the shit out of them, she knew many, many nasty and stupid criminals she would happily offer up for a deal.

And, unlike many criminals who are crooked because they're lazy, feckless people, Tilly was willing to work hard to earn her reward. John was designated as Tilly's lead interviewer, encouraging and manipulating her to release her collection of poisonous names and places, and their stories and thus earn her place in the much-prized Witness Protection Program.

After months of secret testimony, Tilly Good, who certainly hadn't lived up to the promise of her last name, became Emilia Pedella, and left to live incognito in San Miguel de Allende, Mexico.

In defiance of protocol, John stayed in touch with Tilly. Tilly also stayed in touch with John. The relationship was a secret thing, with texts exchanged on burner phones, a borderline flirty —back and forth, back and forth.

Then, one day, two years later, Emilia Pedella disappeared from her hillside apartment in San Miguel de Allende. She had returned to a life of crime, but stayed in touch with John. Tilly had realized that being buried in the WPP was way too confining, and besides, she was a businesswoman, not a victim, not a sit-at-home retiree. John, for his part, told no one about his secret connection with "Maria Espinosa," now ruling from the shadows as a drug queen in a place called Tulum.

John clearly remembered the day he realized why he had kept "the Tilly thing," as he called it, alive. He had been saving her for later, for a time when a friend in the netherworld with Tilly's skill and experience would be helpful. After a year's worth of politicking, John convinced the lords of law enforcement that his Criminal Fraud Group could mount a devastating sting and destabilize a multibillion-dollar money laundering operation called LM Global. But to do this, they would need seed capital of at least ten million.

As the sting was planned, the funds allocated, and the team chosen, John began to be aware that he was hovering near the chance of a lifetime, actually two or three lifetimes. He hadn't set out to steal the money, but he had a fall guy in Flash and—suddenly realizing why he had held on to Tilly all these years—a person who didn't exist, the two essential elements for this kind of theft to work.

So John enlisted Tilly to play shortstop. She was to visit the lovely island of Nevis and make an appointment to meet with a bank manager of the Kits Nevis National Bank at a particular hour on a particular day.

Via the bank manager, Tilly, under an assumed identity and possessing elaborate and pristine documentation authorizing her actions, would take immediate control of a particular account the moment it received a deposit of ten-million dollars. Using a carefully prepared laptop computer, she would redirect the money, sending it around the world through trusts, shell companies, and banks galore. A million of it would zip into her own secret account, and the remaining nine million would reappear on the other side of the world in a blind trust that John had established under another identity.

Tilly had been a secret worth keeping. And at the time of the heist, he was convinced she was even more devious and secretive than he was, which had been curiously reassuring. But over time he began to think that a secret shared with someone else was not a secret.

John approached the Tilly problem like a Rubik's Cube. He worked through many scenarios, imagining consequences—intended and otherwise—until he had conjured a bulletproof plan, a carefully choreographed sequence of events that would, in the end, solve the Tilly problem. He also acknowledged that he would have to walk away from a million dollars. But when you had nine million of your own, who cares?

John had no animus toward Tilly. What he intended was

simply an act of survival. While planning this operation, he saw no need for finesse. Drugs were trouble, morning, noon, and night, as far as Mexican society at large saw them, and the drug world was violent, even more so in Mexico than the US.

John acted accordingly. At the resort, he mounted a set of stolen license plates on his rental. He also had taken delivery of a High Standard HD .22 pistol with a suppressor he'd ordered and paid for online using a fake name. The gun had been delivered in a discreet brown Amazon box to his casita, along with a box of ammunition.

John parked his rented Land Cruiser half a block from Tilly's house with a clear line of sight to the front gate. The time was ten at night, but the sidewalk was still radiating the afternoon heat. He waited patiently in the front seat, looking down the road toward her two-story hacienda. Lights were on upstairs and down. The day was Saturday; she had told him that she gathered her six vaqueros for dinner every Saturday, bragging that she modeled her gang after that of a family, a small Mafia cell, Mexico style.

At midnight, he watched as the guests left, counting heads until he was reasonably sure the visitors were all gone. Finally, when the lights on the veranda went dark, he approached the house. He walked up to the front door, painted turquoise, and with a wrought-iron circular knocker. He knocked, hoping she would think one of her vaqueros had returned.

She opened the door, and he squeezed the trigger four times, tap tap, tap tap, four muffled pops. Her knees buckled, and she fell backward, a red spot spreading across her white silk blouse, just over her heart. He turned and walked out to the street, slid into the SUV, and drove out of the city back to his casita.

Once there, he replaced the stolen license plates, dismantled the pistol and magazine, and placed the disassembled gun in a bowl and poured bleach over the pieces. That evening he again ate in the dining room, had lots of wine and a steak dinner, matriculated to the bar, had two double brandies, got pretty drunk, and returned to his casita to drop into bed. The next day, the pistol parts went into the ocean, and he returned to Seattle with the obligatory vacation tan and stories of old Mexico. He felt like a new man, nothing but smooth sailing ahead.

CHAPTER 15

Paul opened his eyes, sensing someone in the room. Suddenly, he sat bolt upright and sprang out of bed. Two uniformed figures were in the doorway with guns drawn, shouting; Paul stood there naked, staring at them. The nearest person extended her hand, palm out in front of her. "Paul, Paul, stop right where you are! Stop! Get down on the floor. Right now. On the floor!"

Paul began to hyperventilate. He went down to his knees, then fell forward, face on the floor, his nose resting against the dusty wooden planks. He couldn't slow the pace of his breathing, even though he was dizzy. He felt utterly disoriented; his heart was pounding. Blood rushed behind his eardrums, making muffling sounds.

"What the fuck?" he gasped. "What the fuck?"

"Okay, okay. Paul, stay down. Don't move. I mean it!" A second later, the woman's knee drove into the middle of his back. His hands were forced together behind him, and plastic restraints pulled tight around his wrists. The knee was removed, and the woman hauled him up to his feet. He was so freaked out, so amped up with adrenaline, he still couldn't stop his rapid breathing.

He was led into the living room, where Keanu was standing with a cop on either side of him, his hands behind his back. Between gasps, Paul blurted out, "What the fuck, dude?"

Keanu appeared calm. Seemingly at ease, slouching almost, as if he were just chilling on a street corner, hands cinched behind his back—he even grinned, like this might be a Hollywood production, or a joke or something. Except it wasn't a fucking movie shoot, it was life. The kind of scene that could end in a premature death. Paul's breathing slowed a little, running out of juice, as he realized they were under arrest.

Keanu's face grew dark, and he hissed, "Whatever you do, bud, don't say a fucking thing. Got it? Not a fucking thing. Otherwise, that old man will—" Before Keanu could finish, the two cops jerked him backward and out the front door. Paul watched through the grime-encrusted front window as they marched him past the pickup truck to a white patrol car, blue lights rotating.

Kellie Jackson continued to hold Paul. He realized he had recognized her. His mom's friend. She had strong hands. After Keanu was gone, she moved in front of Paul, while the other cop held him by his arms from behind.

Her eyes focused on his, freezing him in place, and she said, "Listen up, Paul. I have a warrant to search these premises. You need to pay attention. You're being arrested for suspicion of possessing and distributing MDMA." She held up a blue backpack, Keanu's stash. "We're taking you two in for questioning. Are you listening?"

Paul nodded. She continued. "We will be questioning you about these drugs and your relationship with Mr. P."

Paul's breathing was pretty much back to normal, and a wave of irrepressible fatigue overtook him. He went limp and almost fell down, but Kellie and her sidekick held him up. Then the three of them moved together out the door to a patrol car, and a hand touched the top of his head as he went to slide in the back seat.

The car door slammed, and Paul looked around at the scene through the protective cage between the back seat and the front. He counted four police cars, all with flashing lights, and at least six cops, with three entering Keanu's house by the front door. All he could think was that his life was over, and his mom would be furious.

"Paul Pookalani, what's with the drug stash?"

"I don't know what you're talking about."

"Don't know? Don't know?" charged Kellie, shaking her head.

Paul's hands were in his lap, fists clenched, as if holding on for dear life. He shifted his weight in the armless steel chair. A recording device sat against the wall at the other end of the room, red light blinking, while other red lights flashed on two small video cameras placed on the ceiling. Paul stared at the tabletop in front of him.

"I don't know what you're talking about."

"Okay," said Kellie. "How about Mr. P. When was the last time you saw him?"

Paul glanced up at her. Her brow was furrowed; she seemed to be thinking.

"You're an idiot, Paul. We found your stash, and Mr. P. has been murdered! We can't go any farther without you having a lawyer. You have no idea what type of trouble you're in here. I'm suspending this interview pending the arrival of a public defender, an attorney of your choice, or your mom's choice."

An hour later, the public defender appeared in Paul's cell. By now, Paul was simply scared to death. He felt brittle and twitchy, and his legs ached. His stomach churned. *Mr. P. dead? What the fuck? What am I doing here? My mom's going to kill me!*

An officer opened the door to Paul's cell, shoved in a folding chair, and let in a young woman, not that much older than Paul. The door closed behind her. She wore a gray skirt, white dress shirt, and black pumps. She was short, thin, with shining, long black hair hanging straight down over her shirt collar. She wore no makeup that he could see.

The woman introduced herself as Janet Nakamura, and she held out a hand to shake. Paul, in a dull green worn but clean jail outfit, was embarrassed—his hand was damp with sweat.

The lawyer then sat in the chair that the guard had slid into the cell. She crossed her legs and took a yellow legal pad and Bic pen from a beat-up leather folio. Removing the pen cap, she locked her eyes on his and said, "Before we start, I need to explain a couple of things."

He sat and listened, catching at least the essence of what she was telling him. She would defend him; he needed to level with her; he was being held for possession and intent to deliver MDMA.

Paul followed as best he could, but when he heard the word *murder*, he blurted out, "Murder?" Shaking his head frantically, he simply shouted, "No!"

"Okay, okay. Look, Paul, we don't have a lot of time here. They'll want to interview you as soon as we're done. Here's what we have to do right now. First of all, you need to tell me everything you know about this. Mr. P. Everything! What you say to me is completely confidential, but I need to know what you know to defend you. We'll soon find out if they have probable cause to possibly charge you for murder, but till then we need to play our cards carefully, and you have to follow my instructions to the letter. So we start with Mr. P., then we talk about the drugs found at your friend's house. Then the interview, and then I apply for bail, and hopefully, we'll have a bail hearing tomorrow. Got it?"

Paul nodded. "Yeah, I get it."

She half-smiled and said, "Now let's start with Mr. P."

. . .

Kellie said, "All right, I have to be a little careful here. I'll tell you what I can, then I'll leave. Mia told me that Paul's public defender will be along later, and I can't be here when she is. It's a conflict, separate interests, like that. But I can give you the same information that we're giving the public tomorrow, and I want to see that Paul gets a fair deal. Actually, I'm sure we all do, all of us at the police department, too. But no kidding, Paul's in serious trouble, and he really needs our help!"

Flash, Mia, Emma, and Kellie were gathered that evening at Mia and Mr. Mia's house, two miles outside of Koloa. The place had been Mia's mother's house until she passed away seven years before; Mia and her husband sold their house, then moved in—the house was larger than theirs and closer to town. They used the cash from the sale to put a down payment on another building in Old Koloa Town, expanding Mia's real estate empire from one building to two, which between them housed a pizza parlor, two apartments, a bar and grill, a shave ice and ice cream parlor, and what Mia called a surf-shit shop. Mr. Mia, whose real name was Reggie Mahow, was a retired surveyor, and he now served as handyman, gardener, and superintendent for Mahow Properties.

After tearing off paper towels and placing one in front of each place around the dining room table, Reggie brought a tray of orange plastic glasses, a mixing bowl filled with ice cubes, and a gallon jug of brewed tea from the kitchen. He distributed the glasses, spooning ice into each one as he passed them around. He went back into the kitchen and returned with a double loaf of mango bread, sliced. He put the bread in the center of the table and encouraged everyone to help themselves.

Flash had agreed to join Mia's Justice for Paul gathering— turned out, he liked being included. Listening to Kellie, he was surprised by his interest in what she was telling them and wondered how he would have played it back in Seattle under the same circumstances.

Flash put one of the six-packs of Foster's he'd brought in the center of the table and released a can for himself. He noticed that Kellie had stopped talking and everybody was looking at him.

He said, "I just thought some of us might like something a little stronger. Feel free. Take one, or two even." He smiled and felt a blush work its way up his neck. Hoping that his tan would provide cover, he sat down, popped open the beer, and said, "So, Kellie, you were saying?"

Kellie told them that Franklin Peterson, head of security at the Nawiliwili Commercial Freight Terminal, had been killed at his home Saturday night. The police thought his death had something to do with Kauai drug traffic, but nothing had surfaced to substantiate that yet.

The police thought that Paul's friend Keanu had been selling drugs, small-time selling, but selling, and maybe Mr. P. had been angry, or Keanu had been angry, over something that had caused a dispute. Paul and Keanu were present on CCD security camera footage talking to Peterson, maybe arguing with him, on the Thursday before his death. That was the entire link to a possible murder charge, so far. For now, that was all Kellie could tell them.

Half an hour after Kellie left, Janet Nakamura was sitting where Kellie had sat. Flash tended to be standoffish around lawyers, especially public defenders, but he liked her. She, all five feet of her, seemed to have her shit together.

Her assessment of the situation was that the stash of drugs found at the house might not be big enough to result in a conviction for selling; the murder, obviously, was more serious, but Paul said the boys had an alibi for Saturday night, that they were at a rave out at Polihale Beach.

Janet said they had to be a bit careful while gathering statements for the alibi. What they needed was written corroboration that Paul and Keanau had been at the rave around 7 p.m.—Peterson's time of death—but she didn't want the statements to suggest that they might have been selling drugs. If one or both of them were selling drugs, that would not be so great.

Flash shook his head. *Of course the kids were selling drugs.*

Janet finished by telling them that Paul had a good chance for bail—he had a clean sheet, and besides, this was Kauai, not Honolulu or LA. Kauai was a tight-knit community, taking care of its own.

Can Kauai take care of its own? Flash wondered. Was that why he was hiding out here? Being taken care of? Was he becoming one of Kauai's "own"? Or was he just on the run and hiding?

Mia said, "I'll find out who saw them at the rave, put together some names so you can take statements. I can do that, no problem."

Janet looked up from her notepad and said, "Great, get names and phone numbers. I'll need at least two—no, better yet, three people willing to sign statements."

Flash said, "I could talk to the boys if that would help. I might be able to reel them in a little, act as a bit of a sounding board?"

"Ah, yeah," said Janet. She made another note, then smiled impishly. "Anything to moderate teen testosterone impulses would be a plus. Do you know the boys at all?"

"No, not yet, but I do know boys. Same tribe and all."

Janet nodded. "Yeah, that could help, but try not to give them legal advice, okay? That's my job. Someone told me you might have been a cop once. Any truth in that?"

"Jesus, Mia, goddamn it!" Flash glared hard at Mia, who just shook her head at him, smiling.

Janet said, "No, not Mia—someone else told me. Oh, never mind, whatever you tell the boys, just leave the lawyering to me."

"Don't worry about that, counselor. I sure as hell don't want to be mistaken for a lawyer—or a cop, either, for that matter."

Emma finally spoke up. "Thanks, Flash. I'm sure you can help. But just to say it, I think Keanau might be a bad influence on Paul. If you can do anything to help Paul, see—Oh, God, what a mess." She covered her eyes with both hands and began to weep.

Mia stood up. "We need to stop talking and get to work," she said. "Reggie will ask around about the Nawiliwili facility. I'll dig out rave names and phone numbers. Can they call you, Janet? Of course they can. Give me some of your cards. I'll canvass for any other information around the island too. We all need to work fast and find anything and everything that might help us. And Janet, you need to hurry back to your desk and go to work."

Mia paused in thought, then continued. "Oh, and also, about the bail? If Paul could get bail, that would be good. You know, Emma, maybe Paul should move back home? He's had enough of the big bad world for now, don't you think? I don't know the Keanu boy, but I'll find out about him, too. Flash can help there, also, so stop crying, Emma. We need to go to work."

Emma looked up and smiled, eyes red and cheeks wet with tears.

Mia said, "Meeting over! We meet again tomorrow evening. Same time, right here. No beer."

CHAPTER 16

The early afternoon sun was shining brightly in Zurich, and the wind was light, so Heinrich Dietrich decided to walk the six blocks from his office to LM Global's headquarters in Trust Square in Parade Platz. Parade Platz was a collection of neoclassical stone buildings, four or five stories high, and for many years it had housed and protected what were mostly banks and banking-related businesses. A monumental capital square, it was open in the center, with block-long buildings standing sentinel on three sides—in short, a Swiss financial fortress.

But Google, Apple, IBM, and others had moved in with the bankers. Trust Square at Parade Platz now was a multiplex of twenty-first-century businesses, although still housed in the neoclassical stone. Dietrich was of two minds about the change. A banker first, he resented the intrusion. On the other hand, the new look of the square's denizens quite excited him. The mix of jeans and Italian suits added both color and a jolt of modernity; the square was more animated than ever. His father, a retired banker, could never have imagined it.

LM Global leased a relatively nondescript suite of offices on a middle floor of one of those block-long stone buildings. Dietrich had an appointment for two o'clock, but he arrived ten minutes early. He didn't want to appear anxious, so he meandered through the building's ground-floor lobby, walking past a flower shop, a coffee shop, and a bookstore, looking at his watch every minute or two. Seven minutes went by.

Dietrich then took the elevator up to the entry of LM Global, a double-sized frontage facing the brightly lit hallway. A sizeable polished-brass plaque with a globe in relief was set in the center of the darkly stained wood door. There was no name, just the globe. An illuminated bell push sat on the wall to the right.

Dietrich took a deep breath and pressed the button. The giant door buzzed and opened inward. Dietrich wondered if he was a fool, petitioning Herr Planc—pleading with him actually. He wasn't used to pleading, or even asking for that matter. He approached the receptionist, a serious-looking man, as the large door slowly closed itself. Somewhere behind this receptionist was Herr Planc, the extortionist who held Dietrich's future in his hands.

He reflected on the idea of karma that the kids always talked about and wondered momentarily whether his treatment of Touma Allen the week before could have contributed to what he was about to experience.

Gathering himself, Dietrich smiled and made his way across the foyer toward the thin, clean-shaven and bespectacled young man behind a dark wooden desk.

As Heinrich approached, the young man spoke. "Who are you, and what's your business, please?"

Heinrich recoiled at the sharp tone and the stern look on the young man's face.

It occurred to Dietrich that LM Global didn't deal with the public; LM Global dealt with billions of dollars and the sort of people who extorted that type of money—not Dietrich's kind of people. He felt an uptick of anxiety, took in a breath, and gathered what control he could muster.

"My name is Dietrich. I have an appointment with Herr Planc, at fourteen hundred."

The young man looked down at a bound diary to his right. He looked up again and said, "Please confirm your identity. Your driver's license or passport will do." He held his hand out to receive the documents, stone-faced.

Dietrich handed the young man his passport with a business card on top, the latter an announcement of who he actually was, the chairman of an important Swiss bank. Then he mused over the reality that in this world, he had no status. This carefully groomed young man wasn't interested in who Dietrich was. The young man was a bully, a gatekeeper, plain and simple.

"Please take a seat over there." The receptionist pointed to an upholstered bench against the side wall. "Herr Planc will see you when he is ready."

After a twenty-minute wait, a cursory exchange of hand-shakes, and a walk into a conference room, Heinrich Dietrich sat looking at his adversary in the flesh. So this was Herr Michel Planc. The two were seated at a highly polished, round wooden table. A crystal chandelier hung over the center of the table. The chairs were dark wood with padded leather arms and backs, secured with brass tacks.

Dietrich gripped the arms of his chair as he listened to Michel Planc scold him and regale him with insults and accusations in a steady drumbeat of abuse. Planc was a small man, just over five feet, but he had big hands and an overlarge head. He was in his mid-to-late sixties, with sparse gray hair, large lips, and brown eyes that went to black as he cursed Dietrich and Banc Schaffhausen GMBH. Planc's voice was rough and loud, his breathing audible between sentences.

Getting a sense of Planc's angry rhythm, Dietrich at one point attempted to interrupt.

Planc slammed his hand on the table. "You shut the fuck up. I'm talking! You are not to speak until I've had my say." And so the monologue went on. Planc had apparently agreed to the appointment not to meet, but to deliver a beating. The old man finally stopped, still breathing hard from his exertion.

Dietrich didn't hesitate, jumping in before the old man could start up again. "I have some answers to the questions you posed through Haysmith, your consultant. Perhaps you would like to hear what we found out about the money?"

The old man took a breath and, in a quieter voice, said, "All right, but this had better be good."

Dietrich slid a brown manila envelope from the black Venetian leather portfolio he held in his lap. He opened the flap and removed an A4-size black-and-white photograph of a woman wearing sunglasses, her face turned down. He then slid out a second photograph and placed it next to the first. It was of the same woman, with long, dark hair, walking across what appeared to be the lobby of a bank. She again was wearing sunglasses, along with a full-length coat and very high heels; she was carrying a box purse. Dietrich next set out a third photograph showing the same woman talking to a bank official at a service desk; both were looking at documents on the counter between them.

Each image had a date and time stamp in the lower right corner in white lettering, the first one reading KNNB 9 Oct 2010, 1750, and the second KNNB 9 Oct 2010, 1752. The third read KNNB 9 Oct 2010, 1757.

"Have you seen these photographs, Herr Planc? Do you know where they were taken? Do you know the woman?"

Planc looked startled, as if he had been caught off-script. The red-faced old man stared, first at the photos, then at Dietrich, still breathing audibly. "What are you playing at? All I want to know is if you've found out how you lost our money, and when you're going to return it. I've never seen this woman in my life."

"First of all, Herr Planc, our investigation confirms that we didn't lose the money, and therefore we are under no obligation to replace it. This woman holds the key. Are you sure you don't know this woman?" This was Dietrich's last stand, and he wasn't about to appear intimidated.

"No," Planc said in a distracted voice. He put his finger on each of the photographs as if to direct his attention, to focus on each one individually. Then he looked back up and barked, "No. This is bullshit! What are you playing at?"

"Herr Planc, this is not bullshit! These photos were taken on Nevis. You may not know her, but you definitely should care about her, because she is your enemy. She is an agent, someone's agent, who redirected your money away from its intended destination to—well, somewhere. We don't know where. The KNNB on the photograph is the clue as to why we can't trace the money beyond this location. These are images made by the Kits Nevis National Bank security cameras, on the island of Nevis, at the Charleston branch, on the afternoon of the ninth of October 2010, the day and time that ten million dollars your client wired to the bank on Nevis went missing." Dietrich was grateful that his voice felt strong. He sounded, he thought, annoyed and assertive. *Good.*

"My client had nothing to do with your losing that money, Dietrich," Planc growled. "We gave your bank ten-million dollars, and you lost it, or more likely stole it."

Dietrich smiled for the first time. "Not so, the security photos tell a different story, don't they? The photographs and subsequent intelligence we have acquired gave us enough information to trace the money back through four shell companies to a source that suggests your client wasn't a client at all." He paused and held eye contact with the old man.

"Your so-called client was really a police sting operation initiated in Seattle, Washington. Those clever lads apparently infiltrated your security, convinced you that they had money to launder, then made the ten-million-dollar deposit. After that, as if by magic—poof, the money went missing. But magic wasn't the cause. That woman transferred the money before you were able to make your move. She could do that because her credentials, vetted by the Kits Nevis National Bank, gave her access to the account." Dietrich was in full stride.

"As you undoubtedly are aware, Nevis is the opaquest of opaque banking centers in the world. So we did what we could do. We traced the money back to its source, as that trail was through less secure channels."

Planc appeared unimpressed. "This is just a fairy tale. Do you think I'm a fool?"

Heinrich Dietrich held out one hand, palm up, and said, "Foolish enough not to vet the people who were asking for your services, it appears."

Planc's red face flushed redder, and he shifted in his chair. He pushed the photographs back across the table to Dietrich.

Dietrich smiled, paused a moment to give Planc more time to squirm, and then said, "This was a private deal with me, remember? You didn't want your LM partners to know about it—paying a bribe, perhaps?" Heinrich held out his hand again as if holding Planc back.

"Okay, okay, maybe just paying off a bet or a debt—I don't care. What I do know is you're a lucky man, Planc. You are fortunate that this woman did show up. Had she not, I'm pretty sure you and your LM Global partners, as well as your intended recipient, would be under indictment and answering uncomfortable questions." Having delivered the coup de grace, Dietrick bowed his head. "You're out of your mind," Planc said by way of reaction. "Get out of my office."

Dietrich looked at Planc in surprise. "Not yet. We're not done," he said, steel in his voice. "This whole mess is your cock-up, not ours. And since you are trying to blame us for the loss, you reneged on your promise to invest in our bank. The whole world will think we screwed this up. I'm not going to stand by quietly and let that happen. You need to make this good."

Planc pushed himself upright in his chair and barked, "Ha! What the fuck do I care what you're willing to accept or not? I don't trust you. I think you're lying about all of this. My board will back me. They don't care where I put money as long as we are paid for it. You and your bank aren't even an afterthought to us."

Dietrich replied, "I wonder what your board would think if I give them this information? Hmm? I wonder what the Seattle people could do if they find out what we know, or Interpol, or the World Bank? You committed to this investment, and I demand that you make good on it, quietly and promptly. If you do, we can all come out of this absurd muddle whole, with some ruffled feathers perhaps, but whole."

"What about my ten-million dollars?" Planc jumped up and began pacing back and forth on his side of the table, hands clasped behind his back. "I'm not whole! Ten million, what are you fucking thinking?"

"I think you didn't actually lose ten-million. The sting lost it. The cops lost it," said Dietrich. "And, to repeat, you're damn lucky they did. Look, you should be thrilled to walk away from this screw-up without incriminating yourselves."

Planc stopped pacing, returned to his seat, and pulled the three photos back to his side of the table. He looked at each of them again, still breathing hard. Reaching down into the pocket of his suit coat, which was hung over the back of the chair, he took out a gold cigarette case and gold lighter. He offered a cigarette to Heinrich, who shook his head, then lit one himself and took a long, deep drag.

Dietrich could see that the old man had run out of steam.

Planc slouched back in his seat. Taking another drag on his cigarette, he spoke in a quieter voice. "What a mess, eh? What a mess. I can see that this must be hard on you and your bank. Let's put an end to this, ah, misunderstanding. This is unfortunate. Life is too short."

Planc slowly gathered the three photographs into a single pile, turned the pile face down, and rested one hand on top of the collection. Then, looking out the window to the square below, he said in a distracted voice, "I need three or four days to do some damage control, understand?"

Dietrich, almost overwhelmed by relief, said, "Yes, and then?"

"Then we'll fix it. We'll make your investment, the Hawaii thing, an island in the air or whatever. In return, you'll have to give me all of this evidence and data in exchange for going forward—all of it—and your promise of secrecy, forever and always, understand?" He looked unblinking at Dietrich.

"And the ten million?" asked Dietrich.

"It's gone." The old man pushed out of his chair. "Now, I have a lot of work to do. Make an appointment with my assistant for next Wednesday, and we'll finish all this."

With that, Planc turned and walked out of the conference room.

In the reception hall, the stone-faced assistant stood at the open door, accompanied by a dark-suited monster of a man. "Herr Dietrich, we will be pleased to escort you out. Come with me, please," said the giant.

Dietrich followed, less relieved than he had felt a minute before.

Michel Planc sat alone in his private office, his door closed. He was still breathing hard, feeling irritated and impatient. *A sting, shit. How did we bungle that? But, come to think of it, nothing has really changed. That fucking money, five-hundred million needs to move.* He'd promised his LM Global partners the money would be invested. With Banc Schaffhausen out of the picture, he needed a Plan B.

Then came the matter of Dietrich. *Isn't he a piece of work? Thinks he is so fucking smart. Not smart enough to emerge from this alive, though. No, Plan B needs that banker to evaporate.*

Planc's job at LM Global was oversight for all capital operations, having first and final say about money in and money out.

He'd assumed the role because he was the founding principal of the firm, having put up the initial capital seven years before, after growing tired of running a drug-smuggling operation that distributed to France, Italy, and Switzerland. In a move to outflank his competitors and strengthen his empire's security, he had divided the cartel into two smaller, tighter, specialized organizations. He'd put his son in charge of one of them and a trusted lieutenant in charge of the other. Drug wars were for younger, more energetic men.

Once the reorganization was complete, Planc set about creating LM Global. The idea was simple, really. Illegal cartels, gangs, and networks needed a way of turning their billions of profits into legitimate investments. Planc's institution, for a hefty fee, would wash their dirty money for others and release the capital out into clean investments around the world.

In the beginning, Planc used the proceeds from his own businesses to prime the pump. Then he attracted two other crime heads, people with whom he had treaties or mutual-protection agreements. LM Global came on the scene just as international financial controls were being strengthened by the IMF, the World Bank, and Interpol.

As a result, money laundering had rapidly become more complicated, fast-moving, and potentially dangerous than ever. A service that could provide cover by associating with legitimate institutions was an attractive alternative to going it alone against the regulators and international police.

Currently, three banks, legitimate banks, accepted LM Global investments, one in France, one in Germany, and one in Estonia. Once the money was inside a legitimate bank, and that bank made its investments, the money would, in time, return to LM Global clean. Ironically, the heightened regulatory practices of these banks provided cover for the LM Global investments.

Planc had been working on the Banc Schaffhausen deal for more than a year, to open up a fourth bank. If the deal had worked, it would have significantly increased their capacity for moving money—in this case, five-hundred-million dollars.

The deal would have some regulatory gray areas, yes, but Banc Schaffhausen was above reproach in the banking world. And since LM Global had a clean track record with three other legitimate banks, this relationship would likely be blessed, exempting it from intense scrutiny. Besides, the world didn't have enough regulators to keep up with exposés like the Panama Papers, the HSBC Files, the Paradise Papers, and other less publicized leaks about illegal capital movements around the planet.

Planc shook his head in frustration. The old crook's large leather chair swiveled back and forth as he moved his legs, trying to burn off the tension. Dietrich knew too much, and now the silly jackass was threatening to blackmail him. He felt fortunate that he hadn't told Dietrich where the ten million was going, or its purpose.

Dietrich had just been guessing when he suggested the money was a bribe. A good guess, though. Indeed, Planc was bribing the head of port security in La Havre in exchange for free passage of special cargo through the port. Free passage meaning an exemption from customs inspections. When the money had disappeared, and the promised bribe never materialized, Planc announced to his partners that careful, last-minute vetting had shown Heinrich Dietrich to be untrustworthy—a mortal sin in the violent world of an illegal enterprise. Trust was either absolute or absent, on or off. So the fourth bank option was dead on arrival.

Planc shook his head again. First, what to do about Dietrich —well, he knew the answer to that. The more challenging issue, the five-hundred-million, which still needed to move, only now without Dietrich.

He picked up the office phone. "Has Dietrich left?" he asked.

"Yes, Herr Planc, he's gone," said the receptionist.

"Good. Tell Haysmith to get his ass up here. I need to talk to him. Also, find out who that Hawaiian developer fellow is, the Village in the Sky person. Get his details." Even if his assistant didn't know what Planc was talking about, he'd come back with the goods.

"Yes, Herr Planc, right away, sir. Would you be able to meet with Mr. Haysmith this afternoon, or tomorrow?"

"As soon as he can get here, this afternoon if he can. No later than tomorrow morning. We pay that creep through the nose to be available. Remind him of it, will you?"

"Right away, Herr Planc."

CHAPTER 17

Malcolm Haysmith sat at his desk, post-its and colored pens spread in front of him. The sun was low over Lake Zurich, casting orange-yellow light throughout the whole room. Last night's meeting with Planc had been exhausting, and afterward he'd slept fitfully. That man made Haysmith nervous. He was visited by a reoccurring regret about putting all of his eggs in one basket—Planc's basket.

Deliver or be punished. Actually, deliver or die was more like it. Planc was not a person who believed in half-measures. Planc was a nuclear-force type of person. Haysmith had told Planc he could do it, but he wasn't sure at all. And fretting wasn't going to make the work any easier—time to get a grip.

Looking at his desktop, the post-its, colored pens, and the possibilities waiting to be brought to life, to be made real, calmed Haysmith some. Yes, he had a lot to do. Yes, the details would be complicated. But this assignment from Planc presaged the big opportunity he'd been preparing for throughout his whole adult life.

Haysmith had studied history at Oxford, then accounting and finance at the London Business School. These subjects had given him a strong foundation in human nature and money and how to manipulate both. His first job had been as a junior bond trader in London for Barclays Bank. That gig had lasted two years. But high-pressure selling and crazy markets caused him fits of anxiety, which were only somewhat mediated by the occasional big commission and the rock-and-roll lifestyle of a trader. After two years of it, he'd been enervated.

His next gig was at Lloyds of London, working with a small group of executives who managed and settled insurance claims. Haysmith's group—there were three of them—were claims adjusters specializing in aircraft accidents. In simple terms, his group settled claims resulting from airplane crashes. Their mission was to do so on favorable terms, meaning by rejecting the claims outright, or at a minimum, settling them as cheaply as possible.

A little-known aspect of claims settlement involved the use of legal and semi-legal coercion. Malcolm Haysmith and his cohort would maliciously invade claimants' privacy, literally taking their lives apart to uncover something, anything, that could give the insurer bone-breaking leverage. In practice, this was quasi-legal blackmail.

For him, this "job training," had been a seminal life experience. He was earning a PhD in human frailty, psychology, and most of all, rule enforcement, where he set the rules, and he imposed them, mercilessly, often cruelly, on the greedy, money-grabbing thieves who were trying to take Lloyds to the cleaners.

Haysmith's last assignment at the firm involved the crash of a private jet and the death of four wealthy men. One of the victims was known to be a crime boss. The crime boss's wife, or rather, her attorney, decided to take a big swing at Lloyds, going after millions against a general liability policy Lloyds held insuring all manner of catastrophic outcomes, including, or so the attorney alleged, the death of the crime boss.

Haysmith went to work digging up dirt on the crime boss. He then started negotiations with the family by leaking some of the juicier bits, mostly true, to a national tabloid. The day after inflammatory allegations about the deceased crime boss were detailed in a four-page special spread—salacious pictures included—Haysmith sent a backchannel message to the attorney and the crime boss's wife that suggested he had plenty more where that came from—they needed to drop their claim, or else.

Two days later, Haysmith was abducted from his apartment in London. As he now recalled it, this experience was the real moment he converted to the one true faith. His captivity lasted three days, during which he was beaten by technicians who knew how to inflict pain without killing him. He was bound and gagged, kept in the dark, deprived of food and water, and repeatedly told how he had erred.

By the third day, Haysmith was a changed man. He understood the facts of life according to the criminal underworld, the real world, as his captors kept reminding him. Bruised and broken, he was returned to his apartment, thrown down on the living room carpet, given one last round of kicks, and left there to consider his options in life—life in the real world. He took a week's sick leave, then resumed his duties at Lloyds. A month later, he quietly settled the claim for the policy's full amount plus a penalty.

Haysmith, the reconstituted Haysmith, quit Lloyds and began a new career as a special projects consultant, a fixer, an information gatherer, a dirty-tricks administrator for the criminal underworld. He realized he had been working for the wrong people all along. The underworld needed people like him, respectable people, who could accomplish tasks on both sides of the law.

His first client was the successor to the deceased crime boss. As it turned out, a lot of dirty work was to be done, with plenty of money in it for him. Malcolm Haysmith was well on his way to wealth, with an expanding client list.

After several years of special projects, building a robust practice, Haysmith was introduced to Michel Planc. He knew this was the opportunity of a lifetime. The price for working with

Planc, however, was exclusivity, a hard pill to swallow. But the payoff potential was enormous.

Haysmith dropped his other clients, accepted a seven-figure signing bonus, a retainer agreement, a fee and bonus schedule, and a salary with perks galore.

Yet when Haysmith met with Planc the previous night, he wasn't prepared for the force of the old man's fury.

"Do you understand?" Planc shouted at him.

"Some of it," agreed Haysmith. "But where am I going to find the ten-million dollars?"

Planc shook his head. "Oh, goddamnit, that's no problem. I'll have it queued up for you in the morning. But be very careful. You need to move it so no one can ever trace it back to us—to me. Understand? And you need to hand the money to him by day after tomorrow, no later than that."

Haysmith said, "Okay, tell me when the money is ready, and I'll send it on its way. What else?"

"Dietrich. He knows too much. I don't want him to be spilling his guts to anyone. Ever."

Haysmith waited, expecting something specific. When nothing came, he asked, "Are we talking about a permanent solution—or what?"

Planc said, "Yes, permanent, and soon."

"How soon?" Haysmith probed.

"Forty-eight hours or less." The old man seemed to settle down.

"Sounds like a job for someone like Erebus," Haysmith observed.

Planc grunted. "*Like* Erebus, maybe, but not Erebus. He's joined at the hip with Dietrich. Oh, and be careful around Erebus, Haysmith, he'd shoot your balls off for fun."

Planc laughed, a rasping laugh that ended in a bout of coughing. He produced a gold cigarette case, extracted an English Oval, and lit it with the lighter from the coffee table between the two men. He inhaled deeply and blew out smoke, then started coughing again.

When the coughing stopped, Planc said, "So not Erebus, but someone reliable. Also, I need to know as soon as it's done. A lot is riding on this. I don't want to hear any details, just that it's done. Oh, and tomorrow, get in touch with that Touma Allen character and tell him you're offering a chance his deal can be resurrected, but he's not to tell anybody until we can draw up a revised partnership plan. Above all, he's not to talk to Dietrich. Tell him that. And tell him that if he doesn't follow our instructions to the letter, the deal will die."

Haysmith was making notes on the back of a utility bill he happened to have in his pocket. He said, "Okay, I need to return to my apartment and go to work. So, let's see, the money transfer, Dietrich, and call Allen. Anything else?"

"Nothing that can't wait. Haysmith …"

"Yes, Herr Planc?"

"Note carefully. You have two days, and the sequence of events is critical. This all needs to happen without a hitch!"

That was how the meeting had gone the night before. In the morning, Haysmith had boiled his instructions down to six bright-yellow post-its. He liked post-its; he could move them around, change the order, make patterns, move the pieces—and a lot of moving pieces were needed to execute Planc's instructions.

He arrayed the six papers on his desktop, creating a kind of post-it outline.

1. Heinrich Dietrich

(48 hour window with 40 hours left.)

2. Le Havre

(Pay in two days max. Shipment due one week.)

3. Touma Allen

(Get LM money in play, with handcuffs.)

4. Erebus

(What to do about him?)

5. John Horan

(The Seattle cop. Anything on him?)

6. Finnegan Michael

(Ex-cop. Missing. Anything on him?)

Haysmith picked up the phone and called Touma Allen's cellphone. The time was 8 p.m. in Honolulu.

"Touma here." The voice was gruff, and Haysmith pegged him as either a former dock worker or a man with a large gut who drank and maybe smoked.

"Mr. Allen, you haven't met me, but I represent the group originally financing your Honolulu project. My name is Haysmith."

"Yes, hold for a moment. I'm with someone," said Touma.

"Actually, I'm going to text you an access code for my encrypted office line. When you're alone and can talk, just hit the link, and we'll be connected."

"I said I'm with someone. I can't talk now." The fat former dockworker, or whatever, was annoyingly grumpy.

"Fine, Mr. Allen. Only you might want to talk to me within the next few minutes because I may be able to help you resurrect your project. You know the one I mean. The one that just died."

"Sorry? Who are you again?"

"My name is Haysmith. I represent some gentlemen who might be willing to fully finance your project, the one you had going with Banc Schaffhausen. You know what I am talking about?"

"Yes—yes."

"I'll send you the link. Call in ten minutes. You need to be alone. This is very important, Mr. Allen. Important for you, I mean." Manipulating people was fun for Haysmith. He felt as if he himself had the five-hundred million to offer or withhold.

"Yes, of course, ten minutes,"

The call came through, and five minutes after that, post-it number three was in play. Allen responded to the news like a drowning man reaching for a life preserver, gasping audibly when he heard that the project could actually be funded within a week. When Haysmith told him not to talk to Dietrich about this deal, the banker's name elicited a string of obscenities. Touma was definitely on Haysmith's side, for now. They would meet by video and begin hammering out the details the day after next.

Allen ended the call with, "Thank you, thank you, thank you!"

Haysmith smiled to himself. *That was easy*. He took a deep breath, then put a finger on post-it number one, the uppermost post on his desktop.

1. Heinrich Dietrich

(48 hour window with 40 hours left.)

CHAPTER 18

Flash saw three parked police cruisers, lights flashing, just off Poipu road in front of an old, white clapboard house tucked in behind the mortuary. Crime-scene tape was strung post-to-post around the screened-in porch. The cruisers were parked on the lawn, one blocking the path leading to the front door.

The cops hadn't been there when Flash had run past just an hour earlier. Curious, he stopped and mopped the sweat from around his eyes.

Kellie and an older guy, both in uniform, were walking down the front steps from the porch toward the cop car.

"Good morning, officers."

Kellie looked up and waved. "Hey, Flash. Flash, come here for a sec."

Flash walked toward them across the lawn.

"Flash, I'd like you to meet Bob Murphy. Bob, this is Flash Thorsten Tucker, Mia Mahoe's renter in Koloa Town, above the surf shop."

Flash nodded his head in a mini bow. "Officer Murphy, nice to meet you."

Murphy smiled.

"Flash is here on a midlife crisis crusade, Bob. You know the drill: Haole escapes the mainland to live the island life."

Bob Murphy was a couple of inches shorter than Kellie and quite a bit older. He was overweight, with weathered skin; wrinkles well-established on his face; a fleshy nose; and bushy black eyebrows. Like so many other cops Flash knew, Murphy had heavily starched his shirt in an attempt to avoid it bunching up over his ever-developing paunch. Murphy smiled and extended a big, suntanned hand in greeting. He had a solid, warm grip. Flash liked him immediately.

"Why do they call you Flash?" asked Murphy.

"Because I am a blazingly fast runner. Didn't you notice?"

"Well, no, that wasn't my first impression."

They laughed. Guessing that he wouldn't get an answer, Flash asked the question anyway. "How's the investigation going?"

Murphy's smile turned to a grimace. He looked down at the ground, as if searching for the right words. "Well, we've done the house. Found some pretty interesting stuff," he said. He looked up at Flash and said, "We have to look at the forensics back at the shop and see what story that tells us. It's a hell of a mess in there. Someone was searching for something."

Kellie grinned and said, "So, Bob, does he look like a cop to you?"

"Jesus, Kellie!" Flash glared at her.

"See, Bob," Kellie continued, hands on her hips, "we think Flash here is or was a cop before undertaking his midlife crisis, just so you know."

Flash shook his head.

Murphy grinned. "How the hell can you have a midlife crisis in Hawaii on a cop's salary? Sounds fishy to me."

"You know, Bob, I couldn't agree with you more. Kellie here has a super-active imagination, that's all."

Murphy rocked back on his heels slightly, still smiling, and said, "Oh, I'd be careful with that one, young fella. Kellie and me, we've been partners for, well, five years?" He paused as if summing up the passage of time. "This old Kellie girl, she's got a good head on her shoulders. I'd be inclined to go with her instincts over anything you might want to push my way—just to say it. But hey—either way, Kellie, we need to get going."

Flash said quickly, in a quieter voice, "Any surprises in the house? Just curious."

"Well you'll be reading about it soon enough, so I guess I can tell you, and besides, if you were a cop and all—"

"Bob, please don't encourage her!"

"Anyway, whoever trashed this place missed finding a shit-load of cash, like forty-thousand or so, and also missed a pretty good drug stash too," Bob continued, taking off his hat and running his hand through his thinning black hair. "Not a professional thief, that's for darn sure. In fact, probably just a dope-head or a drunk. Although we don't see this type of crime around here very often. The real news, anyway, is our Mr. P. is looking a lot like a serious dealer. Don't know how the perp missed the treasure, but there you go—perps, not the best and brightest."

Flash grunted, then asked, "Any news about the boys?"

Kellie said, "The boys. Yeah, well, Paul's out on bail as of this morning. Keanu is still in the lockup, though, for the time being. On the face of it, he looks a lot like a dealer, too, or maybe Mr. P.'s runner. Anyway, he's got priors for possession, two actually, and an assault charge. Even though they both have alibis for the night of the murder. So we're charging Keanu with trafficking. Gotta go, Flash."

Flash thanked them, turned, and began jogging, loping really, back to Poipu Road and up toward Old Koloa Town.

By the time he reached Koloa Roasters, he was walking, cooling down. He spotted Mia, Emma, and Janet Nakamura at Mia's regular table, heads close together, bobbing and animated. Mia looked over at Flash, raised her arm, and made a hand gesture that Flash interpreted as an invitation to join them.

Good, he thought. A lot was going on in his developing social circle, and he wanted to hear the news.

Flash collected his order, a mango scone and large cappuccino, then walked toward the group. As always, Mia stood out, wearing a pink muumuu arrayed with giant, red bird-of-paradise block prints—very Hawaiian and very Japanese. Emma was dressed for work in a blue pants suit, and Janet was looking lawyerly as usual, in a gray skirt with a long-sleeve white dress shirt, her blue blazer hung over the back of her chair. All the chatter stopped as the ladies watched Flash sit down.

Janet broke the silence. "Flash! Hi. We were just talking about you."

Mia shook her finger at Janet. "Don't tell him that. He's very thin-skinned about his reputation, in case you didn't know it. Very sensitive. We all agreed to handle him with kid gloves, him being in a midlife whatever-you-call-it."

"Crisis," prompted Emma and giggled.

Flash looked over at Emma, who was radiant in the early morning sun. He realized that he had come to like all three of these women, even Mia, for God's sake.

"Any news? As if I have to ask," he said.

Mia's hoop earrings swung as she answered with enthusiasm. "Paul is out on bail, thanks to Janet here. That's the big news. Oh wait, and that Mr. P. guy, he's some sort of drug kingpin, something like that. They found lots of money and drugs in his house, that's news too."

Flash smiled and shook his head. "Mia, how do you know? I was just down at Peterson's house where Kellie and what's-his-name—"

"Bob, it's Bob Murphy, Kellie's partner," said Mia.

"Yeah, Bob. Anyway, how do you know about the money and stash? They just found the stuff."

Mia simply smiled at him and continued. "Keanu is not a good boy. We think he's trouble. We agreed that Paul should be made to move back home as a condition for bail. Of course the judge, a friend of Emma's father, agreed. So Paul has moved back into his old room. You know, he is really a sensitive boy, an artist."

Emma added, "Well, he should be home. He's in a lot of trouble. We'll have to wait and see if this whole situation really changes him, though. One thing I've got to say is that he's been a lot more pleasant to me lately."

"Of course he has been. You're a wonderful mother," said Mia.

Janet said, "I think we might be able to get through this without him having a record—I do. He's a good kid, no priors. They found some drugs in Keanu's place, and it was Keanu's pack, not Paul's. I'm guessing." She took a sip of her coffee. "We can have Paul out from under the shadow of the law if he cooperates. If he cooperates and behaves himself."

Mia sat up straight, looking around the table. "I mostly wonder where these darn drugs come from in the first place. How do they wind up in Kauai? Who's poisoning our island?"

"Good question," said Flash.

Janet nodded. "I don't know where they come from—well, I mean, of course most of them come from one of the other islands, probably Oahu—but they're plentiful. I see a lot of telltale signs. Kids strung out. I wonder if someone at the hospital or in the medical community could be a source."

"Is it the tourists," asked Flash.

Janet shook her head. "No, tourists buy drugs, certainly, and an available supply is always around for that group—but the real trouble on this island is among the residents. We have what seems to be a growing drug culture. People who live here are increasingly using meth and crack, and now a growing presence of heroin too. Bad news for all of us. We should ask Kellie. She'd know."

Mia said, "Well, Flash, you'd know all about this, wouldn't you? Yeah, you would. I can tell."

Mia was looking hard at Flash, and Flash, not to be outstared by anyone, accepted the challenge and locked his eyes with hers. "Jesus, Mia."

"Oh, stop with your whining. We're just talking. But this is our problem, and we should talk about it, and do what we can to help the people we can help." She paused, then said, "It's our island, after all."

She continued to look at Flash. "And since you have nothing better to do but be self-absorbed, what with your midlife crisis and all, well, you should think of others, and help us out here. Helping others is good for the soul."

Now that he was bailed out of jail, Paul was back in his room in his mother's house—his old house, his old life. A condition of bail was that he move back home until his case was adjudicated, settled, or whatever. He was relieved to be out of jail, for sure, the place was creepy, really creepy, and smelled funny, with really bad dudes hanging around. The food sucked, too. What a horrible spot.

Paul felt as if he had taken five steps back in life. Just like when he was a kid, he was being told what to do, when to do it, and how to do it. His mom was hovering and worrying. In a way, he was sad about her. This was a mess, and it was his doing, but she was taking it personally, as though he had done terrible things to her. That made his stomach ache.

She'd made him promise to talk to this old geezer, Flash something or other. He couldn't remember the last name. *Flash, Jesus, what a stupid-sounding name for an old guy.* His mom said she and Auntie Mia thought he'd been a cop in another life and could help Paul, talk to him. What could some old haole possibly know about his life? And why exactly would he want to speak to an ex-cop anyway?

He heard a knock at his door. "Paul, can I come in?"

"Yeah."

The door opened, and his mom was standing there as if she

were waiting for permission to enter. Behind her, a head taller than her, stood the old geezer himself.

"Paul?"

"Yeah, yeah. What, Mom?"

"Paul, Auntie Mia's friend Flash has come by to talk to you. Can we come in?"

"Yeah, might as well."

The old guy came out from behind his mom and walked into the room. An old beach bum. Sort of tall, with long, black hair, his nose a little crooked, he was smiling an old-geezer smile. He wore a t-shirt that said, "Hug Me I'm Hawaiian," for God's sake, and hiking shorts. And the icing on the beachcomber cake—he had on Birkenstocks, bent back, broken down by saltwater. The geezer extended his hand, so Paul stood up from the bed and shook.

"Hi," said Paul.

"Hi. I'm Flash, a friend of Mia's and your mom's."

"Yeah."

Flash didn't say anything, just kept on with the old geezer smile, like he was all-knowing or something. It was unnerving.

Finally, Paul couldn't stand the silence and said, "Auntie Mia said we should talk, so…"

"Yeah," said Flash. "Why don't we go someplace? We can take a walk, and we can talk."

Paul's mom drove them down to Salt Pond Beach and told them she would be back to pick them up in an hour. She was going to the grocery store in Port Allen and would come to fetch them afterward.

"How are you holding up?" asked Flash.

"Yeah, fine, I guess."

"I know this is a little awkward, but I might be able to help you some while you work your way through this. The legal thing, I mean. I know something about what's going on."

"How do you know that?" Paul asked, a little resentfully. He was uncomfortable and pissed that he had to put up with this.

They were walking across the grass at the state park. Coconuts were scattered around on the ground. You could pick them up, husk them, crack them with something, and have a free drink and a meal. Paul had done that many times with friends.

They chose a picnic table, where they sat facing each other.

"Let's just say I know things," Flash began. "I'm a pretty private guy, but I might be able to help, really. And if not, I'll leave you alone, I promise. For one, I was busted once—a minor thing when I was seventeen. You're eighteen?"

Paul grimaced. "Yeah, what a way to start life at eighteen. Yeah. That's me now." He could feel the intensity of Flash's gaze.

"So what are they banging you up for?"

"Drugs. Umm, and something to do with that guy's death, Mr. P., but now just drugs."

"Drugs, meaning what?"

Paul squirmed on the bench, then looked away from Flash. Speaking out toward the Pacific Ocean, he said, "Umm, my lawyer says the cops will go for possession, for sure, and maybe selling." He stopped there, alarmed, thinking that Flash would ask him the question he didn't want to be asked.

Flash surprised him. "Yeah, that's what she told me too. So what do you think about all this?"

"I think—I think I fucked up. I think I hate being caught, and I hate hurting my mom." He was still talking out toward the Pacific Ocean, willing himself anywhere but here.

"Yeah, well, for what it's worth, you have a good lawyer and a good mom. And, come to think of it, lots of people who care about you."

Paul looked over at the geezer, who hadn't moved. He was still there, light-blue eyes pinning Paul to the bench.

Paul shook his head and said, "Yeah, I know, but where do you fit in here?"

"I was just passing by and was captured by Auntie Mia. I'm renting a place in Koloa Town from her. Seems that qualified me to become her project while I'm in Koloa. I'm from Seattle. Rains a lot in Seattle."

"Seattle. I know about Seattle. Tech stuff, Amazon. But I've never been there. What do you do for a living there?" Maybe the geezer would say whether he'd been a cop.

"Let's just say I'm retired. For now. This island is a great place. Growing up here must have been fun."

Paul reluctantly broke into a smile. "For sure. Love the water, the waves, the sand, the weather most of the time, my art, everything except what's happening to me right now." The smile turned into a frown.

"Yeah, well, you only have to talk to me for a few more minutes, then your mom will be back."

Paul felt a jolt of embarrassment. The guy wasn't so bad, after all. Paul hadn't meant to hurt his feelings. "Naw, I didn't mean that. I meant going to jail and being bailed out, and maybe having to go on trial. It sucks."

Each time Paul brought his gaze back from the Pacific, this guy was looking at him, quiet-like. A pretty chill guy. His mom seemed to like him too. And then he thought of Auntie Mia. She was a piece of work, but she was really, really protective. If she trusted this guy, well, he must have jumped through a bunch of hoops to get in her good graces.

"Okay, what do you think I should do here? Kellie is pounding on me to give up Keanu, that he's a pusher, not just a user. I don't want to do that. But at the same time, I'm afraid they won't cut a deal for me if I don't." Paul looked over at Flash, who seemed to be thinking.

"Don't know," Flash said at last.

Paul waited for more.

"If you don't want to give him up, that's understandable, I guess. But you know, Keanu has put you in the shit here." Flash nodded.

"Here's a thought. Suppose you don't want to give him up, you might give them something a little less, and see what happens. Like maybe not that he is a real drug pusher, just maybe he sold some E to you or to someone else, but not a pusher, not a runner, like that."

Paul thought that was a good answer, especially the part about Keanu getting him into the shit. But he hated to give up his friend, his friend who gave him a place to live. He said, "And yeah, Keanu gave me a place to live, so I owe him."

Flash smiled and said, "Yes, he did give you a place to live, that's true. But—"

"But what?"

"But you've paid a pretty steep price, and besides, letting you stay didn't cost Keanu anything. As I understand it, he got this house from his grandmother."

"Yeah."

"So how much did it cost him, and how much did it cost you?"

Paul was beginning to see something. Keanu had been a friend in school, sure. But what was the deal about living with him in the house anyway?

"And although I don't know whether it's true that Keanu was a pusher or a runner or what, but if he was one of those things and if he maybe wanted you to help him, well—what was he getting out of the deal besides a roommate?"

"Yeah. I need to think about this. Here's Mom."

Paul and Flash got up from the bench and walked side by side across the grass toward the parking lot. Just two steps before reaching the car, Paul made up his mind.

"So maybe we can talk again about this, before I have to decide?"

"You got it. Give me your cell number. I'll give you mine. How about tomorrow?"

"Good, yeah, tomorrow."

While his mom drove Flash back to Koloa, Paul sat out on the back deck, flipping through *Surfer* magazine. He was surprised that he felt better, somehow relieved. That Flash guy was sort of okay, even if he was an old geezer. He'd given Paul something to think about regarding the Keanu problem.

Until now, Paul hadn't realized that Keanu *was* a problem, but he definitely was. The thing was, Keanu could mess Paul up good if he thought Paul had betrayed him. But—and a *but* always came up. His cell buzzed. The call was from a blocked number.

"Hello?"

"Hey, drug man, how ya doin?"

Paul's heart started to thump hard. Jesus Christ, what was going on? "Huh, who is this, please?"

"Sachiko, drug man, remember? The sexy girl in white at the rave the other night. I need to see you, drug man."

"I'm not drug man, and I can't. I, I don't even have a car." But he did remember. He definitely did remember her.

"Don't be a wuss, drug man. Tell me where we can meet, and I'll pick you up in my new Land Rover. You'll like riding in my new Land Rover, drug man, I promise."

CHAPTER 19

"**N**o, go ahead. Sell the jet."

Minette and Benjamin, sitting across from Touma at his document-strewn desk, nodded in unison.

Touma was on a roll. He felt as though he had been released from death row. The most amazing fortune he could ever have wished for had fallen from the skies. The relief was intoxicating. He was free to fly—that was how he felt, free to fly—and he didn't need a fucking jet.

He was turning over a new leaf here, and the jet sent the wrong message. He was going for a lower profile, everything lower profile. That was how the big guys did it, he'd decided. The really rich ones were like that, staying below the radar. No one actually knew them or knew much about them. Keep a low profile if you have real power and wealth. Sell the jet.

Minette pulled a pencil from behind her ear and made a checkmark on the page she'd opened in her daily diary. She looked up at Touma, pencil poised. "So we'll lose a bundle on this, but I take it you'd rather that than keeping the jet?"

"Yes, yes, yes, sell the jet. We'll take the one-time hit. Cash flow will improve eventually. No jet, no hanger, no maintenance. And a lower profile. Above all, a low profile."

Minette was almost a head taller than Touma, so even sitting, he had to look up at her. She had on jeans, a green-and-brown Hawaiian shirt, several plain gold bracelets, and a red Apple Watch. Her blonde hair was pulled into a bun. She always wore makeup, though on casual days, like this one, the makeup was subtle—a little lipstick and blush-brushed cheeks.

If Touma was asked to describe her, *diligent, perfection,* and *quietly assertive* would be on his list. *Practical, precise,* and *efficient* would be on the list too. She had an MBA from UCLA, was a licensed CPA, and was as dependable, secretive, and discreet as a person could be.

She was also loyal. She had been Touma's finance maven for twelve years. She was a star, and he paid her like one.

Benjamin, on the other hand, was not a note taker. He was action oriented and had a good memory. Benjamin got things done. At forty-nine, he was the chief operating officer, the one who saw that the needful things were accomplished, for the Allen Group generally, and for Touma specifically. He, too, was wearing a Hawaiian shirt with black warm-up pants, and extra-extra-wide size-eight black sneakers.

Benjamin and Touma had met when they were boys—eighteen years old, strong young men employed as stevedores on the docks in Honolulu's busy harbor. Benjamin was a crazy hard worker, and soon he was made a team leader, then a crew leader, then at age twenty-five he was promoted to section captain, overseeing operations of a hundred or so men for a large division of the shipping facility.

As Benjamin was climbing the ladder of success, Touma wasn't climbing any ladder. He was a hard worker, but seriously impatient, a bit of a hothead, and he really didn't like taking orders. Soon, he walked away from dock work to become a carpenter and eventually built houses.

For the next eight years, Touma made his own way as a carpenter, then as a contractor working on one house at a time, and later as a general contractor dealing with multiple projects simultaneously. Eventually he became a developer—Oahu was booming, and he was winning larger and larger projects. Touma's character was suited to boom times. His motto was "all in, all the time."

Such success meant rapidly increasing complexity, more people, more risk, and more chances to fail, which was what brought the two men back together. Who better to handle complexity than Benjamin, who was already managing a hundred and fifty dockworkers? Benjamin became Touma's number two, and Minette had been Benjamin's first hire, as neither Touma nor Benjamin had had any experience with accounting or finance. That had been the genesis of the Allen Group. Benjamin and Minette had been with him ever since.

Benjamin said, "So, T, I don't understand the low-profile thing. What are you talking about?"

Minette sat up straighter and said, "I like it. Being ostentatious and seeking public attention makes you a target. Besides, why waste money on bling?"

Touma smiled. He didn't need to be reminded how cheap Minette could be when it came to spending for stuff she thought was superfluous; anything that didn't have an immediate return, in her mind, fell into that category. On the other hand, she kept Touma and Benjamin on track financially, so they tolerated her unceasing resistance to spending money.

Touma said, "I had a kind of epiphany in Switzerland. First, with Heinrich Dietrich and later with a fellow named Michel Planc, the managing partner of LM Global. Dietrich is a pretty successful guy, buys a new Mercedes every year, has a big house in Zurich, belongs to all the right clubs, makes the social pages in the local papers. But Dietrich couldn't deliver the goods, mainly because this Michel Planc killed it for some reason." Why *had* Planc called the whole thing off? Maybe Planc wanted to do the deal himself.

Touma returned to his point. "Planc is richer than God. He could write a personal check for the whole Village in the Sky project, and it would clear the bank on the same day. Yet as wealthy as he is, he might as well be invisible. Planc is never in the newspapers, or the financial press. He might as well be a ghost for all that anyone has ever heard of him.

"I can't even find out where or how he lives," Touma said. "But he's the person who's going to make our project happen, not the flashy banker. *Below the radar*. The really rich people in the world fly below the radar. We need to be like that. Get me?"

"Yeah, T," said Benjamin.

"I like it," agreed Minette, pushing the pencil back behind her ear. "So, LM will finance it directly?"

Touma's eyes glistened at the thought. "Yup, you'll be getting a draft of the loan agreements tomorrow. I need to sign them and return them to LM by close of business, which is the day after tomorrow in Zurich."

Minette frowned. "That's pretty fast turnaround. You know we need to run it by legal, though, right?"

"No—well, yes. But just a quick look-see. I don't want the attorneys screwing up this thing. Call them, tell them to meet here first thing, two hours max."

"Okay. Not a lot of time, though, for a loan agreement."

"All the time I'm willing to pay for." Touma frowned. "They need to be quick."

"Got it. Have you yourself seen the draft agreement?"

Touma nodded. "Yeah, it's pretty standard. Now, like I was saying, sell the jet, also put the Princeville houses on the market, all except Sachiko's, of course. Also, I want to sell off our four main Oahu properties. We need to build our reserves, harvest the profits. We need to start flying under the radar—with a lot of money in the bank. Get me?"

"Got it," Minette said.

"Good. Go to work."

Touma was almost too excited to go to work himself. He looked at his watch. Time for lunch, but where could he go where he wouldn't be noticed and yet get a Class A meal? The

12th Avenue Grill? His mouth watered at the thought. But he'd know people there. Oh, just this once. A kind of celebration. He'd start flying under the radar tomorrow.

"Now do you remember me?"

"Yes, of course I remember you. Only I didn't recognize you in all black." Standing in the driveway and talking through the open passenger door of Sachiko's SUV, Paul felt uneasy. Good thing his mom was at work, so she wouldn't see him driving off with this woman. He really liked the car though—really liked it.

"Nice car," said Paul,

"Isn't it, though?" said Sachiko.

Just like she'd said, a spanking new, top-of-the-line black Range Rover, a Land Rover on steroids. It smelled new too. She must be loaded.

"Get in. I don't have all day." She smiled at him.

Paul slid onto the front seat and put on the seat belt. Sachiko sped away down the hill, toward the highway. She was beautiful in daylight too. Shining black hair, down to her shoulders. Black silk shirt with no bra, black linen pants, black Keds with no socks, little black plastic monkey earrings. He breathed in a scent, her scent, a hint of tropical flowers, surprisingly subtle.

"So, drug man, what's your real name?"

"I told you before. Paul, Paul Pookalani." He quickly realized she was the type of person who only thought of themselves, not other people—especially him, a kid. So what was she doing here, anyhow? She wanted more E.

"Yeah, I guess you did. I forgot."

Paul nodded. She *would* forget, wouldn't she? "And don't call me *drug man*. I'm not a drug man. At least not—" Suddenly he was tongue-tied. Why had he agreed to her request to pick him up? He couldn't come up with the drugs she wanted. *What an idiot I am!*

She took her eyes off the road and glanced at him, arching

her eyebrows. "Excuse me? There must be some mistake, because I was given this phone number by a drug man, and you look just like him." She returned her focus to the road. Man, she sure was driving fast.

"Yeah, well."

"Well, I want more E."

"I don't have any more E," he admitted.

She gave him an unfriendly look. "So, why did you agree to meet me?"

He shrugged. "You said you wanted to meet me, go for a ride."

"Oh, God, you aren't expecting sex, are you, drug man? Paul —whatever?"

"Well, no, okay, no."

"Good. So, what happened to all your drugs? Tell me, and maybe something good could happen to you this afternoon back at my house, Paul." She released a sort of girlish giggle that ended in a snort.

"Look, that whole thing was a mistake. I'm not selling drugs. Well, I did, once, but not now." They were driving in a nice part of the island he didn't usually go, and despite whatever was happening between them, he really was enjoying the ride.

"Oh, shut up. We'll talk about it at my house. You'll like my house. We'll get a little buzzed, and you can tell me all about your drug thing."

At midnight, a white Toyota van, a Kauai taxi, pulled into the driveway of Sachiko's Princeville house and honked twice. Paul struggled to remember the evening. What had actually happened? He hoped he wasn't going to throw up.

Sachiko kissed him on the cheek. Her lips were warm.

"Thanks for the info, Paul baby. Nice to meet you. The cab's paid for. Go home. Don't call me. I'll call you."

She giggled and slammed the cab door. Paul was blitzed out

on wine. No, she'd called it "Champagne," and they'd had lots of it. They'd finished, God, three, maybe four bottles, and not had sex—that much he remembered, for sure. Oh, and they ate pupu, mahi-mahi, French fries with this amazing mayo, all served by a real maid, Mary Jo or something, dressed in a real maid's uniform.

Sachiko's living room was almost as big as Paul's mother's whole house. They'd gone swimming, drank more, and he thought he remembered telling her all about being a drug man, although in this state he couldn't be sure of anything.

The next thing he noticed was that the cab had stopped, and the driver said, "There you go, buddy." He was home, stumbling to his mother's front door. He wasn't sure of anything other than he needed to get to bed right away, not throw up, and not wake his mom.

Touma's cellphone vibrated on the kitchen table next to a bowl of corn flakes with fresh mango slices and a double espresso— what he called his breakfast of champions. It was Sachiko. He put down his spoon.

"Daddy!"

"Baby, you're up early!"

"Daddy, it's ten-thirty."

"Yeah, like I said, you're up early. What's up?" Sachiko never called unless she wanted something. *Daddy, I want this. Daddy, I want that.*

"Daddy, what's with the For Sale signs on our houses?"

"*My* houses, sugar. They're my houses, and they're for sale." He picked up his spoon and began to eat. This would take a while, and he was hungry, damn it.

"Your houses? They're our houses, Daddy. You said." This was going to be one of those conversations. She was speaking in her whiny voice, the one that always showed up when she felt like wrestling him to the ground over something.

He chewed and swallowed. "No, baby. I gave you one house. The rest are mine, and they're for sale." He felt a pain in his gut and put down his spoon.

"Why, why would you sell them, Daddy, what's wrong?" she whined.

Touma took a deep breath. "Nothing is wrong," he said. "In fact, everything's great. I'm harvesting profits. We're about to start the Village in the Sky, and we need to bank some cash. I'll do well on the houses. I bought them in a fire sale, so time to bring the money home."

"So, does that mean you're selling my house too, Daddy?"

"No, that house is yours, baby, in your name, free and clear."

"So if I wanted to borrow some money, I could do it against my house? I mean, if I wanted to, Daddy?"

What the hell is she thinking? He took a deep breath and said, "Yes, you could, but why would you want to do that?"

"Just kidding, Daddy. Talk soon. Hug hug."

Just kidding my ass, he thought. He put the phone down, finished his cereal, then carried his coffee and a copy of the draft loan agreement out to the pool deck and sat down. The draft was three-quarters of an inch thick. He'd read the first couple of pages. Lots of gobbledygook legal shit, but as far as he could tell, LM Global was agreeing to fund the deal, although they weren't using that name on the agreement, he'd noticed. But all he really cared about this morning was getting the money so he could get going.

His cellphone vibrated. He looked down, expecting to see Sachiko's name. Once she started on something, she never let it go. But the caller wasn't Sachiko, it was Bart. That lifted his spirits. He could tell Bart, who was in for five percent of the Village in the Sky profits, that the money was as good as on the way. He could even brag a little, which would feel great.

"Bart, how are you?"

"Touma. I've got some news. You better sit down."

"Okay, I'm sitting. What is it?"

"It's Dietrich. He's dead. The *International Harold Tribune* said he was killed in a fiery car crash, no other cars involved. Swiss police are investigating."

"What? When?" Touma felt as though a cold wind had invaded his chest.

"Late last night, Zurich time. I don't have any details. Did you hear anything about it?"

"No, not a thing." Touma was stunned. Dietrich, that fucking liar. Dead liar, at least according to Bart.

Bart said, "I'm wondering about our funding, any news on that front? Do you think there's any connection?"

Touma's head hurt. A fiery car crash? How could that have anything to do with him, with his Village in the Sky?

Touma tightened his grip on the draft agreement in his hand. "Nothing to worry about on my end, Bart. We're reviewing the loan agreement as we speak. I expect it will be signed and put to bed by close of business today. Too bad about Dietrich, though. Can't see how, well, that the project would have any connection to a car crash. Can you?"

"No, but the on-again off-again thing with Dietrich's bank was kinda curious. Planc steps in, brings in that Haysmith guy, and then Dietrich goes up in smoke. Just one of those things, I guess, no connection. You're right. Let me know when you have a signed deal, and we'll pop a cork, celebrate."

"Will do, Bart, will do." He put the phone on the tabletop. Then he looked out over the Pacific, his eyes drifting into a thousand-mile stare of peace and relaxation. The gods were in their heaven, and all was right in the world.

Under the radar but higher than a kite! *Serves you right, you liar, Dietrich! You bastard.*

CHAPTER 20

Keanu, yawning sleepily, was standing in the yard for the morning fresh air and smoking break in the correctional facility in Lihue. He knew the minute-by-minute daily routine, as he'd been here before. The schedule was regular, carefully programmed, and rarely if ever interrupted.

But unpredictably, at 10:15 a.m., Keanu and the other inmates watched a black stretch limo pull into the parking lot. The vehicle drove slowly right up to the front door and stopped, blocking the entrance. The driver, in a black chauffeur uniform, emerged and then opened the rear door for his passenger. A dark-suited young man stepped out into the hot morning sun, walked to the front door, and disappeared into the reception area.

Five minutes later, as Keanu was smoking with a group of other inmates, he was directed to the visitor's area by a voice booming over the public address system. He looked up, surprised.

Someone in the yard shouted out, "Hey, Akoni, your limo is ready," setting off a chorus of loud laughter, and a short-lived chant of "Akoni, Akoni, Akoni!"

Keanu made his way through a gauntlet of pokes, catcalls, and sarcastic laughter into the facility. He was accompanied by a guard to a meeting room at the front of the building. He entered hesitantly and casually glanced around.

Seated on the other side of a metal table was the fellow from the limousine, who looked up at Keanu, then stood and extended his hand. "Mr. Akoni, my name is Roger Phillips. I'm from the law firm of Hach, Mulbain, and Reilly, in Honolulu. I've been retained to defend you.

"What?"

"I've been retained to defend you," the stranger repeated.

Keanu was mystified and suddenly suspicious. The guy wore a fancy black suit and had a pricey-looking briefcase. No public defender dressed that nice, let alone drove up in a fucking limo.

Keanu said, "Is this a scam or something? I've got an attorney, a fucking public defender."

Phillips smiled and said, "Yes, that would be—let me see." He pulled a yellow legal pad from the leather briefcase, glanced at the top page, then said, "That would be Ms. Alanai Kahele. I'm taking over for her. I'll be defending you from here on."

"What happened to her? She get sick or what?"

"No, not at all," the man assured Keanu. "As I said, I'm a criminal defense lawyer for the firm of Hach, Mulbain, and Reilly in Honolulu, and I've been retained to be your lawyer. Ms. Alanai has withdrawn. Public defenders are only assigned in cases where private representation is not available."

Keanu was having none of this bullshit. "You're scamming me, man," he told the guy. "Get the fuck out of here. I can't pay no fucking private defense attorney. That's why they assigned what's-her-name, Alanai whatever. Because she's free."

Phillips nodded in agreement. "Yes, of course, I understand. You won't be paying yourself, because your attorney fees are being covered by a concerned friend, Ms. Sachiko Allen. Her father's company is one of our largest clients. She called and arranged to have me represent you, and so the public defender was released. I'm here to get down to work, to come up to speed on your case. Ms. Allen has given me this letter for you."

Keanu was bewildered. He ripped open the envelope and removed a sheet of personalized stationery. The handwritten note read, "Keanu, this guy is the best criminal attorney in the islands. He'll get you off, for sure. Do what he says. Call me at this number, and I'll explain."

"Does the note help make sense of this?" asked Phillips blandly.

Keanu shrugged and took a seat at the table. "Yeah, I guess. What do you want to know?"

"I need to know everything. Everything, starting with when you were arrested and what they've told you so far. Everything. We need to stop this prosecution in its tracks," Phillips said flatly.

Keanu was impressed. He had his own tough-guy lawyer—go figure! He'd call the woman later, whoever she was. He, too, wanted to stop this prosecution, pronto!

Malcolm Haysmith had a secret. He hated flying, and his phobia wasn't improving with age. Five years prior, he'd collapsed on a jet bridge while boarding a flight at the Frankfurt airport. Shot through with pain in the lower chest and gut, he had doubled over and collapsed, hyperventilating. The woman behind Haysmith screamed when he went down and passed out.

From then on, every time Haysmith had to fly, walking onto the boarding ramp felt as if he were entering a tunnel of impending doom. Unable to think his way out of the anxiety on his own, he decided to try a shrink.

His first therapist was a woman. She guided him, rather aggressively, session after session through the uncomfortable pathways of Cognitive Behavioral Therapy. She would command him to relive, analyze, and reimagine or reprogram his experience.

All this did was piss him off. He blamed her for making him uber-uncomfortable, which, predictably, in a relationship costing two-hundred Euros per hour, resulted in her applying the same cattle prod methods to his developing dislike for her.

Eventually, she mercifully ended their work by suggesting he try another approach or perhaps a prescription drug that she, unfortunately, wasn't authorized to prescribe.

He then tried psychoanalysis. Of course, psychoanalysis was an even more expensive undertaking because the course of treatment was a slower and longer process, one that lasted years, not months.

After eighteen months of weekly appointments, Malcolm Haysmith had clarified several issues about his life as a six-year-old but felt he was making little progress on his fear of flying.

His shrink, perhaps jokingly, said, "You know, Malcolm, this thing really has a hold on you. There's an age-old trick that might give you some momentary relief. Why not have a couple of stiff drinks? Choose your favorite libation—I mean, after you've gone through security—then hightail it to the gate."

Haysmith, in fact, was due to fly from Zurich to London that very afternoon. Several bars were located between security and the gate. He had a double scotch at the first, then, he was still feeling anxious as he walked toward the gate, so he stopped at a second bar and had another double. By the time he walked onto the jetway, he was still uneasy, but not panicking.

Haysmith reclassified his problem from critical to manageable, at least for as long as his liver held up. A dedicated cheapskate when it came to his own money, he could do the math: Airport scotch was twenty-five Euros per flight, while the talking cure was three hundred Euros per week and went on forever. He opted for managed anxiety and terminated his psychoanalysis the following day.

In a bad mood and awash in a boozy fog, Haysmith settled into seat 2A. He thought Planc was overdoing it. Why the hell did he have to go to Honolulu in person? He would be in transit for twenty-five hours. Touma Allen wasn't a problem. He'd signed the agreement, and the money was in place. Why go halfway around the world?

Planc had said he wanted to make sure Touma didn't become spooked by the fine print. Fine print indeed. The loan agreement stipulated that Malcolm Haysmith was managing director of the lending institution named Sixty-Four Capital of the Grand Caymans LTD, which owned 100 percent of the Village in the Sky project. The Allen Group was the managing company hired to build the project; it would answer to Haysmith.

In short, Haysmith was on his way to Honolulu to take charge, to have full control over Allen Group decisions, and to hold the purse strings tight. And when the project was done, Sixty-Four Capital would sell the project to the highest bidder, thus recapturing its investment at a significant gain and releasing all of that well-washed money out into the legitimate world.

The really fine print in the agreement stipulated that upon completion of the project, the Allen Group had a sixty-day window to purchase the Village in the Sky property at a price to be negotiated at the time. If the Allen Group was unable to exercise that option for any reason, Sixty-Four Capital was the owner and could exercise its ownership position in any way it chose.

"You really gonna eat all that?" asked Kellie.

Flash, Kellie, and Bob were sitting at a picnic table under a giant Budweiser beach umbrella at Roy's, an island-famous Hawaiian food joint.

"Yeah, sure, why do you ask?" She'd told Flash that locals loved the mixed plate, so he'd gone for it. He'd been rewarded with a large Styrofoam container loaded with chicken katsu, teriyaki beef, fried noodles with greens, potato and mac salad, white rice, and a separate cup of Roy's famous gravy. Why wouldn't he eat it all?

"No reason, just noticing," said Kellie. She had opted for a big bowl of broth, with noodles, greens, and a sliced fried-chicken cutlet with a fried egg and shaved radish.

Bob laughed. He had gone with Roy's cheeseburger topped with a fried egg and a side of French fries in gravy. "Kellie does that to everyone she introduces to Roy's. Only sumo wrestlers finish the mixed plate. You don't look the part. Where did you say you come from?"

Flash chewed, then swallowed. "I didn't," he answered tersely, scooping in the next bite.

"Oh, yeah, I forgot. Well, Hawaiian food is always served in giant portions. That's why so many of us are, you know, big. You might have noticed that, wherever you come from, ya know?" Bob bit into his burger, chewing and talking at the same time. "So Kellie here seems to think you can help us on the Peterson thing? I've been giving that some thought. Do you have any ideas, Flash? How you could help, I mean?"

"Well, for starters, I was curious about something I saw in the *Garden Island*. Your chief said, or at least the paper said he said, that Kauai has no drug problem, organized or otherwise. Does that sound right to you?"

Bob looked over at Kellie, then back at Flash. "How do we get from your helping somehow, to our chief of police? We playing dodge ball here, Flash?"

Ping pong, Flash thought, *ping pong.* Hit the little ball over the net, and he hits the little ball back.

After swallowing another bite, Flash answered. "No, not dodge ball, not at all. Look, obviously, I don't know squat about what goes on here, I'm just a tourist. But I did notice that this recent murder, the only murder for a long time on the island, seems to be somehow connected to drugs."

Flash watched Bob take another bite to see if he would elicit any reaction. Nothing. So he decided to prod a little. "I was wondering what you guys, ya know, think about the drug scene on Kauai, and not to jump ahead of myself, but how that fits with the party line, at police HQ, as they say on the cop shows?"

Bob grunted, cleaned both hands, and balled up the napkin. He cleared his throat. "Yeah, exactly like TV, Flash. Well..." He looked over at Kellie. "The chief is a good man, Flash. Doin' his job. Part of that job is not to scare the tourists away. Another part is to keep things in perspective. For the community, I mean."

Kellie added, "What Bob means is this is a big family here on Kauai. We take care of the family, and we don't air our dirty laundry for others to see, especially the tourists. We make sure the tourists aren't in any real danger from each other or our misbehaving family members, ya know? And the chief doesn't see any point in moaning and groaning about the not-so-good things that sometimes happen here. Simple as that."

Then as if she'd remembered something important, Kellie nodded at Flash and added, "You know the state of Hawaii is nearly the safest in the United States? Yeah, it is. It may not be a perfect paradise, but it's our paradise, and it is probably safer than wherever you came from, haole." She smiled.

Flash thought she sounded like the local chamber of commerce. And this little game of Bob's was silly, really silly. Flash wasn't about to roll over and tell them all about himself. Not their business.

On the other hand, he did want to help. He was walking a fine line.

"Okay, happy and safe island, big family. I've got no problem with that. But if you want my observations, seeing a little more of what you two see on the ground in the community would help me. And just to jump to the end for a moment, I'm not here to be a shit disturber. Mia asked me to help, and maybe I can. Right now, the helping is about Paul and Emma. My questions were more to ask what is it really like here on the island, drugs and all, for a kid like Paul."

Bob was looking away from Flash, as if distracted and only half-listening. But by now, Flash was pretty sure Bob was listening very carefully. So Flash decided to wait him out.

After a long pause Bob said, "Okay, Flash. Fair enough. Help Paul. Yeah, you could help Paul by somehow getting him to give us information about his dope-dealing buddy, Keanu. That would help him a lot, and come to think of it, would help the island family too. Know what I mean?" Then he looked directly at Flash, unwavering eye contact commencing his own waiting game.

"Yeah, I can see how you'd think it would be helpful if Paul rolled over with whatever he knows. Only I don't know if he's willing to do that, and you know, you can't make him. You have to work with whatever he gives you—plus the evidence. That's it. I'll give Paul that advice, to come clean, but I'll give him all the thinking around it, too, and I'm guessing—well, hell, I don't need to guess, we'll just have to see what Paul is willing to say, won't we?"

Bob shook his head. "That's not particularly helpful there, Flash. You need to push him a little, and he gives us Keanu. We nail Keanu for the drugs, find the murderer—whether it's Keanu or not—and presto, the island is a much safer place, and Paul becomes a sort of good guy. Know what I mean? What's not to like about that conclusion?"

Kellie stood up, gathered their napkins and empty containers, and walked to the bussing station.

Bob said, "If you really want to help anyone, make him talk, bottom line. If you really want to help, that is."

"Bob, you know that's bullshit," Flash whispered. "I'll tell Paul what he ought to do, fine, but then he does what he does. You will never convince me to strong-arm him or to somehow try to intimidate him into doing something he doesn't want to do. Got it?"

Kellie returned to the table and stood in the sun, her hands on her hips. "Okay, boys, butt-sniffing time is over. Let's get back in the wagon. First, we need to take Flash home, then we have a hell of a lot left to do today. Murder is murder, and we have a lot of ground to cover."

CHAPTER 21

Kellie pulled into a parking spot right across the street from Poipu State Park.

Flash opened his door and got out, then leaned back in and said, "I'll talk to Paul, but no promises." He smiled, closed the door, and walked over toward Brennecke Bar and Grill, a beer and burger joint across the street from the world-famous bodysurfing beach of the same name. Kellie, watching him go, was pretty sure he wasn't going there for the food.

Back at the police station, before the briefing on the Peterson murder, she went to the crime lab and asked a tech to dust the back seat of her squad car for fingerprints and run them. *Enough of this mystery-man bullshit*, she told herself.

The homicide briefing took place in the station's open-plan conference area.

During the last wave of increased tourism and investment on Kauai, voters had approved a new police building. The whole place still smelled new. The design was the product of a decade of innovation in crime science and technology. The offices and labs bristled with high-tech equipment, while the floor plan provided generous space for present-day work as well as for future growth.

Kellie had been assigned as lead investigator. While Bob Murphy was her senior by a decade and a half, Bob didn't want to be a leader of anything. He just wanted to be a cop. Kellie, on the other hand, was keenly interested in leading, helping cops be better cops. She jumped at any opportunity to have a voice in the department's development.

Chief Samson Aukai was in attendance at the briefing. Aukai was a popular chief. He had been hired away from the Maui Police Department four years earlier, where he had served as assistant chief. He was a vocal advocate for community policing, community integration, and community safety. He was also sensitive to the balance between life on the island for locals and life on the island for tourists. The local newspaper, the *Garden Island*, gave him high marks. Moreover, the city council trusted and seemed to appreciate him, and he and the mayor were good friends.

But murder was murder, and the chief was concerned about the case. He sat at the back of the room, observing from outside the circle. Kellie knew that the chief would watch, maybe ask a question or two, but he would never critique or second-guess her in front of her team. The chief was a big believer in feedback —private feedback.

An hour and a half later, in his office with the door closed, Kellie and the chief went over what they'd learned in the meeting and speculated—speculative collaborating, as the chief liked to call it.

The chief was a doodler. He opened a spiral-bound notebook, took out a pen and began to draw. "Okay, we have prints from the house, and what looks like the murder weapon, a golf club— a putter, with prints," he said. "We know Peterson was killed by a blow to the side of his head. The putter had sharp edges, crushed its way into his skull. The ME agrees it's a fit—blood, shape, everything. Good. That's a start."

"Front door was open," Kellie said, "and it looks like the killer might have tried to set a fire. He is either dumb as hell or was impaired, or both. Who can't start a fire with lighter fluid?" She shook her head. "That old house is a tinder box, too. The front door wasn't damaged or broken, so maybe Peterson knew his killer. The living room and his bedroom were trashed, drawers pulled out, cabinets opened, shelves cleared onto the floor. The whole place was tossed."

"But the perp didn't find Peterson's stash—the money or the drugs," the chief put in. His doodling slowed, then stopped as he looked up at Kellie. "So on the money, any prints other than Peterson's?"

"Tons, but we're still processing the bills, forty-four grand and change. Scanning them takes time. One thing though, Keanu's dabs were definitely on several of the bills. We didn't find the other kid's—Pookalani—at least not so far."

"Paul Pookalani, the old judge's grandson? "

"Yeah. Don't know how deep into this he might be, though. He's out on bail, moved back home with his mom, Emma. Have you met her?"

"No, but I knew the judge. Good man. He'd be distraught to see his grandson involved with something like this. "

"Yeah. Only so far, the evidence doesn't seem to put him in it like Keanu. According to Emma, Paul left home and ended up living with Keanu. They grew up together, went to the same school. Paul's a young eighteen, I think. Naive, maybe. Keanu, on the other hand, is anything but naive. But one thing the two share is a solid alibi for the night of the murder."

"The rave," the chief recalled.

"Yup, the rave, and we have sworn statements. Pretty reliable witnesses saw them out there at and around the estimated time of death."

"Keanu's still in custody?"

"Keanu is still in custody. Yes. We found commercial amounts of E, meth, and crack at his house under a floorboard, stupid shit. And Peterson's prints are on all of the packages, along with Keanu's."

"The judge's grandson's prints on the drugs?"

"No."

"So, Peterson's the drug dealer? "

"Peterson's the drug dealer, maybe a primary supplier. We need to do more digging though. "

"Could Keanu be the main supplier?" asked the chief, looking up from a doodle.

Kellie shook her head. "We don't think so. For one thing, he's not that smart. For another, the drugs at Peterson's place didn't have Keanu's prints on them, but the drugs at Keanu's home had Peterson's prints. Also, Peterson's drug stash was a lot bigger than Keanu's, and he had the forty-four grand. In the harbor security camera footage, it looks like the old man was doing most of the talking—boss talking to the flunkies."

"So, we charge Keanu with dealing?"

Kellie let out a weak laugh. "Yeah, charge Keanu. But here's an interesting twist. Keanu has a new lawyer, a Honolulu criminal defense guy named Roger Phillips from Hach, Mulbain, and Reilly, *the* Honolulu law firm to the rich and famous. He showed up out of the blue at the courthouse three days ago, Keanu's public defender is gone, and the shitstorm begins—motions, a call for a press conference. He's going to be a real pain in the ass."

The chief stopped doodling. "And?"

"And Phillips defending a small-time pusher on Kauai? It makes no sense. Phillips' clients are usually big-time bad people, and by the way, he generally wins."

"What does make sense?"

She shook her head. "At this moment, not much. But we have some leverage. We just need to keep digging, and we need to tie it together into a plausible case."

"You mean evidence puts Keanu solidly in the frame for a drug conviction, right?"

"Right."

"What about the murder?"

Kellie shook her head. "We don't know. But early days. We just started interviewing the neighbors, associates, and so on. We have lots more to learn. Peterson was kind of a hardass to begin with, not well liked, so people are bound to talk. We'll see what we get from the community. Early days. "

The chief made an unhappy face. "Easy for you to say, *early days*—you're not chief of police," he complained. "We don't have murders on the Garden Island. Remember?"

Kellie nodded. "How could I forget? I live here too. We're all-in on this, Chief! We'll figure it out."

Three days in jail, and Keanu was out. His bail had been set by an asshole judge; a bond secured. His hotshot lawyer did that. Dude said some shit to the judge, and after blah blah blah, Keanu was free to go—well, at least until the next hearing.

His lawyer had also said that Paul Pookalani was not his friend, that the little twerp had told the police all kinds of shit about Keanu, and that Keanu needed to stay away from Paul. Then he said that defending Keanu would be more complicated because of Pookalani's big fucking mouth.

Keanu needed to settle up with the little snitch once this whole thing was behind him, and he was confident it would be behind him—what with shark-faced Phillips and all. Dude was a piece of work, a real smart, tough guy. Keanu was sure the fuckin cops on Kauai didn't stand a chance against Phillips, or him. After this was over, they couldn't touch him for nothing. And then—

Keanu walked out of the courthouse into the midday sun and climbed into the stretch limo's back seat. Phillips was sitting in the jumper seat, facing the back, talking to a woman who was also in the back seat, angled in the far corner.

Phillips reached over and closed the door as Keanu settled some distance from the young woman, dressed in white sweats and a black bandana scarf tied like a sweatband around her head. She smelled like flowers. The woman was small, grown-up but small, with Asian eyes and black lipstick.

Keanu nodded at her and said, "Hey," then looked over at Phillips for an explanation.

"Keanu, this is your benefactor, Ms. Sachiko Allen. She's the reason you're out of jail."

Keanu nodded again at the woman, trying to read her. He was a little uncomfortable sitting in a stretch limo. This was a long way from his piece-of-shit pickup truck.

"Hey," he said again. "Hey, thanks. I don't know you, do I?"

The woman hardly moved a muscle, just sat and scanned him with her dark eyes. Finally she said, "You don't know me yet, but you will. And you're welcome."

"So, what happens now?" he asked, looking from Sachiko to Phillips and back. She was weird looking, and he couldn't imagine how she knew him. The whole scene was a little creepy.

Phillips said quickly, "You're free to go. But don't forget your hearing and the bail terms. I'll see you tomorrow morning at ten o'clock, at Ms. Sachiko's house, to collect more information for your defense. She has agreed to put you up in her guest house until the trial. We need to keep you out of your old neighborhood, and we don't want you running into your buddy Paul—and we really don't want you to pal up with any of your old drug buddies. Know what I mean?"

Keanu flushed. The lawyer dude was smirking, arrogant prick, talking to him like he was some bad little kid or something —and a white guy, too, fuck him.

Then the woman spoke, ending the uncomfortable silence. "Roger, let's go to my place. I'll take care of Keanu—what he does and doesn't do. Of course, we'll keep him clean—well, after we clean him up, first." She smiled.

Now he was really embarrassed. Who the fuck was this woman? Then he got it. So this was the rich bitch who was paying the bills. He knew how to handle bitches, no problem, man, no problem at all. She wasn't half bad-looking, either. *Weird get-up, though.*

CHAPTER 22

F lash was in a philosophical space. Not physically—Brennecke's Broiler hardly resembled the agora of Athens. No, he was reflecting, dissecting his new life. He could see that day by day, week by week, he was settling into this little Hawaiian backwater. He knew some people here, not too many, but some. He was helping the odd soul, like Paul, Emma—God help you if you didn't help Mia—and maybe even the cops.

Meeting the cops, now that was interesting. He had no intention of coming clean with them, but much to his surprise, he discovered that he liked them.

"Hey, Flash, what's your fancy? Foster's back, or the topless fruit bomb?" asked the bartender, named Dennis.

"Dennis, let's do a fruit bomb. Extra shake on the bomb, please."

Dennis looked like he'd come straight from central casting for blond pool boy, surf instructor, or bartender. He pushed his blond bangs off his forehead, snapped his fingers, and said, "Coming up, boss. Singapore sling, extra sling, no umbrella."

The Poipu area had a handful of watering holes where one could drink and become lost, as tourists so love to do, but Flash wasn't a lost soul here; he had become a bit of a regular. Being known by island bartenders for his drink order was a bit unsettling, but the familiar banter felt good.

Good wasn't quite right—it made him feel special. He was recognized as being one of the small cadre of locals who frequented these tourist traps. He had to admit to being strangely reassured by these signs of belonging. He took his first sip of the Singapore Sling, tasted the sweet fruit and extra bite of gin, and smiled. Being someone special was okay.

"Hey, buddy. Flash, isn't it?"

Flash looked to his right and saw a familiar face, a deeply tanned fifty- or sixty-year-old white guy seated on the barstool next to him. "Yeah. Aren't you the AA guy?" Flash couldn't remember his name.

"Got it in one!"

"What are you doing here, trolling for members?" Flash couldn't help himself.

"Nah, just checking out the lunch setup. You're starting early. You know, if you ever want to join us, we meet at eight a.m. right over there, at the picnic table, each and every day."

A coffee cup with two plastic cream pods broken open on the saucer sat in front of the AA guy. "You eat here often, bring your buddies here?" Flash asked.

"Oh, no—well, yes. I do eat here often. I own this place. "

Flash grinned. "Really? If you don't mind me asking, how does that work, you being an AA guy and owning a bar?"

"You know, Flash, it works just swimmingly—it really does. Put simply, they drink, and I don't, but I do have to earn a living, and running a restaurant and bar is all I've ever done. I started in Lincoln, Nebraska, built a restaurant and bar, ran it for years, and became really sick of winter, so I bought this place here across the street from old Doc Brennecke's beach. Best move I ever made. It's a good life, isn't it?"

"How long have you been here?" Flash asked.

"Ten years next month. Not long enough to be considered a real local, mind you, but pretty established."

"I give up—what's your name? I lost your card, and the gin isn't bringing it back."

"Fred, Fred Miles. And you're Flash, a friend of Kellie's, not so much Bob, her partner, and a protégé of the indomitable Mia Mahone. See? We're almost related." Fred laughed.

Flash's drink was almost empty. Like magic, Dennis appeared, smiling. He nodded at the glass.

Flash nodded back. "Yeah, thank you, Dennis."

Dennis nodded in return, then asked Fred, "A refill, Mr. Miles?"

"Thanks, a refill would be great."

"Say, Fred, since you've been here ten years, have you noticed any uptick in illegal drug activity on the island? I heard about that murder, and, well, I was just wondering what you see from your vantage point." Flash wondered if his question had gone too far.

Fred shifted on his barstool. He poured two shots of coffee creamer into his refreshed cup, looked at the cup, then said, "Peterson, yes."

"I hear he had a drug stash in the house," said Flash. "What I'm really wondering is if you've seen a bump in the drug culture on Kauai among the locals."

Fred smiled. "Look, I play golf with the chief of police and am pretty good friends with the mayor. These are good men, working hard to make this place safe for locals and tourists alike. So, if you were to ask them your question, what do you think they would say? They would say drugs are everywhere, and it's a never-ending job to keep this place safe in the face of that reality."

Fred looked out through the open windows to Poipu Park, the ocean, and the blue sky. "Didn't I hear you are involved, or sorta involved with the Peterson thing?"

Flash grunted. "More sorta. Mia asked me to help some, only

because Mia asks everybody she comes in contact with to take care of something on her to-do list, you know. She's friends with—"

"Emma Pookalani, daughter of the late judge, a legendary good guy. Yeah, I heard about that. Say, are you a cop or something?"

That was a slap in the head. "No, goddamn it, I am not," Flash barked, then caught himself. "Jesus, sorry, sorry, that was the gin talking, but no, I'm not a cop."

Fred smiled and said, "That's all right. I've heard it before— the gin I mean. I didn't mean to pry—none of my business. Only I'd heard a little about you, but hadn't matched the story to the face. So, here you are now, lounging on Kauai, somewhere between feeling like a tourist and being a local. How is that?"

"Here I am, indeed, almost at my morning limit of Singapore Slings, but since we're talking about it, I'm still curious about the drugs."

Fred sipped his coffee and then answered. "Well, look, the chief and the mayor are truly doing their best. But from where I sit, I'd say yes, signs of an uptick in drug use are evident." Fred stared into his coffee cup for a moment, then said, "Do you have any suggestions about that, even though you're not a cop?"

Flash shook his head. "No, but what about Peterson?"

"Well, I don't want to piss on anyone's grave, but, if I were a cop, I'd be following that Peterson thread a little more urgently. Old Peterson was a bad dude. I can't tell you how I know that, but I do. He was not a good person, and yes, we're talking drugs. I can confirm that."

Flash thought about this, then decided to ask the obvious question, even though it might cost him. "And why might the local police be moving slowly?"

"This is the way I would say it: Our local police force will do their best, only they'll do it very carefully because Peterson was a part of the island family, so to speak. Family investigations are more— What? Subtle, quieter. The cops are very careful not to injure or unsettle islanders. Peterson was part of the family, a bad apple for sure, but still, family."

Fred pushed his cup and saucer away from him on the bar. "The cops will eventually get it right, at least I think they will. But the journey will be a slow and careful one. That's how it works around here. Now, if the person killed had been a tourist, well, that's panic time. Clear the decks and move fast, lots of overtime, urgency, solve the thing as quickly as possible and get the story out of the news. That's the island mantra—don't scare the tourists, whatever you do. I'm a big fan of that mantra, by the way."

"I'll bet," said Flash, rising from his seat. "Well, thanks, Fred. I'll see you around. Oh, and you might think about giving young Dennis a raise. He's damn good for business."

That afternoon, the gin mostly out of his system, Flash took a taxi to Salt Pond Beach to have a talk with Paul. The boy had called him, so that was progress. It would be a chance to find out what Paul knew about Peterson, which would be progress too. He sat down to wait for Paul at a picnic table looking out toward the ocean.

He considered Paul's predicament. If the boy could get clear of murder and drug charges, that would be a big win. But Paul might be facing extrajudicial complications. Everyone on the island now knew that Mr. P. had a huge drug stash and forty-thousand dollars in small bills hidden in his house. The people who supplied the drugs to Kauai would hear the news too. A good chance those people, probably from Oahu, would be looking to make an example of Keanu and/or Paul.

"Hey, Flash. No beer?" Paul asked as he came up beside his mentor.

"Nah, too early for me." Flash smiled.

"Yeah? That's not what Auntie Mia says. In any case I've got my mom's car, so I can drive you back."

"That would be great." Flash looked at the boy. "How you doin'?"

Paul was holding an orange cup with a plastic top and a straw sticking out the top. He slurped, went to the other side of the picnic table, put the cup down in front of him, and said, "Okay, I guess." He slurped again, sat with his back to the ocean, both hands holding the cup, looking down at the tabletop.

Flash waited. The best ploy to induce witnesses and perps to talk to you was silence—just shut up and wait them out.

Paul looked up. "Janet says they might not prosecute. She could make some sort of a deal where they treat me like a minor or something cuz I just turned eighteen. I don't know, but she said she was hopeful. That's good, isn't it?"

"Yeah, it is good, very good. If you don't mind me asking, though, what did you tell them about Keanu?"

"Just like you said. I did the middle thing, path, whatever. I didn't lie, but I couldn't tell them everything I know. He'd be in the shit for sure if I did." Paul smirked and shook his head.

Omertà—the Mafia code of silence—but Hawaiian style. Funny, maybe, but not so funny in this case, at least not so funny if the cops found out that Paul knew more.

On the other hand, the police weren't likely to learn the whole story on their own. That would take digging, maybe digging hard, and Flash suspected that hardassed policing methods were out of bounds among the island family, especially when a revered judge's eighteen-year-old grandson was involved. Flash wondered how the island family dealt with the really bad guys, the Peterson type, for example.

Flash asked Paul, "When do you hear what they'll do?"

"Janet said they're close, maybe a couple of days."

"Good."

Paul smiled and said, "Yeah. She's a tough lawyer. I'm glad she's on my side."

"Me too," said Flash. "Now tell me what you didn't tell them about Peterson, and Keanu, and the rest of it—all of it—because even though you may be off the hook with the law, this isn't over, not by a long shot."

Paul didn't look pleased. "No way. If I tell you—"

Flash interrupted him. "If you tell me, what you say goes no further. I won't tell anyone. But this isn't over. Trust me, Paul, I need to know what you know about Mr. P. and Keanu and the drugs. So why don't you start with Keanu?"

"Okay, Keanu—Look, you gotta remember we went to school together, all the way through. He was my best friend. Then we didn't see each other for a couple of years, then I see him again. I was so happy to run into him, and he seemed glad to see me too. But he wasn't the same dude, really. Something had changed in him. I didn't get it at first, but he used to be a good guy, and now he had a mean streak, ya know? I was afraid of him. I really was. So yeah, about him…"

He sounded as if he was reciting, like he was on stage. His voice was strained. Flash realized Paul had rehearsed the story and was being very careful about what he said.

Paul licked his lips. "Well, he got into a drug deal with Peterson. Peterson and four or five runners. But Keanu became the head runner, and since Peterson was the boss and all, and since he worked as head of security at the docks, well, Keanu ran a lot of the drugs, selling them after the drugs arrived."

Paul slumped a little and gave Flash a calculating look before continuing. "Peterson would give K the drugs, and K would train and manage the runners. Then he'd give the money to Peterson, and if one of the runners stole or took some of the drugs, Keanu would beat the shit out of them, or at least that's what I think."

Flash nodded. "So Peterson bought the drugs and got them to the island how?"

Paul gave Flash a crooked grin. "Yeah, pretty cool, huh? Sit on your ass and the runners take the risk while you take the money. I didn't see much, but Keanu handled a lot of money, and Peterson got almost all of it."

"Maybe not so cool," Flash said dryly. "Peterson's dead."

"Yeah, I know, just talking." Paul shook his head as if waking up. "Yeah, I know, I know."

Once a cop, maybe always a cop. "Where did the drugs come from—do you know? How they came to the island?"

Paul's mouth turned down and his brow furrowed. In an angry whisper, he said, "You're not going to tell anyone about this, are you? Keanu will kill me! For all I know, he might have killed Mr. P."

"No, I'm not telling anyone," Flash answered. "Look, thanks to Mia and your mom, Paul, my job is to help you through this mess. Why would I betray you to Keanu or anybody who wanted to hurt you? If you really think I would, let's stop right here. Don't tell me anything else. But if you trust me, the more I know, the better chance you'll have to get through this mess."

Paul settled on the bench, his dark eyes moving as if searching for something. "Chance? What are you talking about?" he asked.

He was so young. And the young so easily get into trouble.

"This whole thing is a dog's breakfast—" Seeing Paul's confused look, he clarified. "It's an ugly mess, and we need to wake up to how dangerous it is. You and the others think this is all going to go away. I'm not so sure, but I can't help you unless I know what you know."

"You sound like a cop, you know that?" Paul said.

Flash groaned quietly. "I've been told that, yes, but I'm not a cop. Do we keep going here, or are we done?"

"You hitting on my mom?"

"No." Flash watched the boy, saw him shift on the bench, and thought of Pippa, wondering how she would react in a situation like this.

"Okay, the drugs come from Oahu. They come from some big dude there. Mr. P., see, thought Keanu was a dumb kid. Keanu's a jerk, but he's not dumb. He watched the old fart, watched him a lot, and sometimes went to his house. He figured out that P.

paid for the stuff up front, cash, then some time later the stuff appeared on one of the inter-island boats, or a Zodiac boat night delivery. The shipments are easy, cause P. was head of security at the port, no problem there.

"The Zodiac deliveries, well, Mr. P. wasn't exactly a physical specimen. He was a geezer, ya know, smoked and always complaining about his health? So, he'd take Keanu to do the physical stuff—go down to the beach, get the stuff, and bring it up to Mr. P.'s car. P. told K. that he'd kill him if he ever told anyone about the deliveries."

Paul winced but didn't shut up. "Keanu thought Mr. P. was afraid if the other runners got wind of the Zodiac deliveries, they'd rob him. I believed him. Keanu's a jerk, but he was really scared of Mr. P., for sure."

Paul looked up; his eyes opened wide as if asking if he could stop now. The kid was scared, but Flash knew Paul had more to say, and now was the time.

"When is the next shipment? The next Zodiac shipment?"

Paul shifted on the bench, then looked down uncomfortably. Flash had seen the same reaction hundreds of times: some minor crook not wanting to go too far, pleading without words to get out of the interrogation room. He needed to make this a little easier.

"Look, I know you know, just tell me. We can't protect your mom or other islanders unless we know what's going on. When will it arrive, and where?"

Paul's eyes were on the tabletop. "They come in at night, something like midnight. But Keanu didn't trust me all that much, either. I only know this much because he likes to brag when he gets a couple of beers in him."

"Where do they come in?" Flash asked gently.

"I'm guessing here. Keanu described the place once, and it sounded like Koloa Landing. Oh, and when they deliver by Zodiac, P. had to give the people on the boat cash for the next shipment. Cash up front." Paul raised his head and looked at Flash.

Flash nodded. "How often did they use the Zodiac?"

"Pretty often, maybe once every week or ten days."

"How did Mr. P. know when the Zodiac would arrive, or where?"

Paul grimaced. "I don't know. Really. But Keanu might know. He likes to brag, but he didn't trust me all that much. He thought I was kind of a wimp, and his job was to show me the real world, toughen me up, I guess."

"How about the inter-island deliveries through the port? Why the Zodiac thing at all?"

Paul shrugged. "Dunno. Maybe the stuff through the port was like for big shipments? I think K. mentioned something about them being big but irregular? P. was always bitching about it, that they were slow and irregular, couldn't get what he needed when he needed it on the inter-island boats, something like that." Paul sucked the last of his drink out of his cup.

"When was the last time he went for a Zodiac pickup?"

"About ten days ago, just before the rave. He mentioned that after the rave they would be low on junk until the next Zodiac."

As long as Paul was answering, Flash would go on asking. He never turned down information. "What do Mr. P. and Keanu sell? What drugs, I mean."

"Roofies and E, and coke and heroin when they can get em. I never saw the heroin, but a couple of folks at the rave were pissed that I didn't have any. Keanu told me some might be in the next shipment, but that I wasn't going to be running it. H had its own route, a kind of undercover runner. He wouldn't tell me who that was, though."

"Do you know anything about how Keanu would rate a big-time attorney from Honolulu? Like where that would come from?"

"No, last I heard he had a public defender, like me."

Remembering something Mia had told him over coffee, Flash

asked, "Do you know a woman Keanu might hang out with? Sachiko Allen, I think her name is?"

Paul's face fell. He went pale and slouched on the bench. "Shit," he said. "Shit, what the fuck is he doing with her? Oh man, he's going to kill me!"

Shaking his head back and forth, he said, "She knows about the drugs, and she hit on me, for some reason, probably drugs, but I don't remember much. She took me to her house, and we drank a lot. I could have told her anything. Shit." He bent over, head in his arms on the table.

That was a pretty interesting tidbit. "How do you know her?" Flash asked.

After a long pause, without looking up, Paul said, "I didn't, well, I did because I sold her some E at the rave. Only I didn't know her. She called me up out of the blue and we got ripped at her house in Princeville. She's rich. Then she called a taxi for me, cause we were both drunk, and that's all I remember."

Lights started going off in Flash's head. "When was this?"

The words came slowly, in a whisper. "Ten days ago. No idea how she'd know Keanu, unless they were doing something together, trying to find out about me. Shit, he'll kill me."

"No, he won't," Flash said. "Paul, look at me. He won't, because we won't let him. Tell Janet about this, though. You might need some protection at your mom's house. Tell your mom, too, so she can be vigilant, a little more careful than usual."

Flash stood up and stretched his legs. The wooden picnic table benches were murder on your legs and back. The aches reminded him he wasn't as young as he used to be.

Paul bounced up. *No aching joints there*, thought Flash. He thought again about Pippa and smiled at Paul. As they walked toward Paul's mom's car, Paul said, his voice low, "Why are you doing this, anyway?"

"Mia, that's why. Mia. She made me get involved, and now

I'm interested in what's going on. Not quite sure why, but I'm interested in the whole mess."

"In the dog's breakfast?" Paul asked.

Flash laughed and said, "Yes. One part puzzle and one part dog's breakfast."

CHAPTER 23

Flash watched as a green-and-white Toyota sedan marked as a Kauai Cab, pulled into a parking place in front of the Kauai Surf Shop. It was 9:30 a.m., so most of the stores and restaurants along the boardwalk were still closed. Flash recognized the driver, but couldn't remember the man's name. *Paka? Puka? Something like that.*

He walked to the driver's side window. "Sorry, I forgot your name. But okay if I ride in back this time?"

"No problem, Mr. Flash, and the name is Pika, Pika Kekoa." He handed Flash his Kauai Cabs business card, which had his name, his phone number, and the motto *Any Time, Any Day in Paradise.*

They drove out of Koloa past the old sugar mill, then onto Maluhia Road through the tree tunnel, then onto Highway 50, where they began the forty-five-minute drive through Lihue, Wailua, Kapaa, and Kilauea to Princeville.

Pika was a quiet guy. Flash had been in his cab a couple of times before, so he didn't feel the need to chat. Besides, the drive gave him a chance to think, to prepare for Princeville. Kellie and Bob had told him to back off and to let them do their jobs, but he was worried about Paul and Paul's mom. Paul knew too much, or at least Keanu probably thought so, which counted as the same thing.

Flash also saw the signs of an ominous pressure below the happy-go-lucky, day-to-day life of Kauai's family. An active drug presence fuels tension, mostly because of the intimidation, extortion, and desperation that always surrounds the drug trade. With an increase in the flow of drugs, what follows is increased violence—first, among the bad guys, but ultimately out in the community, affecting people like Paul and his mother. And in this particular community, the violence could scare the tourists, too, the goose laying all the golden eggs.

The residents and their police force were acting as though they couldn't see it coming. The Kauai cops were good people, decent people, Flash believed that. They were working the Peterson case, certainly, but seemed oblivious to *why* he was killed, what was happening behind the scene. Flash wondered if they had ever dealt with a severe surge of drug activity before.

His trip today was a calculated stirring of the pot, albeit an unauthorized one. He needed to head one of the bad guys off at the pass.

Due to Kauai's "rush hour" leaving Lihue around the Wilcox Hospital, they were crawling along. The trip would take more than an hour, a lucrative fare for Pika.

Flash said, "So, Pika, do you think the island has a drug problem?"

The cabbie answered in a quiet voice, "No, sir. This is a good place. No drug problem that I know of."

I rest my case, thought Flash.

He had Googled Sachiko Allen, daughter and only child of Touma Allen, a prominent Oahu developer. She was a piece of work, a debutante who became a thirty-something party girl, hell on wheels if the gossips were to be believed.

Every time Sachiko was mentioned in the local stories or the Honolulu press, she was Touma Allen's daughter. Touma was the chairman of the Allen Group, which was currently building

Village in the Sky, a high-rise condominium project on Oahu, a true mega-project. They had broken ground two weeks prior in a big, flashy ceremony, featuring a golden shovel and Honolulu's mayor.

The big surprise in researching Ms. Sachiko was that Flash had heard of the Village in the Sky project before, from the other world, his past life in Seattle, while undercover.

Sachiko's house was a strikingly modern green slate construction. The entry was through a gray-steel, automatic gate that stood open. They drove through the gate and along a hundred-yard-long pebbled driveway to the front door. As the cab stopped, the giant wooden front door opened slowly, revealing a woman in a maid's uniform with black and white fringes. She stood, waiting to greet them.

"Hello, my name is Flash Thornton. I have an appointment with Ms. Allen."

"Yes, Mr. Thornton, if you would follow me, please?"

"Okay, and just so you know, the cab will be waiting to take me back."

"That'll be fine. I'll have him park over by the garage."

Stepping in and following the maid, Flash observed glass, Koloa wood, terrazzo floors, designer rugs, black leather furniture intermingled with white leather furniture, and several huge, fresh flower arrangements in oversized glass vases. The place was a palace, designed by someone who really knew how to spend money.

"If you will wait here, Ms. Sachiko will be with you soon. Can I bring you a juice, or tea or coffee, or perhaps something stronger?"

"Nothing, thank you."

Then came the wait. The I-am-in-control-of-this-situation wait, the this-is-my-fucking-house-and-you-are-an-interloper-so-wait wait. Well, at least she knew how to play the game. He had scored the appointment by telling her he had important information about Keanu's case. Flash was dressed up, wearing a pressed Hawaiian shirt, clean khaki cargo shorts, and Birkenstocks.

"Mr. Thornton?" Sachiko eased her way into the room, wearing a white tennis skirt, white shoes, white top, white warm-up sweater, white everything, including lips and nails. *A pretty clear statement, but of what?* Flash thought. Then he looked around at the furniture, and he got it. Black and white. How about that?

"Call me Flash."

"Sachiko Allen. How do you do?"

She extended her hand. They shook and walked to the couch.

Flash settled at one end of the long, armless, white leather couch. Sachiko propped herself at the other end, hands in her lap. She turned to look directly at him. Flash's impression was that she looked sweet, not the hellcat the paper described. Even her voice was soft.

"So?" she asked.

"So?" Flash gave her his best smile.

"So what is this information you have, and who are you, by the way? I don't think I know you."

Flash let her wait ten seconds or so, and then answered. "I'm a friend of Paul Pookalani, Emma Pookalani's son. He was the other boy picked up by the Kauai police on drug possession charges and suspicion of being involved in Franklin Peterson's murder."

Flash was mildly surprised to hear Flash, the cop from Seattle, speaking again, not Flash, the erased beach bum. He liked the familiar feeling. "Before I share my information, I have a couple of questions. I want to be sure I'm in the right place."

Her assured face started to cloud over, and he noted a tightening of her folded fingers. "Yes?" she said in a sharper tone.

"What's your relationship with Keanu Akoni, and why are you footing the bill for his defense?"

She glared at him, then softened into a smile. "I'm a person concerned about Keanu's well-being and was convinced that the

Kauai police were ready to stitch him up for a crime he didn't commit."

"For the murder? Or for dealing drugs?"

"All the crimes he's accused of, all of them. He's innocent, and I intend to see he's defended properly, especially in this fucking backwater."

Her decorous air had evaporated in an instant. She was still calm, still beautiful, but definitely hostile. Flash asked, "How do you know Keanu?"

"That's none of your fucking business."

"Well, in case you were wondering, he's a scumbag, and he is very likely to be put away for trafficking, no matter how much you pay that Honolulu law firm. Or is it Daddy who's paying the law firm?"

At that, she sat up even straighter, folded her arms, and said, "Look, I don't need to answer any of your questions, and I'm beginning to think you've come here under false pretenses. I think you should leave."

"Okay. In a minute. I understand this may be hard to hear, whatever you've got going on with Keanu, but I want you to be sure to tell him that Paul didn't rat him out to the cops. Paul didn't tell them about Keanu's drug business. He didn't give him up."

"So what?" She looked hard at Flash. "So what? Keanu didn't do any of these things in the first place."

"Nor did Paul tell the police about Keanu being Mr. P.'s main man, or how Keanu helps with the incoming shipments, those brought in by the Zodiacs. Paul didn't tell them any of those things."

She rose from her seat. "You need to leave. You're an impertinent prick—you know that?"

"Yes, I do know. Only I'm not quite done yet. Is Keanu here, by the way? Given your reaction so far, I might be better off telling him the next bit to his face."

"Just get out of here, will you!" she said.

A man's voice from somewhere in the house said, "Yeah, why don't you tell me to my face."

Flash turned to see Keanu standing at the edge of the living room. He'd had a makeover, thought Flash. He had a conservative haircut, combed and parted on one side, and was wearing khaki slacks, a Hawaiian shirt, and expensive-looking leather loafers. Keanu was about a hundred and eighty-five pounds and had big hands. But he didn't look that strong and was soft around the cheeks.

Flash smiled at him and said, "So the toe rag is around. How nice."

Keanu took three quick steps toward Flash, growling, "You fucking jackass, get the fuck out of here."

Sachiko shouted, "Keanu, no, no, leave him!"

Flash, still seated on the couch, put his hands under the lunging boy, grabbed his shirt, and guided Keanu over his head and over the couch's back to an abrupt crash landing on the carpeted floor.

Flash then sprang over the back of the sofa, put his knee in Keanu's back, jerked his right arm up toward his shoulders in a hammerlock, and pressed down hard with the knee.

Flash said, "That was a mistake, you little shit. I need to hear from you in the next five seconds that you'll calm down, or I'll break this arm like a twig."

Flash gave the arm another twitch, and Keanu shouted, "Okay, okay, I give up. Okay!"

Flash released his hold, lifted his knee, and stood up. Sachiko had disappeared. Flash pulled Keanu up by his shirt, guided him to one of the side chairs, and roughly pushed him onto it. "If you approach, threaten, or harm Paul Pookalani in any way, I will rat you out to the cops then come looking for you myself. You leave Paul alone. Don't go anywhere near him, punk, understand?"

"You leave now, or I will shoot, leave now!" Sachiko shouted. Flash turned to see her standing less than ten feet away, holding a Glock 17 pistol with both hands, pointed at Flash's chest. Her hands were shaking.

Keanu, still in the chair, tears running down his cheeks, said, "Shoot the fucker. Shoot him. Do you hear me? He's a fucking trespasser. You gonna take that? Shit, shoot him while you can!"

Flash held out a hand toward Sachiko and said, "Look, I'm through here. Lower the gun, and I'll leave."

Sachiko hesitated, then lowered the gun and said in an angry, frightened voice, "Get out of my house."

"Good idea," said Flash, smiling. "But before I leave you two lovebirds, Sachiko, you be sure to keep boy toy here on a short leash. He's got significant issues with self-control, and if he comes near Paul or me or anyone in the Pookalani family, all hell will break loose on him and you."

"Shoot him, bitch, shoot him!" Keanu shrieked again.

"Shut up, you idiot. God, you're so stupid!" Sachiko looked at Flash and growled, "You, go now!"

Back in the cab, Pika asked Flash if he'd had a good meeting.

Flash said, "Yeah, this was a long way to come, but worth it, Pika." Flash was exhilarated, shaking slightly with the adrenaline that had spiked during the fight.

"Mission accomplished then, sir. Is that it?"

"Yes, Pika, I think so. Mission accomplished."

Message delivered, pot stirred, not bad for a morning's work. But Flash hadn't figured out what the hell Sachiko Allen's game was. What could she possibly want from a toe rag like Keanu? Whatever it was, she clearly had something in mind. Very determined that girl, very determined.

Another thing too—he'd liked the little dustup. That was the first time in a long time he'd been in a scuffle. The action felt good.

Touma arrived ten minutes before the Village in the Sky kick-off meeting that was scheduled for ten that morning. The Allen

Group offices were on the fifteenth floor of the First Hawaiian Bank Center on Bishop Street in downtown Honolulu. Prime building, prime location, with offices intended to impress. They were stunning, modern, all stone, steel, and polished wood, and had cost an arm and a leg. In short, they were totally at odds with Touma's new plan for the Allen Group to fly below the radar.

With a vertigo-inducing floor-to-ceiling glass wall, the conference room looked out toward the Honolulu Harbor and the Pacific beyond. Twenty-five chairs encircled a long maple conference table, with folding chairs lined up along the back wall.

At ten o'clock, Touma called the meeting to order, gave his welcome bit, gave his uplifting let's-do-this-together bit, and began the round of introductions—the meeting had brought together all of the project's primary players, many of whom didn't know each other. Each person at the table named themselves and their organization and introduced colleagues.

As the introductions droned on, Touma noticed a chubby, balding man, dressed in an English tweed suit with a yellow handkerchief stuffed in his suit pocket, seated at the far end of the conference room table. Malcolm Haysmith was in the house.

Soon enough, Haysmith's turn arrived. He rose and said, "I am Malcolm Haysmith, MA, chartered accountant, and managing director for the funding group Sixty-Four Capital of the Grand Cayman." Then he sat abruptly.

So, what the hell was he even doing in Honolulu?

Touma approached Minette during the break, took her by the arm, and drew her out of the conference room into an office down the hall. "What the hell is Haysmith doing here? Did you invite him?"

Minette shook her head. "No. I'm as surprised to see him as you are. He didn't tell you he was coming?"

Minette was clearly unsettled. Touma blurted out, "God no. I didn't even know he was in Hawaii. Why do you think he's here? Why do you think he didn't tell us he was coming?"

Minette took a deep breath, then said, "Well, they put up the money. Maybe he thinks he should watch over it? Could that be?"

"Why would he want to do that? We're watching the money. That's our job."

"Yes, you'd think he'd let us be. Only, the funding agreement does give them a lot of authority, more than usual. They're empowered to monitor and direct our work. You know that, right?"

Touma grunted. Then he said, "Figures. He is a chartered accountant. A Brit, right?"

"Yes, a Brit." She smiled.

"When we go back in, go over and chat him up," Touma instructed. "Find out what his agenda is, will you?"

Back in the conference room, breakout teams were assembled, and the room emptied, except for Haysmith, who remained seated until everyone had left. He then stood and approached Touma.

"Mr. Touma." Haysmith extended his hand. It was damp. "I think we should have our own breakout conversation while the others are working. Shall we?"

Haysmith's suggestion didn't sound like a question. It sounded like an order. A little surprised, Touma said, "Of course. We can go down to my office and talk in private. I didn't even know you were in Hawaii. What brings you here?"

"You do, Mr. Allen, you do."

Seated in Touma's office, Haysmith began what Touma could only describe as laying down the law. Hard. Apparently, Haysmith was going to be Touma's worst nightmare.

The Allen Group would act as developer on the project in name only. Haysmith had set up a satellite office on Waikiki, where he would stay and work while in Hawaii. He expected to spend about half of his time on this project, a venture critical to his masters at LM Global.

As managing director of Sixty-Four Capital of the Grand

Cayman, Haysmith had oversight and operational authority to ensure that the Allen Group made the most prudent and efficient use of the capital raised for this project.

When Touma protested, Haysmith said bluntly, "Read the agreement, Mr. Allen, and you'll see I have that authority. You work for me. That is how this is going to be."

Haysmith had hired a global accounting firm, and they were providing two accounting administrators who would be installed in the Allen Group offices. Reporting directly to Haysmith, the administrators would authorize and sign all checks on the project. They would also carefully monitor subcontractor and service provider selection. Haysmith and the two administrators would be the primary authorizing authority for all services, all money in and money out, starting the following day, when Haysmith's administrators would arrive at Touma's office.

At the end of his recitation, Haysmith said, "Well, we've had a very productive breakout, haven't we? I expect you'll want to brief your staff to prepare for my two colleagues' arrival."

Touma stared at Haysmith, his mind working a mile a minute, trying to assemble his thoughts.

"Oh, and one more item. Since we'll be starting real work in the next couple of weeks, I've a prepared list of preferred contractors for the project's critical parts—civil, concrete, scaffolding, electrical, HVAC, and a few others. Most of them have a Honolulu presence. Your people will need to provide drawings and specifications to solicit proposals and cost estimates from them. We have vetted and pre-approved financial arrangements and contract terms. They're standing by and expect to hear from you by day after tomorrow. You will use them in place of any contractors you may have already selected. This is not negotiable."

Touma was gutted. "Wait a minute, you can't do this. I'm the developer—you aren't. I have the experience and connections here in Honolulu—you don't."

Haysmith's face twisted into a scowl, his little eyes squinting at Touma. "Look, you, this is how I intend to fund and oversee this project. This is not a negotiation! If, as you say, you can't live with my terms, I'll walk and take my money with me, five-hundred-million dollars, and whatever you'll have left of your reputation."

As Touma began to protest again, Haysmith held up his right hand. "Touma, answer now. Yes, you'll proceed with our terms, or no, you won't—in which case I'll go tell your people in the conference room that the project has been suspended. Yes or no? Which is it?"

Touma, in shock, couldn't manage a word. Haysmith shook his head and began to leave the room.

Touma finally croaked out, "Yes."

Haysmith turned, looked at Touma, and said, "Sorry, but what was that, Touma?"

"Yes. I said, yes."

Later that evening, Touma, Minette and Benjamin were discussing the situation. Benjamin said, "You know what this is about? Kickbacks. He's feathering his nest on the side. Who are these people who funded the project, anyway?"

Minette said, "Whose fault would it be if taxes aren't paid correctly or on time? How can I be head of finance when I can't even sign a check? This is nuts, T, just nuts."

Benjamin nodded. "Look, I know most of the contractors on his list. I wouldn't have chosen them. I don't want to work with them. I thought my job was to make those choices."

Minette added, "And I thought I was the chief financial officer of this company."

Touma knew he had to calm his two top executives. "Look, we can figure our way through this," he said, trying to believe what he was telling them. "Let's just do what he says, for now, and I'll try to get us back into the driver's seat."

Minette was shaking her head. "Touma, where is this money coming from, and what happened to Bank

Schaffhausen? These aren't the people you were courting last winter, are they?"

Touma sighed and said in a low, dispirited voice, "Minette, it's the same money, just by way of a different avenue. Schaffhausen backed out at the last minute. I don't know why. Schaffhausen's backers, their investors, wanted the deal to become Sixty-Four Capital. The same money, a different name."

Minette nodded, but her face registered disbelief. The thing with Minette was that she needed certainty, so he repeated, "Same money as Schaffhausen, just a different channel, completely aboveboard."

Minette cocked her head and asked, "You did read the funding agreement, T, didn't you? Sixty-Four Capital is completely in the driver's seat—Haysmith is empowered to do everything that he just shoved down our throats. I read the document. To be honest I just didn't think that you'd sign such a thing like that unless you had some sort of out or leverage. It's not like you."

When they finally left the Allen Group office, the time was eight p.m. Benjamin and Minette were both in deep shock. Touma didn't feel any better. Their dream project, Village in the Sky, had crashed and burned, even before the job trailers were moved on site.

CHAPTER 24

Flash stood in front of the surf shop watching Kellie pull the cruiser into a parking place so as not to block traffic on the two-lane road. This was Koloa rush hour, when seemingly everyone headed to the post office to pick up their mail, shop, use the laundromat, visit the Department of Labor office, or go shopping in either of the two grocery stores in town. Kellie had offered Flash a ride to a meeting/party at Emma's that afternoon.

Flash slid into the front passenger seat. "Where's your partner?" he asked as she backed slowly out of the parking space.

"He's busy, heading up the search for a person of interest."

"A person of interest—like who?"

"None of your business. Well, that's not true. Okay, a heroin addict named Robbie, whose fingerprints were all over Peterson's house. We want to bring him in for questioning."

Flash looked directly at her. She glanced back at him, brown eyes smiling. He said, "You figured out who did it, then? This guy's prints on the murder weapon?"

She nodded, eyes back on the road. *Good cop,* thought Flash.

"Yup," she said. "But we need to see if we can find a motive —well, other than drugs."

"Jesus, Kellie—heroin? Who needs more of a motive than that? Ninety-eight percent of the time when junk is involved, 'It's the junk, stupid,' or so they say."

"Is this your buddy, the cop, talking, Flash? Or maybe *CSI* on television?"

Flash realized he had said too much. "I'm not sure where I heard it." He cleared his throat.

Kellie's voice shifted gears. "Flash, one of these days we'll find out whatever it is you're not sharing with your friends here on Kauai."

"I don't know what you're talking about," he told her.

"Yes, you do know what I'm talking about," she said, giving him a half-glance then returning her eyes to the road. "So here's a heads-up. I ran your fingerprints. The file was blocked by a red flag, meaning *access denied*. I'm not going to ask you if you're in the Witness Protection Program, because that would be against the law, but whoever you are, you're certainly a special sort of person, one whose identity is locked behind a red flag. Interesting, don't you think?"

Well, here we go, he thought. "I don't know what you're talking about," he said. "You know, who I am is none of your business anyway," he added.

She chuckled. "None of my business. Hmm. Well, perhaps. We'll just have to wait and see, won't we?"

"No comment."

He worked to calm himself. She'd surprised him. Not just that she'd grabbed his prints and run them; he would have done the same thing. He was surprised by the red flag. Someone had locked up his identity in the fingerprint system. When he was working undercover that would have made sense, but that was a long time ago.

Kellie was right, red flags were used to protect witnesses. Only, he wasn't a witness—or was he? Perhaps his identity had been barricaded not to protect him but to provide cover for the Seattle Police Department. The police chief could have blocked

his identity, or he might have authorized his favorite lieutenant, the guy in charge of financial fraud. Fucking John
Horan.

Flash, Mia, Reggie, Kellie, Janet, Emma, and Paul were gathered
on Emma's deck, the occasion being Paul's release more or less
from the long arm of the law. Flash had brought two six-packs of
Foster's and found a couple of bottles of sauvignon blanc
sweating on the drinks table, so he deposited the cold beer there.
Janet had brought two large pizzas and eight plastic clamshells
of tossed green salad, each accompanied by a plastic tube of
ranch dressing.

After the food had been distributed, Janet said, using her
courtroom voice, "Could I have your attention, please? Thank
you. First of all, I want to thank Kellie for attending. This will be
an easier meeting than the last one. I'm happy to say that Paul is
no longer a person of interest in the murder, and the prosecutor
has agreed to a reduced charge regarding the drugs— Paul will
be on probation for six months. After six months, assuming that
he doesn't stray outside the lines, his case will be sealed, so he
won't have a criminal record."

That brought a cheer from the gathering. Paul smiled, then
gazed down at the pizza in the middle of the table, looking
embarrassed.

Flash thought the odds were good that Paul would stay away
from the Kauai drug scene. What he needed was to find a job
and move on with his life.

But Emma didn't look happy, which for her was unusual. She
asked, "What about Keanu? What's happening there? I'm
worried about Paul. I think Keanu, or some of his gang, runners,
whatever you call them, might hurt Paul."

Kellie said, "Emma, we'll have your house watched until this
gets sorted out. We have evidence problems in Keanu's case. I
can't go into it, but we're not sure we can convict him on the

drug possession charge. Of course, if any of you have information that would help us, please let me know soon."

Flash asked, "Have you made any progress with the crime scene? Any prints or witnesses? Anything you can tell us about?"

"Yeah, we have. We've issued an all-points bulletin to find Robbie Washburn. His prints were all over Peterson's living room. He's been convicted of heroin possession twice and has been in and out of recovery programs, once on Kauai and once on the mainland."

Flash asked, "Where do you think he's hiding?"

Kellie shook her head. "We don't know that he's hiding," she said. "We just picked up the prints and the witness statements yesterday. We went to Robbie's home, and the neighbors hadn't seen him for a couple of days. He's not popular in that neighborhood, so they'll call us for sure if he shows up. By the way, he was seen near the Peterson house on the night of the murder. Why? Do you know something about Robbie, Flash?"

He laughed and said, "Nope, never met the guy in—oh, wait. I think I may have seen him, though. One morning, months ago, down at Poipu beach, early, near where the AA gang gathers. But no, I don't know him."

"Am I right that you weren't there for the AA meeting? Or were you?" she said, raising an eyebrow.

"Apparently not, officer. Wanna beer?" He reached over and grabbed a Foster's. Smiling, he held it out toward her.

"No, thanks."

Flash smiled at Kellie, popped the tab, and took a mouthful of liquid.

She said, "So, I've got to go. That's what I can tell you all so far. Hey, Paul, you behave. Got it?"

Paul nodded.

Mia had been uncharacteristically quiet, sitting with her arms folded, brow furrowed. Suddenly, her eyes widened. She sat up and said, "You know, Robbie's a second-generation trust-fund baby. His grandfather made a fortune in timber in the Philippines in the early nineteen hundreds. The old man lived in Vancouver, in Canada, but he loved the islands. So he bought a cane plantation up in the hills behind Koloa, fenced it, put up a monumental stone gate at the entrance, private, and built a fabulous house with ten bedrooms, large gardens, a pool, a tennis court—the works."

She looked around, checking that everyone was paying attention. "When the grandfather died, he left the estate to his son, who didn't like it, so he sold it to a hedge-fund guy and left Hawaii. Robbie was twenty at the time and wanted to stay on Kauai. His father said fine, you have your trust fund, go do whatever the hell you want. But Robbie was crushed that his father didn't give him the family estate. So Robbie has money, a nice house over near Poipu, and alternates between being a law-abiding citizen and being a druggie. He binges, and sometimes he misbehaves when he binges, but still, why would he want to kill Peterson?"

Janet said, "Mia, we really shouldn't jump to any conclusions about stuff like this. Right now, we really don't know enough to paint Robbie as the murderer."

Reggie said, "Well, we know Peterson was murdered, and we heard about fingerprints, so that's something."

Flash asked, "If Robbie were hiding, any idea of where?"

"No," said Mia. "But it doesn't feel like the police are moving very urgently. Peterson was a crotchety fellow. No one liked him, as far as I know. But I guess if he was dishing out the drugs, that would make him popular with a particular crowd, wouldn't it?"

Mia then looked over at Flash. "Why are you asking? Are you giving way to your inner-cop thing?"

Flash ground his teeth together before answering. "No, I just wondered if any of us might have information that would help Kellie and the police. I'm sure they're doing their best, but, yeah, slowly. If we can help, we should, you know, and no, it's not some imagined inner-cop thing, Mia."

"Oh, good. You, the good citizen, very refreshing. Can I have one of those beers, please?"

Reggie offered to drive Flash back to his apartment. He said he needed to check on a problem with the air conditioning system in the grocery store. Reggie was a cautious driver, eyes always on the road, and he drove with both hands on the steering wheel and his left foot hovering over the brake, just in case.

"You seem to be settling in here, Flash. Mia said something about you may be looking for a more permanent place to live. Is that right?"

"Maybe, we'll see. I haven't made my mind up yet. I do like this island, though. We'll see."

"Well, I'm sure we'd welcome it if you stayed, not that I'm pressuring you," Reggie said quietly.

Flash smiled. "One thing I like about this place, Reggie, is no pressure. Say, would you mind running me down to Brennecke Bar and Grill instead of Koloa Town?"

"You still hungry?" Reggie raised his eyebrows.

"Nah, I need to meet a friend there. If you don't mind."

"No, not at all."

Fred's office was on the bottom floor, but to reach it, you had to go up the stairs into the restaurant, then descend a narrow stairway in the back of the building. Flash pushed his way through the happy-hour pupu crowd, always a giant money-maker. In a competitive market, happy hours draw customers in, selling them drinks at cost or at breakeven. But Brennecke's didn't have any competition. The happy-hour drinks and munchies were sold at premium prices, and the sunburned, happy beach bodies mobbed the place every afternoon starting at about three.

Fred was sitting on a bar stool off in the corner, overseeing the migration of tourist dollars into his bank account. The pounding bass line of "Stayin' Alive" by the Bee Gees animated the crowd, who were laughing, shouting, and singing. Fred spotted Flash and signaled him over, then led the way down the back stairs.

The office wasn't much—one paneled room, no windows. Stacks of documents were neatly placed around a computer terminal. Fred took a seat behind the modest wooden desk and indicated Flash should take the high-backed visitor's seat.

"Do you know Robbie Washburn, Fred?"

"Yeah, I do," said Fred. "Why?"

"Do you know if he has a storage place or garage or some outbuilding where he might go?"

"Yeah, as a matter of fact, he does. He didn't inherit the great house, but he did inherit a cabin over in Waimea Canyon State Park. They hunt wild boar over there, and his grandfather built a small hunting cabin, way off the road. Why?"

"Can you show me where it is?"

Fred drew a map to the cabin on the back of a paper place-mat. "Why do you want to know?"

"The cops say they want to question Robbie. It just crossed my mind he might be holed up somewhere."

"Okay, but wouldn't that have occurred to the cops too? The cabin isn't a secret or anything."

Flash shrugged. "Dunno. They're probably working through their leads, you know, just like you told me, one by one. Say, another thing. Do you know if Peterson had any family, children, ex-wives, whatever?"

Fred considered the question for a moment. "No ex-wives that I've heard about, at least not in the islands. He does have a son, Jason Peterson. He left Kauai and lives on the Big Island, and last I heard, was operating a food truck in Kona. I'm all ears when it comes to news about feeding the tourists. He had a big argument with regulators and the licensing folks, but apparently, he was granted his permit. One thing for sure, though, he and his old man were like oil and water—never got along. He left Kauai on his own when he was eighteen, an angry young man. But I hear he is doing well on the Big Island."

Flash thanked Fred and politely declined another invite to the AA meeting in the park. He walked back to Koloa, where Pika was sitting in his Kauai Cab, parked in front of Surf Shop. Flash jumped into the passenger seat and told Pika he would be tied up for a couple of hours.

"Good. Time is money, boss. We goin' back to Princeville?" Pika grinned.

"Nope, we're driving the other way. Waimea Canyon."

"Better get a jacket, boss. It'll be a lot cooler up there."

"No problem, I'm used to the cold. Let's go." Flash folded his arms across his chest and wondered why he was doing this in the first place. But he knew why. He was settling in, becoming a local. Part of the family. Well, maybe a half-in half-out member of the family. No point in getting carried away.

CHAPTER 25

"Are they hunting boar now?" Boar wasn't exactly part of the picture of Hawaii Flash carried around in his head.

Pika said, "Nah, hunting season's over. If you want to hunt, you'd have to visit a private reserve."

"Good," Flash answered.

"Good? You want to go hunting?" Pika looked over at his passenger.

Flash laughed. "No, good that the hunting season is over. I don't want to be walking in a forest where beer-drinking hunters are wandering around with high-powered rifles, eager to shoot anything that moves. We're looking for a hunting cabin in the Puu Ka Pele Forest Reserve. I've got the approximate location on my iPhone, so just keep driving. This thing says we'll come to a dirt road about ten miles ahead, on the right-hand side. It's just a couple miles past the Lua Reservoir."

"The boar season is February to May. Boar hunting is a big deal. Free pig, ya know?"

Something in Pika's tone put Flash on the alert. "Do you hunt boar?" he asked.

Pika nodded. "Yeah, me and my brother go out. We bag a

couple each year and put up the meat in a freezer. Like I said, free pig. And it's fun. Hunting boar is an ancient Hawaiian tradition, ya know, but now we use guns, not spears."

"So, you don't fancy going after them with a spear?" asked Flash, amused.

"Ah, no, man. Them wild pigs is dangerous. Mean suckers. You really gotta be careful, ya know. They'll come after you. I like to keep my distance. Guns are good. Boom."

Flash's window was open, and he felt the temperature drop as the cab followed the undulating road up and up, through the pine forest and past breathtaking drop-offs. The region was called the Grand Canyon of the Pacific.

Pika kept up a running monologue about his personal history of the area, mainly adventures that he and his family had experienced, including a life-threatening boar attack that had given his grandfather a permanent limp.

Finally, the chill convinced Flash to close his window. "I got an extra jacket in the trunk," said Pika. "You'll want that when we get there."

They found the dirt road, turned right, and continued slowly —painfully slowly. The road was poorly maintained red dirt, narrow, and riddled with potholes, some of which were deep and caused the cab to lurch and bounce. The light was dimming, as well, eventually giving way to darkness.

Abruptly, they stopped at a large boulder at the end of the road. Flash told Pika to stay with the car while he looked for the cabin.

Pika said, "Hey, glad to help you look, boss," as he pulled a jacket out of the trunk for Flash.

"No, let me look around first, then maybe, if I need help, I'll come to get you."

Past the boulder, Flash saw one trail lead up and away to the left, and one went down to the right. He chose the left one and set out walking. He walked for fifteen minutes, stopping every five minutes to listen. Fred's hand-drawn map showed that

Flash was on the right trail, assuming that they had taken the correct dirt road turnoff. Flash decided he'd keep walking for another ten minutes, putting him twenty minutes or so away from the cab.

At the next stop-and-listen, Flash heard faint sounds, music he thought, but he couldn't be sure. He went farther and quickly confirmed that what he heard was music—if you could call grunge music. Farther along, he saw light through the trees, maybe thirty yards ahead. The old hunting cabin.

Leaving the trail, he circled the house at thirty yards' distance, walking a few steps, then looking and waiting a couple of minutes, watching and listening for any sign of life other than the crap music. He repeated the maneuver all the way around the cabin until he was back at the trail.

Still, nothing moved. The only signs of life were the music and the light—several lights—in the log cabin, a structure twenty by thirty feet with a pitched shingle roof.

Flash moved close to a window and looked inside. He could see the back of a rattan couch with flower-print cushions facing a stone fireplace. A man's head was resting on the back of the couch, unmoving, apparently oblivious to the obnoxious music.

Flash scanned the rest of the room and decided to chance it. He moved around to the front of the house and silently ascended three steps onto a raised porch. He slowly approached the front door and gently turned the front doorknob. The door was open. The music was blaring, so Flash pushed in and moved quickly through the entry, crouching low, not wanting to be framed in the opening.

He was tense and felt clumsy. He hadn't done this sort of thing for a long time. He looked around, then moved over to the man on the couch. It was Robbie, all right. Was he asleep, dead, or what?

He touched Robbie's shoulder, hoping to wake him. Nothing. He shook him. "Come on, wake up, wake up. What have you taken?"

Robbie's head and torso slid down onto the couch seat. He was half-sitting, half-lying on his right side. Flash felt the neck for a pulse and felt a faint but steady heartbeat. He exhaled with relief.

Flash searched the living room and the kitchen, where he found the heroin kit he was looking for. Foil, a pink disposable cigarette lighter, a bent spoon, and three hypodermic needles were scattered on a countertop next to the sink. Obviously, the guy wasn't expecting any visitors, was he? The middle of the woods was a safe place to binge.

Flash pulled out his phone and dialed 911. The call failed—no coverage. He looked around for a phone in the cabin. He didn't find one. He was witnessing a probable overdose, so he quickly resettled Robbie on the couch, placing several cushions behind his back and head, so he was lying with his head and chest raised.

Flash left the cabin and ran back to the cab. He told Pika to take the taxi to where he could get phone coverage, call for an ambulance for a possible overdose, then call the Kauai police and tell them that Robbie Washburn had been found.

"I'm going to go sit with him until the cops and ambulance arrive," Flash said. "The cabin is about a quarter of a mile up the trail on the left."

Back at the cabin, Flash sat in a wicker chair, watching the man's face. He had poured a glass of cold water over Robbie's head. The shock had brought him back for a moment, but soon he was out again. Robbie appeared to be in his forties—a white guy with freckles and curly red hair. He was gaunt, his cheekbones showing a two- or three-day stubble. He was wearing a wrinkled, flowered short-sleeve silk shirt and soiled blue Bermuda shorts with no shoes. His hands were small, a girl's hands, with dirty long fingernails, a couple of them broken. His torso was boney, and he was breathing in short, shallow breaths, softly panting.

All Flash could do was watch and wait. He wondered what

he would tell the cops when they arrived. In his other life, the one that had imploded, he hadn't been a particularly impulsive person. He'd thought of himself as a reasoned and rational guy. And yet here he was, a once-rational man sitting in a remote hunting cabin on the side of a mountain on an island in the middle of the Pacific with a zoned-out junkie.

After Robbie was taken to the ambulance, Bob and Kellie did a preliminary search of the cabin while Flash waited to be questioned. Finally, the three of them were standing on the porch, preparing to walk back to the vehicles.

Kellie said, voice strained, "Well, not-a-cop Flash, what the hell are you up to?" She was pissed.

"I heard you were looking for Robbie Washburn. I know a guy who knows lots of people on the island and who knew about the hunting cabin, so I just thought I'd check it out. I was curious—no crime in that. Besides, I didn't really expect that Robbie would be up here. Lucky I came, though. Otherwise, you might have had another corpse to deal with."

"That's bullshit," barked Bob, standing shoulder to shoulder with Kellie. "Who the hell are you, anyway? What were you really doing up here? You got something going on with Robbie? Let me see your arms." Bob reached out and grabbed Flash's hand, slid the jacket sleeve up to examine Flash's inner arm, first his right, then the left, then he pulled Flash's shirt up looking at his stomach.

Flash remained passive. He couldn't blame Bob for being suspicious.

With no obvious track marks on Flash, Bob said, "You could still be his buddy—or maybe an accomplice. Where were you the night Peterson was killed?"

Flash smiled. He couldn't help himself.

Kellie said, "You know, Bob, I have a better idea. We need to interview him at the police station and get a full statement. We have too many unanswered questions about this guy and Robbie. We need to do this carefully, one question at a time. Come on. Let's go, Flash. Get in the cruiser."

For all their growling, they allowed Flash to go over and pay Pika for the ride—round trip, of course.

The session was more interrogation than questioning for the purpose of obtaining a statement. Flash refused to answer questions about his past. They told him they had followed up the red flag on his files and had been referred to the Seattle Police Department.

Yet Kellie and Bob still weren't given any useful information about his identity. The Seattle police chief's administrative assistant returned their call as a courtesy but stonewalled them. The one concession she made was a promise that if the red-flag status was removed, internal affairs would notify the Kauai police. She said she had made a note on the file in question and then abruptly signed off.

That goddamn red flag. Flash was left holding it, and Kellie and Bob were like marauding bulls. They hammered him about the Seattle police, why they might be involved, and why his fingerprints had led to them. Seattle police, Seattle police, Seattle police, over and over again, question after question.

But Flash knew how to protect himself in these situations. "I have nothing to say," "No comment," and "I don't even know what you're talking about," over and over.

At a little after eleven, Flash signed his statement and was excused. He was exhausted, of course, but actually quite satisfied with his performance.

Kellie volunteered to take him back to Koloa, but Flash told her Pika was just a call away and he would prefer Pika's company, even if he had to pay for it.

John Horan prided himself on having a compartmentalized mind. As he imagined it, each compartment was like a steel-walled, watertight section on an ocean liner. He believed he could, at will, move dangerous or disturbing memories out of the open spaces of his psyche into one of these partitions, and by turning a large steel wheel on the door, lock it shut, sealing the stories, memories, and past sins away—if need be, forever.

Once the section was shut, he imagined nothing could get in or out because he was a well-trained soldier, mentally and physically strong, certainly much stronger than anyone he'd ever known. This act of creative imagery was one of John's several means of convincing himself that he wasn't a psychopath.

No, he was an ultra-intelligent, supremely disciplined human being. Simple as that. He was so strong, he could release one of those threatening memories, let it out to wonder over for a while, and then, once aired, return it to its sealed chamber. All it took, all anything took, he believed, was inner strength and determination.

The other thing that set him apart from others was that most people were wimps. Everyone committed unforgivable sins, some much worse than his, but the wimps of the world cratered, and they were inevitably brought to their knees and punished. All the while, he continued to prosper—proof positive of his invincibility.

John saw Flash Michael as one of the wimps. In fact, Flash had turned out to be the perfect wimp. He had not only caved under pressure, but then he panicked and disappeared, gone forever. Even now, seven months after the robbery, if Flash were to come out of hiding, he would be arrested and probably convicted for John's crime. Who could ask for more than that? Once again, John was bulletproof.

John was forty-six now, divorced, and planned to remain a cop for maybe three or four more years, then fake an inheritance or a successful investment, tap into his trust fund, and bail. This was to say he was cruising, biding his time until he would retire, so to speak, with a nine-million-dollar cushion.

Like many older men and women on the cusp of retirement,

he was becoming a creature of habit. Of the many restaurants and bars he could frequent, four or five nights a week he found himself at Vito's, an old Seattle landmark.

John always sat at the far end of the bar on an old wooden bar stool. That evening, he'd settled in with a bourbon on the rocks, then chatted with the bartender and one of the servers, just chilling out. The cop shop had not been particularly taxing. He was a lieutenant, so he told people what to do as opposed to doing the work itself. If you had to work, his was a good job, especially knowing that he didn't need to climb the ladder anymore.

John ordered a second bourbon, and the bartender brought a menu with it, aware that John would order a meal and some wine next. John smiled to himself when he saw the menu, as if he needed one to order. He took a sip of his drink and pulled out his phone to check texts and his Gmail account.

"Jesus," John said under his breath. "Jesus, Jesus, Jesus."

"Something wrong, John?" asked the bartender.

"Ah, just bit of a surprise. You know, I don't think I'm going to have dinner tonight. I have to take care of something. Could you run my tab?" John slid a credit card across, looking over the bartender's shoulder at the mirror behind the bar and the display of reflected light from bottles, glasses, and a red-and-yellow neon Vito's sign on the far wall.

"Well, I hope you get it taken care of, John. Here you go."

John added a tip, hastily signed the tab, and walked out into the rain.

Back in his apartment, he pulled up the email and printed it. He needed to read it carefully and think. With the printed message in hand, he walked over to the couch facing a floor-to-ceiling window with a view of downtown Seattle, the lights and the goddamn rain, wondering what the hell had just happened to him.

. . .

To: John Horan

From: Tilly Good

Subj: Revenge is best served cold

Hello John,

This is me talking to you from beyond the grave. I know you murdered me. It had to be you, or someone hired by you. Of course, I don't know how or where you killed me, but it doesn't matter. I'm dead, and you did it.

Now, John, my death has set off a series of events that start today and end with your smug, cozy existence going right into the shitter.

Way back in the day, when you were debriefing me about the drug scene in Nevada, I remember answering a question about some complicated deal or another. You interrupted me to summarize what you thought I had said. What you repeated back to me pissed me off, because your summary was shit. It wasn't what I'd said at all, so I went on a rant, correcting you. When I was done, your only comment was, "Oh, what a surprise, Tilly Good gets the last word—again."

You were trying to hurt my feelings, and you did. Now it's my turn, John—to hurt your feelings, I mean.

After you enlisted me to do the Neves Bank scam, I realized I might have made a big mistake. A million-dollar payday can do that to a girl. If I followed your instructions and rerouted the money, the way you planned it, I would end up being the one person on the planet who could ruin your life. How long would you, a bent cop, be willing to live with something like that over your head? Not very long, I figured. So while we were planning the heist, I decided to buy some insurance. If for some reason you turned on me, I could use the insurance to protect myself.

The mistake you made was to give me the coded instructions a week before I left for Neves. I took them to a pro, a hacker, and rejigged your instructions to shunt all of the money, the whole ten million, around the world a couple of times, landing it in my offshore account, not yours. Using the instructions you provided me, he traced the path to your supposedly secret trust fund. He then constructed a fake website that recreated your trust fund's look and feel.

This phony site would act and appear exactly like your account. So when you used your codes to access your account, you would be bounced onto my hacker's fake website. On the screen you'd see a balance of nine-million, you'd see fraudulent statements just like the real ones, and you'd feel good. You know, just like Bernie Madoff, all numbers but no real money. I was pretty sure you wouldn't touch any of the money until you were clear of your cop job, but even if you had discovered my deception, I still had the money. Like I said, insurance.

So there you have it. I have all your money. Poor you, literally!

Don't waste too much time feeling sorry for yourself, though, because the clock is ticking.

Take the date you received this email and add thirty days. That's the day all hell breaks loose in your life. The *Seattle Times* will receive a document dump including my full and detailed confession about the theft, an affidavit that accuses you of my murder, along with copies of documents, emails, text streams, phone numbers, and call records—all of it, every incriminating scrap.

And just in case the *Seattle Times* tries a cover-up, complete copies of the package will simultaneously be transmitted to:

The Seattle Police Department, Chief Forsyth, and Internal Affairs,

Interpol's Fraud and Money Laundering Task Force,

The FBI Washington office chief,

and Finnegan Michael.

I saved it all, John, just in case. Plenty of stuff to convict you of fraud, theft, and, if they're willing to do a little footwork, murder.

The files are all locked and loaded, ready to be fired off in thirty days. Getting worried yet? I hope so.

While you ponder what to do next, you might also be curious about all that money. As you know, I'm dead, so ten-million wouldn't do me any good buried in an inaccessible offshore account. But, hey, look at me now! I may be dead, but I'm playing with house funds. Why not put the money out there, somewhere hard to find, but close enough so you might be able to get your hands on it before you're arrested, or not? Just like a treasure hunt, with real treasure.

Here's a hint to get you started, you might look to your old buddy, Flash. Maybe he could help you. Oh, wait a minute, you screwed him over, too, and you don't even know where he is. That's too bad! Could anyone else help you?

No matter what you do, thirty days from now, everyone will know you're a thief and a murderer, and the nasty old world you created will rise up to eat you alive. I'm looking forward to watching you suffer from wherever I may be.

Have fun out there. :)

Tilly Good

John was sitting in the dark. The printout of Tilly's posthumous email, all three pages, lay on the coffee table in front of him.

He said, "Jesus, Tilly, aren't you an unforgiving bitch!"

He stood up, went over to a liquor trolley against the wall, opened a bottle of Wild Turkey 101, poured a good two slugs into a square crystal rocks glass, and returned to the couch and the view. Watching raindrops break up the city lights, he took a big sip, held the glass in both hands, and said to himself, "Looks like I'm going to have to get really sick, fast."

John took another sip, a longer one this time. "Tomorrow. Emergency sick leave, starting tomorrow. Gotta get that money back." He stood, went over to the trolley for the bottle and put it on the table next to the couch, where he could reach it more easily.

CHAPTER 26

"I don't believe it. This is ridiculous—absolutely outrageous. Kellie, what happened?"

"I'm sorry, I can't explain it," Kellie said, shaking her head. "Either way, we've had to disclose it to his lawyer, the jerk from Honolulu, and bingo, Keanu is off the hook. Charges dropped."

After a run and a shower, Flash had joined Mia's morning mafia at Kauai Roasters. That morning, he, Kellie, Emma, and Janet Nakamura were all gathered around an outside table.

Mia shook her head, scowling. As for himself, Flash was pretty sanguine about the missing narcotics. He knew stuff happened in an evidence lockup. Bureaucracy, lots of details, and every now and then stuff got lost.

Mia, however, was practically apoplectic. She looked over at Flash, squinting, and said, "Keanu's free. Now what do we do to protect Paul?"

Perfume from the surrounding gardens hung in the air, competing with smells of coffee and fresh baking. The time was eight a.m., and Emma, dressed in a blue pantsuit, would be leaving soon for her office in Lihue. In uniform now, Kellie would leave to pick up her partner, Bob, by eight-twenty as they needed to report for duty at the station by eight-thirty sharp.

Janet, who was seated next to Mia, put her hand on Mia's arm. "You know, Mia, Keanu was this close to a big boy jail sentence." She held two fingers up a mere inch apart. "That ought to get his attention, no? He's been warned not to go near Paul. So, I think he'll stay clear, I really do. So why don't we all calm down for a minute and try to get back to normal. Is Paul staying home for now?"

Emma nodded. "Yeah, Paul's done a one-eighty, thanks to you, Janet. Oh, and you, too, Flash. Oh, gosh, you guys have been so great. And yeah, I think Keanu will stay away from Paul. As to whether Keanu has learned his lesson…" She shook her head and said, in a quieter voice, "I just don't know."

Kellie said, "Listen, we told Keanu and his lawyer, too, if Keanu even approaches Paul, we'll charge him in a heartbeat. I don't think he wants to return to the correction unit."

Kellie turned to Mia. "We'll be watching him, I promise." Kellie patted Mia's hand with hers, then took a sip of her mocha. She smiled and wiped her mouth with a napkin.

Mia said, "Okay, maybe, okay. But Keanu. I don't like him. And what was that Allen woman doing anyway, hiring the big-shot guy and coming to Keanu's rescue? And drugs, Kellie, what about the drugs? We're not used to illegal drugs here. What's going on with that?"

"Good question," said Flash, watching Kellie to see how she would react. She didn't offer an opinion, however, which for a cop on the case was the right way to go. The more pertinent question for Flash, though, was what were Keanu and Sachiko up to? Maybe he'd do a little reconnoitering at Keanu's house and then drive out to Princeville—just for a look-see.

A cellphone beeped. Kellie picked hers up from the table. "This is Kellie." She bowed her head and pressed the phone tightly against her ear. Something was wrong. She nodded a couple of times, then shook her head slowly and said in a low voice, "Oh, no, okay. I'll pick up Bob, and we'll be right there, fifteen minutes max." Putting her phone in her pocket, she rose and pushed back her chair. "Ah, look, I've got to go. See you all soon."

Mia said, "What is it, Kellie? You look awful."

"A boy, seventeen, dead of an overdose. Found this morning in Nawiliwili Park. I've got to go."

Today was shaping up to be a troubled day in paradise.

Sachiko said, "I'll get the cash." They were seated at a round wooden table in the garden.

Keanu snorted. "You can get twenty grand?"

"Yeah, I can." Sachiko's eyes met Keanu's. *Well*, she thought, *now is as good a time as any.* "My money, so you understand I'm the boss."

"What? Bullshit! This is my deal. I done all the fuckin' work. I'm the boss!"

"Fine, boss. Where are you going to get twenty-thousand dollars?"

Keanu looked stunned. *What an idiot.* She smiled. "Well, where are you going to get the money, big boy?"

He frowned, his lips pressed tight, his hands joined on the table, his biceps moving as he squeezed his fingers. Sachiko could just make out his pulse beneath his tight puka-shell neck-lace. His hair was thick, black, and combed back, shinning in the morning sun. *He certainly cleans up well*, she thought. *Too bad he's such a numbskull.*

"Look, admit it, you can't do this without me. I'm the boss, or you have no deal. Now that we've settled that—"

"No way. I brought this deal to you," he whined.

"No, Keanu. I plucked you out of jail and saved your ass. You weren't ever the boss. You ran the runners. Peterson was the boss. Now I'm going to be the boss, better than Peterson. Like I said, now that we have that settled— Right?" Her black eyes locked on his. "Right?"

"Right," he whispered. "You're the fuckin' boss."

Sachiko smiled. "Good. Now, are you sure it's tomorrow night?"

"Yeah, tomorrow night at eleven, Koloa Landing. But where will you get the money? If I don't give them money, they won't give me the stuff."

She didn't like how he kept asking about the money—she was beginning to wonder how long she could keep him on a leash. She'd need to take her gun along, just in case.

Sachiko would prefer to go herself and leave dipshit home, but if Keanu wasn't with her, the Zodiac guys might freak. They, whoever they were, must know Peterson was dead. So she would have to be convincing and fast on her feet. She had to convince them that she should replace Peterson.

When Minette had told Sachiko that her father was selling the jet, Sachiko had laughed, thinking Minette was kidding. Minette said Touma was raising cash, selling assets because the Village in the Sky project was in trouble. The idea of Touma reducing risk and selling his precious jet was preposterous, totally out of character. Touma's motto was "Be all in, all the time." And now, Minette was telling her Touma was retreating—why?

What would make Touma want to run and hide? Sachiko couldn't imagine, but she realized that whatever was happening to him might soon be happening to her. She needed to protect herself. Touma's retreat might someday mean stopping her allowance, cutting her off entirely. And then what would she do?

Sachiko went to the Central Pacific Bank in Kapaa and opened an account. She chose Central Pacific because the Allen Group banked with First Hawaiian, and she didn't want her father, or Minette for that matter, looking over her shoulder.

The Central Pacific Bank manager was delighted to have Sachiko as a client. She had a steady income because her monthly allowance was dressed up as a salary paid by the Allen Group. She also owned a two-and-a-half-million dollar home and had excellent credit. She was immediately granted a quarter-of-a-million line of credit.

On a lark, she called that drug guy, Paul. She was just curious. How did the drug scene here work? She got him drunk, and Paul spilled his guts. He told her all about Keanu, Peterson, the Zodiac deliveries, runners, the works. How difficult could it be?

When Peterson got topped, Sachiko had decided that if Daddy wouldn't bring her into the family business, she'd help herself. Business was in the genes—she was Touma Allen's daughter. She could go all-in, all the time too. In fact, she might even do it better than Daddy. She would make her own way, all-in, all the time.

Leaning forward in his office chair, Chief Aukai asked Kellie, "What's the latest in the Peterson case?"

"Robbie has taken a plea offer, manslaughter with a five-year minimum. The prosecutor thinks it's the best we can get. He says a murder conviction would be iffy. Robbie's a junkie. He went to Peterson's house to raid the safe. Peterson surprised him, went for a gun. Robbie got to the putter first and whacked him. Manslaughter."

The chief exhaled. "Well, okay." Then he sat up straighter, shook his head, and asked, "What the hell made him think he could get away with robbing Peterson?"

Bob smirked. He said, "Chief, his story is he got an anonymous tip that Peterson would be out until midnight. He'd seen the inside of Peterson's safe before. Robbie, genius that he is, boosted himself with a little coke and went for it. Just like a junky, he blew it. Peterson came back early, and Robbie panicked."

The chief frowned. "Anonymous tip? Who is he kidding?"

Kellie said, "I think he knew who called. But he's afraid to offer up a name. He'd be a sitting duck in prison." The chief nodded, so she continued. "And, if he's afraid, well, that tells me his caller was someone further up the food chain. Someone up the line may have had it in for Peterson. We checked Robbie's telephone records. He did receive a call at seven-ten that evening. The number was a burner phone, though, so that's a dead end unless he coughs up the name, which, now that he's got his deal, is unlikely."

"Okay, okay, we get a conviction, and Robbie goes to prison. He's out of our hair for five years, that's a plus. Let's inform the *Garden Island* and invite them over for an exclusive interview. Kellie—you, me, and what's the new prosecutor's name?"

"O'Clerk, sir. Michael O'Clerk."

"That's right, O'Clerk. The three of us, we'll give them their scoop, and let's hope it tamps down the flames. Oh, and do you have any news about our overdose?"

"Yes, sir—tourists," Kellie said. "The boy's name is Harry Fitzgerald. His parents are Mary and Sam Fitzgerald, from St. Louis, Missouri. They've been here for a week, staying at the Marriott Vacation Club at Kalapaki Beach. The day before yesterday, Mary and Sam signed up for a tour, Waimea Canyon by van, then a helicopter ride, an all-day thing. Harry didn't want to go, said he'd hang out at the resort, swim, boogie board, whatever.

"When they returned that evening, Harry was missing," Kellie continued. "He was found early the next morning. He had been through a recovery program earlier this year. His parents thought he was clean. In fact, as a condition for living at home, he had to agree to be tested. We didn't find any heroin or paraphernalia in his luggage or his room."

Kellie sighed. "We figure he scored at the resort or one of the nearby restaurants or maybe on the beach. We think it's pretty certain that he got the stuff here on the island. His parents are angry. The coroner's preliminary opinion is that the stuff he injected was a mix of heroin and fentanyl, so that's something to worry about. We're trying to keep the parents in the loop about everything we find—a work in progress. They're really pissed that he could get heroin here so easily. They thought he'd be safe on the island."

The chief looked upset. "Couldn't be Robbie. He was in custody at the time, right?"

Kellie said, "Right, he didn't get it from Robbie. At least not directly, Chief."

The chief frowned and took a deep breath. "Did Robbie give us any names other than Peterson?

Kellie said, "No, only Peterson."

"So who's pushing heroin?"

Kellie and Bob shook their heads.

The chief said, "Jesus. We've got a mess here, and it feels like it's getting worse. That poor kid. Those poor parents. This drug mess has spilled over onto the tourist community, the last thing we want! Who's pushing heroin? Who is pushing? We've got to put the squeeze on this!"

Kellie felt the same way. A rising tide of drugs and drug-related crime was terrible news for everyone.

The chief interrupted her thoughts. "Okay, we need to get through this interview with the paper, first. Then I'll need a day to gather some resources for a drug task force. We've got to move on this. You two make the rounds of shelters and halfway houses, call the social services folks to warn everyone about bad heroin on the island. We'll hold an all-hands meeting tomorrow afternoon. One thing for sure, we're going to have to stoop a hell of a lot closer to the ground to find out how the drugs are entering the island and who's pushing them. What am I missing?"

Kellie said, "What about the Fitzgeralds?"

"Assign a community relations person to meet with them. I'd prefer not to be ambushed, especially by the press. Then, we'll have to wait and see what they want to do, won't we?"

CHAPTER 27

S urveillance in paradise? My own cognitive dissonance at work here, thought Flash. He looked at his phone. Time was passing—but slowly. Flash Thornton didn't know much about surveillance, but he'd been forced to learn from Flash Michael. Flash Michael had insisted that Thornton bring a backpack with a foam pad to sit on, a small flashlight, night-vision binoculars, a cellphone, a light jacket, a screw-top coffee mug filled with decaf and cream, and a bottle of water. No beer. Pack, prepare for a long wait, proceed.

Paul had said he thought the Zodiac came every week or ten days. He also said the last shipment had arrived a week previously. Night one of Flash's surveillance had turned up nothing. Night two—nothing. This was night three.

He checked his phone again. Ten-thirty p.m. With no streetlights other than those on the boat ramp at Koloa Landing, the area was dark. The old landing site was now just a deep cut into the shoreline that served as a boat ramp and a staging place for snorkeling, diving trips, and kayakers. The jungle and stone walls on each side of the descending ramp hid the landing site from Ho'onani Road.

Flash's position was concealed by jungle overgrowth on the cut's west side, near the top of a sloping hill. He had an ideal observation point to see the landing and the intersection of the ramp and Ho'onani Road, as well as Hanakaape Bay, off to his right.

He rechecked the phone—eleven p.m. He thought he could hear an outboard engine out in the bay. The engine noise dropped in pitch and volume. They were running dark, no lights.

Flash saw headlights approaching the landing ramp entrance: a Range Rover—probably black—and he couldn't see the plate number from this distance. The SUV moved slowly down the ramp near the water's edge, where the driver extinguished the headlights. Flash turned on his night-vision binoculars, scanned the bay, and saw a green outline of what might have been a Zodiac moving toward the boat launch.

Two green ghosts emerged from the Range Rover and stood facing the bay. One ghost was shorter and smaller than the other. Flash guessed he was looking at Keanu and Sachiko.

The boat, now clearly a Zodiac, moved slowly toward the ramp. A spotlight from the boat lit up the Range Rover and the two figures onshore—Keanu and Sachiko, dressed in black. *What a surprise—not.* The boat pilot cut the engines. The Zodiac appeared to be about twenty-five feet long, probably a Zodiac Pro 750, with the driver's station in the boat's center. Two men were in the boat, the pilot and the crew guy.

The Zodiac slid onto the ramp. Crew guy jumped off the bow, rope in hand. The boat pilot took out a pistol and pointed it toward Sachiko and Keanu as he made his way to the bow, stepped off onto the boat ramp, and walked to meet them.

At that exact moment, another car pulled onto the ramp from Ho'onani Road, flashing high beams as it moved down the ramp and pulled in behind the Land Rover. A man got out from the driver's side, holding a pistol. He moved forward past the Land

Rover. There, he stopped and shouted something, Flash couldn't make out the words.

Pistol still in hand, the boat pilot approached the threesome. All three backed away a step, hands in the air. Sachiko was holding a manila envelope in one hand. After a minute or so, the man from the car put the gun into his belt, and they continued talking. The boat captain gesticulated and moved side to side while he spoke.

The boat captain motioned to his crew guy to join the group in front of the Range Rover. He gave the gun to the crew guy, walked back to the boat, turned off the searchlight, pulled out a phone, and made a call.

Five tense minutes later, the Zodiac pilot turned on the searchlight, returned to the group, reclaimed his pistol, and used it as a pointer as he talked. Flash heard a yell. The car guy was really agitated. He reached for his gun. The boat pilot stepped forward and smacked the car guy on the side of his head with the pistol. Flash winced. The car guy went down like a bag of stones.

The crewman went to the Zodiac and soon returned to the group with a backpack. Car guy was on his feet, bent over and stumbling back to his car, followed by the pilot, who pushed him into the driver's seat and watched as he backed his black Honda Civic into a turn, gunned it up the ramp, and roared out onto the street.

The captain returned to Sachiko, took the envelope, peeked in, and then handed Keanu the backpack. He waved to the crew guy, who was back in the boat, and the spotlight was extinguished. The Range Rover headlights came on, illuminating the Zodiac and its two occupants as it backed away from the ramp.

Flash noticed that the guys on the boat were wearing red waterproof jackets with HH in white letters on the left side of their chests and a patch he couldn't read on the right side. *A kind of uniform?* As the Zodiac turned toward the open ocean, Flash could just make out the name *Invincible* in red letters near the bow.

Soon the Zodiac was lost to the dark, and the Range Rover made a squealing U-turn and sped up the ramp to Ho'onani Road.

Flash packed up his surveillance gear, climbed the hill to the road, and walked back toward Koloa to unpack what he had seen. One thing for sure was that somehow Sachiko was looking like the new Mr. P., at least as far as this shipment was concerned. *How the hell did she pull that off? And where was the Zodiac headed—all the way back to Honolulu, in the dark, or to a larger vessel offshore? The Invincible? We'll see!*

"Oh, John, I'm so sorry to hear about your health. I so wish I could help."

Hannah Alexander was Chief Forsyth's administrative assistant. The chief had volunteered her to navigate the mountain of paperwork necessary to deal with John's emergency transition. John had told Forsyth he had been diagnosed with Stage 3 pancreatic cancer and needed to take leave immediately. He was going to the MD Anderson Cancer Clinic in Houston, leaving in two days.

The chief had been solicitous, seemingly concerned about John. He said he was upset at losing John, even if it was just for a leave of absence. John knew the chief, however, to be a narcissist with an inferiority complex. Losing a senior lieutenant to cancer would be terrible news, not so much that the lieutenant was maybe dying of cancer, but more that he would have the disagreeable experience of breaking in a new lieutenant.

John said, "You can help by fast-tracking the paperwork and arranging for my leave."

John and Hannah were in her office, with the door closed. She was seated behind her desk and had his personnel file open in front of her. Hannah was thirty-something, with straight brown hair cut neck length. Bangs framed her face and liquid brown eyes. She wore very little makeup except for a flesh-tone lipstick and nail polish.

"Of course," she said. "So, are we asking for sick leave or something indefinite? Sorry to ask that. I don't mean to make it seem, well, final."

"Let's go with indefinite. That way I can unlock my pension now in case I need it," he answered.

"Oh, yes, of course. I should have thought of that. Oh, my gosh!" Hannah started to cry.

"What is it?" he asked. Did he have to comfort her, when he was the one in trouble here? Jesus.

"What a year for Captain Forsyth!" Hannah answered. "He loses both of you. I mean you and Flash. Oh my gosh, this will be so hard for him."

Right. Poor Forsyth. Jesus.

Hannah opened a drawer in her desk, pulled out a tissue, blotted her eyes, and blew her nose. "I'm just so sorry. You and Flash."

"Say, Hannah, have you heard anything about Flash?"

She looked up, cocked her head, and said, "Well, not directly, no but— Well, didn't you hear about the fingerprint check?"

"Fingerprint check, what fingerprint check?" *What the hell?*

"I thought you knew. An ID request was made on the FBI fingerprint system. The request was denied because the prints were Flash Michael's. The requesting agency then called and somehow was routed to this office, maybe because we initiated the red flag. In any case, I told them the prints were sealed and not to ask again."

"Who made the request?"

"My goodness. I'm a little surprised you didn't hear about this, John. Anyway, it seems our boy Flash has made an appearance in Hawaii, on the island of Kauai. The request was from the Kauai Police Department. I talked to—let's see, I have it here somewhere."

She flipped several pages in her daily, put her finger in the center of the open page, and continued. "A Sergeant Kellie Jackson. She didn't seem upset that we couldn't give her Flash's identification, just asked me to call her if the flag was removed, very pleasant. So maybe Flash is having a holiday in Hawaii?"

"Maybe he is," said John. "I sure hope all is well with him."

CHAPTER 28

Erebus read the bulletin that crept across the bottom of his CNN news feed: "Heinrich Dietrich Chairman Bank Schaffhausen dead in a traffic accident." Shocked, he immediately went to Google search and found several news outlets running the same story. In a heartbeat, he realized his stay in Nice was at an end. Time to trigger Operation Last Days.

Of course, Dietrich's death was no accident, and of course, Planc was the one who'd had him killed. And for sure, in just a matter of time, Planc's goons would be coming for Erebus, too. They must know he lived in Nice. Dietrich, groveling Dietrich, desperate for Planc's millions, would have told the old bastard. So Erebus would be next. Only he wouldn't make the same conceited mistake Dietrich had. He wouldn't underestimate Planc or his long reach.

In a wave of nostalgia, Erebus remembered his own first assassination, paid assassination anyway, twenty-five years before. He'd lived in Paris at the time and was hired to kill a rogue agent of the French General Directorate for Internal Security, a man who was sharing secrets with the Russian Intelligence Service. Because the agent was politically protected, the powers that be decided assassination was the best way to stop the leaks.

Since that time, Erebus had lived in five cities, using five different identities. To date, he'd killed thirty-four men and two women.

Erebus treated each assignment reverently. Once retained, he would purchase a new black Moleskine sketchbook and label it in indelible white ink on the front cover and the spine. He would collect the mission notes, background, images, data, details, and planning and record them all meticulously and artistically in the journal. He would often make three or four rough drafts before starting the final, carefully hand-printed draft in the Moleskine journal.

When the mission was complete, he would make a final project list of "lessons learned," then retire the journal into his library of death.

The library of death currently consisted of twenty-eight volumes. *Operation Last Days* would be the final journal. He imagined he would use the library as a reference for a magnum opus about his life as a killer. He envisioned the manuscript being discovered right after his death and becoming a world-wide bestseller.

Last Days was the mission to end all murder missions, and naturally it must culminate with his own death. Well, at least that's what it would look like to the world at large. Another man, a different man, would rise out of ashes created by Erebus's catastrophic demise and quietly wade into the slow-moving river of modestly wealthy Europeans living in Switzerland.

Two weeks later, Erebus arrived at his apartment in Bern, on Kramgasse in the old city. He thought he might live there for the rest of his life. Switzerland was a perfect home base for travel and civilized living. Of course, the occupant of the apartment wasn't known as Zigfrids Erebus but rather Helmut Frone, a retired book dealer who had moved in five years prior and had been mostly absent because of extensive travel. Once Operation Last Days was completed, Zigfrids Erebus would be a ghost, gone forever, having been violently excised from the face of the earth.

Erebus sat at an antique desk in a Philippe Starck chair, looking down four stories at revelers walking through the twilight on Kramgasse. He opened the project journal to a new page and printed "Target(s)" at the top of the page. He then drew two rectangular boxes side by side in the middle of the page. In the first box, he carefully printed "Michel Planc," and in the second, he printed "Malcolm Haysmith."

These two men had pride of place. After they were taken off the board, no one could tie Erebus to the LM Global and Banc Schaffhausen fiasco. In the bottom right-hand corner of the page, he printed the names John Horan, Malcolm Forsyth, and Flash Finnegan Michael, each name followed by a small question mark.

Before going to bed that first night back in Bern, Erebus sent an email to his dark world hacker, Bingwen. Knowing that the hacker's fees would be outrageous, he nonetheless asked for an update on his research into the Seattle cops and a deep dive on Michel Planc and Malcolm Haysmith.

Information was power, and secret information was gold. Erebus's targets had plenty of money to plunder, so in the end, they might well end up paying for their own murders—and then some. Additionally, he might have a chance at the missing ten million. Lots to think about.

Malcolm Haysmith was repelled by the image of Michel Planc, glowering out at him from the video screen. Seeing him on the monitor was almost as bad as being in the same room with him.

Planc shouted, "What the fuck? Four or five years? Why wait? No, sell off the first building as soon as it's fit for occupancy, late next year. Then the next, then the next, as they come online. With four goddamn buildings to build, why wait until they're all built before selling? That could take five years! Crazy! We need that money to move."

"I'm sorry, sir, but he may have a point. The agreement specifies 'project completion,' not individual building completion."

"Haysmith! Haysmith! You aren't listening to me," the old man barked. "I couldn't care less about what the agreement says. That agreement is to protect us, not him, you imbecile! You go over to his office, shut the door, and grab that little fucker by the balls and make him see reason. We aren't waiting five years to sell. We're going to sell as the buildings are complete. That money must start to move, and soon."

Haysmith sighed, transfixed by Planc's demonic face. The old man must have bent in closer to the camera because the video screen was filled with two old, wrinkled, and bloodshot eyes, plus a big nose and angry lips yelling at him.

"Haysmith, are you listening to me?"

"Yes, sir. Yes, yes, I am. But—"

"No *but*, Haysmith! Do it!"

The screen went blank. Haysmith leaned back in his office chair, then swung toward the view of Waikiki Beach below. He had leased two units side by side in an upscale condominium tower called Trade Winds. He'd renovated them to make one large unit, incorporating his private living space and an adjoining office. The living space included a living room, two bathrooms, a kitchen, and two bedrooms, all furnished in a tropical pastiche in shades of coral blue and greens.

The office suite consisted of an executive office, a meeting room, and a reception area. He'd signed a five-year lease with first right of refusal on another five years.

In his mind, he would live there after the Village in the Sky project was sold and off the books. By then, he would be a multimillionaire, and with luck, he'd quietly drift away from that maniac Planc. *Out of sight, out of mind, you bastard.*

On a side table in his office was a scale model of the entire project. He stood up and walked over to it. Tiny palm trees lined a black road, Island Drive, while a green, grassy area ran down to a sandy beach abutting the blue ocean. Haysmith would love to plant himself on that beach forever, not a worry in the world.

He returned to his desk and pushed the Touma button, which was connected to the Allen Group office across town.

A woman's face appeared on the screen. "How can we help you, Mr. Haysmith?"

"Put Touma on, will you?"

"One moment." She disappeared.

Touma's jovial face came into view, the perpetual smile in full force. "Yes, Malcolm, what is it?"

"Touma, we're going to have to reshuffle the marketing and sales strategy."

"Oh? Why's that?"

"I've just received a zinger from on high. We need to sell each building as it's completed, as opposed to waiting until the project itself is complete." Haysmith waited for the eruption, forcing himself to appear calm.

Touma opened his mouth to speak, then abruptly shut it. After a moment he said, "That's not what our agreement says, Malcolm. We've spent a fortune on developing the marketing and sales program. It's in the can. We can't change it now."

"I'm not offering you options, here, Touma. Tell those assholes at the marketing firm to get to work. We'll have a building to sell as soon as Tower One is ready for occupancy."

Touma didn't look happy. "And what if I sue you?"

"We'll stop financing you. We'll take our money and walk, you idiot! You, Touma, will be left holding the bag. Then we'll countersue you for all you're worth. That's what will happen."

Haysmith ended the meeting with a click and sagged into his seat, exasperated.

He stood up and walked toward the window behind his desk. Two nut cases, with him in the middle. He took in a deep breath, then moved over to a credenza beneath a large, framed

Pegge Hopper painting of a Hawaiian princess in a purple jump-suit, seated cross-legged and looking out into the room.

Haysmith opened the cabinet, took out a bottle of MacAllen Rare Cask Single Malt and a crystal sipping glass. He looked into the painted princess's eyes for a moment, then poured himself a generous three fingers of scotch. After one long draw, he took another, exhaled, and returned the empty glass to the credenza. He wondered if he would live to see the end of this project. *Can I really survive four or five years of this?*

He'd scored big on bribes from his handpicked contractors, almost four-million in total. He was skimming at least a hundred-thousand a month by padding invoices for the over-head fees, ostensibly to cover two accountants in Touma's office, the lease of his office and apartment, and other hidden or imaginary costs. So far, he'd accumulated a half-million that way. By the time the first building was sold out, he'd have amassed four to four-and-a-half-million, tax free. That plus the income from another sideline or two. Was that enough to get out early?

How could he and his money break away from Planc? That was the real question. Planc may have once appeared to be the golden goose, but now, after just six months, Haysmith felt he would be pecked to death before getting away with his money.

The scotch was easing his anxiety. He returned to his chair, turned away from his desk, and zoned out, soaking in the beach view, rolling waves, surfers, and palm trees along Waikiki. God, he loved this place. Still, he had to do something about Planc, and soon. It was only a matter of time before the old man was going to push Touma so hard that he would turn on Haysmith and sue Sixty-Four Capital for breach of contract. The money would stop, the city would counter by filing lawsuits against everybody, years of investigations would follow, and Haysmith would lose everything, including, very likely, his life.

Finally acknowledging the likelihood of his own demise, he suddenly considered that he had other options, *outside-the-box* options, as the North American business bullshit machine would put it. Outside the box.

Fifteen minutes later, he awoke from his reverie, reached for a yellow post-it note and a Bic pen and wrote "Z Erebus" on the note, which he carefully placed on top of his desk.

Flash thought the tropical sun must be getting to him. He was imagining himself as Robert Louis Stevenson, who he knew had visited Hawaii, spending the last part of his life in the South Pacific. Flash saw himself in some imaginary upper room, with a fan turning overhead, writing about his friends King Kalākaua, or Princess Victoria Kaiulani, the last heir apparent to the Hawaiian kingdom's throne.

Very romantic, very un-Flash-like too, but still, here he was in the tropics, sort of like Robert Louis Stevenson, seated at his wooden table painted turquoise, which had been purchased at the Goodwill as a desk for his new computer. The table was one of several carefully selected recycled accouterments he'd added to his digs in Apartment B. He'd bought three lamps, a beanbag chair in a floral print, and four small, framed watercolors by a local artist depicting the old sugar mill, Brennecke's Beach, Jump Cliff, and an old funky house he knew to be close to Poipu Beach State Park. Thrift-store chic.

It was midday, and the sun was high. The window was open, and the scent of plumeria, gardenia, and ginger permeated the room. Flash had prepared a list of research items and decided to do a deep Google dive into each, one by one, then spread out from there.

LM Global. He knew a lot about them. He'd been on the team that had selected them for the sting that had led to his present circumstances.

Sixty-Four Capital of the Grand Caymans LTD. He knew nothing about them or their managing director, Malcolm

Haysmith, other than that their name was on the masthead as the funding organization for the Village in the Sky.

The Allen Group. They were the developers of the Village in the Sky, whose managing director was Sachiko Allen's father, Touma Allen.

Invincible. A yacht or working vessel registered under that name—but who owned it?

Bank Schaffhausen and Heinrich Dietrich. What had happened there? And what had happened when the ten-million dollars disappeared?

Later that afternoon Flash was thinking about Brennecke's Kalua pork burger. But first, he decided to see what Touma Allen and Malcolm Haysmith had to say for themselves.

He made up a cover story: that he was a freelance journalist pitching an article about the Village in the Sky development to the international press,—*Barron's, The Wall Street Journal,* and *The Economist.* He would appreciate ten or fifteen minutes as background to assess whether they had a story to tell or not.

His strategy worked—both men bit, agreeing to telephone interviews.

Malcolm Haysmith was a very British chartered accountant who'd attended Oxford and the London Business School. He said he had been managing director of other large projects, though he was unwilling to name any of them as "a matter of confidentiality." He seemed humorless, a bit abrupt, and uptight —especially about his own history, except for Oxford and the London Business School.

Haysmith had been willing to answer questions about the project itself, though he had flatly refused to discuss details about Sixty-Four Capital or his backers other than to say that they had met all of the city's requirements and had been fully vetted and approved to fund the project.

Haysmith had ended the interview by simply saying, "That's all I have to offer you and your readers. Good day."

Touma Allen was a loquacious, upbeat promoter, a pleaser, a

vigorous salesman. He acknowledged the project was substantially bigger than any he had attempted before and was happy to share the story of his meteoric success. He spoke warmly about his COO Benjamin Akamu and CFO Minette Hale. In a solicitous tone, he had recommended that any questions about his partners at Sixty-Four Capital should be directed to Haysmith.

Touma had recounted a harrowing series of events, including the sudden death of one of his backers, which somehow had led him to Malcolm Haysmith.

Hearing that the dead banker's name was Heinrich Dietrich, Flash, burner phone at his ear, pumped his fist in the air. He'd found a connection to the bastards.

When asked whether Sachiko was a member of his project team, Touma had said she was concentrating on her real estate interests on Kauai. And, in answer to the final question, he didn't own a yacht named *Invincible*, but his friend Bart Singleton III, chairman of the Hawaii Board of Trade, owned a ninety-seven-foot yacht by that name.

Curiouser and curiouser. Flash hadn't heard about Dietrich's death. He sure as hell knew about Banc Schaffhausen and their relationship with LM Global, though. As for Michel Planc, well, he was the guy they'd been after in the sting operation. Planc was the biggest bastard of them all.

Flash needed to do further research. Zurich to Grand Caymans to Honolulu to Kauai. *Go figure!*

CHAPTER 29

lash and Minette Hale, were having lunch at the Scratch Kitchen on Auahi Street in the Ala Moana district. Flash had flown to Honolulu from Kauai the night before and checked into the Embassy Suites Waikiki, settling in for a three- or four-day reconnoiter.

"Here we are, blackened ahi salad for the lady, and classic loco moco for the gentleman. Can I get you anything else?"

"No beer?" Flash asked the waiter. His food looked preposterously inviting—the best meal he'd faced in months—but a primo beer would really hit the spot.

"No, sir, sorry, no alcohol. We serve four different types of bottled water and, of course, our famous lemonade."

Minette was a striking woman, almost six feet tall, with shoulder-length blonde hair, and straight bangs across her forehead over blue eyes. Her light-brown skin had no wrinkles, even when she smiled. She carried herself like an athlete or a dancer, and was dressed in a pale-orange linen pantsuit and a collarless white blouse.

Minette's hands moved while she talked, and Flash's eyes were drawn to her red Apple watch on one wrist and two gold hoop bracelets on the other. Her contralto voice was smooth, and she spoke with the cadence of a person used to explaining details, abstractions—like an accomplished teacher.

"Thank you. We'll have two lemonades, please," said Minette, watching as the server moved away from their table. Turning toward Flash, she added, "Sorry about the beer, but the lemonade is justifiably famous, so you need to try it. I like this place because everything is made fresh, from mostly local ingredients. And, as you probably noticed, they specialize in comfort food. Food to soothe the inner beast." She took her napkin from the table, unfolded it, and placed it in her lap.

He raised his eyebrows. "How should I interpret your choosing ahi salad then, as opposed to, say, pork bellies, sausage, and grits?"

She smiled. "Oh, well, I never do pork bellies at a business lunch."

"Really." He couldn't help but smile in turn.

She lifted her fork and said, "Yes, really. It's a rule." The smile broadened.

He could have sworn her eyes flashed. "Well, good to know! I, on the other hand, always go for the pork bellies at business lunches! It's liberating to exercise my inner capitalist pig in public."

They both laughed. Flash was surprised to find that he liked Minette—he wasn't naturally attracted to accounting types. "How did you come to be working for Touma?"

"I was on the fast track toward making partner at Deloitte. They called it the fast track, but it felt more like a slow moving, very rickety escalator, from which, the higher they went, women seemed to disappear. Don't get me wrong, they were pretty accommodating and conscientious about expressing politically correct views about gender bias, but, well, let's just say I wasn't patient enough to see if I could make it all the way up to partner heaven—alive, that is."

She continued, "Touma was a client, had been since his early house-building days. I told him once that he needed a much more robust financial infrastructure to succeed. At the time, his so-called finance department consisted of a bookkeeper and a part-time payroll and accounts-payable clerk. That was it! I meant it as simple advice. He considered my suggestion and made me an offer I couldn't refuse." There came that smile again.

"My mission then, as it is now, was to create a tough and reliable business and financial structure to support Touma's ever-expanding vision. And, with one possible hitch, my time here has been a great ride. We're above water on our balance sheet. We've built a lot of successful smaller projects and assembled a tightly woven operating team. I'm very proud of what we've done. Touma, Benjamin, and I have been through a lot. Our reputation was one of the main reasons we were awarded the permit to build the Village in the Sky."

She picked up her fork again and said, with a flick of her wrist, "Enough about me. How did you become a business journalist?"

Flash laughed. "I went to Wharton and received a degree in finance only to discover I like thinking and writing about business more than I like doing business."

"And?" She put a dollop of wasabi on her fork, skewered a slice of rare ahi, and ate the result.

"And here I am interviewing you and Touma and maybe Haysmith. What is it with Haysmith, by the way?"

"Yes, Mr. Haysmith— Well, look, this would have to be off the record, right?" She looked at him, waiting for him to answer.

He nodded and said, "Okay, off the record."

Minette began, "Haysmith, well..." She put her fork down on the edge of her salad bowl, grimaced, then said, "I know we have a lot to learn about working in the big leagues. This is really big money. But working with Haysmith makes me feel as though we're attempting to do a high-wire act, wearing a strait-jacket and a blindfold, with no net to catch us if we fall. We can only move when he says move, and we stop when he says stop." The words seemed to be pouring out of her.

"We can't choose contractors, service providers, or vendors. We can't spend money or receive money without his explicit permission, item by item. They—Haysmith and the two rent-a-cop accountants he's embedded in our office—are making all of the decisions, and we have to somehow work with those decisions. In short, Haysmith has turned day-to-day operations into a torturous experience. Also it doesn't help that he's rude and insufferably high-handed. And, watching him operate, well, I'm positive he's never run a project like this in his life, no matter what he tells the world. So when it comes to our financing partners, I'm worried. But—" She held her hand out as if to stop Flash from saying anything. "But in spite of it all, we're moving forward and doing our best."

"Do you know why he won't talk to me?" Flash asked.

Minette smiled and shook her head. "No, but it doesn't surprise me. The idea of you writing an article that puts a spotlight on him or Sixty-Four Capital probably makes him very uncomfortable—he's all about secrecy and control."

Flash nodded. "So can you think of a back door I could use to dig out more information or gossip about him or this Sixty-Four Capital, maybe, or friends if he has any?"

"No, sorry, but come on, Flash! You're the journalist. Do your job!"

Flash thought, *Duh, what was I expecting her to say?*

"Look, I've got my hands full just trying to cope with him and his minions. I don't know what working for the Mafia is like, but— Well, you get my drift."

Flash did know what working with the Mafia was like. He wanted to ask her if she thought Sixty-Four Capital was a Mafia front but then thought the better of it. He was a journalist writing a promotional piece about a glitzy development project in Hawaii, not a cop investigating organized crime. He scooped up the last forkful of gravy-soaked rice, ate it, wiped his mouth slowly, and put the spent napkin next to his water glass. "Does the name Michel Planc ring any bells?"

Minette had finished her salad and was leaning back in her chair. She said, "Yes, vaguely. Touma mentioned him. He's a big money guy, in Zurich, I think. He was to be a principal investor in Banc Schaffhausen's investment fund. When Dietrich died, Banc Schaffhausen and the fund disappeared, then Haysmith showed up, and like magic, the deal was back on. Anyway, I don't know if Planc is still involved or not."

"Did you do any research on Planc when you were lining things up with Banc Schaffhausen?"

"No, I didn't. But I'll bet Touma knows more because he and Bart Singleton are best buddies, and Bart was the one who introduced him to Heinrich Dietrich."

Singleton, the owner of the yacht. Of course.

Flash said, "Thanks, this has been a big help, on the record and off. I'm staying at the Embassy Suites Waikiki for a couple of days, in case you think of anything else. Just give me a call and I can meet you wherever."

Flash looked around to find their server. Not seeing him, he turned back to Minette and said, "Oh, one other thing? I understand Touma's daughter Sachiko isn't working with you and her dad. Is that right?"

Minette looked surprised. "That's right. She's learning how to grow up on Kauai—that's what she's doing."

"You don't get along with her?"

For the first time, Minette seemed to pull back. "Oh, we get along okay. It's just that Sachiko has been spoiled since birth. I actually feel sorry for her—most of the time."

Spotting their server, Flash gestured for the check. "Be sure to thank Touma for me, would you? With what I've got so far, I think the Allen Group deserves lots of credit for putting together the Village in the Sky. It's innovative and interesting, and a newsworthy project." He felt a twinge of guilt at the lie.

Minette nodded her head. "Excellent. We appreciate all good

publicity. If I can do anything more, just call. Also, I'm glad to have met you, Flash."

That smile again. She just kept zapping him with brains and charm, over and over. She was amazing.

"Say, Flash this is a little off the wall, but I can't help myself."

Flash felt his face warm. Was there some kind of invitation under her "off the wall" remark? Was he up for it?

"Have you ever been a cop?"

That brought him back down to earth.

"You're a good questioner. You're good at it more than most reporters I've met. I've known a couple of cops, and well—just wondered."

Flash chuckled. "Nope, never been a cop. Although I do get asked that a lot." He smiled at her, holding eye contact until she looked away.

"Oh, well," she said, "so much for female intuition. Thanks for lunch, Flash. Who knows—if business journalism becomes tedious, maybe you have another career waiting for you? Sorting out the crooks from the good guys, promoting law and order, maybe wearing a snappy uniform? Oh, wait—no, you don't look like the uniform type. Maybe a trench coat and a Sam Spade hat."

Minette giggled. Moving away from the table, heading for the door, she turned back and said, "Send me a draft of the article when you're ready to publish. Before you publish. Would you do that?"

He nodded cheerfully. "Yes, of course, I'll send you draft—before we publish."

CHAPTER 30

lash left the Scratch Kitchen and headed for the Waikiki Yacht Club, where the *Invincible* was moored. He'd found an advertisement on the internet for a Hatteras M60 yacht, a bargain, or so the notice suggested, selling for just north of three-million dollars. It, too, was moored at the Waikiki Yacht Club. Flash had called the broker and made an appointment to view the yacht at one-thirty.

Bartholomew Singleton III was a scion of the Singleton sugar fortune, and as such, sat atop heaps of third-generation, white colonialist money. The wealth alone would have made him a Honolulu big shot, a much bigger big shot than Touma Allen. Flash was surprised, though, that Bart was Touma's ex-wife's husband, while apparently remaining Touma's good friend. Go figure. *Pretty incestuous,* thought Flash.

But for all his fame and fortune, Bart was an enigma, and his proximity to everything going on only generated questions: Why would he be a drug czar if he was so rich? How did Touma fit into the drug business, or did he? Were Bart and Touma partners? Was Touma using Bart's Zodiac for the deliveries under some false pretense? The Zodiac Flash had seen the other night was plenty big enough to pound its way across the sixty miles of open ocean between Oahu and Kauai in about two hours, easy, if the seas weren't too rough. Flash needed to make sense of all this, and what better place to start than the giant, black-hulled *Invincible*?

In the yacht club's main building, the receptionist checked Flash's name off on a visitor's list, then gave him a visitor's pass and a glossy brochure about the yacht club. She explained that they were always looking for new members, and while he was inquiring about the Hatteras, he might want to look around the club too.

Flash had lots of sailing experience, but all of it on other people's boats. When work allowed, when he wasn't under-cover, he was a regular crew member on a sixty-foot Grand Soleil racing in and around Puget Sound. He liked the boat scene—easygoing, lots of money, and lots of rules.

Leaving the reception area, he walked through the large trop-ical-themed dining room and out toward the end of one of four long piers that constituted the marina, where he spotted the great white Hatteras and a waiting salesman. The forty-five-minute show-and-tell with the salesman was pleasant enough. Flash was genial, pleasant, and let the salesman down easily; he wasn't buying today, just shopping.

Their conversation turned to the logistics of owning a large yacht—moorage, the crew needed for a boat like the Hatteras, as compared to something bigger, like the *Invincible*. The salesman mentioned that he knew a couple of guys on the *Invincible* and that if she was going out that afternoon, one or two of the crew members might be found in the bar.

Flash went back to the main building, into the bar. A folding wall of wood-framed windows, when pushed to one side, created a large indoor/outdoor space. The bar itself was draped in signal flags, brass fittings, and black-and-white photos of yachts. The time was three-fifteen—the lunch crowd was mostly gone, and the cocktail hour had yet to begin. One solitary drinker, perched on a barstool off to one side, was reading a newspaper and nursing a beer. He was wearing a red polo shirt, blue Bermuda shorts, and blue dock shoes with white socks.

Flash moved up to the bar, sat one stool away, and ordered a Foster's draft and a basket of popcorn.

"Any good news in the paper today?" asked Flash.

The man looked up from his paper and said, "Hell yes, we live in paradise, don't you know that?"

He was in his early fifties, his face an open collection of weathered wrinkles, rugged and tanned. His graying brown hair was parted on the side like a 1950s TV character. "*Invincible*" was stitched in white on his shirt.

"You part of the *Invincible* crew?"

"Yes, sir, first mate."

"How long you been aboard?"

The first mate smiled. "Four years."

"Good life?" asked Flash.

"The best—our owner's a really good guy, and everything about the *Invincible* is first-class, stem to stern. The boat's busy enough to make the job interesting, but not so busy that it's a pain in the ass. Best gig I've had so far."

"How long have you been crewing?"

"Twenty-three years, and no thought of retirement."

"Does the owner rent the boat out, like if I wanted to do a cruise with say, ten people, would *Invincible* be available?"

"Oh, no, Mr. Singleton doesn't do that. He actually keeps us pretty busy entertaining his own clients and customers, and then the family. They use it a lot too."

"You have a tender?"

"Yup, a big Zodiac, twenty-five feet, top of the line. Like I said, first-class."

"Can I buy you another beer? My name is Flash, by the way." Flash held his hand out to shake.

"I'm Dom, short for Dominic." He shook Flash's hand, his grip rough and calloused. "Nice to meet you, too, Flash. No thanks on the beer, though, I'm good. We're going out later, so I've got to keep my wits about me."

"Dinner cruise?"

"Yeah, sort of." Dom went back to reading his newspaper.

"Where do you cruise around here, like this evening?"

"Well, the ocean is calm, so maybe to Kauai and back."

"Sounds nice. How long would that take?"

"Oh, well, we'll leave at eighteen hundred hours, be back here around zero one hundred or so. The guests have their party, then sleep on the boat. We serve them breakfast in the morning, and they'll disembark late morning, early afternoon tomorrow."

"Sounds very luxurious, no worry about drinking and driving."

"That's it, they do the drinking, and we do the driving. Nothing but first-class. Our guests are the cream of the crop socially—important businesspeople, politicians."

"How many guests are you expecting this evening?"

"Last I saw we'll have fifteen guests, that's a good size. Small enough so people don't get lost, big enough to have a real party.

"Sounds like a lot of fun for the guests. Drive carefully," said Flash.

The first mate chuckled and said, "Yeah, you too." He returned to his reading.

The guy didn't seem like a thug, a dope-dispensing slime-ball, or even a heavy. He definitely wasn't one of the two men Flash had seen at Koloa Landing. Maybe he was just what he looked like, a hardworking first mate on a private yacht, keeping his head down and minding his own business. Possibly Dom didn't even know what transpired ashore at the landing. Maybe. Maybe. Exiting the yacht club, Flash had Malcolm Haysmith in mind. He needed to get a beat on Haysmith, perhaps approach him again on neutral turf. A pretty good bet Haysmith didn't cook for himself, so step one was to watch until the Brit left the building, probably to have dinner or whatever, then Flash would decide what to do next.

Walking away from the yacht club, Flash had Malcolm Haysmith in mind. He needed to get a beat on Haysmith, maybe approach him again on neutral turf. Flash made his way to a park on the other side of the marina. At the back of the park was a Starbucks, where he bought a large iced coffee and a *New York Times*. Outside, he installed himself on a park bench that presented a convenient vantage point—he could see the *Invincible* on his right and the entrance to Malcolm Haysmith's condominium tower on his left.

Flash guessed he could just hang out and wait for Haysmith to leave the building for dinner, a drink, or even a late afternoon walk. An hour later, in fact, Haysmith emerged.

Flash watched Haysmith walk along Holomoana Street toward the Harbor Pub. *Where else would he go for dinner?* Flash thought. *Relocated Brit eats at a pub, what a surprise!* He sat watching until the overweight figure pulled open the large wooden door of the pub and disappeared inside.

Flash waited a moment, then took out his phone, and called Haysmith's office.

A woman answered, "Sixty-Four Capital, how may I help you?"

"This is Flash Tucker, I'm the journalist who is writing an article about the Village in the Sky. Mr. Haysmith may have mentioned me to you? He said I could have a tour of your office as background for my article, and as luck would have it, I am nearby. Could I come up now?"

"I'm sorry, Mr. Tucker, Mr. Haysmith is out of the office."

"Who am I talking to?"

"Fiona, Fiona Ryan. I'm Mr. Haysmith's personal assistant."

"Fiona, could you just give me ten minutes and a quick walk-through? It would be a great help. You see, I'm flying out this evening on assignment and don't know when I'll get another chance to see your digs."

After a long pause, she said, "I guess, if Mr. Haysmith promised it, I don't see any reason not to, although I don't think you'll find it very interesting. The offices aren't much to see."

Five minutes later, the building concierge buzzed Flash in and directed him to an elevator, which took him up to twenty-four. The floor consisted of four units, three of which were residences. Flash walked to a backlit glass-embossed sign: Sixty-Four Capital of the Grand Caymans LTD, Malcolm Haysmith, Managing Partner. Flash pressed the doorbell, and a second later, the door buzzed and opened. Inside, seated at a receptionist desk, was a young woman in probably her late twenties.

She stood and said, "Mr. Tucker," and extended her hand.

Flash shook it once, then let go. "I can't thank you enough for this. I'm close to my deadline, and this the last bit I needed, just some visual idea of your offices. Here, here's my card." He half bowed, handed the card to her, and unleashed his warmest smile.

Fiona was a trim young woman, with henna-colored hair cut short, parted on one side, and gray eyes. She was wearing a white raw silk shirt tucked into charcoal-gray slacks, black loafers, and an expensive-looking scarf around her neck. She smiled. "Nice to meet you, Mr. Tucker. As you can see, this is the reception area."

She led him to the door behind her desk and walked through. "As I said on the phone, we don't have much to see. Here on the left is Mr. Haysmith's office, and over there on the right is our conference room and a storage area, beyond. Mr. Haysmith's residence is next to this unit. He has a door from his office into the residence." She unlocked and opened the door and held out her hand into his office. "You can stick your head in, but please stay out here in the hall. Mr. Haysmith would be upset if he thought you were in his office while he was gone. He is a very private person."

"Do you know why?"

"No, other than Mr. Haysmith has a critical position, managing director." She closed Haysmith's office door, locked it, and led Flash down a short hallway into the conference room. Both the office and conference room had stunning views, with large windows looking out along Waikiki Beach.

"And so what is your role in the Village in the Sky Project, Fiona?"

She looked puzzled, thought for a moment, then said, "Well, no direct role, really. I am Mr. Haysmith's PA. I support him. He has others working on the project, Mr. Touma and his people, and our two accounting administrators. They are all located over in Mr. Allen's office. Have you been there?"

"Yes," said Flash, taking a seat in one of the conference room chairs. "I spent the morning there—nice digs."

He was about to ask her if Michel Planc ever visited the office when an electronic bong sounded from somewhere, like a doorbell.

Fiona looked out toward the reception area and said, "Just a moment, please."

She was walking toward the door when Malcolm Haysmith walked in. He stopped, eyes bulging, and barked at Flash, "Who the hell are you?" Looking back to his PA, he said, "Fiona, what the hell is this man doing here?"

Flash rose from the chair, moved forward, and extended his hand. "Mr. Haysmith, I'm Flash Tucker, we've talked on the phone a couple of times. I was just getting a brief tour of your offices for my article."

Haysmith's cheeks were blue-veined and flushed red. He squinted and said, "Get out of my office immediately, or I'll call the police. You have no business being here. Get out!"

Fiona, looking alarmed, said, "I'm sorry, Mr. Haysmith, I understood you had invited him to visit."

"No, I did not invite him, now get out. Get out now!" Haysmith reached out to grab Flash's arm.

Flash moved out of reach. "That would be a big mistake, Haysmith, a very big mistake." Flash squinted, imagining just for a second driving his fist into the chubby man's fleshy face. "I can find the door myself." He turned to Fiona and said, "Sorry, Fiona, I guess I misunderstood Mr. Haysmith's invitation—my bad."

CHAPTER 31

Heart rate still elevated, focus narrowed, Flash made his way back to the park, where he reclaimed his perch. Looking out over the riot of boats arrayed near the yacht club, he spotted the *Invincible*, outlined by hundreds of white LED lights, as the yacht maneuvered away from its moorage. Were they—whoever they were—delivering the drugs or doing a dinner cruise? Or both? Was Singletary onboard? Was Touma on board? Flash looked back at the dock; the Zodiac's mooring space was empty, so it must be tucked in aboard the mother ship.

He pulled out his cellphone and put the phone to his ear.

"Hey, Kellie. Flash."

"Flash, hi. What's up?" She sounded a little suspicious.

Flash realized he'd made the call mostly on impulse. It might have been a mistake. Sure, Kellie was suspicious—fingerprints and the red flag, mystery man and all, who wouldn't be? But he had wanted to warn her that a load of drugs might be coming her way. How could he tell her without opening a Pandora's box? And what if *Invincible* was really just out for a dinner cruise?

"Hello, Flash, what's up?"

"Yeah, I'm here. How about lunch at Roy's, say, day after tomorrow, you and Bob?"

"Well, let me check my busy social calendar. Oh, look, I'm free. So, sure. I'll check with Bob. What's the occasion?"

"I have something I'd like to talk to you both about."

"Is this a prelude to your confession, coming clean with your erstwhile friends, or what?"

"No, no, no, just some information I think might help you guys, that's all. Pick me up at noon Thursday, then?"

"Sure, you buying?"

"Yup."

"Anything else?"

"Nope, see ya."

Jesus, what was I thinking? Just as he ended the call, his phone began vibrating—Fiona Ryan was calling him.

"Flash Tucker."

"Well, you're a right jerk, aren't ya!"

"What?"

"You damn near got me fired, you jerk. I hope you're proud of yourself! You lied to me, and I came within a hair's breadth of being unemployed, thanks to you!"

"Really? Would he really fire you? I mean, you didn't do anything wrong."

"Easy for you to say. He thinks you're some kind of evil person, and like I explained, he's crazy secretive. So he told me, shouted at me, if I ever cause him any aggro again, he'll fire me on the spot, my first and last warning."

Flash smiled. She might be better off if Haysmith *had* fired her, safer at least. No telling what might happen to innocent bystanders if the lowlifes Haysmith likely hung out with came out of the woodwork.

"Look, I'm sorry. I really didn't mean to get you in trouble. I just wanted to see the offices for the article, simple as that," Flash said. This was hardly the moment to tell her to run.

"This is the best job I've ever had—good pay, benefits, and

easy-peasy because he doesn't really let me do anything important. And in an instant, I almost lost it, all because of you!" In spite of her words, she didn't sound all that angry.

"Working for an ogre is the best job you've ever had?" he asked.

"Yes, thank you very much, it is. And now I'm about to go get pissed, but before I do, I wanted to tell you what a shit you are."

"Yeah, good move, way better than phoning after you're pissed," he said.

She laughed and said, "No, it's not that. I just wanted to have the satisfaction of telling you what I think while I'm sober, so I can remember it after."

"I have a better idea," said Flash. He felt the gentle offshore breeze, still warm, his eyes fixed on the fiery sky as the sun set. "Meet me at Chef Chai in thirty minutes. I'll buy you dinner, and if you want to get pissed, at least you can do it with good wine. My treat. It's the least I can do."

"Oh, God," she said. "Wait a minute, what about your flight?"

He'd forgotten about that. "Yeah, change in plans, how about it?"

"Oh, God."

"What's the harm? Some wine, a good dinner, and you'll feel right as rain, maybe even have a laugh or two."

"Are you married?"

"No."

"Okay, but on one condition."

"What's that?"

"Swear you'll never tell Mr. Haysmith I had dinner with you. Deal?"

"Deal."

Flash arrived early at Chef Chai, a fusion restaurant recommended by Minette. Her description had been "mid-level fancy" and "fashionable, but still accessible." She hadn't mentioned white tablecloths and a menu that boasted a vast wine cellar. He ordered a bottle of wine while he waited.

Fiona, still in her work clothes, waved as she entered and then glided to where Flash was seated, in the back of the long, low-lit room.

She sat, hung a red box purse on the back of her chair, and said, "Don't get too comfortable. I haven't forgiven you yet." She removed the bottle of wine from a white marble chiller, read the label, and said, "Peter Michael L'Après Midi, Sauvignon Blanc. Yummy, this might help." She pulled out the cork, poured a slosh into Flash's half-empty glass, and filled a glass for herself. She returned the wine to the chiller, and raised her glass. "Here's to better days."

Flash muttered, "Better days."

Fiona insisted on ordering. They had smoked duck tacos and fresh ahi tartare in mini waffle cones for starters, after which they shared a crispy whole Chilean sea bass with chili ginger sauce, seared greens, and coconut-milk brown rice. As they were finishing the second bottle of Peter Michael—whoever in hell he was—Flash supposed that the trauma of her almost being fired had evaporated.

Fiona was originally from Boulder, Colorado, where she'd studied anthropology. She'd come to Oahu with a girlfriend to celebrate graduation. The girlfriend went back home when the vacation was over, but Fiona wanted to live here forever. That was six years ago.

Emboldened by the wine, Flash waded in. "Is it true that Michel Planc is Haysmith's boss? You know, the guy in Zurich—LM Global. You know who I mean?"

She blinked, momentarily confused, then said, "Yeah, that's the guy. How do you know about him?"

Flaming Sambucas arrived. They watched blue flames for five seconds, then Flash extinguished his drink by placing a hand over the top of the coupe glass. Fiona just waited for the flame on her drink to disappear by itself.

Flash took a sip, then said, "I'm a hard-working journalist. Research is my game. Does Planc ever visit you here?"

"God, no. You must be kidding. If you think Haysmith is a jerk, Planc—well, according to Haysmith, because I don't ever get to talk to or see Planc, but according to Haysmith—Planc is like God with screaming hemorrhoids. He drives Haysmith up the wall."

Flash leaned in and said, "So Planc never comes to Honolulu?"

She shook her head. "No. By the way, I don't think anyone is supposed to know Planc is Haysmith's boss. It's all super hush-hush. Something's mysterious about the whole arrangement. I'm pretty sure Haysmith would go nuts if he knew you knew. You're not thinking of publishing that, are you?"

"No, the city council vetted the deal. That's good enough for me."

"Me too," she said. "Me too. I've only seen glimpses of Planc on Haysmith's screen when they're Zooming, you know? He's old and ugly, and talks—growls—with a thick French accent. Whenever Planc wants to meet Malcolm in person, Malcolm—who hates to fly, by the way, go figure—has to go to Zurich. He's afraid of Planc. I'm sure of that."

Flash realized he had just heard enough to connect most of the dots. Malcolm Haysmith's boss was Michel Planc, who, along with Heinrich Dietrich and the Banc Schaffhausen, had been the targets of the sting operation that had blown up in Flash's face six months before. Now, as hard as the fact was to believe, the shockwave had reached him in hiding, on Kauai.

"Am I boring you?" Fiona's asked, her brow creased.

"God, no," said Flash. "How's your drink?"

She moved her hand back and forth across the front of her neck and said, "Finite, fertig, fini. Done, done, done. I'm full and pissed, just the way you promised. I guess I'll have to forgive you."

"Does that mean we get a sleepover?" Worth a try.

Her smile widened. He was sure she was about to say yes.

Then she said, "No, not on the first date."

He hadn't finished trying. "Okay, so why not be literal? We'll count dinner as the first date and the sleepover as the second one. What do you think about that?"

She said, "Stop the presses, a journalist who can count! One —two— What will he do next?"

The next morning, Fiona left early, telling Flash she needed to go home and change in time to beat Haysmith into the office. Flash went back to sleep. He decided to stay one more day and return to Kauai early the following morning.

Flash slept until nine, then went for a run even though the day was already hot, hoping to sweat out some of the poisons in his system from the night before. Later, he'd go to public records and get a transcript of the hearings approving the Village in the Sky permit and see if he could interview Bart Singletary, maybe stir things up a little.

As circumstances turned out, he didn't have to leave his hotel to get the transcript and an avalanche of supporting documents. God bless the internet and bureaucratic transparency. He downloaded the lot and spent a couple of hours reading. He discovered a very vocal minority had vehemently opposed awarding the permit to the Allen Group. Also, none other than Bart Singletary III had been a strong influence in gathering the votes needed to approve Touma's permit.

By mid-afternoon, Flash had finished his preparations and headed downtown to the First Hawaiian Center, the tallest building in Hawaii, to visit and interview Singletary. In order to ensure that Bart wouldn't turn him down, Flash had called Minette, who petitioned Touma, to see if he could arrange for a short interview with a journalist writing a glowing piece for the Village in the Sky. It had worked.

Bart was ensconced in the Singletary Family office, four

floors above the Allen Group. *Very fitting*, thought Flash. The etched aluminum sign simply read Singletary Family Trust. Flash entered, walking into what he could only think of as a British colonial nineteenth-century library. The room had dark paneling, wainscoting in muted red, and oil paintings in gilded frames lit by invisible spotlights.

The wall-to-wall wool carpet was in dark reds and greens, with black-outlined patterns of tropical birds, mountains, waterfalls, and jungle foliage. Walking on the carpet was like a dream, each footfall sinking a sixteenth of an inch as he made his way to the receptionist sitting at a grand old koa-wood library table with fat, sculpted legs.

The woman glanced at a computer terminal, then back at Flash, and said, "Might I be speaking to Mr. Tucker?"

Her voice was quiet, almost timid. She was very trim, her black hair streaked naturally with white and pulled back into a bun. She had high cheekbones, a small mouth, no visible makeup, and a pink coral-shell bracelet on one wrist. She was wearing a long blue and red shift.

"Hi. Yes, I'm Mr. Tucker, here to see Mr. Singletary."

"How nice of you to visit us this afternoon, Mr. Tucker. My name is Alani. I'll tell Mr. Bart that you're here." She reached to her keyboard and pushed a key. She looked up at Flash and said, "There."

Seconds later, the door to the inner offices opened, and a tall man, maybe six foot four or five, heavyset, wearing a cream-colored tropical suit, a peach dress shirt, and a teal knit tie made his entrance. "Mr. Tucker, how do you do?"

He held out his hand to shake, and Flash took it, finding his hand buried in the big man's fingers and vice-like grip. "I'm Bart Singletary," he boomed. Two hard shakes and Flash's hand, almost numb, was released. "My good buddy Touma says I should help you with your article about his wonderful project. So come in, come in."

Bart's office was at least four times larger than Apartment B.

This room was like no office Flash had ever seen, part royal council chamber and part Oxford's Ashmolean Museum. The decorator must have imagined an encounter between an eighteenth-century gentleman's club or reading library and an old South Pacific museum. The office had no windows.

The walls were dark paneled with several banks of built-in sculpted bookshelves, also in dark wood, attended by a real library ladder on rails. In a separate viewing gallery off to one side were six oil paintings in gilded frames, tribal scenes, one of a stern Polynesian king whose neck was invisible under dozens of flower necklaces looking out into the room through fierce black eyes.

A dramatically lit display of brown, apparently ancient, pots —four of them, each a different size—was suspended in a glass case. Farther along the wall, Flash saw a three-foot-long wooden model of an outrigger canoe— apparently a big one, because it had a large deckhouse and sail, perhaps like the vessels that had brought the original Hawaiians to the Islands.

In the center of the room, under an old crystal chandelier, was another antique carved wooden table, fully ten feet long and four feet wide, that served as Bart's desk. Four hand-carved and upholstered chairs for guests, or supplicants, were lined up in front of the desk.

Bart sat down in an antique leather-upholstered, red wooden throne, whose only modern touch was wheels attached to each leg. Flash took one of the visitor's chairs.

"How can I help you, young fellow?" Bart asked in a deep baritone. His hair was dyed dark brown, and his black eyebrows almost met over his nose. His large square head featured cheeks that folded back when he smiled, and laugh wrinkles radiated out from his brown eyes.

Flash explained his assignment. The man needed no prodding to launch into an impassioned discourse on the value of Touma's project to the city of Honolulu and the state of Hawaii. He announced himself to be a longtime friend and admirer of

Touma and his work, and he appeared genuinely happy to help his buddy.

"Are you an investor in the Allen Group, or do you have a financial interest in the project?" asked Flash.

"Oh, gosh, no. We're in property development, too, and so sometimes we compete with Touma. But we're not in on this deal, no. I just wanted to help my friend."

The two had been talking for twenty minutes, and Flash doubted he would be granted more than a half-hour, so he decided to see if he could shake things up.

"In researching this article, I've been confused by the financing. Originally, the project was presented to the city council as being funded by a Swiss bank, Banc Schaffhausen. I think I saw a letter from a—wait, here—let me check." Flash fiddled with his iPhone for a moment, then said, "Yes, here, the supporting letter in the proposal was from Banc Schaffhausen, signed by Heinrich Dietrich. Do I understand that you introduced Touma to Dietrich? I think I heard that somewhere."

The atmosphere in the room changed at once, as if a dark cloud had fallen over the conversation. Bart creased his brow, looked confused—almost theatrically confused—and in a peculiarly earnest tone, said, "Why, no, I don't know the man. Whoever told you I knew him is emphatically mistaken."

Flash smiled and said, "I don't recall who it was, or maybe I misunderstood. Could it be that you yourself have had dealings with Banc Schaffhausen?"

Bart blurted out, "No, I don't know them. And why are you asking questions about these people? I thought this was about the Village in the Sky project?"

Flash tried to appear calm and as unthreatening as he could and said, "Well, what confused me was that Banc Schaffhausen and Dietrich disappeared at the last minute. And as if by magic, this fellow, Malcolm Haysmith, showed up with Sixty-Four Capital and five-hundred-million dollars in tow. Do you have any idea what happened?"

"Why, as I heard it from Touma, the Banc Schaffhausen people pulled out and recommended Haysmith and his group. How is that confusing?"

"I just wondered, that's all. The change happened pretty quickly, just ten days before the permit deadline. And we're talking about five-hundred-million dollars. That's a lot of money, even in the development world, as I'm sure you know."

Bart's face softened. "Indeed, it is, but they, Sixty-Four Capital, obviously passed muster. They cleared the vetting process, and now we have a wonderful project underway in our fair city."

"The Village is a fine project, and with that, I want to thank you for being so generous with your time and information. Good day to you, Mr. Singletary."

Bart stood up, all smiles again, clearly happy to end the interview. He reached out to shake hands, leaning across the wide table. Flash leaned in for the crushing grip, only he was ready for it this time, tensing his muscles and holding on for dear life.

Just as the death grip was released, Flash said, "Oh, you know, another chap was in the middle of that last-minute shuffle —of the funding, I mean. Do you know a Michel Planc, Zurich, kind of a big-money guy?"

This time Bart didn't bother to put on an act. He just looked right through Flash and said, "No, I don't know what you're talking about. Goodbye now."

Flash walked out of the building and blinked in the afternoon sun. The time was three-thirty. His hotel was a three-and-a-half-mile walk from the First Hawaiian Center. He needed to think, so he ambled more than walked. The breeze was warm and gentle, the sun bright, and the sky almost cloudless. He spent an hour in the park at Lolani Palace and arrived at his hotel at six-thirty. Flash got off the elevator on the fourth floor, walked to his door, inserted the card key, and entered.

Two men were waiting in his room. One of them grabbed him, pulled him into the room, and threw him on the floor. The other man kicked him in the head just as he hit the ground. Flash saw stars and by reflex rolled and curled into a ball and covered his head. The second man came across the room and kicked him in his side, knocking the wind out of him.

One of them pulled Flash to his feet while the other came up behind and pinned Flash's arms behind his back. The man standing in front of Flash then drove his fist into Flash's solar plexus, producing more stars. Flash doubled over, held up by the guy behind him. Both men wore black jeans, black hooded shirts, and black trainers. Flash recognized them: the captain and mate from the Zodiac.

"You are a nosy bastard," said the captain, who was standing in front of Flash. "You need to go back to the hole you crawled out of and mind your own fucking business. You keep asking questions, and we'll track you down and break both your legs and arms before we kill you. This is your only warning. Stay the fuck out of our business."

With that, the captain nailed Flash with a vicious roundhouse to the jaw. the other man let go, and Flash crumpled to the floor, unable to move. The captain launched one last kick into Flash's kidney, and the attack was over. They walked out of the room, quietly closing the door behind them.

Flash pulled himself up onto the bed, lying on his back for a half-hour, letting the pain subside, getting his breath back, checking for broken bones. *The Zodiac guys. Jesus, Bart? But why risk it?*

When Flash finally got up, he stripped down and took a shower, standing in the warm water and steam for fifteen minutes, trying to clear his head and regain his bearings. He probably had a concussion; his headache was escalating. His jaw was swelling, and bruising was beginning to show below his right eye. A big bruise had bloomed in the center of his chest, and another above his right kidney.

He dried off, took four Advil, and decided he would go out for a light meal, maybe to the pub. *No, you idiot, not the pub.* The last thing he needed tonight was to run into Haysmith. Now he *knew* he was concussed. *Get a grip!* He'd go to the Asian Grill, a dark place where he could sit at a table alone and eat slowly, drink some beer, and think. He picked up his phone and noticed that he had a text message from Fiona: Heads up. Haysmith made me call Minette and ask where you were staying in town. He knows where you are. He's climbing the walls, angry about your visit last night. Be careful. PS I might be interested in a third date :)

CHAPTER 32

T
he Einstein Kaffee & Rauchsalon on Kramgasse was twenty-seven steps west of the entrance to his apartment building. Erebus, known in Bern as Helmut Frone, made the passage every morning at ten. Following such a routine was, he imagined, a very Swiss way to behave, to have a coffee and pastry at precisely the same time each day. He'd decided if he was to mimic being a Swiss, he must learn to act Swiss.

Today's pastry was Bundner Nusstorte, a tart filled with walnuts and caramel; his coffee was a double shot of espresso. Accompanying those indulgences was a glass of still water. Erebus had been working at his desk, conjecturing, planning, and researching since six that morning. His head was full; now he would process what he had found. He picked up his fork, took a bite of the sweet tart, and chewed. The sugar soothed him, a sip of coffee braced him, a sip of water cleared the palate for the next round. He proceeded to repeat, pause, and think—very civilized.

The assassin had brought his black Moleskine death book with him, and he opened it to a page with a hand-printed list of essential documents from the Bingwen cache. The first entry, preceded by four asterisks, referred to an email from a woman named Tilly Good to John Horan, the Seattle cop. In the letter, Tilly accused Horan of murdering her and wrote that in thirty days' time, she would publicly release records which would prove that John Horan had masterminded the notorious ten-million-dollar theft. She also hinted that the missing money might no longer be missing, that she had taken the money and placed it where a determined hired gun or lucky bent cop might recover it. Erebus had copied out the sentence exactly:

"Here's a hint to get you started. You might look to your old buddy Flash. Maybe he could help you."

Erebus did the math—thirty days from the email date was the twentieth of May, a Saturday. Only nine days away.

The document cache also contained one seemingly insignificant Facebook interaction between Horan and Flash Michael's daughter, Pippa, which suggested that Flash might be on the island of Kauai, in a place called Poipu.

Erebus sighed, stretched in his seat at the back of the cafe, and turned his attention to the other unexpected bombshell. Last night, he'd received a personal text link for an encrypted video call with, of all people, Malcolm Haysmith, in Honolulu. Curious, he had clicked the link.

Haysmith said, "Mr. Erebus, how are you?" His voice was unrecognizably cordial, which put Erebus on guard, thinking of the fiery car crash that had killed Heinrich Dietrich.

"I'm the same as always, Haysmith, a little surprised to hear from you, though. What is it you want?"

"I have a business deal for you, a contract. I presume you're still in that business, yes?"

Erebus exhaled silently, looking at the piles of paper on his desk. Finally, he said, "Yes, Haysmith, of course I am."

"This is a special, once-in-a-lifetime contract," Haysmith boasted pompously. "Are you available for such an assignment?"

"Depends, Haysmith. Target—fee—special instructions. You know the drill."

Haysmith, apparently incapable of maintaining his façade of bonhomie, nervously blurted out, "Michel Planc, one-million Euros, dead within a week. I don't care how you do it."

Erebus sat back in his chair, astounded. He said, "Too big, too dangerous unless"—he paused for two breaths and lowered his voice—"unless the fee is paid in advance."

To Erebus's surprise, Haysmith had agreed immediately. "The money will be delivered to an account of your choosing by ten tomorrow morning. Do we have a deal, Erebus?"

Erebus didn't wonder why someone would want to kill Planc. The old man was a despicable human being. But murdering a cartel boss was an act of war. Highly likely that Planc's murder would open up the LM Global cabal to all manner of repercussions, perhaps even start an all-out battle among the cartels, leading to the incineration of the LM Global collaboration. Erebus smiled. *The greedy bastards can never have enough! Serves them right!*

Surprisingly, Haysmith's money had arrived early, at eight-thirty that morning, and Erebus had cheerfully swept it into a deeply buried lockbox account. In an instant, Haysmith had unknowingly solved Erebus's short-term funding deficit, with plenty left over to float Haysmith's own demise. Really, the arrangement was almost too good to be true.

The tart eaten and the espresso drained, he took the last sip of water and placed a ten-franc note on the metal tray. The bill was one of the old ones, with an etching of Le Corbusier on its face.

Erebus stood, went to the Kaffee door, turned right, and walked the twenty-seven steps to his building. Morning shop-pers were spreading out on Kramgasse. He almost bumped into an old lady with a red-leather shopping bag. He looked up, pardoned himself, and then stopped dead still in front of his door.

He had it!

While working for Heinrich Dietrich, he had shadowed Planc for three days, following his every move from a distance. Planc and Erebus shared a quality—they were both great creatures of habit. Every day at fifteen minutes after noon, Planc left his building and walked across the plaza to a newsstand, where he bought the *Financial Times* and a candy bar, then walked twice around the outside of the plaza, after which he returned to the LM Global building.

Erebus entered his building, got in the elevator and pushed the fourth-floor button. As the door closed, he vividly imagined a simple, safe, five-hundred-meter shot to the head. That was how he would kill Planc. In and out, and gone like the wind.

Next step: Map out three escape routes, all of which would deliver him first to Honolulu, where he had Haysmith to contend with, and then to the island of Kauai.

John was reminded yet again how much he hated Houston. He had traveled here on cop business four times that he could remember. The city was spread out endlessly, with miles and miles of freeways, housing projects, and strip malls located in a mercilessly hostile environment. And yet, the Texas town was the fourth most heavily populated city in the United States. *People are such sheep.*

Leaving the Marriott located near the MD Anderson Cancer Center, John walked across a scorching-hot parking lot to his rental car. He'd booked a room for a week, paying for it with his Visa card. Just as he would if he was an out-of-town patient undergoing cancer treatment.

His rental car was a white Ford Fiesta, a favorite of police departments and leasing companies everywhere—what a surprise. He got into what felt like an oven, quickly started the engine, and turned the air conditioner on high. *God, what a city!*

He'd made a clean sweep leaving Seattle. His realtor had already received a deposit and a firm cash offer for the condo—

45 percent higher than the price he'd paid just four years earlier. Bingo—an unexpected bonus that would come in handy for chasing down that fucker Flash.

He had needed only four days to sell everything worth selling in the condo, mostly furniture. He'd sold his car to the ex-brother-in-law and canceled all services, subscriptions, his health club membership—the works.

The car cooled down, and he drove out of the parking lot and onto Highway 69, going north toward George Bush Intercontinental Airport. He would fly through Denver to Honolulu, then make a short inter-island hop to Lihue, where he'd booked a four-bedroom, 4,500-square-foot Airbnb, set way back from the road on a private gated drive. The creature comforts included a swimming pool, a game room, and a large entertaining room with an adjacent ultra-modern kitchen.

The house was a big splurge, but it suited his criteria perfectly. He needed a place he could rent for two weeks that was secluded, expensive, and private, so no one would wander in to discover who was there or what they were doing. The knee-buckling rental fee also included a "free" Hertz Jeep Wrangler for the duration of his stay.

John wondered what Flash felt when he'd walked off the map and ended up in Kauai. Then John caught himself. What Flash felt didn't matter. What mattered was that Flash's little escape dream was about to blow up in his face.

During the three-hour layover in Denver, John nursed a beer in a crowded Chili's, absorbed in making plans about what he would need to do once on the ground in Kauai. After some grocery shopping, he would visit a hardware store for duct tape, plastic ties, rope, and a plastic tarp. Also, he had an appointment with a friendly island armorer to pick up a prepaid Glock 17.

Sipping on a second beer, John considered the likelihood that eventually his movements from Seattle to Kauai would be discovered by those sent to hunt him down. By the time those searching for him reached Kauai, though, they would be too late.

He imagined leaving a rat's nest for them to sift through at the scene of the crime. *The scene of the crime*, he thought, that had a nice ring to it. Yes, that was what they would find—a rat's nest, a body, and no John Horan.

When Tilly Good's bomb exploded, John Horan would be long gone. They would find pieces of that fucker Flash, though, or what used to be Flash. John finished his beer, paid his tab, grabbed all his worldly belongings, and made his way to gate B 23. The flight information screen read "DEN-HNL Now Boarding." *Right on time*, thought John—an omen of a perfectly executed game plan.

CHAPTER 33

Sachiko sat facing Keanu across a glass table in Sachiko's newly converted home office in Princeville. She had on a black jumpsuit, white sneakers, white nail polish, and white lipstick. Her hair was pulled back into a ponytail that hung down between her shoulder blades. She was in a pissy mood this morning.

Behind Keanu was a sliding glass door that opened onto a patio, looking out at the garden surrounding Sachiko's house. She was in business mode. She had bought the modern three-feet-by-six-feet rectangular glass table, two black Aeron office chairs, a tricked-out iMac computer, and a koa-wood credenza to signal her new occupation.

She had also moved four large, framed, prints from the guest house and hung them here, two over the credenza and two on the wall opposite. Each print was a single black, Chinese character. She had been told the characters were *Wealth, Serenity, Grindstone,* and *War.* Even though she was the only one who knew what the characters meant, Sachiko liked the austere messaging.

Keanu was lounging in shorts, flip flops, and a faded orange t-shirt under a wrinkled, unbuttoned, Hawaiian shirt. He was eyeing a stack of envelopes that Sachiko had prepared.

"Don't forget. I get paid way more than the monkeys."

Sachiko winced and answered edgily, "Yes, Keanu. Remember? We've already talked about that? You don't need to remind me every ten fucking minutes. Here." She pushed the envelopes and six baggies across the glass table toward him. "It's time to get off your ass and go feed the monkeys." She forced a smile, waiting for him to stand up and leave, but he just sat and smiled back at her. Was he daring her? "And remember, happy monkeys are what we want. Be firm but nice. I put a little extra kicker in Jacob's pay, for his leaving his old gang and bringing what's-his-name with him."

"Robbie, he brought Robbie."

"Right, Robbie. So that's us, six monkeys plus you—we're already growing!"

Keanu still didn't move. He was leaning way back in the office chair, fingers interlaced behind his neck, a smirk on his face.

Sachiko was tired of his acting like the little lord of the manor, yet another reminder that he would have to be demoted soon. She needed to find a number-two person with balls and brains, not just balls. Come to think of it, maybe the balls were the problem. Still irritated, she squinted and said in a louder voice, "Monkeys! This morning, Keanu?"

He rolled out of the chair onto his feet, scooped up the envelopes and baggies, and left.

She wondered if maybe she didn't require a number-two person, perhaps just a gofer, say, someone like Mary Jo, her maid, although Mary Jo might not be able to deal with the monkeys. Then she wondered if Mateo, her tennis instructor, might want to make some real money.

Her cellphone vibrated; it was Bart.

She answered in a demure voice. "Yes, Stepdaddy?"

"Sachiko, a couple of things." Bart always sounded like a football announcer.

"Yes?"

"I've been looking over this spreadsheet you sent me."

She smiled. "Yes, Stepdaddy?"

"Are you sure you want to do business this way? You know I still want payment up-front. This idea of you being a stocking distributor is interesting, but it's a lot for you to bite off. Also, remind me how this benefits you or me."

Sachiko cleared her throat. "Well, it benefits me because you're giving me an extra ten percent discount due to the volume. The quantities we're talking about are the equivalent of ten Zodiac deliveries in one shipment. It benefits you because you greatly reduce your transportation costs, one jumbo delivery instead of ten small ones. Lastly, we both benefit because it reduces the risk of discovery." She had thought the whole proposal through and was quite proud of herself. She was a natural.

Sachiko went on. "One landing versus ten means people are less likely to notice the activity at Koloa landing. Also, given the demand we're experiencing, I'm planning, over time, to put our competition here on the island out of business. Having a larger stock on hand gives me a chance to use my marketing degree and squash the competition. So as I demolish the competition, I buy more product from you. Any questions about that, Stepdaddy?"

"No," Bart conceded. "Sounds like you're on top of it. Assuming you can come up with one hundred and ninety thousand, that is."

She smiled to herself and thought, *Gotcha, Stepdaddy!* "Piece of cake."

He exhaled in something between defeat and agreement. "Okay, when do you want it?"

"Friday night?" she suggested.

"All right. So you can come up with the money by then, right? I don't want any surprises at the handoff, got it?

"No surprises, just money, Stepdaddy."

"Okay, last item. I want to be sure we're on the same page about your dad. Touma can never know I'm your supplier."

"The last thing I want is to have Daddy, Touma Daddy, looking over my shoulder and trying to tell me what to do or not to do. Now, any chance we can stop talking about this and get back to making money, Stepdaddy?"

Bart chuckled. He said, "Expect your jumbo delivery Friday night at eleven. That amount will probably take three backpacks. We'll load up with the regular mix of goodies and a special load of snow, and a small brick of horse."

"Okay, Stepdaddy. I'll be there with bells on."

"With the cash, right?"

"Right."

The Moku Kitchen was what you got when you put money guys together with trendy eclectic chefs, inspired designers, and far-out architects, all focused on a modern, fun Hawaiian buzz. The restaurant had dramatic beams, crisscrossed columns, a wild mix of light fixtures, a fifty-foot-long bar, cushioned bar chairs, and the table and booth seating upholstered in red and white and green.

Minette found a table in a corner, away from the bar. Touma didn't like the bar, but he liked the restaurant. She signaled to a waiter as Benjamin sat in one of the chairs opposite. His gabardine suit was wrinkled after a hard day in the office. He slouched and leaned against the wall, a position that looked uncomfortable to Minette but apparently suited his rotund body. He put one elbow on the table and said, "Big Beck's, please, and some fish tacos and fries."

After the waiter brought the food, Benjamin's liter of beer, and Minette's gin and tonic, Minette told the waiter a third person would be joining them.

Benjamin took a big swallow of beer, replaced the glass on

the table, picked up two fries, and plopped them into his mouth. Chewing, he said, "Mind if I salt these a little?"

Minette smiled. "No, Benjamin, you always salt them, and I never mind."

After salting the fries, Benjamin looked up at her. "Okay, Minette, out with it. What do you think is happening with the boss?"

She took a sip, put her glass down on the table, picked up one of the fish tacos and put it on her appetizer plate, then carefully pulled one French fry out of the stack, and ate it, slowly, to give herself time to think. Finally, she said, "Haysmith, that's the problem. Haysmith. Touma, well, not just Touma, we're all getting a good dose of what it's like to work with an evil idiot." She shook her head, then saw Touma, his teal-and-purple striped knit tie loosened and his dress shirt unbuttoned at the neck and sleeves, working his way along the long bar toward their table. She waved and said, "Here he is."

Touma was as disheveled as he ever got—an ominous sign, she thought. He stopped at the end of the bar, said something to the bartender, pointed to where Minette and Benjamin were seated, then moved to join them.

Touma took the seat next to Benjamin and blurted out, "No shop talk until my drink arrives. I need to catch my breath. What a fucking day!" He reached over and took three French fries, popped them into his mouth, and chewed deliberately, as if he were savoring his last bite before something horrible happened. The waiter set a martini with three olives in front of Touma, who said, "Go get me another and bring it in ten minutes, yeah?"

"Yes, Mr. Touma, ten minutes, sir."

Minette's anxiety grew as she watched Touma knock back half of the double martini and then eat one of the olives.

She glanced at Benjamin, who was gazing silently at Touma. "Are we in that much trouble?" she questioned.

Touma didn't answer right away, another out-of-character bit of behavior. Minette prodded him. "Touma, I asked, 'Are we in that much trouble?'"

After a second slug of martini—the glass almost empty now —Touma said, "You tell me, Minette, Benjamin. You tell me."

Benjamin, his brow furrowed, looked surprised by Touma's answer.

Minette, who thought she understood what Touma meant, said, "Well, boss, why don't we start by you telling us what went on with our marketing friends today, then we'll talk about what working under Haysmith is looking like from our perspective. How's that?"

The waiter arrived with the second martini. Touma took a handful of fries, put them on his appetizer plate, selected one of the fish tacos, took a bite, and put the remainder on top of his fries. He said to the waiter, "Bring us some Szechuan stir-fry beans, lobster deviled eggs, and another order of fish tacos."

After the waiter had gone, Touma said, "Well, to summarize, our dear former friends Jack, Marilyn, and Keoni, the best sales and marketing folks in the islands, by a long shot if you ask me, are pulling the plug. They told me that Haysmith is withholding a big payment they're due in an attempt to force them into starting all over again with a new plan, but cutting their rates by thirty percent. Worse, Haysmith is demanding a bribe—a-hundred-and-fifty-thousand dollars—as the price of admission, or should I say, readmission."

Benjamin shook his head. "I knew it, son of a bitch, I knew it! His contractors pay him to play, so he gets rich, and we're dealing with crooks. Every one of the contractors he's approved will be paying him off. But since Jack, Marilyn, and Keoni were already under contract with us, he hadn't gotten his hooks into them yet."

Touma nodded. The second round of appetizers arrived. Benjamin started on the second liter of beer, and Minette asked for a glass of white wine to slow her alcohol intake. Getting smashed wasn't a luxury she felt she could afford, at least not yet. "So, Touma, what do you think this means?"

"That's why I said *you tell me*. I have a feeling that things are a lot worse than I imagine, but I'm not running the job or the numbers day-to-day. You guys are, so you tell me."

Benjamin didn't need any prodding. "Well, boss, we have two types of issues. First, we didn't choose these contractors. For the most part, they know it, and so we have no leverage with them. Second, if they're paying to play—and I'll bet they've paid through the nose—as far as they're concerned, Haysmith is the big boss, and we're more an irritant than anything." Benjamin took another swallow of his beer before going on.

"The signs are already apparent," he said. "We're falling farther and farther behind schedule. Almost as if they're doing it intentionally, slow-playing the job. That Haysmith converted all of the contracts to cost-plus doesn't help, since now, who cares how long they take to get the job done? Except us, of course."

"Are you sure about this?" Touma asked darkly.

"Yes, boss." Benjamin nodded. "I know these guys, the workers, the superintendents, the project foremen, they're the ones telling me. They don't know about the bribes for certain, but even they think something dirty must be going on."

"Well, we certainly had confirmation of that today," Touma said. "But if this is the mess we're in, how do we get out of it? What do you think?"

"Tell the cops about the bribes. It's illegal. Then sue em," said Benjamin.

Minette shook her head.

Touma said in exasperation, "Yeah, sure, throw the people who are funding us to the tune of five-hundred-million dollars under the bus." He shook his head slowly. "I don't think so. We'd never get another nickel in funding, ever, if we did something like that. Ratting out Haysmith would be suicide. And on top of that, the feds, the cops would bundle us up with Haysmith and try to take the whole bunch of us down. Jesus!"

Minette decided that was the moment to make it clear to Touma that they were in real danger. She said, "Sorry to pile on, but we have another Haysmith problem. We write the checks, but Haysmith's administrators release them. They hold the checks for as much as ninety to one hundred and twenty days before sending them out, just because they think they can.

"The equipment rental firms and material suppliers are screaming bloody murder. They may well gang up and file mechanic's liens on the project preemptively, which, as you know, would stop everything until the liens are released. The construction bond on this project is in the Allen Group's name, not Sixty-Four Capital's, so we'd have to defend ourselves if we defaulted through nonpayment. So we take the hit, and Haysmith and his money folks just walk away."

Touma gave her a weak smile. "Look, we've been in the shit before. We'll find our way through," he said.

He leaned over and slung his arm around Benjamin's shoulder, while holding out his hand toward Minette. She took his hand, felt his warmth.

Touma took a deep breath and said, "We have to stick together, join ranks and stick together. Somehow, we'll beat this, the three of us." He squeezed Minette's hand again and released it, gave Benjamin's shoulder one last pat. "Now, let's eat."

Two hours later, Minette asked the restaurant for taxis to take them all home. Benjamin had left the table for the restroom. "How is Sachiko doing with her property business?" Minette asked.

Touma shrugged. "I don't know. We don't talk much these days. She's still pissed that I haven't brought her into the business."

"Just so you know, about a month ago, I had a call from a friend of mine at Central Pacific Bank," Minette said. "Apparently, Sachiko opened a commercial account and secured a pretty hefty line of credit. Is she buying property, do you know? My friend called me back today and said Sachiko pulled out a hundred-and-ninety-thousand for something."

Touma frowned. "I don't know anything about it." He shook his head as if to shake off the matter entirely. "It's her house and her money, anyway. None of my business."

All the dirt might as well come out now. "Okay. Well, one other thing—she ran up a thirty-thousand-dollar bill with Hach, Mulbain, and Reilly and charged it to our account. Did you know about that? Just wondering."

Touma sighed heavily. "Look, I don't know about that either. Let it go. It's peanuts, but tell them to call you for authorization next time she wants to use the law firm and charge it to Allen Group. You said thirty-thousand, right?"

"Yes," Minette said, deciding not to mention that it had been for criminal defense work. He'd had enough for one day, and for that matter, so had she. Not for the first time in the last three months did she wonder if she'd be looking for another job soon. This whole spectacle had the feel of a volcano about to erupt. She hoped her own reputation would be left intact.

CHAPTER 34

Flash watched the rain, waiting nervously for Kellie and Bob on the covered boardwalk in front of Mia's building.

Soon the squad car turned left in front of Sueoka's grocery store onto Koloa road and stopped in front of him. Kellie was driving, with Bob riding shotgun. Flash ducked into the back seat.

Kellie said, "Roy's is out—the rain and no inside seating—so Bob suggested Grandma's Japanese Cafe in Hanapepe. It's actually closer, and they have tables inside."

Hanapepe, Kauai's biggest little town, or so the welcome sign said, was located off Highway 50, tucked into a bend of the Hanapepe River. The town had two streets, each lined with old buildings, some eighty years old or older. These aged structures had been converted into art galleries, souvenir shops, clothing stores, small restaurants, and Talk Story—the westernmost bookstore in the United States.

Some buildings leaned, and many were weather beaten; a few were freshly painted, though their roofs sagged. The small island village was, at the very least, picturesque.

After parking in front, the three of them ran through the rain to the front door of Grandma's. The inside was newly remodeled, with white walls and local artists' paintings hung for sale on the walls. Tables were set with paper placemats, plastic water glasses, forks, and chopsticks.

After they focused on the menu for a couple of minutes, a young girl wearing jeans and a colorful Hawaiian shirt took their order. Kellie ordered a veggie roll and cucumber salad, Bob a shrimp tempura bento bowl with added avocado slices, and Flash the sautéed steak bento bowl with added shrimp tempura.

Kellie ordered their drinks. "Lilikoi Limeade—three please." She looked at Flash. "It's the house special. You got to try it."

Bob quietly and carefully straightened his table setting. Then, without looking up, he asked, "Okay, Flash. Whattup?" And Flash wondered if Bob had in mind Flash's still bruised eye.

For sure, Flash would have liked to have eased into this conversation, but Bob wasn't the easing-in type.

Kellie said, "Hey, Bob, Flash is buying lunch, so let's maybe remember our manners, shall we? His credit card, his meeting."

Kellie focused her gray eyes on Flash and said, in a quieter voice, "What's up, Flash?"

He caught a reprieve, though, as the food and drinks arrived. After the server left, Flash took a sip of his Lilikoi Limeade, wishing it were laced with vodka or gin, or rum, or anything alcoholic. "I used to be a cop in Seattle—fraud, money laundering, and organized crime." He sighed deeply—maybe in relief at getting that initial admission over with.

"I was given the equivalent of early retirement after fifteen years on the force. At the same time, I got divorced, and my whole life seemed to explode. So I decided, what the hell, get lost somewhere far away from my screwed-up life. I chose Kauai. My name is Flash, only it's Flash Finnegan Michael, not Flash Thorsten Tucker." He gulped another swallow of the house limeade.

Kellie was beaming. "I knew it, I just knew it. But why the name change?"

"I wanted to be erased, to get lost. I did a couple of tours working undercover, so I knew a lot about getting lost and thought I would—uh, get lost, I mean."

Bob, who wasn't beaming, said in whisper, "So why are your fingerprints locked up? Who did you screw in Seattle?"

"No one. I didn't ask them to lock up my identity. Someone in Seattle did that. I'm not quite sure why. But like I said, I wanted to be erased, so when I learned the files were red-flagged, I considered it a plus and didn't bother to call them to find out why."

Bob jumped right over the top of Flash's explanation. "So you're either a crook, or you're in the witness protection program. Which is it?"

Flash shrugged. "Neither, as far as I know. I have a release, signed by the Seattle chief of police."

Bob scowled and shook his head.

Flash could see that he wasn't making much headway with the two. So he decided to stop trying. If they wouldn't listen, to hell with them. All he really needed was to convince them to put him in front of Chief Samson Aukai, their boss. He could talk till he was blue in the face, and Bob would never be satisfied or convinced of his good intentions.

"Look, who I am isn't really important here," Flash said. "What's important is that I've stumbled onto evidence of a drug operation on your patch. I know where the drugs are coming from, where and how they arrive, and when the next shipment is likely to take place, I believe."

Bob was still scowling, but he did lean forward an inch or two. "*I believe?* What the fuck does that mean?"

"It means I'm sure there's going to be a delivery, and it will take place in the next three or four days, in the evening, at eleven."

Kellie jumped in. "Where are the drugs coming from? Who's delivering them?"

Flash noticed neither was eating, so maybe he did have their attention. He picked up his chopsticks, pinched a piece of rare beef, and put it in his mouth. With his mouth still half full, he said, "Coming from Honolulu. No surprise, I'm sure. Delivered by watercraft."

"Who's delivering them? Who's supplying them, and where are they landing? Stop slow-playing this, will you?" Kellie stabbed at her veggie roll and put a piece in her mouth. She didn't look happy.

Flash decided he'd gone as far as he could with them. "Look, I need to meet with Chief Aukai. You two can come. I don't want to tell this story piecemeal to you, him, and anyone else he may wish to include in the loop. The bottom line is I need to know if you—meaning the Kauai Police Department—are willing to act on my information. And since the chief is the only player who counts in that game, let's finish our lunch and go see him."

"Shit," said Bob.

"Agreed," said Flash. He gave them both as much of a smile as his still-aching jaw would allow.

Two hours later, Flash, Kellie, Bob, and Samson Aukai were seated in the chief's office. Flash told an abbreviated version of his release from the Seattle Police Department and showed them a copy of his release and the nondisclosure agreement. He told them about seeing the delivery at Koloa Landing, about the Zodiac and the *Invincible*, about Sachiko and Keanu, and what he'd learned at the Waikiki Yacht Club. When he mentioned Bart Singletary, the chief suddenly looked as if he'd swallowed something unpleasant.

Flash carried on, nonetheless. "I expect a delivery at Koloa Landing on one of the next three or four nights. That's as close as I can guess right now. When the shipment starts to move, I can give you two hours' notice, so you'll hear from me at nine for an eleven o'clock landing. I propose that intercepting the Zodiac, the *Invincible*, Sachiko Allen, Keanu, and his helpers would cut the head off the snake, at least this snake."

The chief said, "Okay, no question I'd like to cut the head off that snake, but how do I know you're for real? For example, how do I know you aren't the leader of a rival drug gang, say."

Flash laughed, trying not to jar his injuries. "Good question. For one thing, you ought to call Chief Forsyth in Seattle, just to make sure I'm not a thief or the head of a drug gang. You definitely should make that call."

The chief nodded stiffly. "I intend to," he said. "Is there something else?"

"Yeah, I read in the paper that you've formed a drug taskforce. If you compare what I've told you about how this ring operates with information your taskforce already has about the drug scene around here, you'll know this is good intelligence."

Flash detected a hint of interest in the chief's eyes. So he went on. "Peterson's death unsettled things, but Sachiko and Keanu stepped in as easy as can be. The only way that can happen is if the runners are in place, and—this is the crucial part—the supply is reliable, tightly monitored and controlled, and somehow protected. In other words, a professional, carefully orchestrated supply operation. Singletary, a ninety-seven-foot yacht, the Zodiac, and at least two henchmen. Sound right to you?"

"So far, yes," Chief Aukai said in a tense voice.

"If you act on this, you're likely to impound a big drug shipment you wouldn't otherwise have known about and arrest a bunch of local pushers and intermediaries. You also have a chance to roll this ring up all the way to Honolulu." He looked the chief in the eye. "The optics are pretty good for you, don't you think? The headline reads, 'Drug Taskforce Scores Big.' I want to help you do that."

"You want to help by doing what?" asked the chief.

"By giving you details, giving you the signal when the drug shipment is a go, and filling you in about how this may be connected to an international money-laundering operation currently dumping tons of dirty money into the state of Hawaii."

The chief stood up, went to the door of his office, stuck his head out, and asked his personal assistant to call Chief Malcolm Forsyth in Seattle and if he wasn't there, to ask for a call back, that it was urgent. Aukai closed the door and sat down. Looking at Kellie and Bob, he said, "Well, what do you think?"

Kellie said, "I've known Flash pretty much since he arrived on Kauai, not well, but we're in the same social circle—you know Mia Mahoe and Emma Pookalani. I can't vouch for him professionally, but he was a big help when Paul Pookalani got into trouble, and you know he ended up finding Robbie Washburn and all. Depending on what the Seattle chief says, we might want to go with this." She looked at Bob. "Your thoughts?"

Bob said gruffly, "Well, I always thought he was a cop, but I don't like people who play games, and this whole nervous-breakdown-erased thing sounds to me a lot like self-absorbed bullshit to cover up a drunken binge. On the other hand, if the Seattle thing checks out, well, what can we lose? One thing, I'm pretty sure—he isn't a rival drug guy. And yes, we really could use a win for the Drug Taskforce. We all know we have a growing problem here."

Sally, the chief's PA, stuck her head through the door and said, "I have Chief Forsyth for you, Chief. Where do you want to take it?"

"I'll take it in your office, Sally." Aukai got up and went through the door, closing it behind him.

Flash said, "If he goes for it, I'm sure we can pick these guys up. Surer even than I might sound. I know how this group works."

Bob gave Flash a long unflinching look. Flash thought it probably worked well with the perps.

Kellie said, "I hope you're right, Flash. But if this is some sort of game, well, you can guess what might happen."

Flash smiled. "Yup, I really do know how that works, Kellie. Better than you can imagine."

They sat in silence for five minutes, then the chief returned, sat down, looked at Kellie and Bob, and said, "Forsyth says he's clean, confirms what Flash said about his time on the police force and his departure from Seattle." He paused and looked closely at each one of them—including Flash. "Are we all agreed to give this a try?"

Kellie and Bob both said in unison, "Yes, sir."

Flash waited two beats, then said, "Yes, sir, when do we start?"

"We'll meet tomorrow morning at eight, the taskforce plus Flash. Meeting adjourned."

Later that afternoon, Pika drove Flash to Emma's house. She greeted him at the door, apparently having heard the cab pull into the driveway.

"Hey, Flash, come on in." She'd changed out of her work clothes into a loose green-and-white print jumpsuit, and her feet were bare. She'd put her hair up into a bun with a bamboo stick.

The two of them walked out onto the back deck. The rain was long gone. Small puffy clouds highlighted a blue sky all the way out over the ocean, and the air was pleasantly warm.

"Can I get you a beer?" Emma asked.

"Yeah, thanks. I don't need a glass."

Emma brought a frosted Foster's can and a wine cooler from the kitchen. She sat across from him, her back to the view, and sounding tired, said, "Day is done. Here's to that." She held out her half-filled glass of wine cooler.

Flash touched his beer can to her glass. "Chin chin," he said. "Long day?"

"Yeah." The sides of her lips turned up slightly. "But we all have to work for a living, don't we? Whoops—sorry, Flash." Her smile broadened. "*Some of us* have to work for a living. And today was a little over the top. Year-end is rapidly approaching, and our investors are eager to see the numbers."

She took a sip of her drink. "So, what's on your mind, Flash? Sorry, that's awfully direct, isn't it? To what do I owe the honor of your visit? You said you wanted to talk."

He didn't know quite how sugarcoat the issue, so he just blurted it out. "I wonder if you can think of someplace Paul could stay—maybe off-island or someplace away from this house—for a week or so?"

Emma straightened in her seat, alarmed. "Why? Is something wrong? Has he done something?"

Flash shook his head. "Nope, he's good. But in the next few days, the police are going to lean on the island druggies. I'm guessing our buddy Keanu and some of his friends are likely to be—well, *inconvenienced* at a minimum and maybe arrested."

Emma said, "Good. That's good, isn't it? Keanu threatened Paul. He's a drug dealer. Everybody knows it. He got off because the evidence went missing, not because he was innocent."

Flash nodded in agreement. "Yeah, you're right," he said. "But chances are, when the police do move, Keanu might try and lash out at Paul. I'd feel a lot more comfortable if Paul was some-place where Keanu and his buddies couldn't find him."

"Reggie and Mia will know a place, maybe up near Kilauea or Hanalei." She paused, thinking. "When are the police moving?"

"It could be as early as tomorrow night. He'd have to stay hidden, out of circulation for at least a week."

"I get it," Emma said. "I'll talk to Reggie and Mia as soon as you leave. When Paul returns from surfing, we'll pack him up and get him ready to move tonight, or tomorrow morning at the latest." She reached out her hand and put it on Flash's arm. "Thank you for your help. Paul really does listen to you, you know. And thank you for helping me protect him."

Flash patted the back of her hand, wondering how she was

going to feel about him as soon as she found out he'd been lying about his past ever since he'd arrived on the island.

Erebus was seated at his desk, checking through the many details of his Last Days odyssey, when he was interrupted by a text message ping. An invitation to an encrypted video session. Irritated, he clicked the link and was surprised to see Michel Planc's large cartoonish face.

The face said, "Erebus, I have a job for you."

Joyfully, Erebus thought, *In two days, this angry old man will be dead and out of my life forever.*

"What kind of a job, Monsieur Planc?" Erebus asked

"Don't be so fucking disingenuous. What kind of job do you think? I want someone off the board. The sooner, the better, *capiche?*"

"Terms?"

"No trace, within a week, two hundred fifty."

"Who?"

"Malcolm Haysmith. You can find him in Honolulu, Hawaii. Make him disappear."

"Malcolm Haysmith? I don't understand, monsieur. I seem to recall he was your fixer. Why would you want to take him off the board?"

"None of your fucking business. Yes or no?"

Erebus smiled. "No. Five hundred. Paid in advance."

"What? That's extortion!"

"I'd call it leverage, monsieur. A fair fee with a little extra to help me stay clear of you and yours if you ever decide to turn on me for some reason. Remember Heinrich Dietrich? I do! Five hundred delivered midday tomorrow. Yes or no, monsieur? Last offer."

Planc's eyes narrowed. "I'll have my personal assistant call for transfer instructions," he said. "Don't cross me, Erebus. I do remember Dietrich. No trace, one week! Any questions?"

"None, monsieur."

The screen went blank.

The gods giveth, and the gods taketh away. In this case, each god pays for the other god to be killed. The assassin imagined a divine intersection of two evil spirits, and he, Erebus, the instrument of justice. The central theme of his Last Days crusade—because that was what it had become, a crusade—was to kill two odious dragons and inherit the treasure.

CHAPTER 35

Trams, cars, and crowds all contributed to the midday cacophony on Parade Platz in the heart of Zurich's financial district. Erebus, three stories above the square, was relying on the noise to cover his rifle's report. Standing in a room-sized service closet in Planc's own building, he shouldered and sighted the CheyTac Intervention M-310SS sniper rifle, placing its bipod on a stone windowsill. The window was tilted open.

Erebus tracked the old man, easily holding the crosshairs right on Planc's head, wondering if he should shoot while Planc was walking toward the newsstand or after, when the old man took his daily constitutional around the square.

This might be my last pure assassination, he thought, feeling nostalgic. Then he noticed he had a clear shot, perfect angle, right at that moment. *Just shoot the fucker*, he thought. He exhaled slowly and squeezed the trigger. The rifle recoiled; the old man collapsed onto the paving stones near the middle of the square.

Erebus chambered a second round, aimed at the center of the crumpled black mound on the ground, exhaled, and squeezed; the rifle recoiled again, the black-suited body jerked. *Yes!* He was elated.

He pulled the rifle down, closed the window, wiped the gun with a rag, and put the gun and the rag into one of the cleaning-supply lockers.

He picked up two shell casings and the oversized courier bag he had used to transport the disassembled rifle into the building, slung the bag over his shoulder, donned his motorcycle helmet, and walked out through the closet door into a long hallway.

So far, no alarm—more good luck. He entered a stairwell and skipped down the stairs two at a time to a service entrance at the back of the building, where his motorcycle was parked. He threw a leg over, turned the ignition key, started the engine, and roared out, melding into oncoming traffic.

"Flash, you think the next delivery will be when?"

This was their second and last planning session in preparation for the intercept at Koloa Landing. Kellie, Bob, Chief Aukai, five other police officers, four Hawaii Harbor Police, and a chief petty officer from the US Coast Guard Fourteenth District all sat in a semicircle in front of three large electronic whiteboards in the incident room.

Flash stood to address the group. "Chief, most likely tonight or tomorrow night. Eleven days have gone by since the last delivery."

Each whiteboard displayed an image of the target zone: one a ten-mile radius from Koloa Landing, the second a closer view, and the third a detailed view of the landing itself. The maps were marked with symbols for units and movements to proceed during the interdiction.

The Harbor Police and the Coast Guard were to coordinate the on-water part of the operation. Once the drugs were ashore, the Coast Guard's eighty-seven-foot patrol boat *Kittiwake* would stop and board the *Invincible,* while the Harbor Police would move in between the drug runner's Zodiac and the *Invincible.*

The Kauai Police would arrest the suspects while the exchange was taking place on Koloa Landing.

The *Kittiwake* and the Harbor Police Zodiac had already been temporarily assigned to Nawiliwili Harbor on Kauai. The Honolulu harbormaster had been brought on board to alert the task force operations center any time the *Invincible* left port.

Flash continued, "Once the *Invincible* sets off, the signal for all units to move into place will be given when Sachiko and Keanu leave Princeville. The drive from Princeville to Koloa Landing at that time of night is sixty to seventy-five minutes. I have someone watching Sachiko's house and will give you a heads-up as soon as they're on the move."

"Who's that?" Chief Aukai asked.

"Pika Kekoa, who drives for Kauai Cabs. He's agreed to stake out the house from a safe distance. He'll call me, and I'll call you."

"Okay," said Chief Aukai. "We'll go with Pika. I'll put a speed trap on the highway near Kilauea so we can confirm their progress farther along the route."

An hour later, the plans were finalized. Roles were defined, agreements confirmed, and the sequence of events and timing had been reviewed and critiqued three times.

When the meeting adjourned, Kellie walked over to Flash, smiling. She said, "Well, here we go. Like I said before, I sure hope this isn't some sort of a game."

"Jesus, Kellie, would you knock it off?" he said in a low voice, turning so that others wouldn't hear him.

"Maybe," she said, rolling her eyes at him. "Maybe I'll knock it off—if this really goes down like you say it will—Maybe." She was no longer smiling.

Flash realized she was nervous, too. She would be one of the arresting officers on the landing when the trap was sprung. It also occurred to him that no matter what happened, she might *never* trust him.

Then she surprised him. "By the way, I had a call from a friend of yours, someone who said he was looking for you."

"What are you talking about?"

"Someone, a man, called my cell. The number was blocked. He claimed to be a friend of yours from Seattle and wanted me to tell him where you were staying. He said he had just arrived on Kauai and hoped to get in touch."

Flash was startled. "Shit, who was it?"

"He didn't say, just said he'd gotten my number from a mutual friend in Seattle. Course, the only people in Seattle who have my number are at your old cop shop. So I asked if he was a cop, and he hung up, just like that."

Suddenly, Flash's head hurt. He clasped his hands behind his back and squeezed his fingers hard.

"So who is it, this long-lost buddy? Is it that guy, John, whatever his last name was? Why would he be here?"

Flash's ears were ringing. Through a fog of adrenaline, he said, "I don't know. It could be anybody. A lot of people were involved in that"—he paused for a breath—"fuck-up, back in Seattle. Did you tell him where I live?"

"No. Like I said, he hung up."

Flash grunted. He looked at Kellie, her gray eyes scanning his face Finally, he told her, "I really don't know who it was. It's not very comforting that he hung up all of a sudden, though. But what the hell. Once you start lying, you're at the mercy of the world around you."

"Indeed," she said with a half-smile.

He had the strange feeling that Flash Michael was merging with Flash Tucker. After all, he had chosen to break cover and blow the whistle, setting this operation in motion. The adrenaline was making him more alert, clear-headed, notwithstanding his months of hard drinking and indulgence. Flash Finnegan Michael and Flash Thornton Tucker were both on the lookout.

At five-thirty that afternoon, Flash received a text from the Honolulu Harbor Police telling him that the *Invincible* was leaving the harbor. *Good news,* he thought. If he had this figured right, Sachiko would leave her house in about four hours. He decided to go down to Brennecke's and have dinner, hang around a while, then make his way over to the hillside above Koloa Landing to watch and wait.

He walked down toward the beach wearing black sweat-pants, a black t-shirt, a black Oakland Raiders windbreaker, and carrying an old black North Face rucksack. He was a little over-dressed for happy hour, but perfectly dressed to be a forward observer in the dark.

The restaurant was alive with early revelers. The music system was cranked up to happy hour volume, and Kim Carnes was singing "Betty Davis Eyes."

Flash found a place at the bar and was greeted by Dennis, the bartender. He nodded to Flash, not wasting time with the regular drinks ask.

Flash said, "Hamburger with onion rings, soda water, please."

Dennis, his short blond hair pushed up at the front the way a twelve-year-old kid would wear it, frowned just for a second, then said, "Got it, boss—burger and rings, and ah, soda water?"

"Yes, Dennis, soda water. I'm conserving brain cells for later."

Dennis smiled and moved away.

Flash looked to see if Fred Miles was in the house. He stood up on his tiptoes to check out the crowd, but no Fred. Dennis delivered the soda water and made a pointing motion toward Flash. "I got your order in. It'll be up in ten." Then he leaned across the bar and said in a quieter voice, "You know, a guy was in here looking for an old buddy of his named Flash. He asked if I knew anybody by that name. I told him no, because, you know, bartenders' oath of confidentiality and all, but he sounded like he knew you. He definitely knew what you look like. You expecting a visitor?"

Flash was shaken. "No, Dennis, I'm not expecting anyone. And since you and I are old friends, I'd appreciate your ongoing discretion. Just out of curiosity, though, what did he look like?"

"Um, six feet, short brown hair, conservative-looking dude— like his shirt and jeans were pressed. About your age, good-looking guy, maybe one hundred and sixty pounds give or take, big hands, he had big hands. Do you know him?"

Flash tried to appear unconcerned. "Nah, I don't think I know the guy. But just so we get this straight between us, Dennis, I didn't come to Kauai to meet up with old friends from my past, if you know what I'm saying." *John Horan—but why?*

Three hours later Flash was sitting at a table under the banyan tree at Koloa Roasters, his phone in front of him next to a frothy cappuccino, his second. The clock on the phone said nine-fifty when it started to vibrate.

"Hi, Pika, what's up?"

"They're on the move, boss, just pulled out of the driveway. I'll follow them to the highway to make sure they go left toward Koloa. Then I'll fall back and see if I can track their progress, you know, like from a distance."

"Pika, check to see they turn left, yeah, but don't follow them. They might remember your cab from our visit to her house, which would be bad news. The cops will take it from Princeville to Koloa."

"Okay, boss."

Five minutes later, Pika confirmed that the Land Rover had turned left. He said he would hang around Princeville for twenty minutes or so before he headed home.

Flash stood up from his table and made a call to the police operations center. When the duty officer answered, Flash said, "This is Flash. They're leaving Princeville and are on their way. They should pass through the speed trap in about twenty minutes. I've got my radio and will join the operation network from my assigned location in about thirty minutes."

He picked up his rucksack and left Roasters, walking along Poipu Road toward the ocean. From experience, he knew a thousand things could go wrong in an operation like this one. His job was simple enough, though, just observe and report from a vantage point on the hillside above the boat ramp.

At Ho'onani Road, Flash veered off to his right, leaving the pavement and following a dirt footpath up the embankment through the jungle overgrowth above the landing. He found a rounded stone he'd placed next to the trail to mark his lookout, turned toward the landing, and pushed through the heavy undergrowth onto a hidden bump on the hillside—his observation post.

He then cleared away several branches that might obscure his sightlines. Flash then moved some earth with his hands to make for a more comfortable seat and settled into his position. Next, he opened the backpack, withdrew a police radio headset and earphones.

He turned on the radio and said, "Radio check. Flash in place, observer position A, standing by, over."

"Roger, Flash. You're connected to the mission ops network, commencing now." He checked his phone; the time was ten-twenty-five.

Flash listened to the radio traffic as the other units took up their positions. The Coast Guard cutter *Kittiwake* tracked the *Invincible* on radar as it made its way along the coast of Kauai toward the landing. *Invincible* was two miles offshore, estimated to be adjacent to the landing site at ten-forty-five. *Kittiwake* was three miles offshore and slightly behind the *Invincible*.

The Harbor Police Zodiac was a mile up the coast, tied up at a small stone jetty near the Beach House Restaurant at Lawai Beach. The arrest team was stationed in two SUVs currently parked in among civilian vehicles at the Shops at Kukui'ula parking lot, five-hundred yards or so from the entrance to Koloa Landing.

Chief Aukai, also in the shopping center parking lot, was in his mobile command center. The SUV bristled with electronics. He would be in contact with all units, with individual team leaders, police headquarters, emergency medical services, and Coast Guard headquarters in case they needed more help.

After about ten minutes, Flash's eyes had adapted to the dark, and he saw four separate lights way out on the water. A warm, gentle breeze was blowing in from the ocean. He looked down toward where he knew the boat landing was—still dark, no sign of life or light, yet. Part of his assignment was to call in any sightings of the *Invincible*, the Zodiac, or the Land Rover, or any other vehicle. And now was the time to wait. And wait.

Twenty minutes later, Flash heard an outboard motor out in the bay. He tried to see through the dark, but nothing. The unseen boat came closer and closer, then veered off, and the sound moved away.

The *Kittiwake* reported, "Radar shows *Invincible* two miles offshore, a smaller boat, probably the Zodiac, launched and headed to shore. The small boat veered away from the shoreline, is now heading back toward *Invincible*."

Flash wondered if the bad guys were waiting for some sort of signal from Sachiko—radio or cellphone or light—or were just taking a quick look-see to make sure the ramp was unoccupied.

Chief Aukai's voice came over the communications network. "Hold positions, hold positions. No lights, no sounds, no movement."

Ten minutes later, *Kittiwake* reported again. "Radar shows a smaller vessel, probably the Zodiac, moving away from *Invincible* again, heading toward shore, slowly this time."

Chief Aukai again said, "Hold positions."

Flash was straining to see if he could make out any shape in the bay. He did see a far-off light, perhaps the *Invincible*, but he had no way of telling at this distance. He struggled to hear the sounds of an outboard motor. But he detected nothing.

Then he heard a sound from the landing below, tires slowly moving on gravel. He saw a dim glow, probably dashboard illumination, like a distant, slow-moving cloud drifting through the entrance onto the boat ramp, creeping down toward the water. Then it stopped, and the cloud went dark.

Flash reported, "Possible sighting. Vehicle, lights extinguished, entered the ramp, stopped thirty feet from the water's edge."

The Coast Guard reported, "Zodiac continues slow approach, now seven-hundred yards offshore. Over."

Aukai said, "Harbor Police, move out. Slow and easy does it. The *Invincible* will be watching on radar. Coast Guard, move slowly off-station toward *Invincible*." They were all keenly aware that the *Invincible* was most likely heavily armed, while the Zodiac crew would likely have handguns.

Flash saw the interior of the vehicle on the ramp light up. He could identify Sachiko's Land Rover now for sure. The passenger side door opened and a man got out, then closed the door. He lit a cigarette. Keanu.

Flash toggled his mike. "Land Rover in place, parked down near water's edge on the ramp, confirmed it is the Land Rover."

Aukai relayed. "All units, the Land Rover is on the ramp."

Five minutes later, the *Invincible*'s Zodiac nosed up onto the ramp. Flash couldn't see it because it was running without lights, but he heard the scraping sound as the bow slid onto the concrete, followed by a soft whining as the twin outboard motors were elevated. A spotlight from the Zodiac flashed twice. The headlights of the Land Rover blinked twice and then remained on. The Zodiac searchlight switched on again, lighting the ramp, the Land Rover, Sachiko, and Keanu.

Flash reported, "Target Zodiac landed, light signal acknowledged by Land Rover. Headlights from the Land Rover show two men from the target Zodiac on the landing, one man remaining on board. Three men in total."

Aukai gave the command, "Mobile one and two, go! Mobile one and two, go! Proceed with lights and sirens down onto the ramp behind Land Rover. Block the ramp exit. Harbor Police

Zodiac proceed toward the ramp. Be prepared to light up once mobile one and two move down the ramp. Block target Zodiac exit. I repeat, block target Zodiac exit! Go, go!"

Flash watched as Sachiko and Keanu walked slowly toward the Zodiac. Two men had jumped from the boat onto the ramp. One of them was holding the bow rope, carried it up the ramp, and looped the end around a dock cleat embedded in the concrete along one side of the ramp. He then joined his partner as they walked farther up the ramp to meet Sachiko and Keanu in front of the Land Rover.

Someone shouted something Flash couldn't hear. The Zodiac extinguished its searchlight, but the headlights from the Land Rover adequately lit the scene. The four stood face to face, talking. Sachiko, who was carrying what looked like a canvas shopping bag, handed it to one of the men, who looked into the bag and held it out to his partner, who also looked. Then the first man turned and walked back down the ramp and put the bag into the bow of the Zodiac.

Flash could see pulsing blue lights in the distance from his elevated seat on the hillside, and then he caught the faint note of a siren. The people on the ramp didn't seem to notice, as they were fifty feet below street level on the enclosed ramp near the water's edge. Keanu walked down toward the Zodiac to meet a returning crew member who was carrying three mid-sized backpacks. Keanu took the proffered bundles, turned, and began walking up the ramp toward the Land Rover.

Sachiko was still talking with one of the Zodiac men when the two mobile units, lights and sirens going, arrived at the top of the ramp. One vehicle swerved at an angle, blocking the exit entirely; the second moved down the ramp right behind the Land Rover and then also turned sideways.

A loudspeaker screeched, "Get down on the ground, hands above your head! Get down on the ground, hands above your head!" Three officers in tactical vests, guns drawn, made their way down the ramp from the cruiser at the very top of the ramp.

Car doors opened on the other cruiser, and four vested and armed officers rapidly exited and took up positions using the SUV as a shield, guns at the ready.

Out on the water, Flash saw the Harbor Police approaching the *Invincible* Zodiac. The police boat had blue lights flashing and lit up the scene with two powerful searchlights. Keanu, who had reached the Land Rover, opened the door, threw the backpacks into the back seat, pulled a gun from somewhere, and using the door as a shield, fired four shots at the officers up the ramp. Five or six shots answered, and Keanu's gun flew out of his hand as he spun out from behind the door and fell screaming and holding his leg, thrashing about on the ground.

The officers behind the SUV nearest to the Land Rover filed out, ducking low, and one by one sprinted down the ramp to the rear of the Land Rover, using it as cover. The two Zodiac men had turned and were running back down the ramp toward their boat. Halfway down the ramp, one of the men veered off and ran over to his right to release the bowline, which had been sloppily secured with a large loop. He reached the cleat, flipped the loop off the cleat, then turned and ran toward the boat.

The Harbor Police Zodiac was at least two hundred yards away. The twin outboard motors on the *Invincible* Zodiac had been raised when the boat was moored. They were now slowly being lowered into the water.

Flash threw off his radio headset and jumped onto the sixty-degree incline between him and the landing. He slid almost uncontrollably, slowed only by the undergrowth. At one point, as he regained his footing, he tripped when the uneven ground caught his foot, and he tumbled and somersaulted through one painful rotation, again landing on his feet, grabbing a branch to break his fall and keep running.

He hit the ground at the edge of the ramp. The twin outboard motors were now fully lowered. The bow rope was moving slowly down the ramp as the Zodiac slid into the ocean. Flash grabbed the looped end of the rope and threw it over the last cleat on the ramp. He then threw himself back onto the vegetation on the side of the ramp, hoping to avoid any gunfire.

The Zodiac captain threw the motors into reverse. The boat lunged back, then abruptly stopped, the bow rope pulled taut. One of the men pulled out a knife and began sawing frantically at the rope. By now, the Harbor Police's Zodiac was closing in. The loudspeaker boomed, "Turn off your engines, get down, hands over your heads, get down now, or we'll open fire. Get down now, or we'll open fire. Turn off the engines."

The bow rope snapped where it was being cut by the deckhand, and the Zodiac lunged down the ramp. Simultaneously, the Harbor Police's Zodiac rammed into their rear, knocking all three men down and driving the boat aground. The twin outboard motors, propellers out of the water, whined and screeched, metal on concrete, metal on metal.

Two officers jumped from the Harbor Police boat, guns aimed at the three crewmen, who were down on their knees, hands behind their necks.

Three officers moved out from behind the Land Rover and approached Sachiko and Keanu. She had her hands in the air; he was writhing on the ground next to her. The officers put her in handcuffs and led her up the ramp toward the nearest SUV, its blue lights still flashing.

Two EMTs, accompanied by Kellie and another officer Flash didn't recognize, moved toward Keanu. He was yelling. Kellie checked to make sure Keanu wasn't armed, then motioned for the EMTs to move in to examine him.

Flash was scratched, bruised, and bleeding from a cut on his forehead. Kellie and Bob made their way over to him.

Bob looked him up and down and said, "I never thought I'd see the day. The Lone Ranger rides again! Nice rope trick, kemo sabe."

Kellie said, "Jesus, Bob. You okay, Flash?"

Flash smiled. "Hi Ho, Silver."

CHAPTER 36

Fiona's cell phone chirped at seven-ten. She was seated at the counter in her kitchen, drinking a cup of English breakfast tea with milk and four spoonfuls of sugar. She believed in the power of caffeine and sugar in combination to kickstart the day.

"Shit," she said, then pushed the green button to accept the call. "Good morning, Mr. Haysmith. How can I help you?"

"Fiona, the office is closed today, so don't come in. Take a sick day. You'll be paid, but the office won't be open for business."

She hardly recognized his voice. The sound was scratchy, constrained, almost forced. That he would pay her for not working struck her as even more baffling. *What is going on here?*

"Closed? Why closed, if I may ask, sir?"

"We've just received word that Monsieur Planc has passed away, quite suddenly. So as a matter of respect and security, I've been ordered by Zurich to close the office for at least today. Maybe longer. I don't know. But you'll be paid, as I said. No need for alarm on your part."

That was when she knew something must be really wrong. Malcolm-the-cheap-bastard-Haysmith trying to reassure her? *No way.*

"So I'll just stand by and wait to hear from you? I have quite a bit of work to do, sir."

"Yes, ah, no. Ah, yes. What I mean is wait, yes. I'll call and tell you when to come in. Oh, and we may be receiving some visitors from Zurich in the next few days to sort out the new organizational structure, what with Planc gone and all." She thought she heard someone else in the office—a man's voice, unfamiliar, with an accent, maybe German or Slavic?

Haysmith signed off with an uncharacteristically cheery, "Have a good day."

Have a good day? Her brain was spinning, boosted by the caffeine and sugar. She went online and quickly found the article on CNN Europe. Planc had been shot while walking in the center of Zurich. The Swiss police were assuming the incident was a targeted assassination. The victim had long been suspected of being a drug lord, although he had never even been indicted. The article went on to suggest that his death might be a precursor to an internecine conflict among the forces of evil. *So Haysmith's boss was a big-time European drug lord?*

She grabbed her phone and dialed the one person in her universe who might be interested in this news: Flash One-Night-Stand Tucker.

"Hey, Flash, got a moment?"

"Fiona, I'm with some people. Let me call you right back, two minutes."

Two minutes later, he called back and said, "Hi, there! This is a pleasant surprise. How are you?"

"Did I catch you at a bad time?"

"No, no, no—love to chat, perfect time. In fact, it couldn't be a more perfect time. It's a great day to be alive on Kauai. What's up?"

Fiona relayed her news, and waited for Flash to say something.

"Flash, you there?"

"Yeah, I am, just thinking." After another long pause, he said, "Fiona, do you have any idea what Haysmith is up to?"

"No. Not a clue. I just this moment heard from him, and then put two and two together with the CNN story. Apparently, the authorities think Planc was a drug lord. What does that make Haysmith, I wonder?"

"Well, you're a bright person, and you know more about him than anyone else I know, so what do you think?"

"I think it explains why Haysmith is such a jerk, for one thing. I mean, if Planc was a drug lord, well, Haysmith is a drug lord's flunky, a pawn, or something like that."

She waited for his answer, but all she got was another long silence. "Hey, Flash, it's your turn to talk now!"

"Yeah, I know. Remember, we talked about this the other night. Haysmith is definitely a crook, and now something bad has happened in the kingdom. The king has been shot, and one of his flunkies is acting— what? Out of character? Frightened maybe? I mean, why shut down the office when the Village in the Sky is in full swing?"

"Dunno. You're the journalist, not me. What do you think?

"I think you may be in danger. I'm thinking you might go into the office and find yourself in the middle of a war zone. Fiona, what would you say about taking an unscheduled vacation, like maybe on an inter-island getaway, a secret getaway?"

"Sorry? What are you talking about, Flash?"

"I think anyone around Haysmith or that office is in mortal danger. We know he's been getting paid under the table, collecting illegal bribes from contractors—that's bad enough. Then his boss, Planc, is murdered, leaving Haysmith unprotected. Planc's partners won't take long to figure out that Haysmith has been fleecing the project and jeopardizing their investment. The situation would be bad enough if he were stealing from a legit business, but, Fiona, he's been stealing from the nastiest people on earth."

Fiona was stunned. She took the last sip of tea, put the cup on the butcher block counter, and stood, looking down at it, as if it were a curious artifact. She said, "What should I do?"

"Pack an overnight bag with clothes for three or four days and fly to Kauai this afternoon. I'll put you up for a while. You have to get out of Honolulu until this blows over."

She said, "Okay, Flash, okay. You got a house or apartment? I can't afford—"

"Don't worry about that, I'll put you up. Nothing fancy. But don't tell anybody you're leaving or where you're going. Oh, and turn off your cell phone and don't turn it on for any reason. Call me from a pay phone at the Honolulu airport with the flight number. Use a pay phone, not your cell. A guy named Pika, from the Kauai Taxi Service—he's a buddy of mine—he'll meet you when you land."

"God, okay, I'll call from the airport. Flash, are you sure about this? You're really scaring me!"

"Good! You should be scared. Now please get off the phone, turn it off and leave it off, and get moving! See you later this afternoon."

The morning light on the Pacific Ocean across Waikiki Beach was sparkling, otherworldly. The view calmed Erebus just enough for him to get a grip and look more critically at Haysmith, who was pale, perhaps hung over, fragile, and near breaking. His jowls were veined and pink, most likely from high blood pressure.

Earlier that morning, Erebus had surprised Haysmith in the Brit's bedroom, shouting at him, shaking him awake. "Get up, get up, you fool! Don't you know what's happened? The good news is Planc is dead. The bad news for you is Planc is dead!"

Haysmith had been startled, disoriented, and frightened out of his wits, shocked awake by the last person he would want to see, Erebus, the killer.

"What—what are you doing here? God, don't kill me, don't kill me, please! I have money!"

Erebus couldn't have asked for a better reaction. The priggish bastard was almost catatonic with fear, curled up in the fetal position. As if he could protect his delicate parts, stomach, lungs, balls, by rolling himself into a protective ball like a stinking sow bug.

"I'm here because Planc is dead. You paid me to kill him, remember? And I did kill him! But I don't want to kill you, Haysmith. I've come to save you."

"What, save me?"

"Mm-hmm, to save you, for a fee, of course. What did you think would happen when Planc was knocked off? Did you believe his partners at LM Global would grant you a free hand with their treasure chest? Haysmith, Planc's partners hated him! And they hate each other too. Planc's presence was the only force that kept them together, mostly through intimidation. When you ordered Planc's execution, which I am pleased to say was a thing of beauty, you released the furies. And now they're coming to get you." Erebus laughed, a little out of control.

"Now, Haysmith, we're going to spend the morning working to keep you alive," said Erebus. "You can count on the fact that Planc's partners have already sent out their killers and torturers to take control of his empire, and you are without a doubt number one on their list. After all, they sequestered half-a-billion dollars in Sixty-Four Capital, with you and Planc as the only key holders. With Planc out of the way, you are the only thing standing between them and their gold. So our first order of business is to release control of that money, to get you out of the way."

All of the blood had drained from Haysmith's face, even his veined jowls. Seated behind his desk, the Brit looked like a partially deflated blow-up doll, cow-eyed, mute.

Erebus knew that shock could be life-threatening, and Haysmith was in shock, even though he'd hardly been touched. Before he died, however, Haysmith had to give up the codes to LM Global's investment chest and his own cache of stolen money. Shock, in this case, was Erebus's best friend, and he would use it to force the fat man right up to the edge of the abyss.

"Here's what will happen. You will release control of Sixty-Four Capital's bank accounts by sending the access codes and authorizations to each of LM Global partners at the same time. That will provoke a free for all, a feeding frenzy, as they all dive in and fight with one another to gain control of the money. During the ensuing battle, we should be able to spirit you away safely. I've rented a boat to ferry you off Oahu to a safe house on Kauai. If they can't find you, they can't kill you. Are you listening, Haysmith?"

"Yes," the weaselly blob mumbled.

"Fine." Erebus moved to Haysmith's side of the desk and placed his face close to Haysmith's. In a growling voice, he said, "Now pull up the document with the codes and instructions to access the Village in the Sky investment fund. Do it now!"

Haysmith winced, then he began typing on his keyboard. After a couple of minutes, he turned the monitor toward Erebus. The three-page document looked legitimate, with the proper codes and instructions present.

"Okay, attach that to an email to LM Global, attention all partners, subject: 'Sixty-Four Capital access codes and authorizations.'"

When he stopped typing again, Haysmith looked over at Erebus as if awaiting a signal.

Erebus looked at the email, nodded his head, and said, "Send it."

Haysmith pressed a single key on the keyboard. The click was accompanied by the electronic swooshing sound that signifies *Sent*. Erebus smiled. He felt a surge of vengeful energy as he imagined simultaneous alarm bells sounding in the dens of the LM Global drug lords on the other side of the world.

"Good," Erebus said. "Next, we're going to have to move your private stash to a safer hiding place." Erebus reached over and put one hand around Haysmith's throat. He said, "I happen to know that Planc knew you were taking bribes, and he somehow knew where you'd hidden the money."

Erebus tightened his hand as he continued. "If your new enemies find out what you've been doing, they will roast you slowly over an open fire for your sins. So we have to move that money and close the accounts. Do you understand?"

"Yes," Haysmith whispered.

The fat Brit took two hours to unearth nearly six-million dollars and move it to another offshore account. What Haysmith didn't know was that Erebus had enabled a back door to that new, supposedly secret and secure location. But in the long run, Haysmith wasn't going to need the money, anyway.

Three hours later, at one-thirty in the afternoon, Erebus and Haysmith boarded a gleaming-white forty-six-foot Cantius cabin cruiser at the Waikiki Marina. Haysmith stood shakily holding the gunwale as Erebus moved to the captain's chair in the cockpit. He turned the starter switch, and twin 435-HP Volvo Penta engines roared to life.

Erebus, thinking of himself as *Captain Erebus*, eased the boat away from the dock and guided the cruiser toward the harbor mouth.

Over his shoulder, Erebus said, "Why don't you fix yourself a drink? We have a full bar here, beer, good scotch, vodka, mixers. Relax, we're home free now."

Haysmith opened the bar, his hands shaking. He took a high-ball glass, opened a new bottle of Johnnie Walker Blue, half-filled the glass with the amber liquid, and drank it down as though it were water. He carried the bottle and the glass to the rear of the bridge and fell onto a white upholstered couch, exhaling as he sat.

Erebus felt a wave of release, a kind of pre-ecstasy, as he guided the cruiser into the open ocean, turning toward Kauai, sixty nautical miles to the northwest. The crossing would take three and a half hours. Near the halfway point between Kauai and Oahu, he'd just throw this worm overboard. No need to bloody the boat.

An hour and a half later, sweeping over the open sea, no land in sight, Erebus saw a waterspout ahead, then another, and another. They were approaching a pod of humpback whales. He eased back the throttle so as not to come too close. He could count three or four geysers at any one time and imagined he smelled their fishy breath, even from this distance.

Erebus felt like an excited child—he'd dreamed of someday seeing whales up close. He wanted to jump up and down and clap his hands. "Look, look, look," he heard himself shout. "Look!" He was alive with joy, so much so that the feeling was almost painful. *I never, I never imagined I could really see these giants up close in the ocean. I never, I never imagined. My God!*

He might not have imagined seeing whales in person, but while reviewing the pilot's manual for cruising Hawaiian waters, he'd taken note of the federal law that prohibited boats from approaching whales any closer than one-hundred yards. Mindful of the law and not wanting to disturb the majestic monsters, he pulled the throttle back farther.

His shouting had apparently jolted Haysmith alert, and the Brit yelled, "What is it? What is it? Why are you shouting? Why are we slowing down?"

The sound of the worm's voice startled and angered Erebus. This irrelevant semi-human was ruining his reverie. He looked back to see the Brit roll off the couch and move unsteadily into the cabin toward Erebus. With each stumbling step Haysmith took, Erebus could feel his anger grow.

He turned and approached Haysmith, then abruptly twisted him around and pushed him out of the cabin to the rear deck, holding him by the shoulders. Erebus didn't ever want to look at that disgusting face again.

He said, "See, Haysmith? See the pretty whales? See them?"

Haysmith appeared disoriented as he stumbled up to the gunwale. He said, "No, oh, oh, wait! Yes, I see—"

Erebus slammed Haysmith with both fists hard between the shoulder blades, and the Brit, who had tried to turn sideways, cartwheeled into the ocean. Erebus walked back into the cabin and advanced the throttle just a bit, enough to move away from the thrashing, screaming Haysmith.

The sound of Haysmith splashing into the blue Pacific released a rush of pure ecstasy! First Planc, then Haysmith—the two main targets in the Last Days death book were dead! He felt a wave of sentimentality. He was nearing the end. He gunned the engines, steering out around the pod, well outside the one-hundred-yard limit. The engine roar drowned out Haysmith's screams and cries for help.

Bart Singletary was startled awake by his phone buzzing on the night table next to his bed. He and his wife slept in separate bedrooms. Theirs was a dynastic marriage; they were a power couple, not an "in love" couple.

Drowsy and still a little drunk from the evening's dinner party, Bart looked at the screen, trying to force his eyes to focus on the message: Invincible boarded by Coast Guard, underway to Nawiliwili Harbor impounded.

He sat up, heart thumping, scanning the screen for more information, wondering what the hell was going on. Impounded? Then he remembered. Sachiko's jumbo shipment was scheduled for last night. *What could have happened?*

His yacht did double duty as a moveable drugs warehouse. He firmly believed it was more secure than a stash on land. A ninety-seven-foot yacht had a myriad of invisible voids and spaces. During the *Invincible's* construction, he had ordered modifications to the superstructure to secretly hide hundreds of pounds of special cargo. At any sign of danger ashore, *Invincible* could just quietly put out to sea and dump or transfer stock. He'd never imagined that the yacht could be impounded. How could the cops ever justify it? No court in Hawaii would dare to consider granting a search warrant for his yacht, let alone impound it, never!

Only here the message was, *impounded*.

He checked his watch; it was two in the morning. Disregarding the time, he called Sam Hatch, his long-time lawyer, defender of the Singletary Family Trust, and senior partner of Hach, Mulbain, and Reilly. His call went to voicemail. "Sam, it's Bart," he barked. "We have a big problem. Call me tonight. This is an emergency!"

He punched out the same message as a text to Sam, followed by four exclamation points.

John had spent the last two days searching for Flash. He'd concentrated on the busy tourist hangouts around Koloa, Poipu, Brennecke's Beach, and the Grand Hyatt at Shipwreck. Each time John asked someone about his "old buddy from Seattle," he knew he risked that word might find its way back to Flash and trigger him into action, like hiding or preparing for a battle or both. So with each query, his anxiety grew, amplified by Tilly's time bomb ticking away in the background.

Tilly's package would be released in two days. John's plan was to surprise Flash and take him to the Airbnb and get on with the work of recovering his fucking money. Surprise was important. He needed to capture or lure Flash up to the rental before Flash knew what had hit him. That was the plan.

Several people he'd asked said they knew a fellow named Flash. He'd heard that Flash was a kind of beach bum, that he drank a lot, that he, unlike most of the locals, liked eating at tourist dives, and that Brennecke's was one of his favorites for drinks and food, in that order. John had asked a bartender at Brennecke's about Flash and noticed the fellow did a lot of thinking before saying he didn't know anyone by that name. John had had a strong hunch the bartender was lying.

John sat in the park across the street from Brennecke's at

lunchtime and watched the entrance. Nothing. He returned at four in the afternoon and watched again. Bingo. There he was, Flash Finnegan Michael, that son of a bitch, big as life, greeting people outside on the sidewalk, then entering the building.

John was dizzy with relief. He walked to the adjacent parking lot where his Jeep was parked. Just as he opened the driver's side door, he felt raindrops. He started the engine and moved the Jeep to a parking space where he had a good view of the restaurant's front door. He could follow Flash in the car or on foot. *This is it*, he thought. *Almost home free.*

CHAPTER 37

Fiona was frightened. She had rushed to Daniel K. Inouye Airport and just made it onto the aircraft before they closed the door. Several times during the thirty-minute flight, she asked herself, *Are you out of your mind?* The best answer she could come up with was, *Shut up, will you? I'm trying to think!*

She deplaned to a sunny afternoon on Kauai. She passed through security doors into baggage claim, through agricultural control, and out to the sidewalk. A tan, cheerful-looking fellow was holding up a sign: Ms. F Ryan. He had on white pants, a flower shirt, a white shell necklace around his rather thick neck, Air Jordans, and a beaming smile. Where the hell was Flash? He had frightened her out of Honolulu. The least he could do was—

"Ms. Ryan? Ms. Ryan?"

Fiona forced a smile and said, "Yes, Mr. Pika—Flash told me. I'm Ms. Ryan."

Pika held a finger to his lips and motioned her to come closer. "I'm at your service. Flash sent me to pick you up and take you to where you'll be staying, with Ms. Pookalani. Follow me, please, and I'll drive you in my cab."

They walked across to the parking lot where a green-and-white Kauai Taxicab was baking in the afternoon sun. He took her carry-on bag and put it in the trunk. She clambered into the back of the car. Then he went around to the driver's seat, closed the door, and started the engine. He rolled down the windows and turned on the air conditioner.

He handed her a phone, then began to drive. He said, "That has an unregistered SIM card. No one can track you with it. Right now, the access code is one one one one one one one. You can change it if you want. We've put several local phone numbers in the address book for your safety and convenience. Me—Pika—whenever you need help or a cab. Flash, of course. Ms. Emma Pookalani—you'll be staying with her. And Mia Mahoe, Auntie Mia to all of us, a very resourceful local lady who's Flash's landlord and honorary queen of Koloa. You can also call Officer Kellie Jackson, a Kauai policewoman, and Janet Nakamura, Flash's lawyer. They all know you're visiting in secret and have volunteered to help."

Fiona was more than a little overwhelmed. "Why are all these people doing this? Helping me, I mean?" she asked.

"Oh, cause of Flash," Pika said, sounding quite enthusiastic. "He's all of a sudden a local hero—busted up a big drug ring. We're his friends, even though he's an incomer. You know, a mainlander who got washed up on the island and didn't start out so good. But pow! He got those drug pushers, caught 'em in the act. I'm his personal assistant and chauffeur—when I'm not on a call, that is. This is my cab."

Fiona turned on the phone, put in the code, and called Flash, but the call went to voicemail. "Hi, Flash, I'm here driving with Pika to Emma's house. You've got a lot of explaining to do, but thank you for Pika and the phone. Looking forward to seeing you this evening— Bye now."

The rain stopped, so the windows in Brennecke's were thrown open all across the front, and the cool evening air, redolent of plumeria, jasmine, and ginger, rushed in to mix with the smells of beer, rum, and barbecue. Flash was running out of gas.

He'd spent the morning at Kauai Police HQ participating in meetings to rehash and document the drug bust. All those involved were in good moods, especially Chief Aukai. They had cut the head off the snake, with no injuries to the good guys and only one non-fatal bullet wound to the bad guys. They'd captured the largest quantity of illegal drugs ever taken on Kauai and recovered one-hundred-ninety-thousand in cash.

Flash had spent the afternoon making a formal statement for the police, giving an interview to a reporter from the *Garden Island*, and arranging for Fiona's arrival. Afterward, Kellie had driven Flash back to Koloa; he had dragged his aching body up the stairs, fallen onto his bed, and crashed.

After sleeping like the dead for an hour, he awoke somewhat refreshed and definitely hungry.

He arrived at Brennecke's just as the rain started. Ducking into the entrance, he climbed up the stairs to the nightly party in progress, where he was greeted by spontaneous applause and cheers. He felt as though he'd begun his fifteen minutes of fame. The adulation, slaps on the back, and being the center of attention almost made him forget that he had come to Kauai to be erased.

By eight-thirty he'd talked and was talked to, nonstop, for two hours. He'd had a blackened ahi sandwich with fries, nursed four pints of Foster's, and was thinking fifteen minutes was more than he had bargained for, and another pint wasn't going to make it any better. Time to leave. He pulled out his phone.

"Pika, you anywhere near Koloa or Poipu?"

"Yes, boss, how can I help?"

"Sorry to do this on short notice, but I think I need a ride back to my, uh Mia's, building. I'm at Brennecke's."

"Be there in fifteen. I'm up the road at the Hyatt. It's pretty slow here tonight."

Flash pushed off his stool, waved goodbye to his adoring fans, and descended the staircase toward the open door. The quiet on the sidewalk and the warm, wet, ocean breeze were just what he needed. *What a relief.*

A familiar voice yelled from across the street, "Hey, Flash, how ya doing?"

Flash waved his hand in the air. "Yeah, I'm good, thanks, I'm good." He looked around but couldn't see anybody in the park or on the sidewalk. Then he saw a man lean out the open window of a white Jeep Cherokee parked across the street.

"Hey, Flash, over here. It's me, John! How you doin', buddy? I've been looking all over for you!"

Flash crossed the street, walking slowly and unevenly toward the voice.

"John? John! What are you doing here?"

"Hey, buddy, I've got a gift for you from Pippa. Jump in. She really misses you, ya know."

"A gift from Pippa, how—"

"Jump in, Flash. I told her I might see you, so she gave me a gift to bring."

Flash made his way to the passenger door, opened it, and looked in. John Horan, his once-upon-a-time partner, John. Flash shook his head, trying to make sense out of what he was feeling. His immediate reaction was joy—his old friend, his partner.

"Jump in. I was beginning to think I wouldn't be able to find you. How are you?"

Flash slid into the seat. When Pika couldn't find him, the man would just move on. Flash would pay him later. "I'm okay, but what are you doing here? How did you find me?"

"What do you mean, how did I find you? I'm a fucking cop, Flash—that's how."

Flash felt as though he'd reunited with a long-lost brother. It was John Horan, his partner. Then another thought edged in. It was John Horan, the partner who'd betrayed him, siding with

Chief Forsyth, perhaps convincing Forsyth that Flash was a crook.

John started the car, shifted into drive, and pulled slowly out of the parking space. He said, "Let's go to my place and have a drink. Pippa's gift is there. We can have a couple and catch up. I'll bring you back after. This'll be great. Boy, is it ever good to see you, Houdini!"

"Where are you staying?" Flash was thinking the Hyatt or maybe the Koa Kea. John liked expensive.

"An Airbnb up behind Kalaheo, in the hills, just ten minutes, not far."

"You resisted the call of the beaches?"

"Yeah, well, the beaches are free, you may have noticed. You can see them from up in the foothills too. But you can get the spaciousness and privacy of a house and a pool up there. Someone spent a packet on this one, probably laundered money."

Flash looked over at John—he wasn't smiling.

"Are you alone over here?"

"Yup, just me, myself, and I."

"Doesn't sound like you."

"Yeah, well, times change, and so do people, Flash."

Again Flash looked over at John. That didn't sound like the John he knew. His answer sounded, felt, out of place, like a steak entree at a vegan restaurant.

John seemed preoccupied with driving. His hands were on the steering wheel, at the ten and two positions. He leaned forward and looked both ways at the intersection of Koloa Road and Highway 50, even though they had a green light. Satisfied that the way was clear, he slowly accelerated across the intersection up into the hills. With no streetlights here, the world around them was impenetrably dark. And as they climbed, the houses were spaced farther and farther apart, many of them well back from the road, making the scene even darker.

With a glance at the dashboard, Flash could see they were

only going twenty-five miles per hour. At that moment, it occurred to him that John was driving just like his dad, Tom. John, who a speed merchant, was always driving too fast. What'd happened to John? Tom was a sixty-seven-year-old widower, for God's sake, and John was what—prematurely old at forty-four?

Then John spoke. "I recently discovered that I have pancreatic cancer. The type they can't cure."

Flash looked over at John, too shocked to say anything. He saw the unsmiling profile of a man he thought he had once known. The face was cold, stern, somber.

"I've been given six months, maybe a year to live. So saving for retirement didn't seem like a high priority with whatever time I have left, know what I mean?"

Flash felt a pain in his stomach. Hearing the news hurt.

"Jesus, John, I'm sorry. Are you sure that—"

"Yeah, yeah, I'm sure. The doctors are sure, everyone is sure."

John didn't look sick, but it was dark. Who could tell?

Flash thought back to that morning in Chief Forsyth's office. John the accuser, not John the friend, and Chief Forsyth in full dress uniform, sitting in judgment, with John acting as the chief's mouthpiece, passing a life sentence on Flash. To be spent either in jail or forever banished, branded as a thief and a traitor.

Flash said, "Why did you turn on me? You must have known I didn't do it. I didn't steal the money."

John looked at Flash, then back at the road ahead. "The evidence, buddy, the evidence. It had to be you. You must have done it."

"But I didn't do it."

"Oh fuck, Flash, let's not rehash that whole thing." John looked at Flash as if waiting for an answer. "Here, let me say it this way. At the time, it sure as hell looked like you did it. Nothing even suggested a plausible alternative explanation, so what the hell were we to do? There, is that better?"

Unbidden, the ease with which he could always talk to John

flooded back again, the give and take between the two of them, thought patterns running side by side. Fifteen years of friendship and mutual support. Fifteen years of give and take, sharing and arguing, but always covering for each other, no matter what. And yet John had betrayed him.

"Did you steal the money, John?"

"Do I look like a ten-million-dollar man, Flash? No, I didn't! We thought you did it, remember?"

"How can I forget? But do I look like a ten-million-dollar man to you, John?"

"Well, it's a little hard to tell. You've been gone for what, six months? You could be a twenty-million-dollar man for all I know, don't you think?"

"So you still think I stole the money, is that it?" Flash looked out into the dark and then back at John.

"What does it matter what I think, Flash? If I think you stole the money, then I'll suck up to you like crazy, and try to get a little sunshine from my millionaire buddy. Maybe that's why I came looking for you—who knows?"

"Yeah, but you've never been the sucking-up type, except with Forsyth, that is. I always wondered how he never saw past the relentless onslaught of obsequious bullshit you kept feeding him morning, noon, and night."

"Fuck, Flash, as if you didn't agree with me! Admit it, you thought he was a prick. He's still a prick! As for the obsequious bullshit, well, it saved your bacon a couple of times."

That was the showstopper. Because on that day in Forsyth's office, John had been on the other side of the table, pushing Flash Finnegan Michael out of a job and out of his life. Flash didn't need to look at John playing at being an old man driving. Flash knew what he looked like, then and now. This encounter didn't make sense, John just happening to come to Kauai —unless…

Flash said, "You know, John, the last time we saw each other? No one was saving my bacon, least of all you. In fact, you were throwing me and my fucking bacon into the fire. Maybe you've forgotten that part."

"Flash, if Forsyth could have had you shot for treason that morning, he would've done it. He was so fucking scared of a public relations fiasco, he would've happily burned you at the stake and had it televised. I'm the one who saved your ass. Of course, you didn't read the situation very clearly, so you just kept saying, 'I didn't do it, I didn't do it, I didn't do it.' How far did that get you, Flash? Huh? I'm the one who came up with the *quid pro quo* that freed you up to run away and hide out with a new life here on Kauai. The alternative was you rotting in a jail cell forever, which was Forsyth's preference, by the way."

John slowed and turned right onto a gravel drive blocked by a gate. John rolled down his window and entered a code. The gates slowly opened inward. A sign over the entryway read *Hale kau lā'au*.

"What does *hale kau lā'au* mean?"

"Treehouse, can you believe it? Treehouse, because the house is among many trees. It was built by a developer, some wealthy guy who hit it big in Lincoln, Nebraska. No kidding. Well, maybe Omaha. I forget. According to the Airbnb material, his daughter named it. Cute, huh?"

The driveway passed through the trees, bending to the right at the first twist, then bending left, then breaking out in front of an ultra-modern, open-beamed steel, glass, volcanic-stone two-story edifice. As the Jeep turned in front of the house under an overhang, the entire bottom floor lit up—outside and inside lighting, all ablaze.

Flash was shocked. *Christ, the place is a mansion!* The house belonged on the cover of *Architectural Digest*. Flash said, "So maybe you're the ten-million-dollar man, after all. Where did all this come from? Renting it must have cost you a fortune."

"Nah, this is the off-season, so it was relatively cheap. Besides, I don't have to scrimp and save anymore."

Flash opened his door and got out, stretched, and walked

with John to the front door. Watching John enter a code in a keypad, Flash began to wonder again what the hell was going on with John. This house was so far out of John's league, well, it was preposterous.

The front door clicked open, and John led the way, motioning Flash to follow him. Flash thought back on his impressions of John so far. He hadn't detected any tics, no noticeable tells, except for the weird driving. He'd thought he knew John really well, and this seemed almost like the old John, though not quite.

They walked into the great room, and John said, "Have a seat over there. What do you want to drink?"

"Beer. Foster's if you've got it. If not, any beer." Flash looked around the room. The space was encased by glass walls, and an open staircase at the back led up to a second floor. The room had three seating areas, with modern European leather chairs as well as couches and one-of-a-kind tables. Each section featured not just furniture, but eclectic pieces of art, tastefully chosen. The whole space was lit from above.

Flash sat in one of two high-backed leather upholstered chairs placed perpendicular to each other with a smooth, green plastic cube table between. On the table were three glass bowls fired in rainbow colors, one filled with Belgium chocolates, another with lemon drops covered in powdered sugar, and a third offering colored marbles—or were they also candies?

John handed Flash a big Foster's can and sat in the other chair. He was apparently drinking a G and T with lime. "Cheers. Here's to better times, as long as they last," he said, and held out his glass.

Flash clicked his beer against the glass and said, "As long as they last."

They both drank, then sat in silence.

Flash said, "So, John, what's all this about? You can't afford this, or at least the John I used to know couldn't afford this."

"Nah, I told you it was cheap. Off-season."

Flash squinted, seeking to make eye contact, but John looked down at the G and T in his hand. Then John put his glass on the table next to the bowl of marbles and nonchalantly reached behind his back, producing a Glock. He pointed it at Flash's chest.

Flash took a deep, slow breath, smiled, then said, shaking his head in disbelief, "Oh. Now I get it. You are a stupid shit, aren't you? You're the one. You rigged it. You stole the money, didn't you, John?"

John's face was impassive. He said nothing, just sat calmly holding the gun steady.

Flash said, "You stole the money and framed me. So you really are the ten-million-dollar man, eh, John? Well, why bother with all this?" Flash indicated the giant great room. "And the cancer, John? You don't look sick to me. What the fuck are you doing here, and why me, for God's sake?" Flash folded his arms and sat back, his eyes drilling on John's again.

In the silence that followed, John's expression changed. His face went from impassive to uncertain, from stoic to startled.

Just like in the old days, Flash picked up on his old best buddy's mood—he was awash in confusion and uncertainty too.

Why was John there in Kauai? Why, and why the gun? And why did John suddenly look as if he'd made some miscalculation?

CHAPTER 38

"What's with the gun, John? Afraid I'll steal your money?"

John grimaced.

"Or is this the gift you supposedly brought from my daughter?"

Flash was sick of this game. John had the gun, so Flash wrote it off as something he couldn't control. What he could do was needle the bastard and see what developed, maybe grab the gun.

"So, John, you took the money and put it somewhere. You bulldozed me into taking the blame. I left town, changed my identity, and did my best to erase myself. That's my story—so what's yours? What have you been up to since I saw you last, huh?"

Flash was breathing faster. "Come on, John! I've shown you mine, and now you show me yours. What have you done, buddy? Tell me."

John rested the gun on his right thigh, still keeping it pointed at Flash. He blinked erratically and swallowed twice before he said anything. Then, as if he had just decided, John nodded and said, "Okay, let's do this. I stole the money, for about three minutes, I figure. Then someone else stole it from me."

"What? What are you saying? Three minutes?"

John sighed. "For all I know, it might have only been one minute. Tilly Good. She was my accomplice. I set you up, and she set me up. You made the initial transfer, and the money arrived. Then she swiped it. She made it disappear into her hiding place, wherever that was. So, yes, one minute I had it, and the next, as things turn out, it was gone. Fucking magic. I didn't even know it was missing until—well, recently."

Flash had heard a lot about Tilly Good, mostly from John, but he had never met her, although he would have jumped at the chance to do so. At this moment, however, Tilly wasn't the most pressing issue; Flash needed to keep the conversation going. As long as they were talking, he continued to breathe, a good thing.

"You always said she was wicked intelligent, but John, what the hell? Did she bewitch you or what?"

Glowering, John said, "I don't know! Bewitched, bamboozled? If I knew, I sure as hell wouldn't be sitting here holding a gun on you, would I?"

Flash smiled, a big gleeful smile. "You're not going to blame all this on Tilly, are you? I mean you and the gun and double-crossing your best friend, violating your oath—all the shitty things that go along with being a deceitful asshole—that's on Tilly? I don't think so."

John shook his head slowly, but he said nothing.

Flash pressed on. "Okay, so Tilly double-crossed you. I got it. What's the next part? Why are you *here*?"

John shifted in his chair and grimaced again. That was a tell, the grimace. Flash said, "Did you hear me, John? Why—are—you—here?"

More silence.

Flash said, "Look at me, John! You certainly can't think I have anything you want! I'm just an ex-cop, retired early, thanks to you, living like a beach bum on a half-pension, again thanks to you, asshole!"

John's face was pink in the bright light, and Flash could see he was growing angry. Finally, John said, "A little birdie told me that you have my money, a little birdie I shot—with a gun just like this one, by the way. Where is my fucking money, Flash?"

Flash chuckled. "What little dead birdie are we talking about now, John?"

"Tilly Good, of course, the, the—the late Tilly Good!" John waved the pistol at Flash as if trying to push out the words. His lips were white, turned up at the edges, his front teeth half-showing, feral. Flash had never heard John stutter before.

"John—You realize I've never even met Tilly. All I know is she was a perp whose testimony supplied you with lots of convictions, an early promotion, and lots and lots of vainglorious stories. So given that I've never even spoken to this woman, how exactly did this little Tilly bird sell you on the idea that I, of all people, have the money?"

Flash sat waiting, his eyes locked in on John's, watching for an opening, any distraction, something to give him a chance.

John said, "She took my money, and she told me she was giving it to you."

Now Flash was really confused. He chuckled and said, "Really, John? Tilly, who already tricked you and stole the money out from under your nose, somehow convinces you that she gave it to me? How in hell does that work?"

John's face turned a darker shade of red, sweat appearing on his forehead. He moved the gun up, aiming it at Flash's face, and said, "It's a long and complicated fucking story. Too long. I know you have my money, and you're going to tell me where it is and give it back, or I'll blow your fucking face off. Where is the money, Flash?" His gun hand shook, knuckles white with strain. The scowl on his face deepened.

Flash could feel his heart pounding against the inside of his chest. He wondered how long he could continue to poke at John without being shot.

Flash took a slow deep breath, gathered himself as best he could, and said, "So, John, let's assume for a moment that you really believe I have the money. Then, what's with the gun? We both know you can't shoot me because then I'd be dead, and you'd never find the money. You're really painting yourself into a corner, John. You'd actually be better off hightailing it out of here while you have the chance—because I don't have the money. I will say one thing, though—Tilly Good sure screwed you up big time!"

John suddenly lunged out of his chair, shouting, "You son of a bitch, listen to me!" He pushed the Glock hard against Flash's mouth, twisting the barrel, cutting Flash's lip, and grinding it against his teeth. John was standing over Flash with one hand on Flash's throat, the other holding the gun barrel, twisting it back and forth in the blood and spit as if trying to push the gun through his mouth, down into his throat.

In desperation, Flash brought his right leg up with all his force, pile driving his knee between John's legs. John grunted and began to double over. Flash twisted his body out from under John's and smashed at the gun with his fist.

Flash reached up with his other hand and punched his thumb into John's eye as hard as he could. John screamed. This was the chance Flash was waiting for. Flash lunged for the gun, which had fallen on the floor. He reached it, turned quick as a snake, and shot John, then swiftly scuttled back out of reach. He held the gun on John, who was on the floor, screaming, holding his right upper arm, which was bleeding and limp. Blood was pouring out of his right eye.

Flash rose to his feet and looked around the huge room for something to restrain John. Over toward the kitchen he saw a large, blue, plastic tarp spread out on the white terrazzo floor with a chair placed in the middle. On the edge of the tarp was a roll of duct tape, a coil of rope, a bag of two-foot-long plastic zip ties, an aluminum baseball bat, and a plastic bottle of Drano. It was like the stage setting for a macabre play titled "Torture." *Jesus Christ.*

Flash pushed the gun under his belt at the small of his back and moved quickly to the tarp, where he picked up a couple of the zip ties. He returned and bound John's hands in front with one tie and his feet with the other, then zipped them both tight.

John was cursing, pleading, accusing, making a hell of a racket. Flash grabbed a flowered throw pillow from a nearby couch and placed it beneath John's head, all the while thinking he would rather smash the bastard's head in.

But the fight was over, wasn't it? He felt relieved that he'd resisted the bloodthirsty urge, even though he now understood why John had sprung the big bucks for an immense, private, isolated, gated, *Architectural Digest* Airbnb: the perfect place to torture and murder someone.

John was cold from shock and bleeding. He was blind in one eye, his head felt as though it had cracked open, his right arm burned where he had been shot, and his shoulder had gone numb. The zip ties were cinched tight around his wrists and ankles. The combination of pain, shock, and despair was so toxic he couldn't speak. He raised and dropped his head on the pillow and growled like an angry dog. The plan had been absolutely perfect; he had been so close!

Suddenly, a foot kicked the pillow out from under his head. Stunned, John looked up through tears and blood and saw a man standing over him, pointing a gun at his head. Not Flash Michael! The man was dressed in black, with dark eyes, an evil smile, and long black hair. John thought he could only be the devil, come to take him to Hell. He let loose a long, hopeless moan that ended with a sob.

Flash had lost his cell phone in the struggle but spotted a landline on the side of the kitchen counter. He went and picked up the handset. John was moaning. Flash was about to dial 911 when a deep, unfamiliar, operatic voice out of nowhere ordered, "Put down the phone, or I'll shoot him."

Flash looked back to see a stocky man dressed in black standing over John with a pistol aimed at John's head. "Hang up the phone, or I will shoot him." The man had long black hair parted in the center, was dark complected, and his accent was vaguely Eastern European. He had a two- to three-day growth of stubble, black eyebrows, high cheekbones, and thin lips. His face was equal parts handsome and menacing.

Flash carefully replaced the handset and put his hands up halfway. "Who the hell are you?"

The man smirked and said, "Not your business. Go sit in that chair over there, the one on the tarp." He pointed toward the tarp with the gun, then lowered it and pointed it again at John's head.

"No, I won't. What do you want?"

"I said go over and sit in that chair, the one on the tarp. Do it now!" The intruder's baritone reached every corner of the great room; his voice was magnificent, imposing, and deeply ominous. Even John stopped whimpering and cursing. The dark man raised his gun and aimed it at Flash. "Now!"

"No, I won't—but look, we might be able to find a way for all of us to come out of this alive, if you'll just tell me what you want," said Flash.

The two men stared at each other; seconds passed. Flash couldn't tell if the man's eyes were black or dark brown. Then the man slowly lowered his gun, aiming it again at John's head. Not for a moment breaking eye contact with Flash, the dark man shot three times into John's prostrate body. The body bucked with each report.

Flash dove around the end of the kitchen counter and reached for his gun.

Staying low, Flash quietly scrambled down the full length of the counter, twelve or fifteen feet, hoping to fire a shot from the other end before the man could close in or secure a better angle for his own shot. He cautiously peered out from the far end. He saw the man had ducked down and was scanning the kitchen area, looking for his prey.

Erebus was riding the wave of destiny. He had expected a real fight, knowing he would find two of them, ex-cops, probably with guns. He would have to surgically neutralize Horan in order to get at Flash—and the treasure.

When Erebus arrived he found Horan wounded and tied up, with Flash wandering around the room, half-dazed. One, two, three shots, and Horan was out of the picture. This was too easy. He almost laughed.

Erebus went down to one knee, gun at the ready. He'd seen Flash duck behind a long counter. He felt like an android, scanning, sensing, ready to react to the slightest movement at the speed of light. He felt immortal. The gods were with him. This Flash was no match for Zigfrids Erebus.

As his wave of destiny was cresting, he'd wound the ex-cop, torture him until he gave up the money, then one, two, three more shots would finish the mission. Having discovered the whereabouts of the treasure, Erebus, Erebus the Great, would melt into the night, disappearing forever—the perfect plan aided by the gods, who giveth and giveth and giveth.

Suddenly, from the other end of the counter, Erebus saw a movement and swung his gun into action, pulling the trigger. Two shots, one on top of the other, exploded in the great room.

The pain. Oh, my god, the pain.

Flash shot just as the stranger fired. The glass bowls on the green end table exploded, and the man screamed and grabbed at his face with his free hand as if trying to tear his skin off. Blood appeared from his forehead, around his eye, and his cheek—cut flesh hung from his face, exposing bone.

The man ran at Flash, holding his face with one hand and the pistol with the other, screaming. Flash fired twice more, this time hitting the man once in the chest and once in the head. The body continued forward as it dropped to the floor and slid to within five feet of where Flash was crouched. The gun slid farther and came to a stop against Flash's knee.

Flash felt as if the life force had been sucked out of his body. A debilitating spell seemed to have hit him, and for a moment, he was sure he would pass out, or perhaps even die. He collapsed, prostrate, the pistol in one hand, a hand barely able to hold onto the gun.

Lying there with his cheek pressed against the cool terrazzo floor, Flash wondered if he had been shot and was in shock. Perhaps thirty seconds later, he revived slightly and raised his head, then lowered it. Next, he tried to move his arms, and they moved. Then he gingerly tried to move his legs, and they moved too. This was enough of a confirmation. He wasn't shot, and he probably wasn't going to die.

Flash exhaled, inhaled, and exhaled again. Yes, he was definitely alive. Unexpected tears stung his eyes and he felt a warmth flood his body. This was good. This was all very good.

Eventually, Flash pushed up to his knees, rose shakily, and staggered toward the phone. He had to call 911. He stopped at the counter, still holding John's Glock, the gun that John had intended to use on him. He shook his head, reassessed priorities, then turned and walked toward John to check for a pulse. John, bound hand and feet, was posed in the attitude of a person sleeping on his side. John had been shot in the head, the neck, and through his upturned shoulder. He had no pulse.

Flash then checked the dark man, who lay spread-eagle on the floor, a pool of blood growing around his head. The exposed side of his face wasn't severely damaged other than two shards of colored glass partially buried in his forehead. He might have been in his late forties, early fifties. He had age wrinkles around his eye, and a deeply creased cheek. He lay there like a carved statue of a fallen hero or warrior. The word, however, that came to Flash's mind, was *murderer*.

Flash went into the kitchen and opened drawers until he found what he was looking for—Ziplock bags would do. He took two, put one on each hand, returned to the dark man's body, and gently frisked him. First, he found two sets of keys in the pocket of the running jacket. One was a key ring with several keys and a tear-shaped fob with a plastic tag that read, "Waikiki Marina White Cantius 46." The other was from Hertz Rent-A-Car.

The man's light windbreaker had an oversized zippered pocket on the inside. Flash fumbled with the zipper through the plastic bags. Finally, he pulled it open and extracted a black Moleskin journal held closed by an elastic strap. Hand-calligraphed in white ink on both the cover and the spine was the title, *Last Days*.

Slipping off the band, Flash opened the first page. Here was the same title, *Last Days*, hand-lettered in jet-black ink. Below it, *Volume 29—Volume twenty-nine*? Flash fanned through the pages. The journal was three-quarters full, all hand-printed, with lists and diagrams. Several pages included photographs, and others appeared to be catalog entries or compilations of documents. Near the center of the book, Flash found a diagram drawn on two adjacent journal pages, titled "TARGETS."

Even through the powerful effects of shock, Flash felt a dark cloud inside. He was looking at a map for murder—careful, meticulously engineered murder. His eyes jumped to the lower right-hand corner, a rectangle not connected to the rest of the diagram, containing three names, each followed by a question mark: John Horan, Flash Finnegan Michael, and Malcolm Forsyth. Tilly Good was one of elements, and a dotted line ran from her name to John's.

Flash turned back several pages until he stopped at one labeled "Essential Documents from Bingwen Cache." The first item on the list was proceeded by four asterisks, so it must have been important:

"Email Tilly Good to John Horan. JH murdered Good. Good's revenge (Documents and transcripts) to be made public on 20 May."

There she was again, Tilly Good, and his once best buddy John. His heart hurt when he thought of John. And who or what the hell was Bingwen, and where was this so-called cache? So many questions, questions, and more questions.

Then he saw it, an answer, not a question. *Today is Saturday, May 20*. If the assassin's book was right, perhaps the world was about to learn the truth concerning the sting, about John Horan the rogue cop, about Flash Finnegan Michael, who was not a rogue cop, all from documents and testimony collected by the vengeful but indomitable Tilly Good. *Tilly's revenge. Go, girl!*

Flash closed the *Last Days* book, slipped the elastic back in place, and decided. He wasn't going to give it to the cops. It was personal. It was the key, albeit a cryptic key, to everything that had happened over the preceding eight months. He had to have it.

That settled, he looked around the great room. The scene was almost exactly as it had been when Flash killed the assassin. This was important because forensics would be all over every detail, every spec of visible and invisible detectable evidence. Every theory, accusation, and explanation would be constructed from the forensic evidence and, of course, Flash's testimony.

Flash removed the baggies, putting them back in his pocket, went to the phone, and punched 911. He reported the incident briefly to the operator, asking for immediate assistance but stressing that no residual danger remained as the combatants were both dead.

He found and retrieved his cell phone and called Janet Naka-mura. The call went to voicemail. Flash said, "Janet, remember that retainer letter we signed? It's time for you to get on your horse and ride. I am at a homicide scene, where two men are dead. One of them is John Horan, my ex-partner at Seattle PD. The other is a hired killer, I believe. I've never seen him before. I shot and killed the assassin in self-defense. I also shot and wounded John in self-defense. The assassin later killed John. I've called 911, and the cops are on the way. I'll be on my way to the police station soon. Come and find me there."

Then he took the *Last Days* book over to a couch on the other side of the room, sat, and began photographing first the cover, then all the pages one by one. He'd realized the only way he was going to be able to cut through the tidal waves of suspicion and confusion that would be generated by the evening's shootout was by giving the black book to the cops. By giving them the book, he significantly improved his odds against being framed in yet another institutional cock-up.

Between the last page and the inside cover, he found a folded receipt.

Einstein Kaffee & Rauchsalon,

Kramgasse 49

3111 Bern, Switzerland

11 May

He photographed the receipt, refolded it, and placed it back next to the back cover, and closed the book, replacing the elastic band.

Flash turned to the assassin's keys. He removed the tear-shaped fob and all of the keys except the boat ignition key from the ring, put them into one of the plastic bags, zipped it shut, and put the bag in his pocket for safekeeping. He placed the boat key with the marina tag and the Hertz keys back into the assassin's pocket. He replaced the *Last Days* book in the oversized pocket, knowing his fingerprints were all over the book. That way, when he gave his statement, the cops would know he had seen the book and knew something about its contents, making it harder for the investigation to get too far off the rails by attempting to construe that Flash was somehow complicit with John or the assassin.

Looking around the room, Flash placed the Glock in clear view on the kitchen counter. He walked through to the front door, found a switch for the front gate and pushed it, went to a nearby chair, and collapsed into it, exhausted. The house was silent.

Flash sat, both feet on the ground, arms folded, grateful for a moment of peace before the arrival of the cavalry with their sirens blaring, blue lights flashing, and guns drawn.

CHAPTER 39

After an early morning visit to the Wilcox Medical Center to have his lip stitched, Flash went with Janet to the police station to give his formal statement about the shootout. Flash was voluntarily fingerprinted and gave a DNA sample to match against blood or whatever they would find on John's Glock.

Officers took photographs of Flash's face, showing the split lip, which by now was swollen. Flash was shocked at the photographs. By five that afternoon, his statement was drafted, checked and rechecked by Janet, and transmitted to the case administrator. As a courtesy, Janet also called Kellie to tell her that the statement was complete and in the Kauai Police Department case management system.

The next day, Monday, Flash and Janet were back at the police station first thing in the morning. After the ground rules were hammered out, Kellie, Bob, a detective from the Honolulu Police Department named Charity Han, and a forensics specialist named Jason began sifting through documents, asking questions, and making notes. They were thorough, direct but civil, building the record answer by answer as a foundation for any future prosecutions.

During a break, Kellie said, "Just a heads up about that Seattle Police Department sting that went off the rails—a data dump of evidence from someone called Tilly Good was released on the internet yesterday."

Flash did a double-take, surprised and relieved. He looked at Janet. She was stoic, but he knew this was good news.

Kellie handed a memory stick to Janet and said, "This is your copy of everything they sent. It's all over the internet, by the way. The *Seattle Times* and *The New York Times* have teaser stories out about the money-laundering operation, the sting gone bad, John Horan and Malcolm Forsyth, and our very own beach bum Flash, who is, by the way, one of the stars of the show."

Flash smiled even though his stitches tugged.

After seven hours of questioning, Flash was free to go. He and Janet returned to her office. There, they reviewed the day's events, and Flash further educated Janet about drugs, money laundering, and his own back story.

Flash was relieved to be in a room with a window and wondered if he could find a beer someplace in the building.

"Why do you think Tilly said you might be able to help John get the money back?"

Flash rocked a moment in his chair. "Well, in hindsight, seeing how the story played out, I think pointing the finger at me was brilliant. Tilly knew that John, having found out she'd stolen his money, would be unhinged. Suggesting I might know where the money was would send John after me with a vengeance. And that's pretty much what happened."

"So?"

"So, long story short, I think she was hoping I'd kill him."

"Really? Wow. That's pretty devious. Pretty iffy too. What if he'd killed you first?

"C'est la vie. She could have cared less about me. But think about it. Sending John after me was her best chance to murder him from beyond the grave. And look, it worked. John died a messy, public death. And even if her plan hadn't worked, and

John somehow lived, well, he'd be condemned to an anxious life on the run, without the money, forever looking over his shoulder."

Janet cocked her head, and she asked in a quieter voice, "You *do* have enough money to pay your ace attorney, don't you?"

"Yes, in my retirement account."

Her face brightened. "Would you be willing to put, say, seventy-five thousand into my trust account? And would you be willing to document where the payment came from so we can be ready for them when they ask?"

Flash smiled weakly. "Yup, I'll do it this afternoon." He could tell she was relieved. He leaned back in his chair and added, "Well, there you have it, yet a further example of Janet's superpowers. She adroitly heads the bad guys off at the pass long before they even show up."

For the next two weeks, Flash was besieged by questioners from officialdom, starting with the FBI agents from Seattle. They were well prepared, having brought stacks of documents bristling with yellow post-its. The interrogators took turns firing off questions, switching back and forth, one then the other, repeat, repeat, repeat. The FBI seemed unable to resist the appeal of trying to overwhelm him with their choreographed, nonstop, fastball attack.

Flash batted the balls back at them hour after hour, until two days later, they gave up.

Flash and Janet watched as the agents, frustrated and unhappy, repacked their fat briefcases with documents and notes and departed.

For Flash, his days of idleness were over. He'd had stitches on his head and lip. He'd endured an onslaught of interviews, formal or otherwise, received warnings against leaving Kauai, and most noticeably, he'd watched as the mystique of being erased was itself erased. Now, everybody knew Flash. When the

Seattle Times launched a series of articles titled "Sting Uncovers Police Incompetence," Flash was named as a prominent actor.

Knowing that Pippa would be worried and upset, he called her. He felt a lump rising from his chest up to his throat as soon as he heard her voice.

"Oh, Dad, I've missed you so much." And she began to cry.

After she recovered, she asked, "Dad, did you really get ten-million dollars?"

"No, honey, just like the story said, Tilly Good got the money. I just pushed a button to send it to some bad guys. It was a sting. We were trying to follow the money back into the bad guys' den and arrest them." Did everyone in Seattle now believe he was sitting on ten-million?

Father and daughter made a date for her to fly to Kauai for a two-week visit.

Flash, whose recent life had been spacious, aimless, and remarkably undemanding, was now feeling the pressure of being oversubscribed. Everybody had a piece of him. The new normal included a daily run, then Koloa Roasters, followed by checking in with Janet, working through the myriad of details attendant on his testimony and witness statements, reviewing evidence, straightening out his real identity, petitioning for forgiveness for having purchased the fake ID, and hopefully cutting deals with the Kauai Police, the FBI, and others.

Mia held court at their morning confab, reading articles aloud, acting as moderator, and calling time at eight-fifty-five, when almost everyone had to go to work. She routinely ended each gathering with some version of "Don't forget that I found Flash, and he's my renter." Or "Flash isn't going anywhere, even though he's famous. He has many months left on his lease, so he has to stay here where he belongs."

Janet announced that Sachiko and Keanu were being held on drug trafficking and a multitude of charges in Lihue. Rumor had it she would claim that Keanu beat and intimidated her into coming up with the money for the drug deals. Apparently, she'd appeared at her hearing sporting a black eye.

Keanu, having been tossed under the bus by Sachiko, was back in the Kauai Detention Center. Again, he was represented by Alanai Aukai, the same public defender who had been assigned in his drug possession case.

The Honolulu Police were holding the Zodiac crew without bail and investigating *Invincible* and its crew members. An arrest warrant was issued for Bart Singletary, who had agreed to give himself up in Honolulu in the company of his legal team. Finally, the Kauai Drug Taskforce was assigned to write a comprehensive report about the drug bust and submit it to the city council and the mayor.

Three weeks after the drug bust and Malcolm Haysmith's disappearance, Flash read in the Honolulu paper that construction on the Village in the Sky had stopped. Contractors had filed lawsuits left and right, construction claims were being prepared, and liens were placed on the property, the construction materials, and all the equipment left on the site. Also, the city was being sued by everybody, as were the Allen Group and Touma Allen, personally.

Minette, though, and Benjamin were still being paid, because the court needed them to clean up the mess and find documents required for the ongoing litigation.

In a separate column in the paper, Flash saw that Bart Singletary was likely to receive a long prison term as the feds and the local police were piling on with drug trafficking and multiple violations under the Money Laundering Control Act. What agency wouldn't want to grab a piece of that?

· · ·

A month later, Pippa had come and gone, her visit a big success for both of them. She'd stayed two weeks. They'd toured the island, hiked, swam, bodysurfed, snorkeled, taken a helicopter ride, and ate local food at local famous places.

The day Pika drove Flash and Pippa to the airport, Flash was already missing her. Afterward, his morning run was slow, the Koloa Roasters gathering felt pointless, and Apartment B felt empty. While he was collecting his phone and wallet to go for a second run, he heard a knock at his door.

A voice called out, "FedEx for you, Flash."

He opened the door and found a FedEx envelope on the landing. He picked it up. It felt light, a standard letter-sized bubble-wrap envelope with a bulge in the middle. He closed the door, went to the turquoise worktable, and pulled open the envelope. Inside was a small bubble-wrapped bundle, encased in an excess of packing tape. He cut through the layers of tape with scissors, revealing a red plastic memory stick that dropped onto the tabletop. He turned it over and saw "Bingwen" embossed in gold letters on a red casing. Flash looked in the envelope for a note or letter, but found none.

He walked across the room to a bookshelf, took out a metal Ikea letterbox with a hinged cover, opened it, and brought it over to the worktable, pushing aside the iMac keyboard. The box contained several keys taken from the assassin's keyring, a gray tear-shaped fob, and printed copies of the pages from the *Last Days* book.

He checked the spelling of Bingwen on the memory stick against the page titled "Essential Documents from Bingwen Cache." The Bingwen in the book was the Bingwen on the memory stick.

Flash hesitated, wondering if the memory stick might be some hacking device used to inject a computer virus, or worse. After a minute or so, he decided. He told himself, *Only one way to find out*. He plugged the memory stick into his iMac, afraid doing so might be the death of his computer. The screen lit up and read:

Please answer all four of these questions:

Last four digits of your SS#?

Mother's Maiden Name?

Your Cell Phone Number?

Your SPD Badge Number?

After he answered the questions, his cellphone vibrated. A text appeared on the phone. It consisted of a series of numbers and letters, which he carefully typed into a box that had appeared on his computer screen.

The iMac screen cleared, and another link appeared. He clicked it.

A message appeared, with a countdown clock blinking in the lower right-hand corner, ticking down the minutes and seconds.

The message read: "In one hour's time (exactly) you will receive another link, which will take you to a secure communications video channel with Bingwen. Between now and then, do not under any circumstances push any key or button on this computer. Leave it on and untouched until you receive the link."

An hour later, the new link appeared. Flash clicked it, opening a video channel displaying an image of a silhouetted male figure speaking in an electronically modified voice.

"Flash Michael, I am acting as an agent on behalf of Tilly Good," the voice said.

The voice went silent, and the silhouette appeared frozen for so long that Flash, who was feeling creeped out by the mechanical voice and the reference to Tilly, blurted out, "Okay, okay, so who are you and what do you want?"

"I am Bingwen."

"Bingwen, who does what exactly?"

"I am a hacker."

"Where are you?"

"Not relevant. I have news for you from Tilly Good. Do you want to hear it or not?"

After a brief internal debate, he said, "Yes—I do."

"She has made a bequest to you. To receive it, you must follow my instructions precisely."

"Instructions like what?"

"Instructions like providing me with an offshore account number and transfer instructions. You provide the information, and I'll make the transmission."

"How much are we talking about?"

"Half."

"Half? Half of what?"

"What do you think?"

"Jesus, you're kidding. How do I know this isn't a sting? Or worse?"

"You don't, but either way, it's your choice. Get me the account info, and you'll find out for yourself. Refuse to do so, and, well—you'll never know, will you?"

"Assuming this is for real, what happened to the other half of the money?"

"Once I discharge my contractual obligation to Ms. Good, I get the other half."

Flash was speechless.

The mechanical voice said, "I need your answer. Yes or no, Mr. Michael?"

"Yes, yes, but why do you get half?"

"For services rendered, specifically this service."

"How can you possibly justify scooping up five-million dollars?"

"The same way you will justify it, Mr. Michael."

Flash was about to ask another question when the mechanical voice said, "It's finders keepers, Mr. Michael—the law of the universe. No elaborate justifications or self-aggrandizing explanations are necessary. *Finders keepers* is all that need be said."

END

ABOUT THE AUTHOR

 Walt Sutton is a retired business executive who lives with his wife and small dog Maude on Bainbridge Island, Washington. He is the author of the Flash Finnegan series of crime novels, *Finders Keepers* and *Losers Weepers*, with *Knick Knack Paddy Whack* coming out in 2024.

To learn more about Walter Sutton and discover more Next Chapter authors, visit our website at www.nextchapter.pub.

Made in the USA
Las Vegas, NV
06 December 2023

82213559R00204